C000218900

MURDERS AT THE WINTERBOTTOM WOMEN'S INSTITUTE

A PRUNELLA PEARCE MYSTERY

GINA KIRKHAM

BLOODHOUND
— BOOKS —

www.bloodhoundbooks.com

Print ISBN 978-1-914614-96-5

ALSO BY GINA KIRKHAM

*For my hubby John
My best friend and reluctant muse...*

Have I told you lately that I love you?

PROLOGUE

December 1979

*T*he whiteness crunched underfoot, a sound that Maisie found quite comforting. She quickly took her eyes from the ground, raised her head and tilted her chin to look ahead. It momentarily hurt, making her blink rapidly. The whiteness had no end. It stretched from the carefully crafted stone edges of Magdalen House, across the vast gardens, over the boundary hedges and then draped itself on the bare branches of the dense trees in Winterbottom Woods.

She could almost imagine her life being completely white.

No darkness.

No fear.

No desperation.

Just white.

She bent down, her small fingers curled around the icy cold snow, patting it into a little ball. Once it was the right shape and size she took aim. Bringing her arm back, she tested her own flexibility before launching it at a squirrel that had until that moment been sitting unaware of her on the fence, a small acorn between its paws. The snowball missed, but it was enough to startle it. The grey flash disappeared over the hedge, leaving the top of its foraged nut peeping out from the snow.

She wasn't sure why she had done that. Now she was alone again. It was only a squirrel, but better some company than none at all. She glanced back to look at the windows of Magdalen House. They were the eyes of her world.

Sometimes they allowed her to see out.

Sometimes they looked out to see her.

Like today.

Today they were watching her.

She turned her back, not wanting to see their disapproval, not wanting to feel their wrath.

Kicking at the ridged drifts with her red wellingtons, Maisie cleared a circle of grass, the lush green stark against the nothingness of the snow, before beginning to roll another ball. She pushed and rolled, her body radiating a welcome warmth from the exertion as her masterpiece grew. A second ball, slightly smaller, was her next project which sat atop the first as she patted and shaped extra snow around it.

Standing back, she placed her hand into her pocket, her fingers grasping at the treasure she had stolen from the kitchen. She held it in her hand, marvelling at the vibrant colour of its flesh. She slowly turned it, examining it from all angles; the shape was imperfect but it was perfect for its purpose.

She liked how that sounded. It reminded her of herself. Imperfect, but perfect for purpose. She just had to find out what her purpose was. Plunging the carrot as if it were a dagger, she pierced the centre of her snowman's face. Two pieces of coal purloined from the cast-iron bucket in the scullery gave him eyes and completed his glare.

There would be no mouth, no smile, no downturned sadness or upturned joy.

Maisie knew that mouths were trouble. A mouth could be opened, and words could spill out, and everyone knew that wrong words hurt.

She buried her own mouth into the rough folds of her red tartan scarf, desperate to keep her words inside as a solitary tear spilled over and trickled down her flushed cheek.

Be afraid of the silent child for they are the ones who think.

LADIES OF THE WINTERBOTTOM WI

'...nd the nominations for our next president are...' Kitty Hardcastle crinkled the white sheet of paper between her finger and thumb, savouring the silence that enveloped the wood-beamed parish hall. Scanning the eager faces of the ladies displayed before her, sitting in regimented lines on the Winterbottom Women's Institute pink velour padded chairs, she paused for effect. When she felt she had reached just the right level of heightened expectation, she clucked ever so slightly and cleared her throat.

'...Felicity Broadbent.'

A polite ripple of applause undulated through the audience. Kitty smiled in appreciation before continuing.

'Mabel Allinson...' A hesitant solitary hand clap followed that revelation. As expected, it was not the most popular nomination, but it was a nomination nevertheless, and according to the rules had to be presented.

Kitty surveyed the expectant faces. Their collective cheeks shone back at her across the hall, alternating between flushed pinks of excitement and the rosy powder of over enthusiastically applied Revlon Rouge, through to the veined and hardened floridness of weather-beaten farmers' wives. They were an eclectic lot that gathered every three weeks from their respective cosy Winterbottom cottages, bungalows, retirement apartments, farmsteads and even, dare she say it, from the local council estate.

She gave a small sigh in an effort to catch and keep to herself what she knew was an outdated, snobbish opinion. It took all walks of life to make a jolly good, well rounded and fun WI, even if that did include Chelsea Blandish, a brassy blonde who was slumped in her seat at the front, sandwiched between the wives of the village vicar and his curate. Her presence really did make for a rather displeasing and untidy front row, with her sausage legs encased in leopard print Lycra leggings and her ample bosom spilling over the top of a cream plunge-neck poly-ester blouse. Add those assets to her ridiculous eyebrows and dermal-filled lips that could easily suction a blocked drain with an overly enthusiastic pout (though rumour had it that she reserved that kind of thing for the local butcher), then you really did have the epitome of a tart on the cherished nominal roll of the Winterbottom WI, albeit not the deep-filled strawberry variety. Through her slightly hooded eyes, Kitty watched Chelsea filing her pink talons with a brightly patterned emery board.

Thank goodness she wasn't on her list – 'Chels' Blandish as a prospective WI president would certainly never do!

Feeling a prickle of irritation, Kitty quickly brought herself back to the task at hand. Her eyes scanned the list of names. 'Avery McIntosh.'

A gentle hum spread through the first few rows, coupled with a combined nodding of several lilac-rinsed heads giving their seal of approval. A sudden grating sound from the far corner of the hall as the hinges of the barn-style kitchen door loudly groaned their displeasure, forced Kitty to pause before she could follow up with the next nomination.

'Tea and cake in five...' Brenda Mortinsen's chubby hand

brandishing four plump fingers and a thumb waved around the door in an effort to endorse her warm verbal command.

Exasperated that her moment of glory was going to be cut short, Kitty riled slightly. 'Brenda, please. I feel this is slightly more important than your cake!' she barked.

Brenda pursed her lips and wobbled her head. 'It's lemon drizzle...' she proffered, '...and it's to die for!' she added, before disappearing back inside the small kitchen to finish laying out the cups and saucers.

Kitty rolled her eyes and gently moistened her lips with her tongue. 'Phillipa Jackson, Betty Prince, Rita Charlesworth and Bryony Richards.' She rushed the last few names, grateful to be able to complete her task without further interruption. 'So there we have it, ladies. Our full list of nominations for president next year.'

Happy that their little group would continue for years to come, safe under the control of several good potential candidates, the ladies of the Winterbottom WI broke the silence by scraping their chair legs against the wooden flooring as they rushed to sample Brenda's tea and cake, neatly laid out on the draped gingham tablecloth. Their chirpy voices reached a musical crescendo as it filled the A-structured eaves and just as quickly bounced back, muffled by the ornate and intricate hand-embroidered tapestries draped on the walls that proudly celebrated their hundred years of WI existence. The excited conversation evidenced their ecstasy, and in some cases their palpable relief that they hadn't been called upon to accept the nomination of future mentor, boss bird and organiser.

They were all delighted as to how the evening's meeting had progressed and to the choices made.

Apart from one.

In the far corner sat a very irked Winterbottom Women's Institute member who was not excited, not ecstatic, and was most definitely not delighted. The generous slice of cake she had just received lay untouched on the delicate china plate that tremored slightly in her left hand. She remained stoically silent, her lips thinned and met, pinched tightly down lest she should accidentally release her bitter disappointment. She gripped the worn leather straps of the tapestry bag nestled on her knee with her free hand, her nails biting into the skin of her palm. Her throat constricted as she fought back tears that threatened to spill and betray her stoic façade.

Another year where she had been overlooked.

Another year where her stalwart presence and gentle kindness had gone unappreciated, unnoticed and unrecognised.

Another year of being 'Phyllis the Bloody Invisible'.

PHYLLIS

*K*itty flung her arms around, fingers pointing, wrists flowing, directing the remaining ladies like a well-rehearsed orchestra. They eagerly followed her instructions to stack chairs and fold the delicately embroidered WI tablecloths to bring the meeting to a close. The vase of freshly cut roses from Kitty's cottage garden that had until five minutes previously adorned the president's table, was gifted to Avery McIntosh for her imminent seventy-fourth birthday.

'Well, ladies, it's been a very enjoyable evening. Don't forget at our next meeting we'll be collecting donated blankets, sheets… and, er… oh, Phyllis, hold on, I forgot to say, can you lock up this evening and give the tables a bit of a wipe before you go?'

Phyllis didn't hear much more of Kitty's simpering request; she had developed an uncanny knack over the years of being able to block out her voice when it suited. And right now it suited. She slammed the kitchen door pointedly behind her, chuntering quietly to herself as she collected the dirty tea towels.

'*Phyllis* my arse, twenty-seven years I've been a member here, and the stupid mare still can't get my bloody name right. It's Dilys… *D-i-l-y-s!*' she spat.

She'd lost count of the number of times she had corrected not only Kitty but the rest of the ladies too, yet they still insisted on calling her Phyllis, as though her real name would stick on their tongues and choke them. That's if any of them could remember it. Christmas cards, birthday cards; they all carried the 'Phyllis' moniker. Every single card, every single letter, every single whiteboard entry in black marker pen.

Phyllis!

She gave a wry smile, remembering the one year when she had been called something other than Phyllis. It was the year when Hilda Jones, in the early stages of dementia, had dedicated a lovely charity-shop Christmas card to her. Hilda's careful but rather shaky handwriting had offered her blessings,

To dear Phallus,
Wishing you a very Happy Easter
Hilda (J) x

Phyllis carefully tapped down the lid on the sugar canister and returned it to the cupboard. The authorities had gone to so much trouble to give her a new identity all those years ago, only for it to now be changed on a whim by those that couldn't be bothered to get it right.

So 'Phyllis' she had become.

It was so much easier just to let the hurtful mistake pass.

She very much doubted there would be any change from 'Phyllis' or 'Phallus'; she was just any old Tom, Dick or Harry to them. Her comparison made her chuckle, but the moment was only fleeting as the realisation once again welled up in her heart. That was the trouble with being meek, timid and unassuming. You became overlooked. Never ignored, just taken for granted, sort of insipidly unappreciated, which in her book was so much worse than being the former. To be ignored could be a blessing if the ignorer was not essential in one's life. Releasing a gentle sigh, she gathered the tea towels into a bundle and made her way back into the main hall to lock up.

'Phyllis... oh, Phyllis?' Mabel Allinson's shrill twittering voice cut through the silence of what Phyllis had assumed was by now, an empty building.

'Yes, Mabel?'

'You couldn't hang on, could you? I just need an extra five minutes to box up the leftover cakes.' Mabel began to stack the Tupperware boxes on the trestle table, matching up the lids by size. Several half-eaten tasty bakes were lined up and waiting to be packed away.

Phyllis nodded and took her place behind Mabel, waiting.

'It's so exciting, isn't it?' Mabel trilled.

'What is?'

'The nominations for president, of course! I can't believe I've been nominated. Ten years I've been a member, and at last I've been recognised for my contribution. It's absolutely marvellous, isn't it?' She tamped down the lid on the second box. 'I think we're all such deserving nominees, don't you? Well, of course you do, why wouldn't you?'

'Yes indeed, why wouldn't I?' Phyllis simpered, feigning interest whilst rummaging in her tapestry knitting bag for nothing in particular, more as a diversion from Mabel's smugness.

As Mabel droned on and on, listing the qualities that she believed she had for the all-important role of president of the Winterbottom WI, Phyllis could do no more than examine the back of her head. She watched it wobble, she watched it nod, she noticed the grey touching the roots of her rooster-red dyed curls. The *click, click* of the lid finding purchase on the box edge to form a seal hit every nerve she had. She continued to watch as her right arm unconsciously and gracefully moved upwards in slow motion, whilst an unnatural, long forgotten but familiar rage burned in her chest.

~

'Oh dear, what a shame,' Phyllis mused to nobody in particular at the terribly inelegant way Mabel Allinson had slumped forward, face first into Brenda's legendary lemon drizzle cake. The 3.5mm crochet needle protruded from Mabel's wrinkled neck, just below the hairline of her dyed, teased and heavily sprayed bouffant. Her dull, unseeing eyes bore the expression of a woman most put out to have been on the receiving end of a sudden and grisly demise, when only moments earlier she had eagerly accepted her potential success as a presidential candidate for her beloved WI.

'Gosh, how on earth has that happened...' Phyllis smirked as she checked her nails, buttoned up her camel-hair coat and adjusted her crochet beret. She'd dropped a few stitches from her work in progress, but that was something she'd worry about later. *'Don't forget to lock up,'* she mimicked out loud in a posh imitation of Kitty Hardcastle's voice as she glided around Mabel's body. *'And whilst you're at it, can you wipe down the table surfaces and make sure the tea towels are clean for our next meeting.'*

'Of course, Kitty, anything you say, Kitty,' she meekly whispered in reply to herself.

Leaving Mabel nose-deep in the remnants of the crystallised lemon drizzle, she carefully used one of the tea towels to wipe the visible end of the crochet hook and clean the crimson pool that had spread across the melamine surface of the table, doing exactly as she had been told. Just as she always did.

'Oranges and lemons say the bells of St. Clement's...' she trilled to herself as she busied with her task.

Holding the bloodied fabric up to the light, she sneered.

Brenda had been closer to the truth than she had realised when she had highlighted the quality of her baking. Phyllis picked at a small crumb of sponge from the side of the plate and popped it into her mouth.

Mmm... yes – it certainly was to die for.

PRUNELLA

$\mathcal{T}$he church clock gave a mellow clang as it counted out the hour.

One, two, three, four.

Prunella Pearce's deft fingers danced across the spines of the books that sat regimented on the shelf of the *Crime, Mystery & Thriller* section in the village library. Pausing to make space between Peter Cheyney and Agatha Christie, she carefully popped Lee Child back in his rightful place. She loved the fact that the Winterbottom villagers still valued books and their magic. Having fought to retain some semblance of culture when their main library closed, they had ensured its future by housing it in a little converted shop with limited stock and reduced opening hours, a compromise the council was happy to agree upon. She checked her watch, twisting her wrist so that it caught the light. Why she did this she had no idea as the church clock was never wrong, but she longed for the day that she could catch it out.

Another half hour and she could turn the sign to 'Closed', pull down the blinds, tidy away the tin of shortbread biscuits that saw her through her days, and shut the door behind her, the tinkling brass bell signalling home time.

Prunella, a strikingly pretty woman with mesmerising green eyes, was just entering what she had been told was the prime of her life. She was happy to welcome her forties, but not so happy to greet the wisps of grey hair that had started to pepper her chestnut curls, and even less happy to have to check daily for the odd stray wiry one that had the audacity to sprout from her chin.

'Is it time for me to go now, Pru?' Mr Tytherington folded the library copy of the *Winterbottom News*, returned it to the growing pile of papers on the mahogany desk and switched off the green shaded reading lamp.

'You don't have to rush off; there's plenty of time yet, Mr Tytherington. I've still got a few books to catalogue.'

She knew that he spent more time than necessary poring over the weekly newspaper, not because of any interest in local gossip, shop opening times or what was on at the cinema in town, but because of the free heating and a respite from Mrs Tytherington's sharp tongue at home. Ever since he had retired as the local pharmacist, Pru had acquired a 'second set of hands' and genteel company almost every day. She didn't begrudge his presence at all, but sometimes she longed for a Tom Hardy lookalike to come begging for her company instead, to rustle her pages, excite her spine and stroke her cover. She let out a ridiculous girly giggle. A Tom Hardy would be a rare and fought-over commodity in Winterbottom, judging by the very scarce single and available male population that was on offer. In the twelve months she had been in the village, she hadn't really managed to integrate herself into its ways, or any part of its social life at all. Maybe it was time to sort out her own life, just as she had sorted out the shelves of the Winterbottom Community Library.

Her excitement had known no bounds when she had taken on this position and moved, or more aptly run, from the hustle and bustle of London to the serenity of the village. She had craved a quieter, more sedate life after her long-term relationship with the dashing Tom Elliott had come to an abrupt and heart-breaking end. She had caught all 6'4" of him potholing (no illuminated helmets required for this little pastime) with her BFF Madison Gale, when she had returned to their apartment a day early from a midweek literary festival in Edinburgh. She had stood horrified, the breath catching in her throat as a naked Madison, erotically straddling an equally naked Tom, had arched her back and thrown her arms up to the ceiling in ecstasy, pausing only to squeal in horror upon seeing Pru's shocked face reflected in the mirrored bedhead.

Pru, on the other hand, had suddenly become mesmerised by Madison's exceptionally hairy armpits, something she had never noticed in her best friend before. Either she had been cultivating them as a sexual prompt for Tom, or Poundland had run out of Veet. Whichever it had been, that scene, along with Madison's King Kong armpits, had sounded the death knell on their twelve-year relationship.

She closed the dust jacket of *Gone with the Wind* and stacked it on top of several other books that needed stamping. Nature had stopped at Tom's height when gifting him bodily dimensions to brag about, but he had been a warm and imaginative lover which more than made up for his lack of size in other departments. She gave a wistful sigh. Above anything else he had made her believe in herself, and she didn't doubt that he had loved her too, right up until the time Madison had chosen to crush his diminutive hairy chakras between her rugby-player-sized thighs.

The long-ago sadness suddenly returned and overwhelmed her. She had not only lost what she thought was her life partner in that awful mess, she had also lost her life friend. Betrayed by the two people she herself had loved and trusted.

'Oh my goodness, oh dear, I can't believe it, how absolutely awful...'

The half-glazed door to the little shop burst open, forcefully hitting the display cabinet and knocking a row of books on to a tilt, making Prunella startle before bouncing back into the upturned hand of Mrs Tytherington, the owner of the high-pitched, panic-stricken voice. The brass bell jangled uncontrollably as though it was heralding the second coming of Jacob Marley.

Albert Tytherington, surprised by his wife's sudden appearance, visibly blanched. Reaching for her, his gentle voice tried to soothe her. 'Calm down, Ethel, what on earth has happened? Deep breaths, dear, deep breaths.'

Ethel Tytherington, her shiny plump face flushed between shock and what Pru suspiciously thought could also be a touch of excitement, clutched at her chest, patting herself gently to assist the flow of words. 'There's been a murder,' she gasped. 'A murder at the Winterbottom WI.'

MURDOCH HOLMES

*D*etective Inspector Holmes adjusted the white slip-on foot covers so that the elastic tightened securely around his heavily polished brown brogues, before tentatively stepping on to the first of several metal plates that had marked out the common approach path to the body of Mabel Allinson.

'What have we got?' He nodded in acknowledgement to the new detective sergeant on his team, Andy Barnes.

'Elementary, boss, it's a dead body...' Barnes smirked before adding, '...and one hysterical Mrs Mopp.'

The muffled sobbing, peppered by a keening wail every few seconds, drew the attention of Murdoch Holmes to the open serving hatch of the kitchen area that currently housed the distraught Ellie Shacklady, the unfortunate cleaner of Winterbottom Parish Hall and discoverer of Mabel's rigid mottled body.

'D'you know, Barnes, for all the fun you lot have over the vague, and I mean very vague, similarity of my name to a well-known fictional detective, I'm surprisingly quite capable of recognising a stiff when I see one.' Holmes tapped the side of his nose knowingly before slowly moving around the trestle table, which was occupied by the plump upper half of Mabel, a squashed lemon drizzle cake, several Tupperware boxes and half a jam sponge. Taking in the angle of the murder weapon, the point of entry, and the lack of any sign there had been a struggle, he quickly scribbled his initial observations in the small black notebook before returning it to his jacket pocket and zipping up the forensic suit. 'Taken by surprise I shouldn't doubt, or she knew them.'

Barnes nodded and pointed to the crochet hook. 'Agreed. No sign of resistance and an unusual murder weapon too, but I suppose it's in keeping with the WI ethos. It's better than being whisked to death with a blender.' He laughed at his own joke.

'All right, Barnes, less of the dodgy wit. Shame about the cake, though; one of my favourites is lemon drizzle.' Under other circumstances the temptation to try a piece would have won the day, but to be caught with a mouthful of potential evidence at a murder scene would, at the very least, see him busted down to constable, if not required to resign.

'Uniform are sorting the witnesses and door to door, but apparently there was a WI meeting here last night with over sixty members in attendance. I've asked for the membership list and their register for the evening.' Andy checked his own notebook. 'It's definitely going to keep us busy, boss.'

DI Holmes watched as the forensic team began to work effortlessly around him, the arc lights casting eerie shadows around the hall breaking the late afternoon gloom. The spasmodic flash of the camera bounced unforgivingly off the waxed features of poor Mabel Allinson as a small, unnoticed strand of mauve wool quivered in the stagnant air.

The hum of expectation, curiosity and general nosiness circulated rapidly around Winterbottom over the following days. What each and every resident didn't know about the very sad demise of one of their own, they happily invented during their little gatherings that were arranged under the guise of the newly and hastily created *Mabel Allinson (deceased) Support Group.*

Phyllis sat in the bow-fronted window of The Twisted Currant Café; her fingers curled around a rather decadent hot chocolate with a lovely swirl of cream decorating the top. Previously she had never dared to sway from her usual peppermint tea, but the excitement of this ever so naughty adventure she had inadvertently embarked upon had given way to a most surprising feeling, one of utter delight and devilment. She licked her top lip and savoured the taste, keenly watching the comings and goings at the parish hall directly opposite.

The blue and white police tape that still barred entry for ordinary mortals to the building fluttered in the breeze. A large police van, rear doors wide open to accept the stream of sealed bags being ferried by people in white boiler suits and masks, blocked some of the view, but she could see enough to hold her interest. Her tummy suddenly spasmed with a gut-wrenching sense of fear. Gulping a rapid intake of breath, she quickly pushed any thoughts of discovery to one side.

Why on earth would anyone suspect an overlooked, unappreciated and insipid older woman? She thought. *After all, murder most horrid is rarely attributed to the female of the species – and I am most definitely one of those.* She stifled a chortle as she peered down her paisley blouse to check her own pendulous 36Fs, happy to confirm her status as a woman. Once upon a time they had been so pert they would wedge themselves on top of the table when she sat down; now they just adorned her upper thighs, causing hideous chafing if she moved too quickly.

She opened her tapestry bag and rummaged into the depths, her fingers touching her prize. Pulling out a small notebook decorated with pink roses, she licked the end of her pencil and set to work on the uniformed lines of the pages.

1. *Mabel Allinson*
2. *Felicity Broadbent*
3. *Avery McIntosh*
4. *Phillipa Jackson*
5. *Betty Prince*
6. *Rita Charlesworth*
7. *Bryony Richards*

She carefully placed a tick against poor Mabel's name, feeling a very slight twinge of remorse that lasted for almost two seconds before it quickly evaporated.

Seven presidential candidates. Seven women who probably had been no less deserving than herself, but they were still seven very good reasons to feel aggrieved.

The unnatural rage that was now growing so familiar began to burn once again in Phyllis's heart as revenge quietly took on its very own persona.

DESPERATE NEEDS

'I knew who had dunnit before I got even halfway through!' Pru banged the lid onto the kettle and flicked the switch, multi-tasking as she popped a teabag into each mug and shook out several Variety biscuits on to a plate.

Bree grinned, flashing teeth that had been whitened to within an inch of their lives. 'Is that the librarian or the would-be detective in you? Honestly, Pru, can you not just take a book at face value? Do you always have to delve into hidden meanings, or destroy all the hard work the author has put in to make it a mystery?'

'I don't!' Pru took a bite from the Jammie Dodger and wiped the crumbs from her chin. 'I just, well, er... I just have a very inquisitive mind, that's all.' She offered the plate to her friend, the only person in the village she had so far managed to form an attachment to: Bryony (Bree) Richards, thirty-seven years old, mum to a lippy thirteen-year-old called Nathan, merry divorcee, film researcher and fellow gin aficionado.

Her vibrant red hair, a mass of tight curls, had been the first thing that Pru had noticed when she'd literally bumped into her at Betty's Village Store during her first month in Winterbottom.

Pru, who had been happily chugging on a bottle of passion fruit smoothie at the point of impact, proceeded to slop it all down the front of Bryony's pretty blouse.

Profuse apologies had then taken place between them, both desperate to personally adopt the blame for their mutual clumsiness, followed by three hours in the Dog & Gun drinking copious amounts of Edinburgh gin with elderflower tonic, whilst giggling like two schoolgirls.

And so a special friendship had been drunkenly created.

Bree watched Pru intently, head cocked to one side. 'Well, my lovely, if working in a library and then spending your evenings reading your dusty tomes is all that fills you with excitement, I think you seriously need to get out more,' she gently chided as she ran her fingers across the stack of books on the built-in shelf unit. 'I've lost track of the number of times I've suggested the Women's Institute to you. We do have a laugh, and it leads to a lot of other social activities too.' She popped what was left of a ginger nut biscuit in her mouth and followed up with a slurp of tea.

'The WI... oh good God no! It's bad enough that every third month I have to deal with my own chin hair, without having to endure sitting next to several OAPs cultivating copious amounts of upper lip foliage that waft in the church hall breeze. It's still a big fat no from me, I'm afraid.'

Bree was having none of it. She was still surprised that people carried such a dated view of the WI. Granted, each group had their fair share of older members that tipped the scales in their favour, but they were working hard to attract new, younger members to make the Institute a vibrant and fun place for women of all ages. 'You know what they say: don't knock it until you've tried it; you just might enjoy it.'

'I take it we're still talking about the WI here and not some exotic bedtime gymnastics,' Pru snorted. 'Talking of which, did you drool... er... I mean see, the younger of the two detectives over at the parish hall yesterday?'

'Mmm... did I? What a dish. I wonder if he's spoken for.'

'Hands off, Bree! I saw him first and I think my needs are far greater than yours.'

Bree giggled, catching herself in the mirror that hung above the oak beam of Pru's fireplace. She pouted, fluffed her hair and coyly looked over her shoulder. 'Let me see. Mine was a balmy summer night two years ago after the village dance with... oh shit...' The sudden recollection of who had eagerly ripped her Marina Rinaldi blouse from her shoulders made her blush and shudder. 'It was just a bit of a flirt, fumble and a fu... er... bonk. It was forever ago and nothing to write home about, so best forgotten.' She waved her arm, indicating a time long past. 'I really don't think you can better that, so my lustful need will be massively greater than yours!'

'You didn't have the pleasure of meeting my ex, did you?' Pru bent the little finger of her right hand and jiggled it to show Tom's minute manhood, making Bree collapse on to the sofa laughing. 'Honest, Bree, even if I'd jumped into bed with him and indulged in the dastardly deed yesterday, my need would still be bordering on the totally desperate!'

Pru left her draped across the sofa, pausing long enough to grab a cushion and cuff her across the head with it before making her way into the kitchen. Maybe Bree was right. Her social life really was quite dire. Apart from the occasional night they shared, either in the pub or at their respective cottages, drinking wine or gin or whatever they could lay their hands on, she actually did very little else. The most excitement Winterbottom had seen for many a year was the unfortunate and extremely sad death of Mabel. She'd gleaned enough from Mr Tytherington, who in turn had gleaned the information from his wife, that it was being treated as murder. Murder by persons unknown.

Taking two glasses from the cupboard and the corkscrew

from the drawer, she rolled the wine bottles in the rack to read their labels. Picking a nice merlot, she back-heeled the kitchen door to open it, a smug smile touching her lips as the glasses chinked together. If truth be known, she was not only good at solving whodunits, she was also pretty darn good at gathering lots of other information.

Well, if a murder it truly was, then the delectable Detective Sergeant Andy Barnes would be around for some time to come.

How exciting.

AVERY

'Oh, Winston, you naughty boy!' Avery McIntosh held her hands firmly on her ample hips whilst surveying the fresh deposit that Winston the Yorkshire terrier had left for her in the kitchen. 'And behind the door, too.' She shook her head in exasperation.

It was bad enough that Winston had suddenly started producing Rover's leftovers in surprising locations around her much loved and neat little cottage, but this one had well and truly taken the biscuit. The large rainbow-shaped arc was smeared across the old quarry floor tiles. 'Well, I certainly won't find a pot of gold at the end of this one, will I, Winston?'

Winston sat in his luxury dog basket. His soft brown eyes carried a haughty expression and, if she dared to think it, one of triumph. Rummaging around in the cupboard under the sink, she pulled out her well-used Marigolds, a red plastic bucket, scrubbing brush and a bottle of bleach, and set about the task in hand.

Her days were ones of routine. She wasn't a particularly early riser, but after a light breakfast she would lace up her walking shoes and take a gentle stroll by the river with Winston, calling in at the Winterbottom Infants' School on the way home to collect any PTA correspondence that needed her attention. She would then partake of a nice cup of tea and cake for her elevenses at The Twisted Currant Café, followed by lunch at home, which usually consisted of soup and a wholemeal sandwich whilst reading a few chapters of the latest book she had withdrawn from the Winterbottom Community Library. Needlework crafts and baking would fill an hour or two of what was left of the day before retiring to bed with a large cup of cocoa.

As the retired headmistress of the local school, she had found her days long and unfulfilled during her first few months of leisure, so she had taken it upon herself to assist with the PTA, school charity events, summer fairs and Christmas parties. Avery was assured that her help was very much appreciated, but if she had had the notion to eavesdrop on the staffroom chatter, she would have realised that this was not the case. The staffs' feelings ranged from pity for the lonely spinster who had been unable to come to terms with losing her position of authority within the community, to outright exasperation at her constant interference.

'Come, Winston, time for dinner.' She swilled the bucket into the grid of her small but perfectly laid out garden, and with a wet thwack removed her Marigolds, placing them over the fence to dry. 'It's chicken today, although why I think you should deserve such a treat is beyond me.' She bent down to ruffle behind Winston's ears as a painful sadness overwhelmed her once again. She looked up, taking in the two rickety wooden garden chairs under the rowan tree, one of which would never support the well-padded bottom of her oldest friend ever again. 'Oh dearest Mabel, I do so miss our little chats. I still can't believe you're gone and in such a dreadful, dreadful way.' She brushed away a tear that had unexpectedly trickled down her cheek.

From village gossip and the appeals placed in the *Winterbottom News*, Avery knew that the police were no further along in their investigation. The murderer of her dear friend Mabel Allinson remained at large. Suspicion would clearly fall on whoever could be proved to have been the last person to see her alive, but so far nobody had come forward or had the finger pointed at them. It had just been a collective group of middle-aged and elderly women from the WI who had traipsed out of the parish hall together, carrying remnants of cake and muffins in plastic boxes – all at the same time.

Or had they?

Avery stopped suddenly, her hand wavering on the barn door handle. They hadn't all left at the same time, she was sure of it. There was that woman, what was her name?

Phylicia, Phyllida, Phil, Phil-something...

Winston sat beside her, furiously wagging his tail. His mistress had mentioned food and had then become annoyingly distracted. He pawed at her leg.

'Yes yes, Winston, just a minute, Mummy's trying to remember something.'

Her heart skipped a beat and then thudded in her chest. It was definitely that quiet-as-a-mouse, strange woman, the one that was always just there, either hovering in the background or, as Kitty once laughingly put it, blending into the magnolia walls of the parish hall. She remembered now; that particular night she had momentarily turned to look back into the hall and wave at Mabel as she buttoned up her coat. Standing behind her had been...

'Oh come on you silly old woman, think!' She quickly made her way back into her cottage, thoughts only of remembering the name so she could telephone the police as any good citizen would do. She actually felt excited that she, Avery McIntosh, Headmistress (Retired) could hold a vital piece of evidence that could solve this whole dreadful event.

Picking up the old black receiver, her finger hovering over the circular dial, she paused.

'Phyllis! That was it, it was Phyllis!'

The usually welcoming and comforting squeak of the hinges to the barn door and the low grumble that Winston produced momentarily puzzled her as she stood stock-still, listening intently before slowly turning to look behind her.

'You called, Avery?'

The figure of a woman loomed large in the doorway between the kitchen and the hall, the sunlight radiating behind cast an eerie, almost angelic, aura which belied the sudden grip of fear that Avery felt.

'Mmm... *Phyllis*. Only it isn't, is it? Such a shame you'll never have the opportunity to rectify that mistake.'

Avery stumbled backwards, dropping the receiver against the console table with a clatter as a brightly coloured and, even if she did say so herself, very professionally knitted mauve scarf was quickly wrapped around her neck.

As the soft fabric tightened and Avery's eyes bulged, the receiver swung like a pendulum acting as a metronome as it knocked against the under-stairs cupboard.

Tock, tock, tock.

You owe me five farthings, say the bells of St. Martin's... Phyllis couldn't stop that earworm from floating around her head. She would have also said, *Oh dear, how did that happen?* but she didn't need to this time. She knew exactly the how and the why.

The 'how' was with one of her beautiful chunky knit, extra-long scarves that had been lovingly created and knitted by her own fair hands during the lonely winter nights that she had endured year after year.

The 'why' was quite simple, really. The realisation that Avery had seen far too much and subconsciously knew too much, had flared in her brain during the wee hours of her sleepless night. Knowing Avery's scholarly brain would soon start to piece things together was a risk she couldn't take. Besides, she had anyway been number three on her list. The opportunity to silence her was just in time.

Phyllis was a little perturbed that she had been forced to make the decision to take action and not follow the regimented order of her list, but it had to be done. This had given Felicity Broadbent, sitting at number two in her notebook, a little more time on this mortal coil, but at the expense of poor Avery who, at the grand old age of 73 years and 361 days, was now quite dead, swinging from a metal coat peg in the under-stairs cupboard of Rosehip Cottage, 3 Cholomendy Lane, Winterbottom.

LUCY

'*R*ight, listen up ladies and gents...' DI Holmes, outlined by the sharp light of the projector on to the whiteboard in the incident room at Winterbridge nick, rubbed his hands in anticipation of silence and rapt attention from his team. He nodded to Andy Barnes to start the slide show from the open laptop. A slightly blurred colour photograph appeared on the wall behind him. Keeping his eyes focused on his detectives, he began his briefing. '...Avery McIntosh, single, female, seventy-four years, local to Winterbottom.'

A low-level snigger ran around the room.

'Something funny?' Holmes sarcastically questioned his gathered audience before turning to look at the projection himself. The photograph that had been hastily obtained from an old album at the crime scene had slipped into zoom mode, and rather than the face of the recently deceased Ms McIntosh staring back at him, he was confronted by Winston the Yorkshire terrier in the background, wide-eyed and furiously humping a tartan cushion. Giving a wry smile he laughingly chided his audience, 'Okay you bunch of juveniles, settle down!'

'Sorry, sir.' Andy Barnes hastily adjusted the settings so that Avery could have her moment of glory, albeit not one she would have happily chosen for herself. Despite all his years of police service and experience, he still couldn't stay the feeling of sadness that crept over him. That was the thing about a high-profile death: notoriety for all the wrong reasons. Doesn't everyone dream of having their five minutes of fame, to be lauded for something great, something special, remembered for a good deed, a talent or heroics? To be remembered for being a victim and one that was left hanging on a coat peg like an old anorak was just so bloody wretched.

DI Holmes coughed loudly, breaking his thoughts.

'So, we have death by strangulation at her home address, Rosehip Cottage, Cholomendy Lane. She was discovered by...' Holmes pointed to DC Lucy Harris, a recent addition to his team, for the answer. She quickly flicked over the pages of her notebook.

'Er... Eric Potter, the local postie. He usually enters by her back door and then has a cuppa with the deceased.' Catching herself, Lucy blushed. 'Oh no, not whilst she's dead, but normally when she was alive, sir... the tea, that is, drinking the tea not actually entering...' she tapered off amid snorts of amused laughter which added to the general hum of her new colleagues relishing her discomfort. She stretched her neck to allow the warmth of her embarrassment to sneak out over the collar of her blouse before she continued. 'This morning he found the door open, the dog going ballistic, scratching at the under-stairs cupboard and no sign of Ms McIntosh.' Lucy paused to memorise the next few lines of writing. 'He only opened the door when it became apparent that the dog wasn't going to give up and move away.'

A new screenshot projected on to the wall. This time, rather than the smiling, plump face of a retired headmistress in the garden with Winston her beloved pet, it was the crime scene photograph of poor Avery in all her glory hanging from the coat peg, the mauve scarf wound tightly around her neck acting as a noose, her slack mouth held in a lopsided grimace.

Andy stared longer than he should at the photograph, wondering what the last words on her lips would have been. There was certainly no dignity in death, and at the moment there were no leads either.

'Okay, forensics are just finishing at scene, house to house is being carried out by uniform, and key witness statements are being taken as we speak.' Holmes checked the file on the desk, snapped the ring binder shut and shoved his pen back into the top pocket of his shirt. 'Can we just make sure that there's follow up support in addition to our general aftercare for those witnesses that need it? Right, let's get on with it. You've got your briefs, back here at 4pm.' A curt nod indicated dismissal of his team before he strode purposefully from the room.

Lucy remained seated, taking in every section of the photograph still displayed on the wall. She noted the deathly grimace, just as Andy Barnes had. She stood up and walked over to the whiteboard, being careful not to block the projection and disrupt the picture. To the left of Avery McIntosh, hanging on the next peg to her slumped body, was an old-fashioned pair of PE pumps, the type every kid in the 1950s and 1960s had. Black, with side elastic and a rubber toe. She checked her list. They hadn't been booked in as a crime exhibit. Her fingers danced over the laptop keys, zooming in on the relevant section.

Inside one trainer, she could barely make it out but it was there: a word written in black biro that had faded with age to a pearlised purple hue. She'd read about this in the course notes of her last forensic residential; it was called photo-degradation where ultraviolet light causes colour fade.

Those tiny little shoes had once graced someone's feet, but

she knew Avery had never had children. As a retired teacher maybe they were something left over from her days at the school, a sort of keepsake. However, Lucy wasn't happy with that explanation. It didn't gel.

Grabbing her coat, she quickly jotted down a short note to Andy before setting off for Rosehip Cottage.

BLAST FROM THE PAST

*P*ru slumped down on her bed and stared at the ceiling, trying to coax a smidgeon of energy to get ready for her promised night out with Bree. They'd vowed to try at least four different gins, maybe a glass of wine or two and a less than 3 per cent fat packet of crisps at the Dog & Gun.

Kicking one leg up over her head as high as it would go, she strained to touch the bedhead with her toes, but only succeeded in combining the several rolls of excess flab around her middle with her boobs making one large wobbly mass that resembled Homer Simpson's face.

Mr Binks, her midnight-black cat, lay beside her, bent double. He also had one leg in the air. He stopped what he was doing, gave a haughty stare with his unusual copper-coloured eyes, and carried on licking his nether regions.

'Good grief, Binks, oh to be that agile!' She dropped her leg back down on to the duvet. Feeling a twinge, she grimaced and checked her hip was still in its socket before padding across the bedroom to her wardrobe. Age was definitely starting to catch up with her; she could feel it in her bones and her loss of flexibility. She was under no illusion that any future romance and bedroom

romping would not include her much admired and most definitely appreciated speciality of throwing both legs behind the
back of her head for easy access. She sniggered, remembering the
look of utter horror on Tom's face the first time she had
squirmed out from underneath him and gaily flipped both legs
backwards shouting *Voila!* Her excitement and Tom's disap-
pointing reluctance to participate in her bedroom gymnastics
had taken on a more eye-watering turn when it quickly became
apparent that she should have removed her high heels before
performing her *pièce de résistance*. Tom had quickly vacated the
bedroom in panic, leaving poor Pru resembling her nan's old
kitchen chair as she rocked backwards and forwards, stiletto
heels wedged in her neck like Frankenstein's bolts.

She pulled the bristle brush through her hair, catching herself
in the mirror. 'Mmm... the signs had been there, hadn't they,
Binks? No bloody sense of humour, that was his problem.' She
waited for Binks to reply, or at least acknowledge that she had
included him in her conversation. 'Not even a meow?'

Pulling open her wardrobe, she pushed the hangers along the
rail two at a time, looking for just the right thing to wear. She
plumped for a pretty navy-blue-and-white spotted top with a
flirtatious sweetheart neckline and teamed it with her Jamie
skinny jeans and a red belt. Pulling out a pair of flat ballet pumps,
she checked them against her. 'Maybe it's time to be a little more
adventurous, Binks!' She really did need to shake off the staid
librarian look that she sported most days between 10am and
4.30pm. She needed to be different outside her working hours;
she needed to be herself.

Grabbing a pair of scarlet red court shoes with killer heels,
she bounced down stairs barefoot to answer the knock on her
front door.

Pushing open the colourful half leadlight wooden door to the Dog & Gun, the heady aromas of hops and malt mixed with the rich smell of furniture wax wafted out to greet their delicate noses. Pru and Bree stood momentarily in the doorway, searching for a vacant table. It was unusually busy for a Wednesday night with the bar at least three people deep waiting to be served.

'Bree, Bree... over here!' A pretty blonde, her hair bobbed to just below the chin, frantically waved in their direction with one hand, while patting a vacant stool next to her.

'OMG, Lucy, you're back!' Bree squealed and burst into excited schoolgirl mode, flinging her arms around Lucy as she squeezed her tight. 'Just look at you...' She held her at arm's length, taking in the friend she hadn't seen for more years than she cared to remember. 'You haven't changed a bit!'

Lucy blushed. 'I think I might have just a bit, Bree. I've got contact lenses now and got rid of the tash with a handy bit of electrolysis a few years ago.' She undulated her fingers over her top lip and burst out laughing. 'You're looking pretty good too.'

Pru discreetly sat down in the upholstered booth, pushing the table slightly forward to accommodate her knees, and left the stool free for Bree. She watched the two of them animatedly jabbering about times long past.

'Gosh, how rude of me!' Bree caught her breath for a moment. 'Lucy, this is my good friend Pru Pearce. She manages the library in the village. Pru, this is Lucy. Lucy and I were at Winterbottom High School together, many moons ago.'

'Lovely to meet you, Pru. If you're a friend of this loon then you must have the patience of a saint – or be a loon too!' Lucy laughed, holding out her hand.

'Best go with the latter.' Pru smirked. 'It's lovely to meet you too, and if that makes three of us then we'll all get along famously. Right, first things first. Drinks?'

Ten minutes later, huddled together with three decent gins, a packet of crisps each and a large bag of peanuts, they set about catching up. Bree was shocked, but Pru was delighted to hear that Lucy had joined the police force after finishing university and was now no less than a detective working on her first murder case.

'Oh my goodness, how exciting,' Pru gasped. 'I wish I'd done something like that; I don't very often get a rush of adrenalin in the library. Well, I almost did once when the sliding ladder unclipped itself from the rail when I was second rung from the top reaching for *Wuthering Heights*, but that was more of a rush of something else through sheer fright!'

Lucy laughed and shrugged. 'Oh it's not all heroics and excitement. There's plenty of boring stuff like endless bits of paperwork, but I am enjoying CID; it's quite different to uniform. I got drafted up here last week for the two murders. It's not really changed around here, has it? It still looks pretty much as it did twenty years ago.' She took a large swig of her gin, savoured the taste and followed up with a handful of cheese and onion crisps.

'It's awful, isn't it? Two murdered in as many weeks, and Bree knew both of them really well, didn't you?' Pru posed the question through a mouthful of half-chewed peanuts.

'Well, sort of. They were both members of my WI, but it's not like they were friends of mine. Surely you remember Miss McIntosh, Lucy? She was our headmistress at junior school.'

Lucy shook her head. 'I didn't come to Winterbottom until I was almost thirteen years old, when Dad moved here with his work. All my memories are of you and me getting numerous detentions, rolling my school skirt up to make it shorter, having to scrape the ice off the inside of my bedroom window, snogging Billy Loftus behind the bus stop and, of course, Winterbottom High.' She rolled her eyes and pushed the peanuts towards Pru, indicating she should take some. 'Talking of which, whatever happened to that nerd who used to follow you around like a lovesick puppy? He had the most awful festering acne, a permanent bogey hanging from his left nostril, and the worst cheesy feet in the entire year! Mark... Marcus something-or-other, God he was such a bloody dork.'

Bree almost choked on the mouthful of gin she had just gulped. 'I don't know how to break it to you gently, Luce – I married him!'

A BIRD IN THE HAND

Phyllis swept her hand across the rich velvet cushion, thumped it a few times to plump up the feathers, and then set it at an angle on her overstuffed armchair. Standing back, she admired how cosy it looked nestled close to her inglenook fireplace. There was something about worn leather, brick and aged oak that warmed her, took her back to her childhood, the childhood she had once loved before everything had changed, before her dad had suddenly left without even saying goodbye. She involuntarily shivered, eager to dismiss the memory that had suddenly gripped her.

'I think a nice cup of tea and a garibaldi is in order, don't you, Captain?' Tucking a stray grey wisp of hair behind her ear, she ambled over to the large bird cage in the corner. Captain, her irritating but much-loved cockatoo, tipped his head to one side. His piercing black eyes, circled by powder-blue feathers that were stark against his white body, stared back at her. Letting out an ear-splitting screech he started his morning routine, his head frantically bobbing up and down as he pattered from left to right and back again across the thick wooden perch.

Phyllis testily berated him. 'Dearie me, that's quite enough. I think the whole village can hear you!' She tutted as she made her way into the kitchen. Twenty years she'd had that ruddy bird, twenty long years, and no matter how much she had talked to it, encouraged it with titbits, cooed, simpered and whistled, it had never uttered a bloody word. Not one single, solitary word. Just that annoying screech when she least expected it. Phyllis had lost count of the times she'd almost had a heart attack when he'd launched into a frenzied tirade completely out of the blue. She poured the boiling water into the already warmed pot, rattled the lid into place, and carefully set it upon the tray with her cup, saucer and biscuits.

'Even a "hello" would be better than nothing, Captain,' she grumbled from the doorway as she made her way back into the morning room. Setting her tray down onto the small side table by her chair, she raised her eyebrows and waited. 'See, you really haven't invested yourself into the art of conversation at all, have you, you stupid bird.' Plonking herself down onto the chair, she sank back into the cushion and took her first bite of the garibaldi, savoured the moment, and then used the remainder of the biscuit as a pointer to emphasise her dissatisfaction with her house sharer. 'So, I suppose I have no option other than to just continue with our little one-sided chats, have I?'

Captain bobbed his head, stretched out one leg and a wing, and turned his back on her. Even the damn bird thought she was worthy of being ignored. Phyllis sighed and reached for her little notebook, teasing the pencil from the loop at the side. Carefully placing a tick against 'Avery', she scanned the remaining names. She had seen the large hand of her bedside clock pass many an hour the previous night as sleep had eluded her, her mind racing ahead with her plans. She had decided during those long wakeful hours that her list would be fluid; she would take her opportunities as and when they arose, rather than be regimented in order of numbers or preferences. If any of the remaining ladies presented themselves in the right circumstances, she would adapt. After all, didn't that add to the exquisite fear of being caught?

She couldn't remember the last time she had felt so excited, so animated – so... so... *alive...* that was it, she felt alive. She finally had purpose again.

'Never piss off a full blown, professionally certified, time-served psychopath, hey, Captain... no matter how old she gets!' Phyllis didn't so much giggle; she cackled as she reached into her tapestry bag and pulled out her current work in progress.

The chilling sound of her laughter, accompanied by the clackety-clack of the needles as she started a knit-one, purl-one row, eerily drifted out through the open window, across the small front garden, up over the neatly trimmed privet hedge, and faded before it could reach the ears of the busy Winterbottom residents going about their sedentary, peaceful lives.

If only they knew...

Pru turned the floral-headed leaflet over and read the words that had been typed in what she recognised as 'Brush Script'. It had a melancholy feel to it. She wasn't sure if it was the combination of content and font, or simply because she knew why everyone would be gathered at the parish hall.

Winterbottom Women's Institute
Remembrance Meeting 7.30pm
A time to reflect on our friendships and to remember those
who are no longer with us...
Mabel Allinson and Avery McIntosh R.I.P

She twisted the leaflet in her hand. Rolling it into a tube she desperately resisted the urge to blow it like a trumpet. 'I can't believe you've actually got me here,' she hissed through gritted teeth at Bree. 'In fact, I can't believe I'm sitting on a bloody pink velour chair with a slice of...' She poked at what was on her plate with her finger and turned it over '...Jeez, I don't know, something brown, incredibly sticky, and crusty on the outside!'

Bree stifled a snort of laughter, which, considering the sombre occasion, would have been totally unappreciated by the assembled ladies of the WI and the sobbing Kitty Hardcastle, who was currently sitting directly in front of her doing a pretty good impression of a Victorian professional mourner with a lace hanky shoved up her right nostril. 'It's Brenda's latest recipe, Chocolate Delight,' Bree whispered. 'Just shove it in your mouth and be grateful.'

'Ha! It's been a long time since anyone's said that to me!' Pru almost choked on the first taste of sponge, trying not to snigger out loud.

'Oh my God, you are so disgusting!' Unfortunately, Bree couldn't contain her own laughter, spluttering fine blobs of chocolate sponge over the back of Kitty's blouse and causing several other stalwarts on the front row to uniformly turn their heads in their direction and proffer the Winterbottom death stare. 'Look, now you've done it; we'll be pegged as troublemakers.'

Wiping her mouth with a tissue, Pru quickly made a feeble attempt to dab her own eyes too, whilst giving a look of conspiratorial fake misery to the aforementioned ladies. The faces of one or two softened, but the stalwarts gave nothing. 'See, it's death and damnation for us. We're doomed, I tell you; we're all doomed!' Her poor stab at a Scottish accent to emphasise the words only made Bree laugh more. 'So, if I'm here under the guise of paying our respects to Avery and Mabel whilst doing a bit of detective work, why are you here?' She pulled at a small piece of cake with her fingers and popped it in her mouth.

'I'm a member, duh, why do you think?' Bree rolled her eyes. 'D'you know, the more I think about this, the more I'm convinced this isn't going to end well. I can just see us getting locked up rather than the murderer. Can you imagine poor Luce if she's the one that's got to slap the handcuffs on us?'

Savouring the chocolate on her lips, Pru smirked. 'Talking of handcuffs and other bedroom accessories, did I ever tell you about the time when Tom and I indulged in...'

'Whoa, too much information! Let's just stick to what we know, hey?' Bree's voice dropped to a low whisper, 'Right, Mabel was killed with one blow from a crochet needle in the neck, landing face first in one of Brenda's delights–' She mimicked a stabbing motion. '–and Avery was strangled with a hand-knitted scarf and left hanging on a coat hook in the cupboard.' She popped her eyes, stuck out her tongue and tipped her head to one side, her right arm out holding what Pru imagined would be an invisible scarf.

Pru nodded in agreement. 'Mmm... so Avery literally did "peg it" then!' Making air quotes with her fingers she smirked, waiting for a decent reaction from Bree, only to be disappointingly gifted one raised eyebrow. 'Ah okay, not funny? Right, do you think it's safe to say that the murderer is a woman unless you know of any manly men who crochet and knit in between picking their noses and scratching their nuts?' Another chunk of cake went the same way as the first.

'Ladies – really!' Kitty's head swivelled *Exorcist* style. 'This is not an evening for joviality. We're here to pay our respects to–'

'Lemon drizzle cake, anyone?' Brenda interrupted. Standing at the end of the row with a plate piled high, she eagerly wafted it towards Pru and Bree whilst furtively wiping crumbs from her chin.

Kitty took on a slight greenish hue before squealing, 'Brenda, how *could* you?' and promptly burst into tears again.

It was now Pru's turn to roll her eyes as she slumped back in her chair, arms folded. This wasn't going to be as easy as she had first thought. The excitement she had felt sitting in the Dog & Gun when Lucy had asked her and Bree for 'inside' help at the Winterbottom WI was quickly starting to wane. A furtive look around the room, taking in the row upon row of heads that were permed, teased, hot-ironed, feathered and bobbed, all in a rainbow of colours, natural and otherwise, told her the task they had accepted was in fact going to be an absolute bloody nightmare.

HAIR TODAY...

Murdoch Holmes ran both his hands through his hair in frustration. The start of a tension headache held a vice-like grip around his temples. He scribbled key words in his jotter to remind himself of the various lines of enquiry he wanted tied up by his team before the end of the shift, along with a half-hearted shopping list for on the way home. Sweeping his greying quiff to one side, he mentally conceded that a quick visit to Urban Shave for a much-needed trim was in order. Giving his nose a furtive scratch, he also had to admit that their speciality service, the 'Dastardly Duo', might be on the cards too. Just the mere thought of a savage simultaneous wax of his nostrils and ears made his eyes water. He still marvelled at how he was rapidly failing to keep hairs on his head but had no problem at all in cultivating excessively long ones that sprouted in unison out of his olfactory and auditory orifices.

'Boss, I just got the forensics back on the wool fibre from the Allinson job.' Andy Barnes purposefully strode across the office, plonked himself down on the chair next to Holmes and pushed the open report on to the desk. 'It's 15 per cent wool, 25 per cent cotton and 60 per cent acrylic, and it's from the Sirdar Crofter

Double Knit range in Maisie, shade code 099, which is a sort of mauve colour.' He sat back waiting for Holmes to be suitably impressed. He didn't have long to wait.

'Bloody hell, son, a man who sees more colours than just black, white and magnolia, you'll drive the women wild!' Holmes guffawed. 'Joking aside, it's amazing what forensic scientists can achieve these days.' Pulling the file closer to him, he carefully studied it. 'Mark my words, it's well worth the years of study they do, the hours of focused revision and exams, to get a detailed result like that. It makes you wonder how they do it.'

Andy bit his bottom lip. 'Er... from the label.'

'What label?'

'The one they found wedged down the back of the cardigan the deceased was wearing. It must have fallen from the ball of wool the single fibre came from during the stabbing. Well at least we can assume it did from the work forensics have already done.' Andy gestured at the sealed evidence bag containing the glossy paper band printed with the word 'Sirdar', to Holmes. 'They bought another ball and did a cross-match with the fibres.'

Holmes gave an air of indifference. 'Never assume, Barnes, and why shouldn't we?' He stabbed the nib of his pen in the air to emphasise each word.

Andy hesitated, wondering if it was a loaded question. 'Er...'

'I'll tell you exactly why. We should never assume "as it makes a donkey out of you and me".' Holmes sat back, pretty pleased with himself.

'An ass.'

'What?'

'It's an ass.'

'What is?'

'Out of you and me.'

'Now listen, son, I don't know what you're getting at, but–'

The squeak of the incident room door and the sudden breezy

appearance of Lucy waving a sheet of A4 paper cut Holmes short, much to the relief of Andy Barnes.

'Sir, sir...' She paused to catch her breath. The three flights of stairs had pushed her lungs to full capacity. She cringed; the last time she'd panted that hard was with Ben Foster when he'd hit just the right spot in the back of his reconditioned Mark II Ford Escort classic. Well, it had either been him or the rather unfortunately placed fancy gear knob. She involuntarily blushed at the memory.

'Spit it out, Harris!' Holmes barked, causing her face to redden further.

'The pumps I found hanging next to Avery McIntosh have definitely been marked inside with a name, but due to age the ink has degenerated quite badly. We've only been able to make out the first letter of the first name, which is an "M", and the last two letters of the surname we think are "e" and "n". I know it's not much at the moment, but it could be worth following up.' Lucy waited, bending the corner of the paper in nervous anticipation.

Holmes mused on her words, taking the opportunity to use the pause in conversation for a large swig of tea from his mug. Finally, he replied, 'What makes you think it has anything to do with the investigation, Lucy? Why are they any different to the umbrella that was in there, along with two coats, a bag of dog biscuits and–' He turned the page on the crime scene log and studied it. '–two hundred plastic carrier bags in a butterfly pattern dispenser?' He shook his head and grinned, trying to work out how many 5p's that would add up to.

Lucy composed herself. She didn't want her words to spill out randomly and unconnected, resulting in her suspicions and suggestion being easily dismissed. 'They're tiny school gym pumps, sir, the sort a child would wear.' She paused, gathering her thoughts. 'Avery McIntosh didn't have children of her own, and to think she would keep a souvenir from her school teaching days doesn't quite sit well from the enquiries I've made. She was a good teacher and headmistress, but she didn't do sentimentality or favouritism. I think they were left there by the murderer for a reason.'

'Ah, you do, do you?' Holmes gave nothing away. Pursing his lips, he sagely nodded his head several times, thinking. 'So, if we put this together, we've got a wool fibre with a label left at the Allinson scene and a pair of kid's gym shoes at the McIntosh one.'

Lucy could hardly contain her excitement; he was going to take her seriously! Her first big investigation and the DI was considering what she'd brought before him.

Andy interrupted the silence. 'It's worth keeping it in mind, boss. If we're honest, it's all we've got from scene two.' He gave Lucy a conspiratorial smile.

Holmes finally spoke. 'Okay, keep with it. See if they can be sent for enhancement.' He scribbled his signature on the submissions form and handed it to her. 'And let me know of any developments.'

Standing outside in the corridor, the door slowly closed into its frame behind her sending out a muted thud as Lucy punched the air in unbridled triumph.

PIP

*P*hillipa Jackson, or better known to her close friends, family and, of course, her fellow Winterbottom WI ladies as Pip, exaggeratedly smoothed on a liberal slick of Ruby Raisin lip gloss. She smacked her lips together and pouted into the small hand-held magnifying mirror.

'Bloody hell, nooooo!' She grabbed at the single dark hair that was adorning her top lip with the nails of her thumb and middle finger and pulled upwards, which only served to elongate said lip so that she gave a pretty fine impersonation of Elvis Presley. Panic quickly set in as she frantically rummaged around in her make-up bag.

'Voila!' She turned the tweezers to catch the light and clicked them together to ensure they still had holding power. She rarely used them these days. Years and years of over-plucking to accommodate the 1970s fashion of needle-thin eyebrows had left them bereft of any new growth since 1982. She now had to pencil them in to show the world the delightful variance of her available expressions, which ranged from surprise to compre-hension and from happiness to sheer annoyance. She had thought of the possibility of having them tattooed on, but considering the consternation that had been caused at the last WI meeting when Ethel Tytherington had almost fainted after seeing Chelsea Blandish's recent inked additions, she had abandoned that thought.

She smiled to herself as she pulled on the solitary hair. It pinged from her skin, making her eyes water. Poor Ethel had sworn Chelsea's massive slug of an eyebrow was alive and had moved on its own accord. It had taken two cups of tea and a slice of bara brith to calm her down and convince her that it had been a trick of the light combined with Chelsea's excessive use of cosmetic fillers.

'Well, would you look at that?' She held the tweezers up to the window, inspected the length of the bristle, and tutted. 'Oh dear God, I'll be checking for hairy nipples before you know it!' She tried to make light of her current predicament, but in all honesty there was nothing funny about getting old. She checked her reflection in the mirror again, stretching her neck to iron out her chins – in the plural – whilst tipping the sides of her lips up in a futile attempt to lift the sagging jowls that had suddenly appeared from nowhere.

'This will never do, it really won't!' She felt like crying but held back. Knowing her luck, the effort of sobbing would probably cause an involuntary Tena Lady moment, ruining the fabulous silk Janet Reger fineries that were currently cosseting her ample backside. She spun the aged and worn gold band around on the third finger of her left hand and sighed. She might be a widow, she might be on the wrong side of sixty, but that shouldn't mean letting herself or any other dreadful bodily function go. What if she was successful in her bid to be the next WI president? Imagine standing in front of everyone with a full-blown moustache quivering in the breeze whilst her baggy chins rested on the opening minutes as her bladder gave up the ghost the very first time she coughed and uttered, *Ladies, attention please*? She shuddered and quickly reached for her address book.

Poking her manicured fingernail into the 'W' slot, she flicked the pages and scanned the numbers. The *bleep, bleep* of the keypad to her mobile phone, as her deft fingers quickly typed in the number, was strangely comforting and gave an instant promise of a fabulous solution to lift the fluffy cloud of gloom she was currently feeling.

Brrrrr, brrrrr. Brrrr, brrrr. Brrrr, brrrr.

'Good morning, Wrinkle in Time, Andrea speaking, how may I help you?'

Pip reclined on her bed, plumped and adjusted the large pink scatter cushions behind her and grinned. 'Yes, I would like to make an urgent appointment, please.' Holding her Parker pen in the other hand, she waited expectantly.

But Pip was not the only one who was waiting.

On the other side of the bedroom door, a figure hovered. Holding her breath in anticipation, a can of Mr Sheen in one hand and a yellow duster in the other, Pip's new cleaning lady also waited.

SWEATY BETTY

'ove along now, ladies,' Kitty's voice trilled loudly above the excited chatter from the fifty-two members of the Winterbottom WI annual day out posse. The charabanc was full to capacity, with heads attired in an assortment of colours, materials and fancy additions for the themed hat competition they were attending. Kitty held her clipboard high, standing regally at the front of the bus next to Frank Atkins, the driver and proud owner of Rubber, Springs & Gaskets Coach Tours.

'Millie, oh Millie.' Kitty raised the tone of her voice several octaves whilst frantically waving her free hand in the air. 'Millie, please remove your hairy muff from Clarissa's face, it almost took her eye out. Do try to keep it under control, dear!'

A wave of laughter rippled through the rows of her captive audience as Millie duly obliged by removing her hat and, with a stroke of her fingers, tamed the bright yellow chick that bounced backwards and forwards on the end of a wire. 'It's a hairy puff, Kitty, a puff-ball to be exact and I knitted it myself, look it's even got a little beak.' She held it aloft with a flourish of pride, whilst Clarissa, who was sitting in the seat directly behind her, squinted through her one remaining good eye as she tried to pluck the offending piece of yellow fluff from her eyelash.

Feigning ignorance of her verbal faux pas, Kitty swept her fingers through her hair, and delicately patted her bob upwards with the palm of her hand as she turned her attention to the open coach doors. 'Come along, Mrs Charlesworth, quick, quick. We need to be on the road pronto if we are to arrive in time for the opening presentation.' She gently took hold of Rita Charlesworth's arm as the unsteady OAP negotiated the steps onto the coach. Watching her pause to catch her breath before gathering the energy to tackle the aisle to her seat, Kitty couldn't help but wonder how on earth Rita had been a presidential nominee. Half deaf and with a much talked about bladder weakness that kept her in the parish hall toilets for most of their meetings, if she were chosen she would definitely struggle to call 'Order' and open matters before she would have to disappear into the smallest room clutching her latest Mills & Boon for a minimum of twenty minutes. 'Oh, *c'est la vie*,' she mentally sighed to herself before turning her attention back to the task in hand. 'Here you go, Mrs Charlesworth; you're sitting next to Clarissa.' She manoeuvred Rita towards the seat on the right-hand side of the coach.

'Eh?' Rita waited for a further prompt as she adjusted her hearing aid.

'Clarissa.'

'I haven't missed her... have I?' Rita looked confused.

Kitty let out a sigh of mild exasperation. 'Clarissa! You're sitting next to Clarissa!'

'My sister? I haven't got a sister.'

Kitty looked up to the heavens for support. When none was forthcoming, she changed tack, deciding to shove Rita in the nearest available seat. 'Okay, dear, you're here, right by Betty.'

Rita harrumphed as she slid herself into the seat. Giving Kitty a look of disdain, she savagely positioned her handbag on her knee before turning to her sharing companion. 'The cheek of it, *you* don't think I'm sweaty, do you?'

Poor Betty shrugged her shoulders and rolled her eyes. 'She said "Betty".'

'You too, well I never!' Rita grabbed a small Lily of the Valley atomiser from her handbag, gave herself two blasts of perfume and then blasted poor Betty for good measure.

Kitty beat a hasty retreat from the oppressive scent towards the front of the coach. She checked her list and nodded to Frank, who gave her a saucy wink. She blushed, returning his acknowledgement with a coy smile. 'Right, ladies.' She tapped her pen on the final number on the list and made a cursory head count. 'We're on our way!'

As the coach rumbled along the country lanes, heading out from Winterbottom towards their rural destination of Chapperton Bliss, the WI ladies used the time to unite their voices in song. A shortened version of 'Jerusalem', which was normally reserved to open their meetings, set the ball rolling. As the final line gently faded away to a whisper, Kitty, who had been rigorously conducting the tempo from the front, tottered slightly as Frank rounded a sharp bend.

Grabbing on to the handrail to catch her balance, she inelegantly slithered into the front seat, ensuring Frank was treated to a fleeting glimpse of her shapely pins at the same time. 'Not too far now, ladies; gather your belongings. Don't forget your coats, just in case the weather turns.' Kitty rummaged around in the large blue Ikea bag on the empty seat next to her.

'Pah! That woman would be happy directing traffic if it meant she could send them all down a one-way street – the wrong way!' Ethel Tytherington hissed to no one in particular as she carefully applied a cupid's bow of pink lipstick to her top lip. She smacked them together to even out the application, and after checking her teeth for any residue she snapped the hand-held gold compact closed. 'I just know she's going to die of bloody boredom when she eventually relinquishes her precious presidency.'

Several heads surrounding Ethel nodded in agreement.

'I'm sure old Frank will keep her busy,' snorted Clarissa, indiscreetly pointing to the back of their driver's head, whilst giving a knowing wink and a comical Les Dawson hoist of her boobs using her forearms. 'Dear Kitty has slipped her moorings on many occasions…' she gurned, '… and she doesn't always wait for the tide to rise to do it!'

Her quip led to an outbreak of laughter between them, their voices low and spirits high, clearly enjoying the snippet of gossip that Clarissa had imparted, as Kitty sat in blissful ignorance at the front.

A hunched figure quietly ensconced in the corner seat on the back row appeared to pay no attention to the joviality. Phyllis feigned indifference to their gossipy conversation by looking out through the window as the fields and trees passed in a blur, the road noise and rustling leaves hitting the side of the coach wafted in staccato through the open top window.

Oh what a tangled web we weave…

A PENNY FOR HER THOUGHTS

The large tarpaulin sign flapped in the gentle breeze as it heralded their arrival at The Chapperton Bliss County Crafts Festival. The large red letters, peppered with colourful daubs of paint that were meant to simulate flowers, gave promise of exciting things to do once they entered the field and its tightly packed marquees.

The ladies of Winterbottom WI formed an ill-managed posse as they followed Kitty and the ridiculously large plastic flower she was holding aloft for all to see.

'Follow the sunflower, ladies, follow the sunflower!' she trilled as she strode purposefully across the car park towards the entrance, clearly in her element as leader.

Pru, who had been dragged along by Bree as an *Oooh you'll love it once you get there* invitation, rolled her eyes. 'Follow the bloody sunflower! Jesus Christ, Bree, why couldn't it be "follow the hunky farmer" or "follow this bottle of gin", hey?'

'Yep, you'd be fair galloping for those, wouldn't you?' Bree smirked. 'Just humour her; she means well. We can sneak off once we get in there; they'll be doing the hat competition and the cake stalls, so while they're occupied we can do our own thing.

I've heard a rumour there's a pretty decent drinks tent with a selection of locally sourced and produced alcofrolic drinks.' She grinned and linked arms with her friend.

'Lead me to it!' Pru laughed, giving an over-exaggerated hiccup. 'I'll need more than one though, after suffering that journey.' She vigorously slapped her thigh to bring some feeling back. 'I don't think Frank has had those seat springs refurbished since 1952.'

The lovely ladies of The Winterbottom WI held their formation through the main gates and then splintered into smaller groups once inside, the strict instructions from Kitty to meet back at that location at 4.30pm still ringing in their ears.

Pru and Bree had veered quickly and gracefully towards the drinks tents, faking interest in the arts & crafts stall run by the ladies of The Chapperton Bliss Soroptimist's Society on the way. Tatted lace doilies were pegged out on a fine string to show off their intricate patterns and small hand-knitted animals sat in carefully arranged groups on the table. Bree picked up a plastic doll dressed in a brightly coloured rainbow ball gown and a pom-pom hat. Turning it in her hands, she lifted the crochet skirt and peeked underneath. 'Jeez, where on earth would you entertain one of these in your house?' she sniggered.

'In the toilet,' Pru helpfully offered.

'No way!'

'Yep, very 1970s twee. It's a bog roll hider; no house was without one. To be honest– oh quick! She's not looking!' Cutting the conversation short as soon as she spotted Kitty disappearing into the cake tent, Pru grabbed Bree's arm and gaily twirled her towards the bar. 'Come on, first one's on me!'

The spread of green fields made the uniformed layout of the tents and side stalls appear like teeth, some white, some decidedly discoloured, some in a straight line, some uneven and wonky, depending on who had set them up. The gentle breeze smacked and cracked against the tarpaulin as each tent flapped in its thermal.

Rita, Clarissa and Ethel formed their own small troupe, remaining slightly behind Kitty who was still exuberantly waving her sunflower as she wound her way through the crowds inside the cake tent. 'Plum crumble to the left of me, Victoria sponge to the right,' she warbled loudly.

'And here we are, stuck in the middle with you!' Clarissa half sang, half muttered under her breath, making the others titter like naughty schoolgirls. She rolled her eyes and pointed through the pegged-up flap, just in time to see Pru and Bree disappearing inside the drinks tent. 'Ten minutes in here, quick powder of our noses in the loos, when we find them–' Another roll of her eyes. '–and I propose we join the two youngsters in *that* marquee over there, don't you?' She smirked waiting for nods of approval.

She didn't have long to wait. As Kitty blithely carried on with her tour guide routine, the yellow of the flower bobbing above the crowd of heads, the ladies following in her wake began to discreetly drop away to make their escape and indulge in a glass or two of sweet sherry.

Bree clinked her glass against Pru's. 'Cheers, my dears!' she said as she took her first sip of gin, the ice cubes rattling melodically as the small sliver of lemon swirled around them. She looked at her friend, taking in the sadness of her smile. It didn't quite reach her eyes, it sparkled all right, the sort of smile that always made you want to smile too, her perfect teeth setting off her pretty lips, but it still belied her pensive mood.

'Do you still miss him, Pru?' Bree hoped she wasn't speaking out of turn.

Pru hesitated, taking a much bigger slug of her gin than was really necessary. 'I suppose so, in a strange way. I miss what we had before it all went wrong, but I don't miss what he became, if that makes sense – and I certainly don't miss Madison Gale's festering bloody hairy armpits either!' She shuddered at the thought.

Bree nodded. 'Of course it makes sense. Sorry, I shouldn't have brought it up. We're supposed to be here for a bit of fun, a light-hearted and hopefully drunken afternoon.'

'Did somebody mention fun and being drunk in the same sentence? It's an absolute recipe for disaster in my humble opinion.'

Pru was the first to turn and acknowledge the owner of the smooth voice that held the trace of a local lilt. He held out his hand in gentlemanly greeting. 'Andy Barnes. We met briefly with Lucy a few weeks ago; we work together.' He waited, hoping he wasn't about to embarrass himself.

Bree grinned at him, remembering only too well who he was, but Pru was of no use whatsoever. She had already become instantly mesmerised by his blue eyes that were haloed by a dark outer circle, making them deliciously hypnotic. She sat on the edge of her stool, gawping at him like the proverbial idiot, wanting to speak but not finding the words.

Oh for goodness' sake, girl, get a grip, say something... anything!

She was aware that his image was starting to tilt to starboard. Not dreamily, not in coyness or under the undue influence of alcohol, but with a startling judder as one of the tripod legs on her stool began to slowly sink into the grass. She tilted her own neck in the opposite direction to match and straighten him up, but it was no better. In fact, it was worse.

And then she found the elusive words she had been waiting for, but they were not the ones she would have liked as the leg sank itself another two inches into the turf.

'Oh shit... what a bastard!' she squealed. Tipping forwards like the Leaning Tower of Pisa, she desperately tried to regain her balance and failed miserably.

Andy was quick to react, becoming her accidental hero as he scooped her into his arms, her gin slopping over the side of the glass, falling in droplets over him. 'Oops, are you okay?' he breathed, trying hard not to laugh. 'Maybe take more tonic with it next time, hey?'

'I've only had one. In fact, I've hardly drunk this one at all!' Pru mumbled in embarrassment. She was now mesmerised, not by his eyes but by the chunk of lemon that was sitting forlornly on the shoulder of his jacket.

Andy was acutely aware that this could possibly be the first and last chance he would get to make a good impression. He had to pick his words carefully. He'd just virtually insinuated that the well-thought-of village librarian was nothing more than a lush, and an unbalanced one at that. 'I'm sorry, that's my crass humour; of course I know you're not drunk... just a little tip-sy maybe?' He indicated the stool that was now lying on its side on the grass to prove his little joke before letting out a deep, warm laugh, which encouraged Bree to spray her last sip of gin all over the other shoulder of his jacket as she started giggling, more at his cheesy joke than his timing.

'Tipsy... get it?' He waited.

Pru pulled at her blouse, trying to cover her shoulder and bring back a small amount of dignity to her current situation. 'Mmm... yes, tipsy, I get it,' she murmured. 'Do you know you've got a lemon on your shoulder?'

'Well, I'm more of a detective than a singer, but if you hum it, I'll try!'

The uncomfortable pause in the introductory proceedings suddenly gave way to bursts of laughter and the promise of another round of drinks.

~

The high-pitched squealing of Rita Charlesworth's hearing aid as she attempted to adjust the settings made Clarissa flinch. It was on a par with someone scraping their fingernails along a blackboard. 'When you've quite finished fiddling, Rita, we'll make our way to the loos and then we can indulge in a few sherries before Kitty realises we're missing.'

Rita gave a tut of indignation as she quickened her pace to catch up. 'I wasn't piddling! I know I have a problem, but I can hold on.' She stomped ahead of the group, her stick waving in the air as she had the last word. 'And I'll have you know I was gusset-clutching before half of you were born!'

Clarissa snorted. Considering Rita wasn't that much older than most of their group, she wondered how long her little 'problem' had actually been a problem. 'Okay, ladies, here we are.' She stopped abruptly by the row of Portaloos. 'As usual, there's a bit of a queue so let's assemble some order. Rita, if you're still gusset-clutching, you go first. Ethel, you can go ahead of me, I'm not that desperate. Phyllis, Phyllis! Has anyone seen Phyllis, she was here a minute ago? Oh that woman will be the death of me...'

Phyllis couldn't help but agree.

She certainly was the death of some, not Clarissa in particular but there were still several left on her list, and she couldn't believe how fortuitous today was going to be. Her plan had been for Pip Jackson to bite the dust next, but in all honesty, she couldn't; no, she *wouldn't*, miss this opportunity. Even if death failed to be immediate, a broken hip on most occasions would lead to a promising demise in the elderly.

She positioned herself behind the row of brightly coloured turquoise and yellow toilets, being careful not to be seen. It was amazing how being middle-aged, being ordinary, and being overlooked could almost make you invisible.

She waited.

She watched.

Any minute now.

She held her breath as the target made her way to the fourth toilet along. Her next victim was slow, giving Phyllis plenty of time to manoeuvre herself along the row and stand behind the moulded plastic of Cubicle 4, her fingertips first finding purchase under the rim of the hoisting hook as she unhitched it from the hammered-in metal safety peg. This was going to take every ounce of strength she possessed, but determination can conjure up wonderful things, and without its mooring point it was already nicely unstable.

The seconds ticked by.

When will you pay me? Say the bells of Old Bailey...

...and *voila!*

ANCHORS AWAY

*R*ita, glad of being ushered to the front, slowly made her way to the Portaloo that had just been vacated by a particularly ruddy-faced farmer type. She took in his bulk under the red and black checked shirt, the way he tugged aggressively at the belt on his brown cord trousers and the triumphant grin on his face.

Well he certainly hadn't been for just a tinkle!

She inwardly cringed, wondering what delight he might have dropped in Cubicle 4. Not having the stomach for manly odours, her relief was palpable when the door to Cubicle 6 opened. Neatly veering past Cubicle 4, her sharp-as-a-tack eyes picked out a glimmer in the grass. Deaf she might be, but when it came to cash, she could spot money a mile off.

Bending down, her arthritic fingers plucked at the object. 'Ooh, see a pound and pick it up and all day long you'll have good lu–'

Rita didn't get chance to finish her little ditty before the rush of wind and a loud crash behind her plunged her to the ground awkwardly.

Screams and gasps from the crowd around her, along with the

sounds of utter pandemonium, filled the air. She felt nothing, only a wetness that had begun to seep through her Verity Millington summer dress...

...and the shiny pound coin that was clutched in her outstretched hand.

∿

'Oh my God, what was that?' Bree's head snapped sideways so that she could look through the pinned-back flap of the drinks tent.

Pru dropped down from her stool to quickly follow behind Andy, who had already abandoned his weak tasting orange juice in favour of a rapid sprint outside, the detective in him coming to the fore.

Pushing through the gathered crowd, he came to a halt.

The voice of a very distraught Ethel Tytherington shrieked over the general hum of the shocked but intrigued mass who had made their way to where the excitement was.

'She's dead. Oh my poor Rita! What a way to go!' Ethel wailed before she fell sobbing into the arms of Clarissa, who could do no more than stand there stunned, her mouth opening and closing like a cod fish.

The turquoise cubicle lying on its front was spewing out a blue foamy liquid that was seeping into the grass beside the prone body of Rita Charlesworth. The hum became a babbling crescendo as people shouted for first aid, an ambulance, a seat for Ethel, and even a tot of whisky.

Andy had to holler loudly to be heard. 'I'm a police officer. Please can everyone calm down and step back.' Eager to preserve the scene as even accidental death would require investigation, he became animated in the role that he knew best. Pru stood beside him, there should he need her.

The crowd parted, giving him space to kneel down next to

Rita. As he leant in to check for a pulse, her eyes fluttered open, giving him a start. Her lips parted and closed, emitting a very faint whisper. Andy placed his ear closer to her mouth to try and catch her words.

'I didn't bloody gusset-clutch–' Rita moaned as she lifted up the pound coin pinched between her finger and thumb in an act of triumph, the sunlight glinting from its edge. '– I may have accidentally spent a penny but look – I've made meself a quid!'

Andy knew that as much as his police service had taught him a darker side to humour, this really was a most inappropriate moment to seek it in this situation, so he restrained the snort of laughter that had threatened to escape. 'It's okay, we've got you. An ambulance is on its way.' He turned to Pru. 'Make sure someone has definitely telephoned for one.'

Pru duly obliged by starting towards the organisers' tent, but not before she came face to face with Phyllis Watson who was animatedly surveying the scene.

'Oh dear, had a little mishap, have we?' Phyllis smirked. 'I always said her weak bladder would be her downfall. Not a very pleasant way to go, though, is it.' She didn't so much ask the question; it was more of a statement.

Pru nodded. 'We don't know what's happened yet, but she's very lucky to be alive.'

Phyllis didn't reply, her eyes sparked and narrowed as she took a huge intake of breath before turning on her heel to amble off towards the cake tent, leaving Pru to ponder her strange reaction.

Bree draped her arm across her friend's shoulders to give her a comforting hug. Sensing Pru's confusion, she whispered, 'What was that all about?'

'Honestly, Bree, if I didn't know better, I could swear she looked more disappointed than upset that Rita is still alive.'

Pru made a mental note to do a bit of digging on creepy Ms Watson. She'd seen her around the village, and even though she wasn't the type of woman to mix with others or generally pass the time of day with, there was still a village camaraderie and concern amongst everyone, so there was definitely something very, very wrong in that reaction.

So much so it made her spider senses tingle.

THE TWISTED CURRENT CAFÉ

Florrie Patterson, owner of The Twisted Currant Café, carefully placed two chocolate eclairs and a custard slice on to the gaily patterned plates in front of her. She loved her little shop, the small, intimate tables that had been laid out in a pleasing pattern across the black-and-white chequered tiles, the crisp linen tablecloths laundered daily – no plastic ones in her café – and the small vases that held a meadow flower mix from her own garden.

She was also happy that after several weeks of practice she had finally mastered the art of using her new spring-loaded cake tongues, specifically manufactured for those with arthritic hands and no decent finger squeeze. She smiled to herself, her train of thought coming to the love of her life: Mr Patterson. There had been no complaints from him in that department, but her lack of hand power had caused untold problems in her working day. The new tongues had not been an easy purchase. Just like Avery McIntosh's grouchy dog Winston, they'd snapped at her each time she picked up a cream horn, crushing the delicate puff pastry to smithereens. It was two days, several sticking plasters, a broken fingernail and a hit on the cream cake profits before she'd realised there was a handy wheel to adjust their ferocity.

Thinking of Avery suddenly made her happy mood turn to sad. First Mabel and then Avery, and now the sudden near miss with Rita. What on earth was going on in her lovely peaceful village of Winterbottom? The melodic tinkling of the small bell above the door broke her reverie as another customer entered her haven. Shuffling the plates around on the tray to fit the Lorna Doone chintz teapot on, she made her way over to Table 3 by the window.

'Oh, thank you, Florrie; gosh, they look delicious!' Pru lifted her arms away from the table, which only moments earlier she had been hunched over, elbows firmly planted on the delicate cloth, discussing the previous day's events with Lucy and Bree. She waited until Florrie had moved on to tend to her new customer before she continued with her conversation.

'Apparently it couldn't have been an accident. According to Andy it was a deliberate act. The Portaloo company had a book that was signed off after installing them, showing that all safety procedures had been carried out.' Pru took a bite from her custard slice, mumbling through the next few words as she savoured it before using the serviette to wipe her chin.

Bree and Lucy nodded in agreement. Lucy had read the report that had been given to their team. The DCI had called Murdoch Holmes in for a 'little chat', which in their world meant he had probably been given a good old-fashioned bollocking for not progressing the McIntosh and Allinson jobs. He'd emerged some twenty minutes later with a look of thunder on his face and a file for Rita Charlesworth tucked under his arm. He'd grumbled incessantly for the rest of the shift that there was no 'bloody evidence' that Rita was the intended victim or that it should be linked, but what the DCI wanted, the DCI got.

'I've never actually seen a set up like that for Portaloos, not that I spend my time sneaking around outside bogs!' Bree was quick to add.

Lucy laughed at the thought of her friend skulking around public toilets. 'It's not something that most companies have, but this one has had issues in fields where the ground can be uneven or unstable and to combat strong gusts of wind, so it's just an additional safety feature they dreamt up themselves. The hook on the back clips into a ground anchor, and someone had unhitched it, then pushed it over.'

The three of them sat in silence for a while, enjoying their respective cakes whilst their collective brains ran over the two murders and the non-accidental privy incident.

It was Bree who broke the silence. 'Poor Rita, she thought she'd had an unfortunate breach of the old pelvic floor. It took forever for Kitty to convince her that it was the chemical water from the toilet that she was lying in.'

They looked at each other, trying not to laugh. 'Poor Rita', was right, but on the other hand it was just as much 'Lucky Rita'.

'And if she hadn't bent down to pick up that pound coin, she'd have been embedded and imprinted on that field like a fossil; it literally missed her by millimetres. She was lucky to get away with a couple of bruised knees and a bump on her head.' Bree touched her own forehead to emphasise Rita's injury.

Pru wondered if she should share her concerns again over Phyllis Watson's reaction to finding out that Rita was still alive and kicking. She had lain awake until the small hours, going over and over their conversation, desperately trying to find either confirmation of her suspicions or something that would quell them. By 3:28am exactly, she had tiptoed downstairs for a mug of milky cocoa, and whilst sitting on the sofa with her legs curled up underneath her dressing gown, her hands warming against the sides of the mug, she had come to the conclusion that the only link between Avery, Mabel, Rita and Phyllis was their WI membership.

That had made her laugh loudly.

Running her hand along the back of Mr Binks, watching his copper eyes become hooded in pleasure, a thought had suddenly entered her weary mind.

'Oooh, Murders at the Winterbottom WI... well I never, Mr Binks, that certainly has a ring to it, doesn't it? It almost sounds like the title of a book in our library!' Much to her disappointment, Mr Binks had denied her a reply as he was already fast asleep, leaving her to pad upstairs to bed on her own.

Coming back to the conversation at hand, she looked at Lucy and Bree considering her options. It didn't take her long to decide to keep what she thought to herself for the time being, maybe until something more substantial came her way. 'Luce, are there any thoughts that it might be an "inside" job?' That was a good police term if ever there was one; she'd heard it lots of times watching *Midsomer Murders* on the television.

Lucy shrugged. 'Inside where? The Women's Institute?'

Bree smirked, visions of a rampant killer amongst the ranks of the Winterbottom WI scone makers and knitters filled her with glee. 'Oh come on, Pru. For goodness' sake, half of them can't rustle up the strength to squeeze a teabag, let alone plot and carry out a devilish murder.'

Pru popped the last of the custard slice into her mouth and licked her lips. 'They're not all old and past it. What about that blonde one, what's her name? You know, the one that wears all that leopard print stuff, big boobs...'

'Chelsea Blandish? You're kidding me!' Bree guffawed loudly, which made Florrie raise her eyebrows and almost drop the tea tray she was carrying to the next table. 'Chels can't carry out a conversation without the help of a bloody spellchecker, and even then she struggles if it doesn't have "ugh", "um" and "yar" in it, and the only thing she has a penchant for squeezing is a s-'

'Oh my God, Bree!' Lucy quickly interrupted her. She felt a little mean to laugh, but it was funny watching Bree's expressions as she mimicked poor Chelsea and what she liked to squeeze by indulging in an impromptu play of charades. 'Well, if it does lean towards an inside job, then who better to have on the inside than you two.' She made air quotes with her fingers around the word 'inside'.

Letting her cup rattle back in the saucer, Pru tilted her head and curled her top lip. 'And that would mean I'd have to become a permanent member of the Winterbottom WI, would it?'

'What else have you got to fill your lonely evenings with?' Bree stabbed the air with her fork before plunging it back into the chocolate éclair as she watched her friend blush, the pink spreading from Pru's cheeks to across her throat.

Pru pulled her shoulders up to her ears like a coy child. 'I don't tell you everything in my life, Bryony Louise Richards.'

In anticipation of a little local gossip that might tempt the ears of her regulars, Florrie began to polish a non-existent smear vigorously from the shop window with her pinny whilst straining to catch the conversation.

Bree grinned, waving her hand in front of her, fanning an imaginary hot flush. 'Oh purleese, don't tell me you've fallen hook, line and sinker for the Delectable Detective!'

Before Pru could answer, Lucy puffed out her cheeks and draped her arm around her shoulder. 'Aw my lovely Lunatic Librarian, I think Defective Detective is more apt.' She squeezed her in a bear hug and laughed. 'Yes, the Defective Detective and the Loony Librarian sounds like a winner to me!'

PUSHING UP DAISES

*P*hyllis couldn't have been more cross than if she had paid £2.99 for a multi-packet of cheese and onion crisps in Betty's Store, only to find them fifty pence cheaper in the Pound Shop. Bowling up her path and leaving a flurry of trembling lavender fronds in her wake, with fingers shaking she slotted her key into the lock, turned and pushed hard on the front door, almost stumbling over the polished brass threshold bar. Slamming the door behind her, she leant back on the wood, her head thumping against the glass in the small bullseye window.

That was another thing too, why call it the bloody Pound Shop? Nothing was a pound; they were either 99p or two quid and over.

Subconsciously she dug her nails into the wood. Curling her fingers into a rigid claw, she dragged them in a slow and steady manner across the peeling paintwork, her heart pounding. Her breath, which had been hard and long, began to slow to a shallow hiccup as she brought 'The Rage' under control.

Shuffling along the narrow hallway, Phyllis made her way into the kitchen-cum-morning room and slammed her carrier bags onto the table. One bag toppled sideways, spilling its contents across the red checked tablecloth. Captain sat in his cage in the corner, totally apathetic to Phyllis's arrival or her huffing and puffing.

'See a pound and pick it up, pah!' she imitated in a brittle, high-pitched voice, spittle forming on her bottom lip as she spat out the last word. 'Old Rita the Bleater didn't deserve any bloody luck, did she, Captain, but she got it anyway!'

Captain bobbed his head up and down, but as always stayed silent.

She moved several tins around in the wall cupboard and carefully slotted in the small seeded batch loaf, freshly baked from Ellison's. That's where she had heard them talking, all of them huddled together in Ellison's. The narrow-minded, the ignorant, and the home-grown gossips of Winterbottom Village, all relishing in Rita's good fortune. She shoved the spout of the kettle under the brass tap and turned the spigot. Water bounced from the edges, forming droplets on the back of her hand. 'Just another two inches, Captain, that's all I would have needed, two bloody inches and the moaning old trout would've been pushing up daisies.'

Phyllis shivered. As the sun had dropped behind the trees, so had the temperature. She felt the cold so much more these days. She could happily lament her lost youth, but although she hadn't quite left her flirty forties to jump into the flighty fifties, she still felt older than she should and her bones agreed with her.

'I'm old before my time, Captain, old before my time!'

Lighting a spill, she tentatively touched the balled-up paper underneath the logs that were stacked and waiting in the grate. She watched the flames curl up, fighting to be the first to engulf last week's edition of the *Winterbottom News* before igniting the white stick of the solitary firelighter which she hoped would light the logs.

By the time she had poured herself a cup of tea and made herself comfortable in her armchair, the fire had roared into life, casting flickering shadows across the semi-darkened room. Hypnotised by the dancing flames, her eyelids became heavy, her breath a mere whisper as she drifted off into a troubled sleep...

'Please, Mummy, no... don't do it, please, Mummy, please.'

Her small plump hands pummelled the worn wood of the cellar door as she frantically scrabbled for the latch, trying to lift it before the lock was engaged on the other side, but it was too little too late. The metallic clank of the bolt evidenced the finality. Her chest rose and fell with each heaving sob as big fat tears rolled down her cheeks. Wrapping her arms around herself to ward off the chill, her whole body suddenly became wracked with tremors. A chink of light squeezed through the grated coal drop window above her, vying for position with the darkness. It fell across her pretty summer dress, illuminating the pattern of strawberries, oranges and lemons that peppered the fullness of the skirt.

'Please, Mummy, I won't do it again, I promise.'

A tiny voice that was not heard.

A door that led to nowhere...

...and a small child that was overlooked.

THE BUTCHER, THE BAKER...

Flustered, Pru finished the call and dropped her mobile phone onto her bed. Checking herself in the mirror, she tucked a stray piece of hair behind her ear. Her skin was flushed pink and a slight sheen of perspiration beaded across her top lip.

Jeez, what is wrong with me? It's not like I'm still a teenager!

Quietly berating herself didn't alter the situation or her feelings. The excited, sickly wave in the middle of her tummy, a sort of flutter combined with a dropping sensation, continued to undulate as she smiled, grimaced, pouted and stuck her tongue out at her own reflection.

'I've got a date with the Delectable Detective–' She murmured to the empty bedroom in a half sing-song lilt. '– and I don't look too bad if I say so myself.' She gently patted her cheek and brushed her fingers against her skin. Checking her reflection again, her heart sank. Her peachy complexion was courtesy of a giant streak of mis-aimed hairspray which had coated a haze across the glass, more than good genetics. She sighed loudly, it had been such a long time since she had attracted the charms of a man, or even had to court attention from one. She was definitely out of practice.

Gosh, now she thought about it she couldn't even remember the last time she had flung herself in wild abandonment at Tom before it had all gone horribly wrong. Mentally counting back the weeks and months, the mourning period after discovering him with Madison and the fragility of their relationship before that fateful day due to their respective work commitments, she was surprised to find that it was at least two years, if not more.

My God, I'm a born-again virgin – I need help!

She grabbed her phone. As her fingers typed furiously across the keypad, finishing with an emoji blowing a kiss, she quickly pressed 'send'. Once her cry for help to Bree had gone, she set about finishing the chores she had started before Andy's call had interrupted her less than enthusiastic dusting. Plumping the satin bolster cushion, she positioned it carefully between the two pillows on her bed and smoothed out the throw. This was a cue for Mr Binks to take her action as an invitation to jump up onto the bed and make himself comfy. He stretched himself out, lifting one leg into the air to almost touch his ear.

'Oh, Binksy, I think you've actually seen more action here than I have.' Pru sighed as she unhooked the mirror from the wall and placed it onto the bed. Mr Binks viewed her with his usual indifference as she bent over the mirror and began to vigorously polish the glass, paying particular attention to the sticky smear from her errant aerosol. 'I used to be able to fling my legs behind my head once upon a time too!' She fondly wondered if that ability would still be useful if her relationship with Andy went to the next level. She laughed, feeling quite optimistic.

Good grief, girl, what wicked thoughts when you haven't even been on a first date yet!

She laughed again.

As the glass cleared to a sparkle, Pru gasped in horror, watching her reflection in the now clean mirror, totally fixated by her untethered jowls as they flopped forward and swung like a pendulum with each energetic swirl of her duster.

Oh for feck's sake. If I do eventually get round to straddling the Delectable Detective, it won't just be my hair I'll be tucking behind my ears.

'Well, Mr Binks...' she pushed her fingers either side of her face, stretching her cheeks back as far as they would go, '...there's no doubt about it, it'll definitely be the missionary position with the lights out.'

∼

Andy Barnes scuttled his office chair across the incident room, not even bothering to stand up to do it. He utilised his go-kart foot action from childhood, the four wheels rumbling in unison. It span out of control as it neared Lucy's desk, wobbled as it hit the rumpled carpet tile that had peeled itself away from the floor sometime during 1994, and only came to a standstill when he slammed his hands on to the desk and locked his elbows.

He leant forward, cupped his chin in his hand, and scanned Lucy's monitor, his eyes narrowing as he read the document she had just loaded. 'Is that the report on the kid's gym shoes?'

Lucy set her lips into a thin line and nodded. 'Yep. Not much use so far, though; the writing has degraded more than I thought. There's a possibility of a first name–' She moved the cursor to the end of the report. '–but there's a footnote giving a low probability factor as it's only certain letters that could be classed as a definite.'

Andy scanned the possibilities. Pre the fancy, stick-on personalised labels mums now use on schoolkids' clothing and accessories; the good old black marker pen used to indelibly claim an item with the child's name was always popular back in the day.

Mabel, Maria, Maisie, Mary, Macey, Mandy were just a few off the top of his head.

'So if it's a name, it's one beginning with "MA" and with any number of letters between four and six?'

'Yep, 'fraid so.' Lucy looked dejected. 'And in all honesty, what on earth did I think it would prove?'

'Well, we didn't expect it to prove anything; we just hoped it might be a possible clue to a potential lead. Never dismiss anything, Luce, if your gut instinct is telling you something. Always go with it.' He gave her a supportive grin.

The general hum of the room was a welcome backdrop to Lucy's thoughts as she focused on the trees outside her window, bending and swaying in the breeze. She pulled her notepad towards her and stabbed the nib of the pen she was holding at the end of each line as she read them.

Mabel Allinson
Scene: Winterbottom Parish Hall, 3.5mm crochet hook, lemon drizzle cake, mauve-coloured Sirdar fibre, wool band
M.O: Bled out, stabbed/neck
Personal: Female, 70 yrs, widow, retired social worker, retirement flat, lifelong Winterbottom resident

Avery McIntosh
Scene: Home address, under-stairs cupboard of her one-bed cottage, mauve knitted scarf, pair of small, child-size 6 black PE pumps with faded words inside (possible ownership)
M.O: Strangulation
Personal: Female, 74 yrs, single, retired teacher at Winterbottom Junior School, lived alone, dog called Winston.
Lifelong Winterbottom resident

Rita Charlesworth
Scene: Chapperton Bliss Country Crafts Festival, deliberately unhooked Portaloo, pushed over
M.O: Suspected failed attempt

Personal: Female, 71 yrs, widow, lives alone, two-bed cottage-style bungalow, deaf, retired community nurse. Lifelong Winter-bottom resident

Lucy slumped back into her chair and blew her fringe upwards, pushing it out of her eyes. What was she missing? All female, all roughly the same age, all lifelong residents of Winter-bottom, and, as an aside, all members of the local Women's Institute. Not that the latter was anything unusual; most villages had a good membership from their lady residents, friendship, mutual interests and voluntary work would always attract a good crowd and their days out were legendary according to Bree. She chewed the end of her pen.

Social worker, teacher and nurse. Mmm...

'Andy?' She waited, head cocked, for him to reply.

'Yep?' He did his go-kart roll from his desk to hers again, but added a flourish half away across the room, spinning the chair 360 degrees, his outstretched legs acting as rotor blades to add to the momentum. 'I'm *all* yours,' he enthused, finishing with a very enthusiastic *'Taa daa'* and a cheesy grin as he came to a grinding halt directly in front of DI Holmes.

Holmes was less than impressed having his grand entrance into the incident room rudely accosted. 'Very pleased to hear it, Barnes! Now if you'd like to put the brakes on your chariot and get your face out of my crotch, I've got a briefing to conduct.' He sidestepped a suitably embarrassed Barnes.

Lucy faked interest in a random file on her desk whilst she waited for Holmes to get out of earshot. She patted Andy on the back as a show of support.

'Shit, that's all I need: the Wrath of Holmes.' He grinned.

'Could've told you, sarge, if it has tyres or testicles – it'll cause you problems!'

MIRROR, MIRROR...

*P*ip checked her reflection one last time in the rococo mirror in her hallway. She had a great fondness for this particular mirror as it was her magic mirror. She didn't have to sing to it or chant a rhyming couplet for it to reply as to the measure of her beauty. She just had to stand in front of it.

The youthful vision that was always reflected when she posed was probably more to do with the amber glass in the transom window over the front door that softened the reflected sunlight as it burst through the small mosaic pieces than any actual magic, but it always made her feel confident and happy with herself. That was until she nipped into the morning room to grab her handbag and caught sight of herself in the large oval mirror built into the old-fashioned mahogany mantelpiece. She stood forlornly in the middle of the room as it revealed its cruelty with every furrow and wrinkle of her skin.

'Tsk. If I'd known I was going to live this long, I'd have taken better care of myself!' she snorted whilst pulling the side of her eyes upwards in an attempt to iron out the ridiculously named laughter lines. How anyone could make getting old sound funny was beyond her way of thinking. Pip couldn't remember where she'd heard that quote, but it sure as hell summed up how she was feeling at this particular moment. She checked her handbag for her house keys, applied another slick of Ruby Raisin lipstick, and snapped the clasp shut.

Today was her much anticipated appointment at Wrinkle in Time; in a few hours her youthful skin and *joie de vivre* would be restored, and all would be good with the world. She hated to be thought of as vain, but in her line of business as the owner of an upmarket boutique, she had a particular style and appearance to maintain – her clients simply expected it of her. After all, who in their right mind would take advice on being stylish and chic if those pearls of wisdom were given by a pruned up old trout? She shuddered. The knock-on effect to her private life was just as dire. Her wardrobe was full of Janet Reger satin and lace, a fair plethora of colours and fabrics that should excite any gentleman caller, but she had long since reached the conclusion that it was pointless to dress the beetle bonnet and headlamps with fineries whilst the bodywork was woefully in need of a good welding and a dab of filler.

Standing by the open front door, she cleared her throat to enable her best 'employer' voice to gush forth and travel up the stairs.

'Oh, Phyllis, once you've finished the bathroom, could you be a dear and throw your dishcloth over the cooker?' She paused before quickly adding, 'I know it's seen better days, but I'm sure you can work your magic and just lock up after you've finished, I don't know what time I'll be back.' She skipped over the step, carefully avoiding the new coir mat, and slammed the door shut behind her.

Phyllis strode into the bedroom, pulled back the net curtain and watched Pip glide down the path and through the garden gate. As her grip on the flimsy material tightened, 'The Rage' began to swell and burn in her throat, rising to a determined growl. 'Believe me, Philippa Jackson, owner of La Belle Femme

Boutique, presidential candidate and Botox Barbie, it's not just your cooker and foo-foo that's seen better days, my girl.'

～

'Hi, Mrs Jackson, lovely to see you again; it's been quite a while, hasn't it?'

The pretty girl with dazzlingly straight teeth offered her best smile to Pip who gave a curt nod and then wondered if maybe she was being a bit petty. In her present state of body dysmorphia she had immediately assumed it was a dig at her for showing signs of facial neglect and not, as intended, a standard greeting or that she had been truly missed. She forced a return smile and then immediately pinched her lips together as she remembered her slightly crooked top tooth.

Mumbling, Pip opted to take it as the latter. 'Yes, it has been a while, er–' She peered closely, squinting her eyes at the name badge. '–Chantelle. We've had several extremely busy months in the boutique, lots of delightful new stock in too.' She was never one to miss an opportunity to promote her latest Italian collection and obtain a new client in the bargain. After all, when it came to fashion and cosmetics the youngsters these days seemed to have money to burn.

Chantelle ticked her appointment book and pulled two pure white fluffy towels from the wall cube behind her. 'Oh gosh, really?' she gasped. 'I'll let my nan know as soon as I get home.' Turning on her heels, she beckoned Pip to follow her.

Pip childishly pulled a face behind Chantelle and then quickly checked for any cameras. She could always claim to be exercising her facial muscles if caught but having her tongue hanging out almost touching her chin would be a little more difficult to explain.

'Here we go, Mrs Jackson. If you'd just slip off your blouse and make yourself comfortable, Victoria will be with you in a moment.' Chantelle adjusted the mood lighting in the treatment room. 'Is the music just right for you?'

Pip nodded, taking in the restful space where she was going to spend the next two hours being wonderfully rejuvenated. She had opted for a 'Genie' facial in an effort to turn back the years. She smiled to herself, calling it 'Genie' must be a play on words. Maybe the clients were hoping for three wishes and a little magic. Well, she certainly wouldn't be giving the lamp a gentle stroke to let the little bugger out; it would be more of a vigorous scrub to cater to her needs. Swinging her legs up onto the treatment bed, she lay back, and whilst the minutes ticked by she studiously examined the ceiling, tracing the small hairline cracks that spidered across the plaster, just as she had traced her own facial cracks that very morning.

'Afternoon, Mrs Jackson, lovely to see you again.' Victoria breezed into the room, giving off a trace of sweet-smelling perfume as she approached Pip who was serenely lying in repose, perfectly chilled. 'Right, let's get down to business.' She grabbed the side rail of a metal contraption displaying a host of dials, switches and trailing wires that had been lurking in the corner. Pulling on the flex, she checked the wiring and plugged it into the wall socket, trundling it to the side of Pip's treatment table.

Victoria gave a knowing grin. 'Now just relax, go with the flow. It'll be worth the effort in the end.'

Pip held her breath and waited.

GO WITH THE FLOW

*P*ip had never really considered herself to have a foul mouth. She rarely cussed, and if she did drop the occasional bomb it was normally a mild expletive.

Well I can honestly say I've just bloody excelled myself! she mused.

Lying in the afterglow of her treatment, damp pads covering her eyes and a cooling gel mask over her face, neck and décolletage, she relived the previous half hour, quietly berating herself for not requesting more detail as to what the treatment had entailed. She couldn't believe that on her way out of Wrinkle in Time she would be parting with the best part of £120 of her hard-earned cash just for the pleasure of being legally electrocuted.

Once Victoria had stuck the little pads to her face and checked that the wires dangling down were attached to the machine, she had switched on the current and ever so carefully turned the dials. The gentle pulsating throb as Pip's facial muscles began to work had been pleasantly addictive – that was until it was suddenly wanged up to the top-notch setting, sending her into a spasm as her face ticked, jerked and grimaced all on its own accord.

Horrified, she had tried to alert Victoria that all was not well, but each time she'd rounded her lips to form a word, the jolt of electricity had shoved her top lip up her left nostril whilst the rest of her mouth went into overdrive, as though she were exaggerating the five vowels in an amateur production of *My Fair Lady*.

'*Pleesh, urgh ... ahhhhh ... fffff ... eeeooooweeeew ... mmmmfff ... fffeck meeeeee...*' she had howled, waving her arms to signal her growing agony and her resemblance to Quasimodo with each passing second as her right eyelid drooped onto her cheek. Shocked, Victoria had hurriedly shut down the machine and torn off the pads, the ferocity of the adhesive stripping with it several stray facial hairs, two blackheads and what Pip had always believed was her one and only beauty spot.

Now alone in the room, the spa music and gentle aromatherapy oils that had been massaged into her neck and shoulders easing her anxiety, Pip breathed deeply and focused on the blackness at the back of her eyelids as she wondered what effect an unfinished treatment would have on her face.

She groaned.

Bloody hell, that's all I need – a half-jowly gob and a ruddy Elvis lip.

Phyllis waited. Silently, like a church mouse. Unheard, unseen, overlooked.

The red plastic bucket hung from her fingers; the mop leaning against the storeroom wall had left a small damp patch on the woodblock flooring. She was thankful for the smell of various oils, creams and lotions in that small space. It lifted the darkness just a little, and it never ceased to amaze her what the senses could do for you in times of uncertainty or fear.

She heard the door to Treatment Room 3 click shut. Popping

her head out to peer around the corner she saw Victoria breeze out into the corridor and make her way down the stairs to the front of the salon, pausing on the half-landing to acknowledge a second girl. Phyllis strained to hear what they were saying.

Victoria's was clearest of the two voices. 'I've left her meditating; she's had a full neck and shoulder massage and the mask and eye pads can come off in–' She checked her watch. '–about fifteen minutes.'

The other girl nodded in acknowledgement. 'It'll give her time to get over the shock of her treatment, I suppose.' They both burst out laughing as they disappeared down the second set of stairs and out of sight.

Phyllis held her breath, counting the footsteps. Once satisfied she was alone, she stashed the bucket and mop and quietly made her way to Treatment Room 3.

Sometimes being overlooked can have its advantages; add a costume, props and an insignificant role, and suddenly you become completely invisible to those that don't care.

Gliding silently towards the treatment couch, Phyllis checked that it did indeed hold the form of her intended victim. She would have loved to get a little closer, to stare at Phillipa Jackson for a few moments more, to watch her chest gently rise and fall as she dozed in blissful ignorance. Just a few moments more would be enough to appreciate the effect her next action would have on that simple but important evidence of life.

But time was of the essence.

Slipping the frayed wire into Pip's half-curled hand, she held her own breath as she waited for any sign of disturbance from her sleeping victim. Pip's lower jaw dropped, allowing a small snort to escape from her slack mouth. Phyllis knew from watching her employer during her afternoon 'power naps' that this indicated she was in the next stage of sleep.

Perfect.

Tiptoeing over to the wall, the cable trailing through her

fingers, she placed a brochure on the table next to the cream leather tub chair and gave one final backward glance at Pip before carefully pushing the three-pinned plug into the wall socket.

When will you pay me? Say the bells of Old Bailey...

Phyllis dramatically pointed her index finger in the air and did a little dance of triumph before elegantly flicking the switch and...

Pow!!

~

Pip truly didn't know what had hit her.

That's if the 'what' was actually something physical. She really had no idea, but based on her half-hour 'Genie' session with Victoria, she was in no doubt that it was a similar, if not more vicious, experience. Her eyes popped open as her face contorted, the eye pads and mask flicking to the side with the sheer force of her body jerking into a violent, uncontrollable spasm.

She could feel the sheer strength of what she now realised was electricity burning along her arm, finalising itself with a powerful burst of unbearable pain in her chest. Her mouth curled up, giving her the dreaded Elvis Presley lip again, which tightened further to set in a rictus grin. Her feet banged down against the padded, heated leather of the couch, her knees locking straight, every bone in her poor body rigid.

In the briefest of moments, the sad realisation came to her that she would soon breathe her last.

Pip's final thought before the nothingness took her was not of an old age she would now forego, nor of her fancy new Italian collection still in boxes awaiting her attention at La Belle Femme Boutique, and not of her sexy Janet Reger underwear which she was currently sporting – although she was smugly content to know that she would at least look presentable when the under-taker arrived.

No, it was none of those things.

The only thing that passed through Pip's brain – apart from 240 volts of electricity – was the bloody annoying melody of the 1957 Elvis classic 'All Shook Up'.

What a way to go!

MORIARTY'S MIRTH

*T*he high-pitched scream of Chantelle Blakeley, beauty therapist and receptionist at Wrinkle in Time, carried through the open window of Treatment Room 3, out on to the main street of the little village of Winterbottom, paused, and then drifted upwards and beyond.

Sitting at the window table in The Twisted Currant Café, Phyllis adjusted her position on the floral cushion of the shabby chic chair, barely taking her eyes from the front of the salon opposite as she sliced through the generous helping of Black Forest gateau that Florrie had just served her. Whilst savouring the first mouthful, she absent-mindedly stirred her tea, her eyes still intently covering the high street, the salon and the parish hall next to it.

Waiting.

'Oh my goodness, what on earth was that?' A flustered Florrie almost leapt from behind the counter. Hurriedly drying her hands on the pinny she was wearing, she yanked open the café door and made her way outside. Whilst the other customers joined her, either in surprise, shock or just general nosiness, Phyllis chose to remain where she was.

Waiting.

Seconds passed with a hiatus of silence before the ensuing chaos began in earnest. The front door to Wrinkle in Time flew open, spewing out a visibly distressed Victoria and a sobbing Chantelle on to the pavement. This was closely followed by the wailing of sirens in the distance as they filled the air, their two-tone blaring heralded their urgency. Florrie, a gingham tea towel flapping from the waistband of her apron, ran across the road. She was met seconds later by two other women who came from the nearby library.

Phyllis carried on watching. She knew Bree well; after all, she was on the 'List', but she was still unsure of the other woman with her: *Prudence, Prune, Pru...?* something like that, she couldn't quite recall, but she could remember the look of suspicion that she had given her after the little mishap with Rita and the portable toilet.

As first an ambulance, closely followed by a police car, arrived in a hail of blue lights outside Wrinkle in Time, Phyllis took the opportunity to wrap the remains of her cake in the serviette and position it carefully at the bottom of her bag so as not to squash it. Leaving a ten pence piece under the saucer as a tip, she slipped out, unseen, unnoticed and invisible.

～

'Right, listen up.' Murdoch Holmes, his lips set in a thin line, a grey wash to his skin, waited for the incident room to fall silent.

The gathered Murder Investigation Team, fuelled by the latest death, continued their hushed conversations with a hum of expectancy accompanied by chairs scraping or rolling across the threadbare carpet tiles as they formed their preferred positions in the room.

'I said *listen up!*' His patience clearly stretched; Holmes' bulbous eyes scanned the room. Once silence and rapt attention were gained, he continued. 'Thank you, ladies and gents. Phillipa Marian Jackson, sixty-one years, widow, owner of a local ladies-wear shop.' He stabbed a finger at the black-and-white photograph pinned to the board, showing a rather youthful Pip in a regal pose, her head tilted, eyes reflecting the light of the flash.

Lucy, who had pulled her chair forward to sit next to Andy, had her notebook out and pen poised waiting for anything Holmes would throw their way. She tucked her hair behind her ear and bit down on her bottom lip.

Holmes pointed to a series of crime scene photographs from inside Wrinkle in Time. 'Cause of death, electrocution. You'll have the finer details in the handout that DS Barnes will pass round.' He gave a cursory nod towards Andy. 'This is our third murder within as many months.' He ran his fingers through his greying quiff and turned his back on his audience, eyes scanning the board. 'All female, all roughly within the same age bracket, all living alone, all residing in Winterbottom and–' He swivelled on his heels to face his team. '–all members of the local Women's Institute. What does that tell us?' He jutted out his chin and stretched his neck, waiting for a response.

An uncomfortable silence hovered over the room.

'Come on, give me something, anything. You're supposed to be bloody detectives.'

'Er… three unexpected WI vacancies?' Tim Forshaw, the new trainee investigator piped up from the back, eager to show keenness to his hard taskmaster and get himself noticed.

An infantile snigger raced around the room as Holmes looked fit to burst.

'No, you blithering idiot. It tells us we have victim similarities or things in common, a profile of sorts, which should, if the good book of *MIM* is true to its word, give us an insight into the mind of the offender with a potential profile!' Holmes shook his head in exasperation.

'What's a "MIM", sarge?' Directing his question to Andy, Tim kept his voice low, not wanting to single himself out for ridicule yet again.

Andy turned to face him. Leaning in, eager to impart an important snippet of information to the newbie, he cleared his throat, enabling him to sound more commanding. 'It's our training bible, stands for *Moriarty's Investigation Manifesto*, Holmes treats it like a work of art, so if you ever mention it to him, don't use the acronym, give it its full title, the full welly.' He tapped the side of his nose knowingly. 'I'm telling you; he'll be well impressed.'

'Oh great. Thanks, sarge, I'll remember that.' Tim bristled with glee as he swivelled his chair back to face the front, failing to notice Andy's ensuing smirk.

Lucy stifled a snort. 'Oh no, how could you? You are wicked!'

'DC Harris, is my briefing interrupting your conversation?' Holmes homed in on poor Lucy, who had the good grace to blush profusely. 'Sorry, sir, I was just comparing notes.' She felt like a naughty schoolgirl caught cheating in an exam. 'I was just wondering if their professions might be worth looking at.'

Holmes paused for a moment, turning over the sheets in front of him. The room remained silent in anticipation of his response. 'Okay, you take that one up, Lucy. Andy work with her, see what you come up with. Start with where they worked, if they worked together at any point,' he waved his hand indicating an 'etcetera' to his sentence. 'You know the drill.'

'Sir, sir!' Tim shot his hand up into the air.

'What's the matter, Forshaw, do you need the toilet?'

Waiting for the laughter to die down, Tim shifted eagerly in his seat. 'I was just wondering: would your *Moriarty's Investigation Manifesto* allow for intelligence-led lines of enquiry, like if we put out a media appeal?' He relaxed back in his chair, mightily pleased with himself. Hardly five minutes had passed and he'd managed to act on the sarge's advice.

The collective intake of breath coming from nine detectives, two sergeants, one intelligence analyst and a forensic officer was deafening. Lucy pulled her mouth down and shifted her eyes sideways towards Andy, who in return rolled his eyes and blew on imaginary burnt fingers.

'Forshaw, how long have you been with the team?' Holmes was measured, but everyone could see he was trying not to laugh.

'Er... two days, sir.'

'Well, son, if you'd like to see a further two days and maybe even a future career as a detective, you might want to read up on some of Sir Arthur Conan Doyle's greatest novels, and while you're at it, the definition of a "jolly jape" wouldn't go amiss either–' Holmes stacked his reports into his clip file and casually flicked off the projector. '–and intelligence works both ways, Forshaw – maybe you'd like to find some before our next briefing.'

HAIR TODAY, GONE TOMORROW

'What about this one?' Pru held the coat hanger under her chin, letting the floral fabric drape to below her knees.

Bree was less than impressed. Lounging across Pru's bed, flicking through a magazine, she briefly gave her undivided attention to the task in hand. 'Urgh… only if you're thinking of channelling his grandmother. Jeez, Pru, all you'd need is a set of pearls, a pair of bloomers and tell him to call you Nancy.' She rolled over onto her back. 'Ooh, Andy, take me now!' she breathlessly imitated her friend, flinging her arms up over her head. Giggling, she thought for a moment. 'Hey, it wasn't modelled on Norman Bate's mum in *Psycho*, was it?'

Pru threw the offending dress at her, laughing as it hit Bree in the face, knocking off her reading glasses. 'What then? I don't want to be his nan, and I certainly don't want to look like his mum, but neither do I want to have the whole shelf of goodies on show for a first date.' She exuberantly pushed the line of hangers in the wardrobe to one side and pulled out her 'go-to' little black dress. 'How about this one?'

'Mmm… have you de-fuzzed though? It is a bit short.'

Pru rolled her eyes. 'Of course I have, but funny you should mention that. I had been thinking of getting laser hair removal, but the shocking demise of old Pip has put me off that.'

Bree pushed herself up onto her elbows. 'Nooo, who in their right mind would want to laser their beetle bonnet? It'd kill; you wouldn't be able to sit down for a week!'

'My legs, you numpty, not my mimsy!' She stepped into the dress and wriggled it over her hips, wrestling one elbow through the armhole. 'Anyway, whatever happened to the good old days where a Bic razor was all that was available? That did the trick, didn't it?'

'Yeah it did, but it itched like a bugger for days, and then the regrowth acted like bloody Velcro on the lace panel of your knickers. Not good when you were desperate for a wee. Three cubicles down could hear you ripping them off!'

Bree swung her legs over the bed and sat up, giving Pru the once over. 'Yes, that's lovely, but where is he taking you?'

'I'm not sure; he said for a drink and a bite to eat. D'you think I'm overdressed? I could always wear my old favourite.' She rummaged around in the wardrobe for the tenth time in an hour and brought out her navy and white spotted blouse and Jamie jeans. 'These?'

'Perfect. Not too much and not too little. Add those red killer heels you wore with it last time and you're good to go.' Bree gave a sigh of appreciation. 'So, can you remember all my tips and advice?'

'Yep, it's all up here.' Pru tapped the side of her head. 'And if he tries any funny business, I'm to make my excuses, say something's happened and I've got to get home – keep him keen.'

Bree proudly grinned at her protégé, although in all honesty, divorced herself and very much lacking in the man department, she really wasn't the best person to advise on affairs of the heart or any ensuing bedroom gymnastics.

'Ladies, ladies may I have your attention, please.' Kitty Hardcastle rang the brass bell with gusto, bringing the members of The Winterbottom WI to order. The word 'please' had morphed into an exasperated plea rather than a polite request. She had lain awake the previous night, desperately trying to think of an uplifting and motivational speech to give to her ladies at the opening of this evening's meeting. The tragic and dreadful murder of Pip Jackson had caused as much, if not more, consternation than the previous losses of Mabel and Avery. She looked out on to the sea of expectant faces sitting in regimented rows before her.

Uplifting and inspirational – who the hell am I kidding?

Kitty quickly pushed away the bleak thoughts that had wormed their way into her soul and plastered on her best presidential smile.

'As I am sure you are all aware, our little village has been struck once again with a further tragic and untimely death, the sad loss of another of our Winterbottom Women's Institute members: Pip Jackson.' She dutifully paused to give reverence to the proceedings. Several heads were bowed in thought. Rita Charlesworth on the second row was making vigorous use of her handkerchief as she blew, wiped and waved the embroidered square sheet with theatrical aplomb. The rest sat in stony silence.

'I am assured by Detective Inspector Murdoch Holmes from Winterbottom CID that they are doing everything within their power to bring the offender to justice. If anyone has anything they think might help their investigation, no matter how trivial you think it may be, then contact them as a matter of urgency.' Kitty picked up the stack of cards that DS Barnes had left with her that morning and began to sort them into smaller piles. Each one bore the Crimestoppers' logo, the force crest and a number. 'I have here the direct line to Winterbottom CID. Please take a card each. Keep hold of it, and if you should think of anything, please, please let them know. No doubt in due course we will all be interviewed again too.'

Clarissa Montgomery, perched on her seat at the end of the second row, eagerly accepted the first batch of cards, took one for herself and passed the rest down the line. Rita, a cup of tea in one hand, quickly shoved her handkerchief into the sleeve of her three-button pink cardigan in order to have a free set of fingers to grab a card for herself. She turned it over in her hand, carefully taking in the small print.

'It says Murdoch Holmes not Sherlock Holmes. I thought she said Sherlock Holmes!' she quizzically declared, confusion spreading across her face.

Clarissa closed her eyes and took a deep breath. Years of sitting next to Rita at their WI meetings had taught her to expect at least one moan, gripe or misunderstanding during the few hours they spent together. 'Sherlock Holmes is fictional; it's from a book. His name just happens to sound the same.'

'Oh aye, now I see.' Rita fiddled with her hearing aid, forcing a shrill whine of feedback that made everyone wince. 'I loved Basil Rathbone in the film, not so fussed on that Crumbledick Bender-batch, though. Telly always ruins everything,' she harrumphed.

'It's Benedict Cumb... oh forget it; just phone the number on the card if you think of anything, Rita.' Exasperated, Clarissa stood up and made her way over to Kitty to sort out their next proposed day out.

As the rest of the ladies huddled around tables, catching up on the latest news and gossip whilst adding their amateur sleuthing to the mix, Betty Prince kept notes on who they believed could be responsible for whisking Mabel, Avery and Pip prematurely off this mortal coil. She looked down at her own neat hand-writing.

1. *A Murderer*
2. *A Man*
3. *...Or a Woman*

She poked her pencil through the wire spiral that held the sheets together on the pad. Mmm... that wouldn't get them very far, would it? They had sadly been stating what her old hubby would call 'the bleedin' obvious'.

As their voices settled to a level hum, their heads almost touching in conspiracy, Phyllis sat unobserved at the back. She would only become visible when everyone wanted their tea and cake, as yet again she'd been nominated to the role of head cook and bottle-washer. Listening to the proceedings, she had felt a surge of power, knowing that she was the one to cause so much disruption, so much chaos, so much fear. It actually warmed the cockles of her heart to think that the ladies of Winterbottom WI did not sleep well in their beds at night because of her.

And do you know what made it all the more sweet?

She was amongst them.

She was one of them.

And they didn't suspect a thing!

THE DELECTABLE DETECTIVE

*P*ru sat awkwardly in the window booth of the Dog & Gun, twisting the rose-gold watch strap around her wrist in a subconscious act of nervous anticipation. What exactly she was anticipating wasn't quite clear yet, but she did suspect that it might have something to do with the rather magnificent shape that the rear of Andy's jeans had taken on as he stood at the bar with one foot on the polished brass rail, ordering their drinks. He definitely had buns of steel. Resting her elbow on the table, she cupped her chin in her upturned hand and sighed.

Mmmmm, the Delectable Detective...

She reluctantly turned her attention away from Andy's 'assets' to the window beside her so that she could enjoy the lanterns outside as they glowed through the sections of leaded glass. Dusk was quickly descending, giving an ethereal look to the gardens beyond, as shadows cast and a slight mist followed the ground. She could almost imagine the fairies from her childhood story books dancing and taking flight amongst the flowers and trees, such happy carefree days when she didn't have the trials of being an adult to contend with, when the only thing she had to worry about was if her pocket money stretched to a bag of aniseed balls and a copy of *Bunty*.

She wondered what she should expect, or in fact what she actually did want from her first date with Andy. Her long-term relationship with Tom and his subsequent infidelity with Madison, aka the Yeti, had left her rather lacking in the trust and confidence department. Could she really see herself revealing her 'other' side to Andy, the side that enjoyed wantonly throwing her legs up behind her head in a moment of passion whilst shouting *voila*?

'Here we go, gin and tonic with a strawberry.' Andy placed the large gin balloon down in front of her, the ice making a delicious rattling sound as the red fruit, surrounded by bubbles, bobbed up and down.

Completely thrown out of her daydream, Pru blushed, utterly convinced he had just fallen upon her secret thoughts and could read her mind. 'Oh, gosh, yes, well, I've always been double-jointed!'

'Pardon?'

'Double-jointed, you know, sort of hyper-mobile, that's why my legs can go behind my head.' She visibly cringed, wondering why on earth she had imparted the former and then followed up with the latter.

'…and I need to know this because…?' A wry smile touched Andy's lips, his rather gorgeous lips in Pru's opinion.

She gave him a coy smile in return.

Oh well, in for a penny, in for a pound!

She tipped the glass and took a sip. Fixing him with her intense green eyes she stretched out her leg and jiggled her red stiletto-clad foot. 'Just so you know to take my heels off first.' She grinned.

∾

'What was his reaction?' Bree stabbed her fork into the chunk of cheese and popped it into her mouth. The pickled onion that sat next to a rather limp-looking piece of lettuce rolled towards the edge of her plate. She over-exuberantly flicked it back into the middle with her thumb and middle finger; it skipped over the ham and shot across the table, dropping over the edge on to Pru's skirt. 'Goal!' She punched the air in delight.

Hastily retrieving it from the folds of her best librarian-style outfit, Pru flung it back at her, it missed its target and disappeared under the next table. Fortunately, in the after-lunch lull at the Dog & Gun, their childish exchange went unwitnessed.

'He just kissed me on the tip of my nose and left!' Pru tipped her head.

'That's it? That's all you've got to tell me? Bloody hell, mate, I thought you might at least have had a bit of a firkle.' She crunched down as a slice of celery went the same way as the cheese.

'He's a gentleman, Bree, albeit a very sexy and desirable one! We had a lovely night, lots in common and he made me laugh. What more could I want?'

'Er... I don't know. How about a no-strings-attached, good old-fashioned bonk?' Giggling, Bree gave a show of jazz hands to accompany her suggestion.

Pru side-angled her fork and squished the paper napkin onto her empty plate. 'Maybe I don't want no-strings-attached. Maybe I want something more than just a one-off roll in the hay... or, in my case, a king-sized memory foam mattress with a pocket-sprung base!'

Bree nodded in agreement; she knew only too well how loneliness could rear its ugly head at the most unwelcome of times. Her single life was very much self-imposed as she had her son to think of; he came before any thoughts she might have of romance for herself. A sadness fleetingly crossed her face as she remembered her happier times with Marcus. The times before she had realised he would rather fiddle with his own joystick whilst interfacing with his Dell Pentium computer than swap dirty data with her.

'Penny for them.' Pru looked concerned for her friend.

'Ach, just ignore me.' Bree waved her hand in dismissal. 'I was actually thinking I could have done with a memory foam mattress myself. I'm sure rumpy-pumpy would be a delight on one of those. Just think of the imprints!'

'I highly recommend them; are you having trouble sleeping?'

'Nope, I'm having trouble bloody remembering!'

RITA

'Come on, Todger, time for tea.' Rita tinkled the fork against the ceramic feeding bowl; her daily signal for the huge ginger cat to come running was timed to perfection. Head cocked in anticipation, she waited for him to come lumbering along the hall into the kitchen. 'Ah, there you are.' She bent down and gave his head a rub and tickled his ears. 'Chicken in gravy, your favourite.' She pushed the bowl towards him.

Todger gave her a look of indifference. If cats could talk, and Todger very much wished he could, he would impart to his human slave that chicken in gravy wasn't actually his favourite. It never had been, and, if truth be told, neither was his name really Todger. He'd unfortunately obtained that ridiculous moniker when Rita had failed to change the batteries in her hearing aid on the day she had acquired him. Just as Jolly Jilly from the Winter-bottom Cat & Dog Rescue had handed over the small bundle of fur, the legendary high-pitched squeal from Rita's outdated earpiece had completely drowned out Jilly's kindly words as she had stroked the little kitten's head for the very last time whilst announcing, 'Here we go, Roger, off to your new home.'

Ambling back to her abode, her new acquisition safely

cocooned in a blanket inside her wicker basket, Rita couldn't help but feel the name 'Todger' was rather familiar to her, but for the life of her, she couldn't remember why.

So there you have it, 'Roger' had become 'Todger', which in turn gave endless hours of laughter to the local youths when each evening Rita would stand on the doorstep of her neat little cottage bungalow, hollering into the darkness asking if anyone had seen her wee Todger.

As if on cue, Todger sniffed the air and blinked his pale gold eyes in an attempt to impart his knowledge to Rita through mental telepathy. When no reaction from her was forthcoming, he dived nose first into his bowl.

Leaving her much adored pet to dine in peace, Rita shuffled her way into the sitting room and made herself comfortable in her fireside chair. Adjusting the cushions, she picked up her book from the two-tier trolley beside her, the well-thumbed pages curling at the edges, and pulled out the bookmark. Checking the time, she was happy to know she had just long enough for a chapter or two before supper. Being a spinster had its merits – for one, she only had to be concerned about herself: when she would eat, when she would sleep, how she would live her days.

She loved the blissful feeling on autumnal mornings when she would wake, slip on her candlewick dressing gown, and pop into the kitchen to make a nice cup of tea and a piece of toast. Waiting for the kettle to boil on the stove, she would watch the wind whip the trees outside in her garden, bending them first one way and then allowing them to snap back to stand momentarily still, waiting for the next gust to catch them. She would marvel at the leaves as nature tore them away from the branches, throwing them up into the air, scattering them across her small lawn and turning it into a patchwork quilt of colour, a mixture of reds, golds, greens and browns. Once the whistle and steam signalled her brew makings were ready, she would return to her bed with the small tray that was hosting her chinaware and snuggle down under the counterpane, listening to the rain gently tapping at her window, content to remain there and with no one to tell her she couldn't.

Yes, being alone did have its benefits, the tranquil silence she was currently enjoying was another of them, although most of the time she couldn't be sure if it were a natural silence or if her batteries had run out. She twiddled the infernal pieces of equipment in her ears and took the conscious decision to remove them; after all, she had no one that she wished to hear and they rubbed terribly, causing little sores that itched. Maybe one day she might look at the new-fangled ones that were apparently virtually invisible to the naked eye.

She smiled to herself; her peaceful hour always gave time to appreciate the good things in her life. She turned the next page in her book, only to realise that she hadn't actually read the previous one. Her thoughts had distracted her and brought all her memories to life again. It was unfortunately one of the prerequisites of old age: a dreadfully short attention span. Her thoughts were now of Jim, the one man that would have offered her a less lonely life if his untimely, and very inconvenient, death during a brief dalliance with Edith Bromilow the village tart, several bales of poorly stacked hay and a pitchfork, hadn't put a spanner in the works.

She laid her head back and closed her eyes, and he was there, just as he had been in the heady days of their youth.

Jim. His dark curls bobbing atop his head as he chased her across the field, the summer sun warming their bronzed skin.

Jim. His inviting smile filling her heart as he tenderly kissed her ever so softly on the cheek.

Jim. Taking her hand and leading her to the hay barn, his arm around her, nuzzling into her neck as he gently dropped her down into the rough, warm straw, the shoulder of her dress slipping to expose her breast, his breath becoming urgent.

Jim. Teasing at the buckle on the worn leather belt of his trousers to reveal…

Oh bloody hell nooo!

Her eyes snapped open.

Suddenly, and without a by your leave, Rita had washed away fifty years of memories, and with a startling clarity had just remembered why her beloved cat's name had always seemed so annoyingly familiar.

A WOLF IN SHEEP'S CLOTHING

*P*hyllis carefully closed the small wrought iron gate behind her and made her way along the narrow garden path, paying particular attention to where she placed her feet. The lavender blue flowers of the multiple campanulas that edged the borders had spilled on to the crazy paving, flourishing in every direction. She couldn't bear to crush anything so delicate underfoot.

She paused momentarily, just slightly shy of the front door and tilted her head, listening. When she felt safe to do so, she edged her way along the building line, through the ornamental rose arch and into the back garden of 26 Tarporley Lane, Winterbottom. The rear garden was laid to grass, surrounded by trees. A wooden bird table, bleached and weathered, tilted sideways, forcing the peanuts and treats to roll towards the lip and remain in an unruly pile. From memory, Phyllis found the window she was looking for. She had almost gone to the wrong one before she had remembered that her previous visit had been from inside, so she had to turn her mental compass around to accommodate her current view from the outside. Keeping her back to the wall, she flattened herself alongside the frame of the leadlight window and tentatively peered in.

My oh my, it couldn't be any better. There she was, eyes closed, serenely posed in her armchair, book dropped on her lap, with a half-drunk cup of tea and a pair of hearing aids on the table beside her. Perfect, just as she'd hoped.

Phyllis had to agree, even though it galled her to do so, that her original idea for Rita hadn't been a very dignified one at all. She had eventually conceded her relief when her attempt to despatch her at the Chapperton Bliss Country Fair with a vividly coloured chemical toilet had failed. She smiled to herself.

This time I won't fail; it will be a 'resounding' success!

It had taken some planning and it hadn't been an easy task to obtain what she needed to fulfil her desire to send Rita to her Maker. She hadn't wanted anything straightforward or boring; after discovering Oscar Wilde's *A Study of Duty* her research had actually become quite exhilarating and her modus operandi had been born. Poison! She had pondered the logistics of ingestion, such as Lord Arthur Savile had embarked upon in that very story, but as his attempt had failed she had decided to move on swiftly to the possibility of subcutaneous introduction. She had spent hours poring over various books in the Winterbottom library, researching medical, herbal and botanical agents and making notes on dosage, application and the all-important method of supply. Although her research had been diligent, it had actually been Rita herself who had put the final nail into her proverbial coffin, when, in the absence of her hearing aids, she had complained very loudly whilst poking her fingers into her ears in Doyle's Dispensary that her auditory orifices were causing her pain. Clarissa in her role as pharmacy assistant had dutifully inspected them and warned her not to poke, prod or otherwise introduce anything else into the open sores to avoid infection.

Ah, what a revelation, and how blissfully unaware Rita and Clarissa had been of her presence – as always...

Phyllis moved cautiously towards the kitchen door and tentatively tried the handle. It gave slightly, allowing her to gently push down, being careful not to let it ratchet back and alert the sleeping Rita, although she was pretty confident that without her hearing aids in, the chances of her even hearing a nuclear blast would be a million to one. Passing through the kitchen, she paused briefly by the tempting wholemeal sandwich wrapped in cling film that sat on the countertop, before making her way into the sitting room. She took a moment to stand and stare at Rita's slumped, sleeping form before pulling a small vial from her pocket and gently picking up Rita's discarded hearing aids.

Less than five minutes later, Phyllis jauntily skipped through the gate of 26 Tarporley Lane, and closing it behind her made her way into the village singing to herself. The haunting melody lifted high and drifted on the gentle breeze before disappearing into the trees.

When I grow rich, Say the bells of Shoreditch...

'Good grief, Todger...' Rita checked the clock on the mantelpiece. '...that was a little bit more than my usual forty winks.' She yawned, stretched and eased herself up from the chair, giving herself a few moments respite as she waited for her bones to catch up. 'A little bit of music, I think, whilst I get our supper. What shall it be? The blues or a rousing symphony?'

Todger barely lifted his head from underneath his tail, but allowed for the squint of one eye. Watching his human fiddle with the knobs on the transistor radio, he knew it would only be a matter of seconds before his own ears would be subjected to 110 decibels of Tchaikovsky's 1812 ripped out at full blast. He wasn't wrong.

'Goodness me, my hearing must be getting worse, can you hear anything, Todger?' Rita turned the dial up and strained. She could swear it was on. She twiddled the knobs further and marvelled at her ceramic Lady Grey figurine as it bounced across the top of the sideboard, the vibrations she could feel in her fingers giving the ornament a merry dance. 'Oh dear, silly me!' She poked a finger in her right ear and then checked her other one. 'Mummy has forgotten to put her ear trumpets back in again, hasn't she?'

Todger couldn't have shown less interest if he had tried. He didn't even bother to look up as Rita found her hearing aids and tentatively shoved one in each ear. She grimaced.

'Ouch, that stung a bit. I really must see Doctor Forsdyke about some new ones, or at least find out why these darned things are hurting me.' She pushed them a little further in, fiddled until they felt relatively comfortable, and set the volume dial.

Fifteen minutes later Rita was ensconced in her chair again, a half-eaten wholemeal ham and mustard sandwich accompanied by a very rosy Gala apple and a nice cup of cocoa sat on the tray beside her. She had taken a respite in her dining due to coming over a little queer. She brought her hand up in front of her and wriggled her fingers, marvelling as a tingling sensation spread along the skin of her arm and flushed to her cheeks. Beads of perspiration peppered her forehead and top lip as she struggled for breath.

As her heart began to race, pulsating like little feet dancing inside her chest, her breath became shallower and tighter with each strain of her lungs.

Oh my goodness, what is happening to me?

She wanted to wail, shout for help, but the words were only forming in her brain not on her lips as she moaned and keened. The pulsating of her heart became a throbbing beat. Squeeze, release, squeeze, release.

Phone, I need to get the phone...

Gripping the arms of the chair, she tried to pull herself forward, stretching as far as she could, the effort radiating pain in every muscle. Her fingers brushed the grey coil that led to the telephone handset, touched it momentarily and then lost their hold, her arm dropping limply into her lap as she slumped back against the red tapestry cushion. Her eyes slowly glazed; a small flicker of awareness that was barely perceptible passed over their rheumy blueness as a slow paralysis swept through her whole body.

Rita wasn't really an academic. She read consistently but had never pushed herself forward in life with her knowledge or views; she had just lived a life that she believed was simple and complete, but right at this particular juncture she was firmly of the opinion that a few extra years to have the chance to shine a little more would have been so very much appreciated.

Alas it is not to be, for I have a feeling I'm about to kick the bucket imminently.

Her eventual acceptance provided her with a strange feeling of tranquillity. She had found peace in her measured last breath as her chest rose and fell for the last time, allowing a perpetual silence to envelop her.

'Life is pleasant, death is peaceful – it's the transition that's troublesome.'

— *Isaac Asimov*

KICKING THE BUCKET

From her earliest memories as a child, the one thing that Pru loved about books, besides the content, of course, was their smell. Musty, new, vanilla-sweet, fruity, nutty, earthy; her 'sniff list' was endless. Just when she thought she had covered every aroma there could possibly be, she would pick up a new book, inhale deeply, and discover yet another scent.

She carefully rearranged the shelf and pushed *The Stranger* by Harlan Coben in between Ann Cleeves and Patricia Cornwell. Amused, she wondered if Mr Coben would be impressed to be squeezed between two fabulous women writers in a village library. Her next book to be catalogued and shelved was one she adored herself by crime writer David Jackson. She admired the atmospheric cover of *Pariah* before opening it in the middle so she could press her nose to the page.

'Oh my God, I'm a secret sniffer.' She chuckled to herself.

'You're a what?'

Startled, Pru dropped the book onto the top plate of the ladder. She hadn't heard the door open, let alone the bell that was supposed to alert her to patrons wanting to avail themselves of the library and its contents. 'Oh gosh, Andy! I didn't hear you come in.' She quickly descended the small ladder so she could stand on firm ground and be on a level footing with him. 'It's nothing weird, well, not that weird; it's not a fetish or anything. It's just I like to sniff–'

'Whoa, don't ruin the moment whatever you do.' He put up his hand, palm towards her, in a staying motion. 'Please allow me a little fantasy, hey?'

She laughed, thoroughly enjoying his quick retort. 'It's the books; I just love to sniff books. It's a childhood thing.'

Andy picked up the dropped copy of *Pariah* and gave it a once over. 'Mmm… in my childhood it was more about go karts, catapults and large paper bags full of gobstoppers, although I must admit I did enjoy a quick sniff of the rubber sling on a catty once.'

Pru had a saucy retort of her own to that comment but decided to wait until they were better acquainted before she got too risqué with him. 'Actually, I'm glad you popped in. Would you like to come for dinner at mine one night this week?' She knew she was taking a chance; her cooking skills were legendary amongst the London social crowd she and Tom had been part of. Her last offering before their split had ended in a rushed telephone order to the local Indian takeaway after she'd invested the best part of four hours cooking a lamb Kathmandu from scratch, only to find ten minutes before everyone was due to arrive the carefully diced and still raw cubes of meat on a side plate in the utility room and the Whiskas chicken in jelly intended for Mr Binks smothered in spices and smouldering in the oven at 180 degrees.

'That would be lovely.' Andy gave her his impish grin again. 'Does Friday night sound good?' As he waited for her reply, his police radio burst into life.

'DS Barnes from Delta Charlie…'

He gave Pru an apologetic smile and mouthed the word *sorry* in an exaggerated fashion before responding to the call. 'DS Barnes, go ahead.'

'Sarge, we've had a report of a sudden death. The DI has asked that you be notified.' Jules from the divisional control room cleared the air, waiting for his response.

Andy grimaced and clicked to respond. 'Sudden death or a suspicious death?'

'It's just listed as sudden at the moment, but it's the lady that was the subject of the near miss a few weeks ago at Chapperton Bliss. DI Holmes needs you to go to the scene; it's a precautionary measure.'

'Right, throw me the address and I'll start making my way there.' Andy crooked his middle fingers into his palm and gave Pru the thumb and little finger sign to mimic a telephone. She nodded and watched him disappear through the door as silently as he had arrived.

She had barely turned to face the oak bookcase to continue with her cataloguing when the door was flung open with gusto, bouncing back against the 'Book of the Week' table display and making it wobble. The one edition that she had carefully placed in the clear plastic stand on top of the neat stack fell backwards with a clatter, but before she could politely reprimand the culprit, Bree's excitable voice heralded her arrival.

'Bloody hell, you'll never guess what the latest gossip is!' Breathless, she flung her tasselled boho shopping bag on to the counter and made an exaggerated show of fanning herself with the library copy of *The Winterbottom News*.

Pru gave a wry smile. 'Another of our lovely WI members has snuffed it?'

Bree looked crestfallen. 'Well, thanks for piddling on my bonfire. How did you know? It's only just come hot off the press. Well, actually from the gob of Chels Blandish in the newsagent's, if it's to be believed.'

'It true, apparently. You've just missed Andy. The call came through whilst he was here. He's gone to the scene; they don't know if it's a sudden death or a suspicious one.' She quite liked the way that sounded, as though she had been privy to a secret inner circle.

Bree took a few seconds to digest that snippet of information. 'It's Rita. You know, the deaf one with the cat called Penis.'

'Todger, it's called Todger.' Pru smirked. 'I thought as much; they said it was the one that had a near miss, and poor Rita was the only one I could think of.'

They both stood in mutual silence, sad that another member of their community had passed away. Pru could see that her friend was desperately trying to think of something upbeat to add to the conversation, but for once positive words seemed to be failing them both.

'It could just be natural causes, you know; she was getting on a bit.' Bree doodled a flower on the scrap of paper in front of her, adding a leaf as a final flourish.

'Mmm... but what are the odds, considering the spate of murders we've already had? Jeez, we seem to be giving good old Chief Inspector Barnaby and Midsomer a run for their money: four murders in a small village. Now, if you ask me, that's got to be just a little bit suspicious.'

Bree looked aghast. 'Er... no shit, Sherlock – that's like saying Pizza Hut sells pizza!'

Andy surveyed the scene. The distinctive smell had already begun to permeate both nostrils. He made a show of rubbing underneath his nose to give the impression to the uniform lads holding the cordon that it was itchy, when in reality he had just furtively spread a thin layer of Vicks VapoRub from the handy tin he always carried in his inside jacket pocket.

'Do we have a time of death and a possible cause yet?' He gave Melv Hibbert, the on-call CSI, a cursory nod whilst taking in the scene cordon and the ridged metal step plates. 'I take it we're going with a sus death?'

'Yep. Murdoch's on his way here with a forensic pathologist. Can't see any obvious signs of trauma but take a look at this.' Melv leant forward, with his gloved hand holding a pair of large tweezers. He probed and peeled back the top slice of bread from the curled-up sandwich next to the body of Rita Charlesworth. On top of the ham, which had since taken on a silver-green hue, was a slip of paper smeared with dried mustard. 'Somehow I don't think the deceased was in the habit of using A4 lined instead of tomatoes to enhance the experience of fine dining!'

A flash from the CSI assistant's camera caught the unveiling and subsequent retrieval. Andy studied it. The neat, careful writing with a flourish of loops and curls spidered across the lines.

Sorry you had to go tits up, Rita
  See you on the other side
  You might even 'hear' me coming next time...
  M.M

'Bloody hell, that's a bit casual for a murderer, isn't it?' Andy reread the words, taking in the distinctive handwriting. 'It's not exactly a love note, but it shows familiarity.' He took a snap of it on his mobile phone.

'The cross bar on the letter "T".' Lucy was standing behind him, peering over his shoulder. 'It's quite an aggressive sort of tick, isn't it? It's not a gentle flow, more of an angry dash.'

'Blimey, Luce, you're like creeping Jesus. I didn't hear you come in. Is Holmes with you?' Andy watched Melv carefully place the note in a clear evidence bag.

She nodded. 'He's outside suiting up with old Barnacle Bob

and he's brought Tim, Tim Nice but Dim with him.' She rolled her eyes and grinned. Wrinkling up her nose she sniffed the air. 'Rita's a bit ripe, isn't she?'

Andy handed her his little tin of Vicks. 'Yep, Melv reckons she's been dead at least a couple of days. It was the cat that alerted one of the neighbours; it's been turning up looking for food.' He gave the curled-up ham butty a cursory glance as his stomach gave an unexpected heave. He swallowed hard. Death didn't really bother him; he would enter the place in his head that was his 'go-to' at incidents like this. His professional place. It was the smells he couldn't be doing with. He'd been like this since his first sudden death as a probationer when he'd embarrassingly hurled without warning, depositing his recently devoured cheese and onion pasty over the very deceased Miss Blundell and her expensive Persian rug. He had endured the psychological correlation of deathly odours and barfing ever since, along with the bollocking he'd got from the sarge for contaminating the scene and the mickey-taking from the lads on his section.

'Any ideas yet on cause?' The paper boot on Lucy's left foot caught on the rug. She bent down to readjust the elasticated edge over her own shoe, her eye catching the small glass vial peeking out from behind the leg of the chair that was currently housing Rita's rather expanded body. She quickly indicated her finding to Melv, moving out of the way to allow him access. 'Glad Barnacle's the FP. He's thorough–'

The rest of Lucy's sentence was drowned out by a loud clattering of metal, followed by Holmes's voice booming from the kitchen. 'Bloody hell, lad, watch where you're treading. Keep to the plates; they're there for a reason.' Holmes used his gloved hand to move the aluminium mop bucket that Tim had just kicked halfway across the quarry tiles. He needed the common path they were using free from obstacles so they could navigate the bungalow in accordance with forensic preservation. Tim sheepishly obliged. Leading with his right foot, he skipped on to the first plate, hovered momentarily, his left leg held up behind him as he judged the next plate to hop to.

'For Christ's sake, Forshaw, walk like a man. Don't flutter like a ruddy fairy at a ballet class, lad!'

Andy and Lucy recognised the bristling annoyance barely hidden in Holmes' voice, and mutually decided it would be sensible to remain silent. He appeared in the doorway between the kitchen and the sitting room. 'Right, let's see who's kicked the bucket.'

Tim sniggered loudly and waved his hand in the air as a signal of admission. He animatedly swung the aluminium pail that he had only moments before rattled across the kitchen floor, towards Holmes. 'Er... I think that would be me, boss...'

BETTY

The discovery of poor Rita had caused much consternation amongst not only the remaining ladies of The Winterbottom WI but all the residents of the once safe village. A strange phenomenon had sneaked its tendrils through the narrow lanes and cobbled streets of Winterbottom, drifting over fences, hedges and walls, finding its way into homes and shops like an early morning field mist, eerily silent, but felt in the bones of everyone it touched.

Fear.

Betty Prince, proprietor of Betty's Village Store, inhaled deeply, pushing away the nervous fluttery feeling that was gnawing at the pit of her stomach. She touched the cotton fabric on her patterned curtains, brushing her hand down the neat folds so that they sat in perfect alignment. She had been watching the small groups huddled together outside her ground floor apartment on The Green. Being a much sought after residential and recreational location in the centre of the village, it was a meeting place for anyone who sauntered past on their daily comings and goings. Where once they would have paid attention to the mamma duck with her ducklings gaily quacking their way to the edge of the pond, or would take a brief respite in their day to sit on the bench watching the huge willow tree sway in the breeze, they were now merged in angst and suspicion, totally oblivious to anything nature had to offer.

She could almost imagine their conversations, held in hushed tones, scared that if overheard, they might fall foul of their nemesis and be the next victim, afraid that the person they were talking to, be it friend, neighbour, work colleague or just someone to pass the time of day with, had potential to be what was now being dubbed the 'Ladykiller'.

'There was a note...'

'She'd been there for days...'

'It's got to be someone they knew, how else could they have got into their houses...?'

'Poor cat...'

In truth, Betty knew they were not their conversations but her own. The conversations she had with just herself. No one to acknowledge them, no one to dispute them, and no one to reassure her. Since the passing of her Jack some years before, she had tried to keep him alive in her memories; little things around her home that would suggest he was still there. His pipe sat clean and empty, balanced on the edge of the ashtray by his armchair. His grey tartan slippers neatly positioned side by side and perfectly aligned, had remained where he had left them on that fateful day.

'Just taking Hugo out for a walk, Betty, won't be long.' Hugo, their little white-and-tan terrier, had run around the coffee table in excitement, eagerly waiting for Jack to clip on the lead and take him on their daily adventure.

Jack had laughed a hearty laugh at his four-legged companion whilst duly placing those same slippers carefully underneath his armchair, just as he had done every single morning for the previous thirty-seven years. He'd shrugged his arms into his jacket, popped his flat cap upon his head, and had turned to plant a kiss on her forehead.

Just as he had done every single day of their married life.

But he had been long. The minutes had become an hour, the hour had become two, then three, then four. As the clocked ticked loudly on the sideboard, she had waited. His morning cuppa had gone cold, his toast had become brittle and her vigil at the window had been in vain.

Jack had never returned home – and nor had Hugo.

He was gone, just like that. Courtesy of the level crossing and the 9.32 Winterbottom to King's Cross express that had been ahead of schedule. No by your leave, no thanks for over thirty-seven years of marriage: nothing. Just an empty place beside her in bed at night and a broken heart.

A tear slipped onto her cheek, pausing momentarily before her fingertips gently wiped it away, stopping its journey.

'This will never do,' she loudly berated herself. 'Kettle on, I think. A decent cuppa will always put the world to rights.' She plumped the cushion on the chair, more out of habit than the fact it needed plumping, and made her way into her small kitchen. Placing two plates, two cups and two saucers on the tray, she shook two digestive biscuits on to the floral-patterned china. Pausing, she checked how many were left and threw caution to the wind by adding another two.

Glancing at her watch, she was glad to see that she had just enough time to quickly powder her nose before the arrival of her visitor.

'Quite dead, not a breath to be had, I believe.' Ethel Tytherington took a bite of the digestive biscuit and a sip of tea. 'Well, I suppose you wouldn't have any breath if you were dead, would you?' She attempted a small laugh, spraying crumbs over her skirt.

Betty looked on in amusement. Ethel hadn't stopped chattering since she had burst through the front door full of gossip, half-facts and downright invention. The four murders had clearly brought out the best in her; she was animatedly animate. She wondered if you could actually have both those words together, or whether it was what they called 'grammar suicide'. She wasn't sure, but she didn't really care because 'animatedly animate' sounded simply perfect.

'Anyway, my Albert was saying that Winterbottom hasn't seen the likes of this since that dreadful incident, ooh now, when was it? He did say, oh well.' She waved her hand dismissively. 'Ah yes, that terrible incident with, er... um, now, I've forgotten the name of her, too. Well, it was that woman that was found at the bottom of the cellar steps up at Magdalen House in the late 1970s or early 1980s, remember?' Ethel tilted her head waiting for a response from Betty.

'Ethel, how many "ooohs", "umms" and "ers" were included in that sentence? My dear, if you can't remember and you're telling the tale, how on earth am I supposed to?'

Ethel thought for a moment, using the hiatus to take another bite of her biscuit. Pointing the remaining section at Betty, she continued. 'Well, they thought it was an accident, didn't they? That she'd lost her footing and fallen. Those steps were quite steep and rickety, you know, but when the undertaker got her on the trolley to hoist her up the stairs, they realised that the large kitchen knife embedded in her back might have been a contributory factor!' She finished her sentence, feeling pretty pleased with herself.

Betty took her time to reply, still unsure if Ethel was being tongue-in-cheek or was actually quite stupid. 'So it was a murder then?'

'Mmm... Well, some thought maybe she'd been peeling spuds or something, then gone to the cellar for supplies and had slipped and accidentally stabbed herself.'

'In the back?' Betty couldn't hide her disbelief.

'Ah, well yes. I suppose if you put it that way, but you don't have to be so bloody pedantic, Bet!' Ethel indignantly harrumphed, the expression on Betty's face rankling her even more. 'I think I might need a trip to the little girls' room, I seem to have a bladder the size of a peanut these days.'

Whilst Ethel availed herself of the toilet facilities, Betty took the opportunity to open the patio doors that led out on to her small garden to let fresh air in and allow some of the midday heat to dissipate from the room. One of the benefits of having a ground floor apartment was the outdoor space; gardening was one of her small pleasures. She had pruned, teased and loved her flowers into bloom and they had repaid her with an oasis of colour, scents and tranquillity year after year. She heard the lounge door close shut, breaking her train of thought.

'I'm out in the garden, Ethel.' She bent down to dead head her favourite rose: High Society. She loved the creamy yellows and raspberry reds of the inner petals.

Ethel swanned out into the courtyard garden, sweeping around the four sides to take in the colours, the sunlight dappling between the branches of the large hawthorn tree falling in patterns on the small patch of grass. 'I used to be a bit of an expert on all thing flora and fauna, you know, Bet.' She drifted through the wooden arch, pausing to admire the white blooms cascading down.

'Did you really?'

Ethel smiled and nodded serenely, touching the delicate petals. 'I sure did.' She pulled at a tendril, the weight of the flowers making it sway. 'I must admit, though, it's been quite a while since I've seen your clitoris looking so flush and healthy.'

Betty sniggered. 'Good grief, Ethel, I know we're close friends, but seriously we're not *that* close!'

Totally oblivious to her snorts of laughter, Ethel continued to caress the flowers on Betty's rather grand climbing clematis, whilst rapturously sniffing its abundant blooms.

WHAT'S YOUR POISON?

'*A*conitine poisoning.' Robert Limpett (MRCS, MB, BS, RCPath), also known as Barnacle Bob to his friends, peeled off his latex gloves, stamped down hard on the pedal bar of the medical waste bin, and dropped them inside.

Andy nodded. Rita's autopsy had taken place the previous day and, as promised, the findings had been quickly pushed through. He had managed to wangle the good fortune of watching Rita's deathly repose from the viewing gallery above rather than have to suffer the delectable odours of cavity clearance and organ weighing first-hand. He jotted the name down in his notebook. 'Do we know how it was administered?'

'Subcutaneously, through the open sores in her ears via her hearing aids; they'd been laced with it.' He indicated to the close shot photographs. 'See, here… and here…' He jabbed his finger on the coloured paper. 'Very unusual way to go about it. Ingestion is by far the best method.'

'So, where would the–' Andy paused and checked his notebook again. '–aconitine come from?'

'Well, it has various names: Devil's helmet, Monkshood, Wolfsbane. It's from the plant *Aconitum*, and highly poisonous, although in China it's used in small doses as an analgesic and blood coagulant, not that I'd recommend that. It's mainly found in damp woodlands, ditches, meadows; it's one of the most toxic plants in the UK.' He clipped the photographs into his file. 'I'll get the report sent through ASAP, but there's no doubt about it; you've got another murder on your hands, and whoever carried this one out went to an awful lot of trouble. All I can say is thank Christ I don't live in Winterbottom!'

'Is there anything to link to the other jobs, Bob?' Andy was desperate for anything. He felt like the proverbial lame duck, just waiting for the smallest bread crumb to be thrown his way.

'Forensically from the body? No, but I think your best bet is going to be what comes back on that note left at the scene.' He clipped his briefcase shut.

Andy raised both eyebrows in unison and bit down on his bottom lip. Murdoch Holmes would go ballistic. The lack of progress on the previous three murders was quickly becoming a talking point throughout the whole force area. Any longer without something to push the investigation along and they'd be a complete laughing stock. He gave a cursory nod of thanks to Bob and hurriedly made his way out of the hospital complex, desperate to inhale fresh air. He wasn't looking forward to having Murdoch to contend with once he landed at HQ, but as soon as his shift was over he had an evening with the provocative Prunella to look forward to.

Sprinting across the car park he smiled to himself as the sun washed over his face and the breeze filled his lungs.

Life really wasn't that bad.

Andy watched Pru's unbelievably long and slender legs as she stretched to reach for a bright green plastic bowl from the wall cupboard in her kitchen. He'd already made himself quite comfortable and at home on the squishy sofa, reclining with a nice glass of Shiraz in his hand. As Pru moved from the cupboard to the breakfast bar, he adjusted his position and craned his neck to continue his view.

Mmm... gorgeous, funny and a great conversationalist, I must be punching well above my weight!

He tipped himself a bit further to the left, trying to keep the level of the wine in his glass horizontal whilst continuing to study his beautiful host. The last thing he needed was to slop it over Pru's cream rug whilst admiring her as she bent down to check the oven. The tight red dress she was wearing began to slowly ride up, making Andy flush with excitement as he waited for a few more centimetres of thigh to expose itself. Suddenly his five seconds of voyeurism was abruptly cut short as his vision was plunged into total darkness and a searing pain clutched at his scalp.

'Bloody hell!'

Grabbing at whatever had attached itself to his head, he plucked at the massive ball of black fluff and held it aloft in front of him whilst spitting hair and... he glanced at the undercarriage of the angry cat, *bleurgh...* goodness knows what, from his mouth. The cat fixed him with fierce copper eyes.

'Oh blimey, Mr Binks, you naughty boy! I'm so, so sorry!' Pru rushed to grab the offending animal from his outstretched hands, completely forgetting that she was still wielding the stainless-steel Ikea spatula she'd just used to baste the potatoes. She grimaced as it promptly smacked Andy hard across the side of the head.

'Yeeeooooow!' Andy flung his hand up to quell the stinging heat that was quickly blooming around his left ear.

Mr Binks, totally nonplussed by his dramatic introduction to the usurper that was ensconced on his side of the sofa, wriggled in Pru's arms, slowly elongating himself until his back paws rested upon Andy's knees. He held his copper gaze directly into Andy's eyes.

'He gets a little uneasy with strangers, I'm truly sorry, Andy. He will get used to you; I promise.' Pru gave a coy smile, waiting for what she hoped would be an understanding response. 'Sorry for twatting you on the ear.' She allowed Mr Binks to drop gently to the floor. 'I must say, it's got some oomph behind it, hasn't it?' She grinned and made a play of swishing the spatula through the air as if to prove her accidental assault on him might not be a one-off if he didn't behave.

Andy couldn't help but forgive her. He loved her smile; it was open, honest and fun, which made a nice change from the usual stuff he had to deal with day in and day out. He loved his job, but sometimes the deceit, dishonesty and downright cruelties of human nature hit him hard. 'You can, er... twat me anytime, so to speak. I'm assuming it has a more innocent meaning for you?'

Pru looked puzzled. 'Well, it's got two meanings hasn't it; to hit someone or it's a pregnant fish?'

'Yup, if you say so.' He took a slug of wine and laughed. 'No doubt you'll be researching that come Monday morning?'

She nodded and flopped herself down next to him, clinking her own glass against his. 'Definitely, I'm a librarian; words are my life!' Binks snuggled down next to her, still keeping a watchful eye on Andy. 'Talking of life, any update on our little village murder count?'

He took another sip of wine and licked his lips. 'Not much, really. It's a case of piecing everything together as it comes in. We're still waiting for forensics from the Charlesworth scene, and without restricting our investigation, we're going with the one offender slant for obvious reasons.'

'Lucy is convinced there's a back story to it all; that it's not random. She thinks the victims and the murderer are all connected somehow.' Pru jiggled slightly, adjusting the cushions which gave her the opportunity of moving closer to him.

He looked pensive. 'I know. There's definitely a common link between all the victims, not only the WI connection. We just haven't found it yet.'

A comfortable silence fell between them; even Mr Binks had relaxed a little. Pru leant against him, draping her legs across the arm of the sofa whilst simultaneously kicking off her shoes. Her pretty painted toes pointed in ballerina pose as she reached up to him, his blue eyes making her heart dance. With her lips pursed and eyes closed, she waited.

He didn't disappoint.

A NIGHT TO REMEMBER

'So...' Bree couldn't contain herself. She dropped her elbow onto the table and settled her chin into her upturned palm, waiting.

'So what?' Pru was giving nothing away, her lips met tightly together stifling a knowing smirk.

'Er... we're waiting...' Lucy grinned.

'A lady should never tell!' Pru blushed profusely and began to swirl the ice and lemon in her gin and tonic as a means of distraction, a smile twitching at the corner of her mouth.

A mutual exchange of glances followed until the penny dropped.

'OMG you've done it! You've succumbed. You've been naughty and had nuts on your waffle, haven't you?' Bree shrieked loudly, waving her hands in excitement, almost knocking her own drink over.

Pru grinned. 'Shhh, everyone's looking, I don't need half of Winterbottom to know about my sex life!' The collective whoops, sniggers and table slapping that came from her friends filled the snug of the Dog & Gun.

'Why not? It'll make a change from gossiping about Chelsea

Blandish's weekly leg-overs with Beefy Bruce from Sheraton's Butchers,' Bree quipped, then quickly followed up with a snort. 'And she has the cheek to tell everyone she's giving him a yoga class!'

Pru pondered on that awful vision. She could just imagine Chels' Lycra-encased thighs flinging around in wild abandonment under the guise of executing the Flying Lizard position whilst her surgically enhanced boobs flopped forward to suffocate the poor boy underneath her. She shuddered. 'Mmm… yep, Chels and the word "class" don't really sit well in the same sentence, do they? That girl's got less culture than a pot of yoghurt!'

'Oooh… bitchy…' Lucy took a sip of her lime and soda, quickly catching the drip from the bottom of the glass before it fell onto her jeans. '…but true!' She gave a wry laugh and then quickly fell silent, studying the tattered beer mat in front of her.

'You okay, Luce?' Pru was the first to notice.

'Yeah, it's just this murder case, I try to put it to bed for an hour or two when I'm off-duty, but the smallest thing sparks it up and it's back right at the front of my brain.' She tapped her forehead to evidence the location. 'It's like having a little guy in there with a toffee hammer, tap, tap, tapping at something I'm supposed to see, something that's smacking me in the face, but I'm just not putting two and two together.'

'What do you mean?' Bree hated to see her friend so distracted.

'It's an itch I can't scratch; that's the only way to describe it. I know it'll come to me; I just don't know when.' Her lips turned down at the corners as she squeezed her shoulders up to her ears, eyes wide, her face taking on a 'beats me' expression.

It was now Pru's turn to look pensive. She was secretly glad the subject had changed from her night of passion with Andy to a more normal – if you can call murder 'normal' – and less embarrassing topic. She didn't have the heart to tell them how her night with the Delectable Detective had really panned out.

The kiss on the sofa had been amazing, making her tingle from her head to her nicely painted toes; he had tenderly caressed her bare shoulders, daring to drop one strap from her dress so his lips could touch her skin. But before she could get the chance to have her breath completely taken away they had abruptly broken from their embrace, not by choice but because Pru's smoke detector had shrieked a warning that dinner was well and truly ready. As the spontaneity of the moment passed, they had diverted their attentions to eating.

He had been such a gentleman. She had watched his face gently lit by the candle in the middle of the table as he gingerly crunched down on what should have been tenderised lamb with a garlic and rosemary marinade, but in reality, by the time she had dragged it smoking from the oven, it had resembled (and tasted) like half an old house brick with a caramelised dollop of cement. He hadn't complained or passed comment, but she was pretty sure that some of it was being discreetly chucked under the table for Binks. She hadn't fared much better with the pudding either when one too many glasses of wine gave rise to a fumbled serving of shop-bought cheesecake. She had stood rooted to the spot as the generous portion toppled over the edge of the cake slice, hit the corner of the table, and landed neatly with a splat in Andy's lap.

The whole disastrous episode had ended with them both crumpled in a heap laughing whilst she polished off the remainder of the Shiraz before seductively dragging him upstairs. Andy had not objected in the slightest. Fumbling with various items of clothing, discarding them randomly on each stair, they'd bounced from wall to wall tangled together before he had eagerly thrown her on to the bed. She had been in seventh heaven as his muscular arms held her tight and just as she thought they had passed the point of no return in their after-dinner foreplay, Mr Binks decided to make an impromptu appearance at the top of the pillow to aggressively headbutt Andy on the nose. Andy feigned ignorance of the pilchard-smelling assailant and had continued to kiss her throat, running his tongue down to stop just above her breasts as a promise of what was to come, until a second headbutt had forced him into action. He'd swiftly picked up the large ball of fluff, who promptly did his usual trick of body elongation to evidence his annoyance, and marched a very bewildered Binks back downstairs to the kitchen. She had giggled uncontrollably at the sight of Andy's rather lovely bare bum as it sashayed out of the bedroom door with the impressive undercarriage and tail of Mr Binks draped down and visible between his own legs giving him a pair of hairy chakras to be proud of.

And then what?

She couldn't remember a thing after that... but the note he'd left for her to find in the morning was sufficient to fill in the blanks.

Morning Pru,

Well, that's a first, a date that's fallen asleep on me before I've even got warmed up! Came back to bed after sorting your furry beast out – and no, that's not a euphemism – and you were in the land of nod (was it really me or could it have been the wine?).

I've given the cat its breakfast. Actually, I didn't; that's a lie, it fed itself on the 'tasty' lamb chunks you left out on the table.

Ring me when you get chance, I really think we need to continue where we left off – but without the cat!

Andy x

PS It licked the leftover cheesecake too!

.   .   .

She involuntarily flushed pink. Okay, so it hadn't quite been the night she had dreamt of for the first time to be diddling Miss Daisy after her disastrous relationship with Tom, but at least Andy had let her know there was still a promise of good things to come...

...and best of all, he'd signed it with a kiss!

'Penny for them!'

Lucy's voice brought her back down to earth with a bump. 'What?'

'Your thoughts. Were they very naughty?' Lucy winked at Bree.

'Maybe.' Pru laughed. 'Look, it was a great night, but I must admit my brief foray with narcolepsy didn't really enhance the sexual chemistry.'

Bree almost choked on the pickled onion crisp she'd just popped in her mouth. 'Eeeeeeew! How gross, sleeping with dead bodies! How on earth did you think that would add to the evening?'

Pru rolled her eyes whilst handing a tissue to Lucy, who had just snorted a fair dollop of lime and soda through her nostrils trying not to laugh.

'Bree, my lovely friend, you really do need to brush up on your English Language skills!'

MOM KNOWS BEST...

*M*urdoch hated the soft-close pneumatic doors to the incident room. If ever there was a time when he wanted to show his frustration, annoyance, lack of sleep, his half-chewed ears from the command team, and ultimately his disappointment with his own team, now was it. In his book, a good old-fashioned slam of the doors as he entered the crowded room would have been a perfect way to show that, but instead they creaked slowly shut with a pathetic hiss of air as they settled in the wood frame.

He jutted his chin out and looked around. Some of his team had the decency to look up, the others remained huddled together discussing God knows what. He opted for the next action available to him, slamming his folders down onto his desk. The resounding *thwack* brought the room to total silence.

He nodded his satisfaction.

'Right, listen up. I'm going to go through a few basics with you all.' He hit the keyboard of his laptop, bringing the white-board screen on the wall to full brightness through the projector fixed to the ceiling. 'This, boys and girls, if you didn't know already, is a dead body.'

The image of Mabel Allinson, face-first in a lemon drizzle cake, filled the screen.

'And this is one too.'

A second image. This time poor Avery McIntosh, swinging from the under-stairs coat peg by a hand-knitted scarf.

'And believe it or not, this is also a dead body.'

Phillipa Jackson lay in repose on the heated treatment bed of Wrinkle in Time with a frayed extension lead welded to her hand, the other end inserted into a three-pin socket.

Holmes looked around the room, taking in the surprised faces of his team. He watched Andy shuffle uncomfortably in his seat before he continued. 'And to make it one more than a hat trick, which is just marginally better than the Winterbottom Rovers match last Saturday, we have yet another dead body.' He clicked the key and the swollen form of Rita Charlesworth slumped in her armchair graced the wall. 'So there you have it. Your first lesson in what a dead body looks like.'

Tim Forshaw's hand hovered somewhere between the waistband of his trousers and the pocket on his shirt, his fingers waving nervously before deciding to just go for it. He shot his hand in the air.

'Toilet again is it, Forshaw?' Holmes looked less than impressed.

'Er… no, sir, I went before I came in, but I was just wondering–'

'Let me interrupt you there, son. Unless the next words out of your mouth are "I know who the murderer is", don't waste your breath or my time!' Holmes was definitely on a mission. He turned his attention to the screen, his back to his audience. 'We have four dead women, four dead local women. These women have families, friends and work colleagues, all of whom need answers, and above all we still have a murderer walking amongst us, so forgive me if I seem a little short.'

Taking in the 5'8" stature of their detective inspector caused a muffled snigger to pass through the first two rows of desks.

'That's enough. Great things come in small packages, so the wife tells me.' He let a slight smile touch his lips; he didn't want to wreck their morale completely. 'I need answers, I need results, so that I can tell those families, those friends, those work colleagues that we've got the bastard.'

'Bloody hell, he's taking no prisoners, is he,' Lucy hissed to Andy.

'He's just frustrated like the rest of us, but he's the one that's getting it in the neck.'

'Got something to add, DS Barnes?' Holmes had snapped round to face him. Seeing his second-in-command making an aside, he was keen to share his observations.

Andy grunted. He felt as though he was back in school, and half expected Holmes to throw a blackboard duster at him for making a spit and thud ceiling dart in class. 'Sir, just discussing a potential lead with DC Harris.'

If looks could kill, he knew Lucy would be making them behind his back. He had no idea why he'd chosen to suddenly say that. Odds on Holmes would want details, and he didn't have any details to give; he'd just blurted it out as an appeasement. As if on cue and before he had chance to think on his feet, Murdoch was straight in.

'And what lead would that be? Pray tell.'

His mind working overtime, Andy desperately tried to think of something plausible.

'Er... it's the note left at the scene of the fourth murder, sir.'

Lucy quickly interrupted. 'The one addressed to Rita. We think there may be a connection with the sign off, the "M.M" on the bottom.'

Holmes looked pensive. 'Why?'

'It's personal; it means something. The suspect used the victim's name and signed off as someone would if they knew her.'

No sooner had the sentence left her mouth than the little guy with the toffee hammer began to tap, tap, tap at her brain. 'And the child's plimsolls at the Avery murder scene; we now know that one of those initials, even though the writing had been degraded over the years… was an…'

The light had been switched on in all its blazing glory.

'Go on.' Holmes waited.

'It was an M… that's what it was, it was an M!' She sat back, puffed her cheeks and blew out with relief, surprised at herself for being so forward with the DI, but also amazed that she had at last got some of the wispy threads in her brain to actually meet up and make a modicum of sense. 'And don't forget, the wool was mauve so we have another M there too!'

'Where the hell did that come from?' Andy hissed out of the corner of his mouth.

'I don't know, it just suddenly came to me.'

Andy grabbed his notebook and a couple of pens from the desk drawer and indicated to Lucy to get her stuff together. She grabbed her jacket from the back of the chair.

'Before you all get back to what you were doing before I came in, remember that even the smallest clue, the tiniest speck, the quickest head-thought are all worthy of investigation. Rule nothing out until it's been proved negative. I need you to work to the *MOM* principle.' Out of the corner of his eye he saw Tim's hand shoot up again. '…And no, Forshaw, that's not something your mother does for you!'

The ripple of laughter around the room eased what had been a tense ten-minute briefing. Holmes felt better about leaving it on a lighter note.

Lucy wriggled one arm into her jacket as Holmes wrapped up the briefing, the scraping of chairs and slamming of desk drawers almost drowning out the DI's last words.

'Means, Opportunity and Motive.' He counted them off on his fingers. 'Get me those and we'll be getting somewhere.'

OH, TO BE BESIDE THE SEASIDE...

*K*itty Hardcastle straightened the white linen tablecloth, using the edge of her hand to press out the creases. She unfolded the beautifully embroidered Winterbottom Women's Institute cloth and draped it across the table so that the name and years active were on full show. Brenda had brought a crystal vase filled with water from the kitchen so that she could begin her display of freshly cut sweet peas. Kitty loved the array of pastel colours; they stirred a memory of her childhood when her grandmother would allow her to pick them from their garden to adorn the table at Sunday lunch.

'Brenda, can you ask Clarissa to bring the chairs just a little closer together?' She held out her hands, making a sideways patting motion in the air to show exactly what she wanted Clarissa to do. 'And no lemon drizzle cake tonight; just stick to the scones and Victoria sponge.' She knew the evening was going to hold a rather solemn meeting, and she definitely didn't want that particular sweet fancy or indeed anything knitted in Sirdar DK Mauve to completely destroy what remained of the usual WI cheerfulness.

No sooner had she thought of the welfare of her ladies than

the large oak doors burst open and the members began to pour in. She was pleased to see that they had begun to adopt a 'safety in numbers' protocol between themselves. Nobody arrived or left the meetings alone. The minimum group number to travel between Winterbottom Parish Hall and their respective homes was never less than three, which made Kitty wonder how vulnerable the last lady in any group would be. There always had to be one left to travel alone, even it was only a few doors away from the last drop. She watched them huddle in groups to pass chatter, before breaking away from each other to form a new dynamic. She glanced at the clock sitting high on the wall, waiting for the long brass finger to jerk towards the number six to bring the time to 7.30pm on the dot.

'Ladies, ladies, please, if we could just take our seats as quickly as possible, that would be grand.' She inched her way behind the table, taking her usual presidential stance and began to ring the small bell vigorously to bring the ladies to attention. 'I have some rather uplifting news for us all, something I think we could all do with.'

Chels Blandish, this time dressed in skin-tight jeans and a very sheer see-through lace blouse, raced to the front and grabbed the seat next to Pru and Bree. She flopped herself down with an over-exaggerated sigh. 'All right, girls, well what a rum do we're having, hey?' She pulled at the crotch of her jeans and wriggled. 'Blimey, these are bit of a squeeze when yer sit down, my taco's munching my thong!'

Bree gagged at the mere thought of what Chelsea's 'taco' was capable of, and more to the point where it had been lately. As if reading her mind, Pru started to giggle, but quickly caught the ensuing snort of laughter by muffling her mouth with the sleeve of her jumper.

Undeterred, Chelsea continued. 'I know everyone is hung up on these murders, but have you heard the latest about Alison

Kilty's hubby, hey? Just wouldn't expect that 'round here, now, would you?'

Pru felt obliged to shake her head, and although not particularly fond of gossip, she found herself engaging with her. 'And what would that be then, Chels?'

'He's a drug addict.' Chelsea looked accomplished in her revelation.

Bree hastily jumped in. 'Why on earth would you think that? He's a lovely guy; you shouldn't spread stuff like that; it could ruin reputations.'

'All right, no need to bite me head off. I'm just telling you as I heard it. He's got one those yellow boxes for putting syringes in. Courtney from down our road saw him trying to get rid of it in Dylan's chemists,' Chelsea just as quickly snapped back.

'Bloody hell, Chels, wind it in, will you? That's a prescribed sharps box.' Bree sighed, annoyed at her assumption. 'It's not common knowledge, but the guy's a haemophiliac.'

Chelsea chewed the inside of her lip and pouted. 'Don't be daft, he can't be; he's married with kids!'

Pru and Bree's attempt at educating Chelsea without laughing was suddenly cut short as Kitty gave another peal of her bell calling everyone to order. Like two naughty schoolgirls they immediately adopted a serious face each. Kitty waited until the last lady was seated and carefully measured her words. She had lain awake the previous night, trying to come up with the best way to acknowledge their losses whilst trying to offer her ladies something to look forward to. The butterflies fluttered in her stomach, a sick feeling worming its way upwards as she took a deep breath.

'Tonight will be a little different from our usual routine. There will be no minutes or orders of business.' She paused, taking in the collective faces and the reassuring nods from her stalwarts. 'I don't need to remind anyone of the tragic events that have plagued Winterbottom and our Women's Institute. We have lost not only four members, but four good ladies and four loyal friends.'

The nodding continued throughout her audience, providing a wave effect to the rows before her.

'The only information I have at this time is that the funerals, when they eventually take place, will be family only affairs, but maybe we could perhaps arrange a collective memorial service for Rita, Avery, Pip and Mabel at a later date.' Kitty checked for signs of approval from her ladies. When it was given in the form of several nods and melancholy smiles, she felt it was safe to move on.

'I think we now need to look forward to our own emotional needs, and with that in mind I have procured the services of Frank and one of his sixty-seater coaches for a day trip to the seaside.'

A ripple of excited ooohs and aaahs undulated through the gathered ladies.

'Methinks she's procured a bit more of Frank's services than just a clapped-out charabanc, don't you?' Bree hissed from the side of her mouth, causing Pru to cover another uncontrollable bout of laughter with the sleeve of her jumper.

Kitty gave a headmistress style glare to the front row before continuing. 'A few hours of fresh air, a change of scenery, and maybe a candyfloss or two will do us the world of good. The funfair will be open too, so don't forget to bring a few pennies with you for the rides.'

The animated chatter that began to fill the rows as the ladies of the Winterbottom Women's Institute excitedly discussed their plans for their day out was all the proof that Kitty needed to show that her fabulous idea had been fully embraced.

THE PROSPECTUS

Phyllis could barely contain herself as she helped stack the chairs at the end of the WI meeting. She had deliberately kept herself to herself throughout the evening, choosing not to engage in any flippant conversation with the others, opting instead to eavesdrop. Kitty had just given her the most perfect opportunity for the eagerly anticipated despatch of presidential candidate number five from her list. She couldn't wait to get home to start planning.

She would have to research what would be available on their day out, but she quite liked the idea of a funfair murder; it sort of had a special feel to it, and listening to the conversations she now knew who it would be. Perhaps she...

'Oh, Phyllida, cooeee!'

Kitty's voice cut through her like a knife, rudely interrupting her thoughts.

'It's Phyllis.'

'What is?' Kitty barely looked up from the depths of her handbag.

'My name. My name is Phyllis.'

'Of course, dear, silly me. Glynis, could you please help

Clarissa move the extra chairs we brought up from the basement. They need to be returned down there, or the caretaker will have my guts for garters!' Kitty draped her handbag over her arm and instantly dismissed any further conversation with Phyllis before making her way over to Prunella and Bree. 'Pru, I've got your WI application here; you've been seconded, so we're all good to go.'

Phyllis watched her flitting between various ladies who were still milling around the hall. She knew they were afraid to step out into the night to chance their safety, afraid that they too might become a victim of the 'Ladykiller'. It was just too funny; she really wanted to laugh out loud at the absurdity of it all, or at the very least announce to them that they were actually quite safe. Well, apart from Felicity, Betty and Bree. They, of course, were quite a different matter. What was even more absurd was the fact that all this palaver and murderous mayhem could have been avoided if only they'd had the decency to notice her, to get her name right, to include her.

'Phyllis', 'Dilys', 'Glynis', 'Phallus'... the list had been endless. She'd never been particularly fond of the name she'd been given, 'Dilys' didn't quite roll from the tongue or sound exciting, and if truth be known, she had probably subconsciously encouraged them to use the mistaken moniker of 'Phyllis' to make up for it.

Picking her way carefully down the rickety wooden steps with two folded chairs under her arm, the maximum weight she felt safe carrying, she hesitated, peering into the murky depths of Winterbottom parish hall basement. She hated going down there; it brought back far too many memories. The darkness, the smells, the scratchy noises. Her skin began to crawl, thinking of what could be hiding in the shadows. She inhaled sharply and closed her eyes. Her heart had begun to thump against her ribs, just as it always did when she remembered, when she became a child again...

Nasty little listeners never hear good of themselves.

She had been caught hiding behind the parlour door, rough hands had clutched at the collar of her thin summer dress before manhandling her along the tiled corridors, pausing only briefly as her small hands had reached out, trying to keep purchase on the spindles of the staircase to stop her journey. But it had continued, her little fingers slipping through the wood as she had frantically grabbed at anything and everything in an attempt to slow her progress. She had lost her balance and fallen onto the Victorian tiles, hurting her knees, her hands grazing the coarse woven mat in front of her, but still they continued, the collar of her dress pressing hard on her throat as she was lifted up and dragged forwards, on through the morning room, through to the kitchen and into the dank scullery where the cavernous mouth to the cellar stood open.

'No, Mummy, please, please, Mummy, don't...'

But she had.

And there had been no one to hear her, only the rats who scuttled in the shadows, waiting.

~

Andy adjusted the height of his chair and rolled himself forward, slotting his knees under the desk. Jiggling the mouse on the mat next to him, his screen flickered, then brightened and the Winterbottom Force logo welcomed him with an invitation to log in. His fingers rattled across the keyboard, ending with a deliberate and confident stab on the 'enter' key.

He clicked on the case number for Phillipa Jackson.

'Morning, sarge; tea or coffee?'

Andy looked up to see Tim eagerly waving the kettle at him. 'Er... coffee, please. Strong, one sugar.' He didn't normally drink coffee this early in his shift, or take sugar for that matter, but his late night with Pru had left him rather jaded and in need of perking up. He let a smile touch his lips remembering her very agile party trick. She wasn't just beautiful, intelligent and funny, she was also a bloody amazing contortionist too – if she could stay awake long enough. He chuckled to himself, remembering her slurred drunken promise of fabulous things to come, only to find her planted face down on the mattress and snoring her head off when he'd returned to the bedroom, after ensuring the dratted cat couldn't invoke a super weird *ménage à trois* by sneaking back in.

'Andy, uniform have just taken this at the front desk. They've bagged and sealed it, but God knows who's touched it since the Jackson murder.' Lucy dropped the clear evidence bag onto his desk, interrupting his rather delicious train of thought, the magazine text obvious through the plastic. 'It's a prospectus brochure for a college in Oxford, one of the girls from Wrinkle in Time brought it in. It was found on the table next to the treatment bed in the room Pip Jackson was in.'

Andy studied it. 'Why do they think it's significant?'

She rolled her eyes and sighed. 'It's a beauty salon; the only magazines and brochures they have are for cosmetic procedures and products. They're selling an image, not a chance for further education and to stretch someone's brain; the only stretching they do in that place is to pull the skin up on your face and tuck it behind your ears!'

He grimaced at the thought. He still couldn't get his head around the fact that women actually paid to end up resembling a startled trout with their taut faces and puffed, pouty lips. 'So you're saying there's a possibility it was left by our offender?' He studied the brochure, pressing out the creases in the evidence bag.

'Maybe. I don't know, but it's worth getting forensics to have a look at it,' Lucy fired up the submission form on her PC. 'There's been something left at every scene so far, apart from Pip Jackson's, so we've got to take a shot at it.'

'Okay, send it in, not that I'm expecting much. Did front desk take elimination prints from the girl who brought it in?'

Lucy nodded. 'Yep, that's all been done.' She pressed print and scuttered her chair across the office, the wheels squeaking as she twirled around to grab the sheet of paper from the printer. 'I forgot to ask, how did your date night with Pru go? You're getting quite cosy, you two.' She grinned, tilting her head and waiting for his reply. She'd gained very little from Pru and was hoping Andy might be a bit more forthcoming.

Andy grinned back. 'Just get on with your work, Harris. Don't be trying your interview techniques on me. Anyway, a gentleman should never tell.'

'A gentleman!' Lucy stood up and grabbed her jacket, tucking the submission form and evidence bag under her arm. 'Andy, you truly are proof that God has a fabulous sense of humour!'

Andy looked momentarily chuffed at that comparison, until the true meaning of what she'd said sank in. Before he had chance to think of a quick comeback, Lucy had disappeared through the door, her cheerful laughter drifting along the corridor.

PUDDLINGTON PIER

he sun shone brightly, picking up the metallic red stripes on the side of the cream bus that were the trademark colours of Rubber, Springs & Gaskets coach tours. Kitty stood in her usual spot at the front, monitoring the excited arrival of the ladies of Winterbottom Women's Institute as they eagerly lined up, waiting to climb the steps for their day out to the seaside. The pages on her clipboard fluttered in the mild breeze as she ticked off each passenger whilst smiling coyly at Frank.

'Come along now, Betty.' She grabbed Betty's arm to assist her onto the first step. Betty grabbed the handrail and glowered at her.

'I'm not that decrepit, you know. The day I can't get my leg up and over is the day I pack all this in!'

Bree almost choked laughing. 'Bet she's not had that particular leg over in donkey's years.' She nudged Pru and winked. Pru playfully punched her on the arm in response.

The pair stood back and waited until the over sixties had boarded, along with Chels Blandish and her friend for the day, Cassidy Parks. Neither really relished the prospect of procuring a seat squeezed in between Chels' over-inflated bosoms and Cassidy's four-inch-long false eyelashes.

'Beats me as to how the hell she can see through those.' Pru was mesmerised as Cassidy paused on the first step and gave Frank an alluring flutter, much to Kitty's disdain. 'Look, the breeze from them almost lifted his toupee at the front.' Without thinking, she pointed wildly, drawing attention to the unnaturally swept and patted down fiery red tresses atop Frank's head.

Frank's toupee was legendary amongst the Winterbottom residents. He had kept the truth of his male pattern baldness a closely guarded secret for years, until he'd forgotten to duck under the low oak beam on the way to the toilet in the Dog & Gun. His rug had been left dangling from one of the obsolete tankard hooks, much to the amusement of the regulars – and to the absolute horror of his Elite Singles online date, who was last seen dodging through the car park at breakneck speed whilst Frank tried to retrieve his ginger pocket pompadour from the seventeenth-century chunk of timber.

'That's enough, ladies!' Kitty gave her well-practised disdainful stare to Pru and Bree. 'Pick your seats and settle down, I'm sure Mr Atkins is raring to go.'

'Haha, not 'arf, missus!' Pru's impression of Frank sent the whole coach into a jovial outbreak of laughter, much to the consternation of Kitty who blushed profusely.

'This is not some *Carry On* episode, you know. There is a certain level of behaviour that is expected from us and–' The gentle hiss of the pneumatic doors as they closed drowned out the end of her sentence. Kitty plonked herself down on the front seat and pursed her lips. Undeterred, she continued with her reprimand. 'We represent the Women's Institute; we are beacons of refinement; we are–'

'Oh blimey, Kitty, give it a rest. Beacons of refinement indeed!' Betty Prince huffed in disagreement. 'We are a group of women out for a bit of enjoyment, something to take our minds off recent events, or at the very least to allow ourselves some small respite.'

Several 'hear, hears' were uttered from the back four rows, forcing Kitty's mouth to go into cat butt mode. Pru watched wide-eyed, half expecting it to become so tight and so puckered that Kitty would be in danger of losing the ability to speak.

She was wrong.

Kitty's face reached a startling shade of purple as the grip on her pen forced her knuckles to turn white. 'Give it a rest! Give it a rest!' Kitty spluttered with indignation. 'I'll have you know that it was me who thought of this jaunt; it was me who made all the arrangements; it was me who had to drop everything and liaise with Mr Atkins–'

'We know; several times, late at night, in his office! What was it you dropped again, Kitty?' Betty was on a roll.

As the banter, largely at Kitty's expense, continued, Phyllis sat quietly at the back of the coach in her usual seat, musing to herself that when her time came to be president, she would ensure that she would never be the butt of anyone's jokes. Once again the trees and fields raced past her window, the lush countryside making way for the rocky coast. She could smell the salt air through the open window as she gazed upon the blue-grey of the sea. If truth be known, she was actually quite enjoying Betty's comedy turn, as were the rest of the ladies, if their laughter was anything to go by. It was strange how she had never really noticed Betty's quick wit and tongue. Under different circumstances she probably would have got to like her; even enjoy her company.

Mmm... under different circumstances.

Now that would have been a blessing, but that was the thing about Phyllis's life: it had no blessings.

Puddlington Pier was crammed full of happy day-trippers, taking in the sea views and the endless sunshine. Not a cloud marked the clear blue sky, which in turn allowed the sea to sparkle as the waves gently washed towards the white sand. Children in bright swimming costumes ran laughing to the water's edge whilst their smaller and younger counterparts played castles with red and yellow plastic buckets. Deck chairs for hire, set in regimented rows of blue and white stripes, added to the scene.

Pru leant over the bleached wood rail, her ice lolly melting far too quickly. 'It's like something from an old 1950s cosy seaside story book, isn't it? Just like Enid Blyton would pen.'

'If you say so.' Bree licked the side of her hand, catching the drip from her ice cream and gave her friend a sideways glance of amusement. 'I'm not the biggest fan of books and reading to be honest.'

'Oh dear, and you being a film researcher too, that doesn't bode well. I'm afraid we can't be friends anymore then,' Pru quickly retorted. 'How on earth can you say to a librarian "I'm not a fan of books"? It's like an arrow to the heart!' She staggered backwards, feigning a sharp object sticking from her chest.

'What I mean is I'm more of a magazine type of gal. I've got the attention span of a gnat, so anything more than ten pages leaves me lost.' Bree watched in despair as the top of her ice cream slid off the cone and splattered on the deck. She surveyed the melting mess. 'D'you think the three-second rule counts with an ice cream?'

Pru grinned. 'Bree, if you're even considering scooping that up off the ground, then you and I really are finished.'

'Come on, ladies, candy flosses at the ready, funfair time!' Kitty, closely followed by Clarissa, and hot on her heels the rest of the Winterbottom WI gathering, marched in unison towards the two bouncing hot air clowns either side of the large overhead sign that welcomed them to enjoy '**The World of Thrills, Spills and Frights at Pudds Fairground**'.

THE DUNGEON OF DOOM

'*A*rms up, girls!'

Terry, the young fairground worker on the ghost train, jumped like a mountain goat from one carriage to another, checking the bars had dropped down and were fully engaged. He fleetingly charmed Clarissa and Brenda who were sharing The Phantom Express carriage. They were wedged in like two balls of dough, Brenda's ample bottom causing a good few inches of spillage over the side whilst Clarissa's enormous boobs began to lift and separate. One rolled comfortably out over the metal bar to finally rest on her knee, whilst the other took refuge under Brenda's left armpit.

'We don't want you beautiful ladies coming to any danger in there, now do we?' Terry grinned, showing a decent set of white teeth against his tanned skin.

'In that case, why don't you sit right here and come through with us?' Clarissa jauntily teased, patting the knee that didn't have a body part rolled over it. 'You never know what you might discover in the dark!'

Brenda looked absolutely mortified, but before she could offer an apology for her naughty friend, Terry had gone, leaping down the snaking train to stop at The Ghouls' Gate carriage that held the giggling forms of Chels and Cassidy, much to the consternation of Clarissa.

'Humph, wouldn't you think he'd prefer maturity over shallow youth, Brenda?'

Taking in the moulded wobbly flesh that was filling their little carriage, their joint penchant for support stockings and the fact that at least one of them had a set of dentures, Brenda gave her a wry smile. 'Not really, we've got to face facts, my dear; we've become old and surplus to requirements in *that* department.'

'Speak for yourself, dearie. I've still got a bit of life left in me; there's a few services I can still provide, even at my age.' Clarissa pouted and winked.

Brenda grinned. 'Only if you took your teeth out first, though. You wouldn't want to lose them amongst the bed sheets!'

Their jovial belly laughs floated along the line of carriages, ensuring each of the Winterbottom ladies joined in; some because they had heard their saucy exchange, others simply because their laughter was infectious. Betty and Ethel had joined forces, and jokingly fought with Pru and Bree for The Dungeon of Doom carriage near the back. Betty had triumphantly won by being surprisingly agile and beating the youngsters to the weather-worn seat. She dragged poor Ethel down next to her.

'Goodness, Betty, mind me Nobbly Bobbly!' Ethel wailed as a chunk of chocolate covered in sugar balls dropped to the floor of the carriage.

'You're a lady, Eth. What are you doing with a Bobbly Nob?' Betty chortled loudly; she was so enjoying this little jaunt. She'd been right; this was just what they all needed.

The sudden clunk as the ratchets caught the rails forced their carriage to jolt forward, making them squeal with laughter.

'Teeth or no teeth, we're off!' Clarissa yelled over the sudden ghostly wail of a white sheeted spectre that appeared from nowhere.

Phyllis had taken up her place in the second to last carriage, aptly named The Grim Reaper. She thought that was quite amusing, considering what she was about to do. As expected, she sat alone, but this time it had been through choice, not oversight.

Millie Thomas had tried her best to partner up with her as soon as they had alighted the coach, even offering a choice of chocolate peppermints or orange creams from the screwed-up paper bag she had dredged from the depths of her handbag. Phyllis had politely declined, but that hadn't deterred Millie in the slightest. She had stuck to her like glue along the pier and into the fairground. She had only managed to shake her off by deliberately spreading herself across the seat in her carriage. Millie had eagerly tried to place the toe of one of her navy-blue Mary Jane's inside The Grim Reaper without success, before it had dawned on her that Phyllis was never going to make way for the other shoe, let alone her posterior and her handbag.

As chagrin set in, Millie had stuffed her sweets into the pocket of her cardigan and set off looking for another carriage that was going solo, leaving Phyllis to furtively cosset the large syringe that was loaded and ready in her own handbag. As the carriages slowly trundled along the track, she settled herself into a comfortable position. Her vantage point, directly behind the animated form of dear Betty Prince sitting in The Dungeon of Doom was perfect. As she watched Betty and Ethel, arms held aloft, she smiled and hummed her signature tune.

When will that be? Say the bells of Stepney...

Unaware of what the following minutes would hold, the ladies of Winterbottom WI set off on a most exciting and spooky adventure as the train and several carriages disappeared through the cavernous mouth and into the darkness.

'Wahooo!' Pru's voice shrieked out, as yet another skeletal form clattered out from an eerily lit crevice to jiggle inches away from her face before disappearing back into the depths of the painted pre-cast rock. The rush of cool, musty air that raced past The Vampire's Vat as the little train trundled along the tracks, blew their hair wildly, adding to the fun. 'Daylight ahead, ladies, our ride's almost over, where to next?' she yelled behind her.

Clarissa was the first to reply. 'Roller coaster for me; anyone else up for it?' Eagerly rattling the bar on her carriage with one hand as it slowly drew to a stop, she glanced at Brenda. 'Oh dear, I think I should've got rid of me candy floss before I got on.'

Brenda sat with a less than amused expression on her face, a spidery smattering of pink froth stuck to the side of her head and a large blob dangling from the rim of her glasses. 'Oooh, you don't say,' she sarcastically retorted. 'That's a bit like saying you should shut the gate after the cat's got out!' She began to pull at the sticky mess.

'It's stable door and a horse.'

'I don't have a horse; I've got a cat.'

'Well in that case, cats can jump over gates; they don't need them to be shut to stop them from getting out!' Clarissa grunted in triumph as she eased herself out of the carriage with the help of Bree.

'Ladies, ladies, come on now, play nicely!' Pru laughed. 'Roller coaster it is, let's just–'

Pru didn't get chance to finish as a loud scream broke through the jaunty hurdy-gurdy organ music.

'I'm not going anywhere until I find it, I can't be seen like this; it's a disaster!'

Cassidy's high-pitched voice brought the undivided attention of the whole group to her carriage, where she was in full flow, dramatically flinging her arms around and wailing.

'It got blown off in there... my eyelash; I'm bloody naked now!' She held one hand over the offending eye to hide her alleged public bareness. The other hand was curled into a ball, with one finger pointing out and stabbing the air. 'We've got to go back in and search for it.' She gave a pouty expression to Terry, who had hastily joined them to see the cause of all the commotion. 'Please help me.' She fluttered her one remaining false eyelash at him.

Terry was completely unmoved by Cassidy's plea. He grunted and shrugged before making his way back to his kiosk with his hands stuffed in his pockets, satisfied that no true disaster had actually occurred.

Bree grabbed Pru's arm and started to laugh. Pointing to Chelsea's ample heaving cleavage in her low-cut top, she grimaced. 'Look, here you go, Cass. Either your friend has saved the day for you or she's got a hairy nipple she's been keeping under wraps.' With her thumb and forefinger, Pru plucked the offending false eyelash that was poking out from the neckline of Chelsea's blouse. 'Oh look, it's waving at me!' She shook it in the warm breeze, so it fluttered wildly, making everyone laugh.

Phyllis, after much huffing and puffing to extricate herself as gracefully as possible from The Grim Reaper used the distraction of Cassidy's lost eyelid tarantula to compose herself before joining the others. She exhaled. She inhaled. She raised her face to the sun and closed her eyes.

Suddenly, and for the second time in as many minutes, their joviality was interrupted by an ear-piercing scream, but this time it was different; it was accompanied by a keening moan from poor Ethel Tytherington.

'Oh, Betty, what did you want to go and do that for? We were having such good fun, too.' Ethel, tears streaming down her face, sat shell-shocked next to Betty Prince who was still unceremoniously wedged in The Dungeon of Doom, her neck bent at an awkward angle, her eyes staring soullessly towards the sky with a half-melted ice lolly in her lap. 'I thought she was just joking, but she isn't. The selfish mare has only gone and died on me, and she didn't even finish her Bobbly Nob either.'

Pru helped Ethel out of the carriage and wrapped her arms around her, offering her as much comfort as she could, whilst Kitty broke into her presidential role to assume the responsibility of managing the aftermath of Betty's sudden and unexpected passing.

As a flurry of activity began to take place around them, Pru couldn't shake the feeling of unease that was gripping her. Once again her attention was drawn to Phyllis. 'What do you think, Bree? Natural or unnatural, given our recent track record? I mean, I can't see any signs of foul play, but you never know.'

Bree looked thoughtful. 'Only one way to find out.' She sighed as she pressed the keys on her mobile phone for the number that would call Lucy. 'Better to err on the side of caution.'

Pru nodded. 'Just a thought. Check out everyone's reaction to Betty popping her clogs.' She waited for Bree to take stock. 'Now look at Phyllis. Does that look normal to you?'

Bree looked at Phyllis and shook her head. 'No, no it certainly does not!'

INSIDE JOB

*A*ndy frantically yanked the oven door open and made a grab for the roasting tin. The searing pain in his first three fingers and thumb, along with him simultaneously smacking his elbow on the door as he hastily pulled away from the spitting fat surrounding the chicken, reminded him of why oven gloves were so useful.

'Shit, shit, shit.' He blew on his hand, and when that had little effect he shoved his fingers under the running cold water in the sink. 'And bollocks!' A second attempt at a dinner date with Pru was already not going according to plan. He watched the half pulled-out tin teetering on the oven shelf and prayed that it would stay put whilst the fire that was currently travelling along his nerve endings was dampened. The last thing he needed was for his lemon and thyme supreme to end up splayed out on the kitchen floor tiles. He took a closer look at the country style ceramic squares and prayed even harder; he couldn't remember the last time he'd given the floor a good mopping. He felt sick, wondering what evils lurked amongst the grout that could be transferred on to the chicken if it decided to take a tumble and belly-flop onto his budget flooring.

Wrapping his hand in a tea towel, he used his foot to kick the oven door shut, which in turn pushed the roasting tin back on to the shelf.

'All's good, no sweat, Moby, another ten minutes and it'll be done.' He grabbed his wine glass and tipped a toast to his goldfish before taking a swig. 'Don't you ever get bored just swimming round and round in circles?' He didn't expect the orange comet to reply, but it did give him food for thought. 'Maybe it's about time I got you a little tank rather than a bowl.' Visualising Moby swimming in squares each time he hit a corner made him laugh out loud. 'Or maybe a mate. Nobody should live alone all their lives, should they?'

Apart from a carefully chosen small selection of girlfriends over the years, Andy had never quite had the desire to be married or even have a permanent woman in his life. His job had always come first. It was difficult to find anyone who wanted to put up with the unsociable working hours, rest days cancelled at a minute's notice, not to mention the stress the job sometimes heaped on his shoulders. It was hard not to plunge into the abyss when dealing with the worst that the human race had to offer; he would never expect anyone to willingly buy into that.

'But she's different, Moby. There's something very special about this lady.' He couldn't quite put his finger on it, but Pru made his heart beat just that little bit faster. 'I really do need to make a good impression tonight. After all, I can't have her falling asleep on me again, can I?'

His man-to-man conversation with Moby was abruptly interrupted by the doorbell loudly heralding the hopeful arrival of Pru. Andy checked his watch.

'Blimey, that came around quickly.' He paused to check himself in the hall mirror, giving himself a wide, inane grin. The last thing he wanted was strings from the celery he'd been nibbling on stuck between his front teeth when he greeted her.

Taking a deep breath, he glanced at his reflection once again and reached for the doorknob.

~

Andy lay staring at the ceiling, content.

Pru was nuzzled into his neck, her breath pulsating against his skin as he gently caressed her bare shoulder, tapering down her back until his hand fell comfortably to rest in a protective position at her waist.

'Congratulations, gorgeous,' he mumbled.

She opened her eyes and searched his face. 'For what?'

'...er... staying awake!'

Quick as a flash, romance forgotten, she was up on her knees in combat position, arms held high before she swung her weapon of choice.

'Oooommmmffffffffff!' Andy took the full force of the pillow in his face. Scrabbling for anything to retaliate, his fingers grabbed at the novelty toy penguin his mum had bought him last Christmas, the one he wished he'd hidden in the wardrobe before he'd enticed Pru into his bedroom. 'Prepare to meet thy doom!' he yelled as he swung it wildly in the air, forcing its googly eyes to spin in different directions. He missed Pru completely, throwing himself across the bed where he bounced on the edge of the mattress and disappeared over the side.

Pru froze mid attack. 'Oh my God, Andy, are you okay?' Her head appeared over the edge of the mattress looking down on him as she desperately tried not to laugh at the naked body of the guy, who only moments earlier had brought her to the heights of complete ecstasy – which incidentally was something Tom had never been able to achieve – to being the comedic lump now lying on the carpet.

He held one hand out as reassurance whilst the other tenderly cosseted his groin. 'I'm good, don't worry.' He grimaced.

'It's your hairy chakras, isn't it? You've flattened them. I'm sooo sorry.' Pru tried to sound truly repentant, but the look on his face and the explosion of penguin stuffing surrounding him just made it all the more comical. 'I hate to be the one to break it to you, but I think your pecker's seen better days.'

He pulled himself up and kissed the tip of her nose. 'I'll have you know my pecker is fine and functioning right at the top of its game, Miss Pearce.'

She dangled the squashed carcass of what had been his mum's lovingly bought stocking filler by its beak between her finger and thumb. 'Now, now, Mr B, less of the saucy innuendos.' She reciprocated with a gentle fun kiss on his lips as they flopped back down together and cuddled up under the duvet.

'Any chance of more than a corner?' He held the edge of the grey and ochre geometric patterned cover in the air. 'I suppose this is just the start of mattress and duvet hogging, and me having a cold ass on wintry mornings!'

Pru paused for a moment, pouting her mouth in thought. 'Maybe, if you play your cards right!' She stretched out her legs and wriggled her toes before turning to him. 'I'm not easy, you know...'

He pushed himself up on his elbow and tilted his head, studying her face. 'Oh dear, are you one of those awkward types to live with? You know, always nagging about the toilet seat being up or dirty undercrackers being discarded on the bedroom floor, or do you talk incessantly over *Line of Duty*?'

She smiled. 'No, I meant–'

He quickly and gently placed his finger against her mouth. 'Ssshhhhh, I know exactly what you meant; the thought never crossed my mind and we wouldn't be here if it had.'

A comfortable silence fell between them. Pru studied the streak of sunlight that had broken through the gap in the curtains, keeping track of the specks of dust as they drifted lazily through the air. For the first time in a long time she was not only happy; she was also content. She smiled to herself, remembering how at one time that word would have made her heart plummet.

Content.

In her youth, only geriatrics and spinsters were 'content'. To be content was akin to settling for something other than excitement or challenge; it was second best to actually living, to really being alive. She traced a small hairline crack in the ceiling as it meandered towards the corner and disappeared behind the wardrobe. So why did it now conjure up feelings of happiness and security, a feeling of belonging. Was this what her mum had meant when she had offered her comfort after her split with Tom?

One day, Pru, you'll meet someone special, and you'll never have to pretend to be anyone other than just you.

'What have you got planned today?'

Andy's out-of-the-blue question broke through her thoughts. 'Mmm... not sure, really. Bree and Lucy have a day off too, so we thought a girly lunch and a bit of digging on why so many of our Winterbottom WI ladies have prematurely reached their expiry dates, with or without a bit of outside help. Talking of which, has anything come up yet on Betty? That was such a shock.'

'The post-mortem is today, so that should give us an idea, but at the moment it's looking like a heart attack.' He curled a section of Pru's hair around his finger. 'It was only treated as a precautionary scene because of the ongoing investigation.' He hoped that justified the ensuing forensic circus that had taken place at Pudds Fairground once Bree had alerted the team. 'Anyway, that's beside the point, I don't really want you getting yourself involved in this, Pru. It could be dangerous; you could make yourself a target.' He flung back the duvet and sat on the edge of the bed, pushing his fingers through his hair. 'Please leave the investigating to us, that's what we get paid for.'

'Oh come on, really? Do you honestly think two women, one a librarian and one who's the mum of a thirteen-year-old would be a threat to the murderer? And anyway, how would they know we're interested? It's not like it's an inside job at the WI.' Pru wrestled with her T-shirt, pulling it down over her head. 'I can't imagine someone like old Ethel Tytherington being the master-mind behind four murders, can you?'

Andy grinned. 'It's inside out.'

'Nope, I said inside job.'

'I know, but your T-shirt is inside out.'

'Damn!'

A BIT OF A PICKLE

*M*elv Hibbert, arms heavy with files and internal envelopes, adopted his usual lolloping gait as he rushed along the corridor towards the incident room. He shoulder-barged the double doors, flinging them open so hard they bounced back against the support posts, almost knocking Murdoch Holmes into the water cooler.

'Sorry, boss, I'm at sixes and sevens here.' Flustered, he dropped everything onto the nearest desk, catching several sheets of paper as they slipped off the edge.

'No shit, Sherlock!' Holmes snapped.

Andy smirked and quickly feigned scratching his nose to cover it.

Holmes could have kicked himself. It was the age-old standing joke to have a laugh at his expense and he'd just facilitated the banter by his own fair hand. For fifty-two years he'd suffered ridicule because of his name, and even more so when he'd decided at the youthful age of twenty-three years and four months to join the constabulary. It had been bad enough when he'd been in uniform, but the derision had tripled as he'd worked the ranks of CID to become a detective inspector. He still couldn't get his head around why his mother had chosen such a name for him. He grabbed a chipped mug from the tray and poured himself a black coffee.

'You tell me, who in their right mind holds a red-faced, screaming new-born brat, looks at it, and says, *Oh I know, let's call it Murdoch*. It's not like they didn't know their own bloody surname, is it?' He slammed the mug down on his desk. 'I ask you; do I look like a bloody Murdoch?'

Andy looked at Melv. Melv looked at Andy, each hoping the other would be the first to have to make the choice of a 'yay' or a 'nay' in response, and risk feeling the full wrath of Holmes whilst he was so explosive. Melv took the initiative.

'Boss, I was in a hurry as I've just got the PM results for Betty Prince for you.' He paused to catch his breath. 'It's not natural causes; it's another murder!'

The room fell silent. The furious tapping from various keyboards was abruptly halted; even the water cooler stayed its usual gurgling, whilst the air was sucked from the room.

Melv handed the file to Holmes. 'It was an embolism; it caused a heart attack which was fatal.'

'I know it was bloody fatal, Melvyn. That's why we've got body number five in the mortuary, enjoying the delights of tray 17b. If it hadn't been fatal she'd be sitting at home now watching *Emmerdale* with a nice cup of tea and a garibaldi.' Holmes ran his fingers through his hair in frustration. He jiggled his hand in a 'give-me' motion and waited for Melvyn to hand him the Prince file. He turned the sheets of A4 paper, scanning the report that Barnacle Bob had prepared. Holmes had erred on the side of caution by asking him to do the PM just in case, believing nothing lost, nothing gained, but in this instance it had been a proven gain. Bob had located an injection site on Betty's neck, which had then led to him bringing in a spirometer for gas chromatography testing, which had confirmed his suspicions.

'Right.' Holmes turned to the wall board, aware that his team were all expectantly waiting for him to brief them. His heart felt heavy looking at the photographs of Mabel Allinson, Avery McIntosh, Rita Charlesworth and Phillipa Jackson uniformly pinned side by side. He reached for the photograph of Betty Prince, which had been clipped to the bottom of the post-mortem file. With an unusual tenderness and respect, he pinned it on the board next to the others, her friends. 'This is Betty Prince, sixty-four years, owner of Betty's Village Store and another member of Winterbottom Women's Institute.' Her unassuming smile and the twinkle in her eyes that shone back at him from the photograph filled Holmes with sadness. Some days he truly hated his job. 'Unfortunately, Betty has just been confirmed as victim number five in our "Ladykiller" murders.'

He scanned the room, taking in the downturned mouths, collective sighs and shaking heads of his team, which in turn only served to heighten his own despair.

~

Pru peeled off the wholemeal slice of bread from her sandwich and investigated the remaining piece and its contents.

Lettuce, tomato, ham and...

'Eeew, who the hell puts this on a sarnie?' She pinched the offending slimy circle of dill pickle between her thumb and forefinger and pretended to gag.

'Mmm... they're lovely, really zingy, although I must admit they go better on a burger.' Bree dabbed the corner of her mouth with the serviette and tentatively inspected her own sandwich. 'Nope, none on this.'

'Here, have mine then.' Pru flicked the pickle towards Bree's plate, but with a bit more gusto than was really necessary. It sailed through the air, bypassed Bree, shot over Lucy's shoulder, and was only halted in its progress by Jason, the rather fit barman of the Dog & Gun. It slapped loudly as it stuck to his cheek.

The girls looked on horrified as a startled Jason, tray in hand containing their round of drinks, froze on the spot. The dill pickle, which by now resembled a giant wart, clung on for a few seconds more before gravity kicked in and it flopped from his cheek to rest on his crisp white shirt.

'Oops, shit, I've just given you a new brand logo. It's the "pickle-ator" instead of the alligator.' Pru chuckled, bringing her hand up to her mouth to execute a pretty poor stage whisper to Lucy and Bree. 'I think that's his best Zara shirt too; it'll have cost a bomb!' As Jason pressed his thumb over the nail of his middle finger, preparing to flick the offending garnish into oblivion, Pru tried to appease him. 'Jase, I'm so sorry, it was meant for Bree.'

Without breaking his stride, he simultaneously eradicated the pickle and plonked their drinks onto the table. 'No sweat, ladies, I'm used to it.' He flipped the tray under his arm. 'I do the school run for my neighbours' kids twice a week; they're disgusting too – and by the way, it's a crocodile, not an alligator!'

'Oooh, don't be so *snappy*!' Bree quipped.

Jason grinned and gave her a saucy *touché* as he made his way back to the bar, leaving them bunched together and giggling like schoolgirls.

'Okay, so pickles and Juicy Jason apart, what's the latest on our "Ladykiller", Luce?' Bree was a lot more forthcoming in her desire to know the finer details of Winterbottom's gruesome events than Pru.

Lucy mumbled through a mouthful of coronation chicken, picking at a stray piece of cress that was dangling from the corner of her mouth. 'Still not much more to go on, apart from what I think are the strange clues left at the scene, which both Andy and the DI are reluctant to believe have anything to do with the case, and there's very little forensically to go on, either.'

A silence fell over the three friends as they digested Lucy's lack of anything decent to add to their own investigation.

Pru was the first to speak. 'It's got history, I know it has.

There's something behind all this that's the catalyst.' She took another bite of her sandwich, pointing the remaining crust at Lucy. 'Anyone got any grievances with the WI as a whole, or with Avery, Mabel, Rita, et al. as individuals or collectively?'

Lucy shook her head. 'Not as far as we're aware. There's never been any bad blood directed at the Institute, or any of the members from an outside source, and by the very nature of the inclusiveness and friendliness of the WI, none between the members either. We just can't find anything that links them apart from their obvious membership.'

The silence resumed, their collective minds working overtime as they relished the remainder of their lunch and consumed the refreshing G&Ts they had treated themselves to.

'What about schools? Did they all go to the same school?' Bree adjusted the cushion behind her.

Lucy was quick to reply. 'They did, but at different times, and we can't find a link there either; nothing out of the ordinary, nothing that would give a direction to go in. In all honesty, being members of the Winterbottom WI was the only thing in common historically that we could find for them.'

The first smattering of rain hit the leaded window to their booth. The diagonal ticks of water formed a random pattern as the wind pushed the sudden squall across the beer garden, making the parasols flap and bend. They watched Jason leaping from table to table closing the folds of colourful fabric down as more dark heavy clouds drifted over the trees towards the Dog & Gun.

'Okay, so how about we do a bit of historical research then? See if we can dredge something up from the past?' Pru checked her watch. 'I'm going to have to skip; I've got a reading group in half an hour, but what about seeing if we can check the parish records? They might have old school documents, ones that list teachers as well as pupils. We could see if there's anything that smacks us between the eyes with a sort of eureka moment.'

Bree dug deep into her bag, rummaging around in its depths for the compact umbrella she'd had for years but had rarely needed to use until now. 'We could, but I can't see how that'll help.'

'It's better than doing nothing. You never know, and besides it'll be fun to find out some of the background to this lovely village and the residents. Come on, Bree, you can't tell me that rummaging through old stuff isn't exciting?' Pru zipped the front of her jacket up and pushed the Velcro tabs together at the neck.

'Mmm... only a librarian could gush over musty things.' Bree smirked. 'Talking of which, how is the Delectable Detective?'

'Very, very delectable, even if I say so myself.' Pru slipped her tongue between her lips and rolled her eyes.

'Oh purleese! You two forget I've got to work with him. I can't be doing with images of my sarge in anything other than a suit, thank you very much.' Lucy pulled the hood of her coat over her head. 'And don't let the world and his dog know that you're poking your noses into what's going on; you never know who could be eavesdropping.'

Bree and Pru gave her a satirical salute of acknowledgement before disappearing through the door to brave the elements.

TEA AT THE SAD CAFÉ

Florrie pressed down the creases in her apron with the palms of her hands, neatened the bow at the small of her back, and then carefully checked the length of the ribbons were equal. She did like things to be perfect on herself, especially in her beloved café. It was after all what her customers expected from her.

She picked up a floral tea tray from the counter that was laden with small, delicate glass vases, each just the right size to hold a pink St. Ethelburga tea rose and a single sprig of gypsophila. She placed one in the centre of each table, eager to set up before her morning ladies made an appearance for their regular tea, toast and jam session. She had already spotted Clarissa Montgomery bowling down the high street as if on a mission, her shopping bag slapping wildly against her thigh as she swerved to avoid becoming a pedestrian fatality at the wheels of Eric Potter's Royal Mail delivery cycle.

Florrie had earlier arranged the tables, just as the ladies always liked them, but this time with a sadness in her heart. The four large round tables had now dwindled to just two, side by side, in the corner next to the aspidistra that had grown to such an enormous height ever since she had re-potted it in her mother's rosebud chamber pot. Florrie smiled to herself, remembering the look of horror on Betty's face when she had announced what she would be doing with it after she had discovered it under her recently deceased mother's four-poster bed. After much consternation from Betty, she had managed to reassure her that after a good swill it would be a perfectly usable piece of vintage for her café. Betty had remained unconvinced and had refused to be seated anywhere near it on her regular visits.

Thinking of Betty made her want to cry; the tears pricked and stung, while swallowing made her throat sore. Just how was it possible for such a lovely little village like Winterbottom to become host to so many awful murders? News had spread quickly that Betty Prince's passing had not been peaceful or indeed natural, and another wave of fear and dread had rapidly washed over the small community. Florrie had paid a fortune to a handyman from the next village for extra locks, both on her own little flat above The Twisted Current Café and on the shop itself. She absent-mindedly wiped the counter with her dishcloth for the hundredth time that morning before the tinkling of the bell above the door broke her reverie and heralded the first of the ladies.

'Morning, Florrie.' Clarissa made her way over to her usual seat, dropped her shopping bag on the floor beside the chair, shrugged off her coat and sat down with determination. 'Terrible news, isn't it?'

'Aye, 'tis that. It's been playing on my mind all night, so very sad. Are the police any closer to catching the culprit?'

Clarissa shrugged and waved to Millie Thomas through the window as she also made her way to the door. 'No, not a dickie bird. Everyone is coming up with suspects, but a lot of that is down to overactive imaginations with a smidgeon of gossip thrown in.'

'Small village and gossip do go hand in hand, though, 'Rissa,'

Florrie offered sagely. 'Mind, I don't suppose we can discount anything or anyone, can we?'

'Oooh discount, is that on the cakes?' Millie poked her finger in a custard slice as she edged between the counter and the table, almost toppling one of the chairs with her plump derriere as she squeezed through the gap. She grinned and patted her stomach. 'D'you know, I actually bent down and got to touch my toes this morning. Admittedly it was with my boobs, but y'know beggars can't be choosers!' She laughed heartily, which brought a rare smile to Florrie's face.

Clarissa patted the chair next to her. 'Grab a pew, Millie. We're just waiting on Brenda, Hilda and maybe Ethel, if she feels up to it. It's hit her hard this, losing her best friend, so she's going to need us.'

As Florrie set up the cups and saucers, along with little individual pots of jam and marmalade, the remaining Winterbottom Tea & Jam ladies made good their arrival, bringing with them a gentle hum of chatter to the cosy café as they took their places, each taking it in turn to hug Ethel Tytherington in a show of friendship and support.

Huddled together, Florrie couldn't help but feel that she was a reluctant spectator to a poignant tableau acknowledging loss, framed by the aspidistra on one side and the ornate coat stand on the other.

Phyllis stood watch opposite The Twisted Currant Café, hidden from view by the large thick trunk of the oak tree that overshadowed the boundary wall of Winterbottom St. Michael's churchyard and the side of the parish hall.

A tightness squeezed at her heart. She had never been asked to accompany any of them on their regular gatherings at the twee and ridiculously named café. Never, not once. It was rare that she would give into sadness. In her world, any form of emotion that gave way to feeling something, be it love, fear, want or hurt, was a sign of weakness. Once upon a time she would have enjoyed being part of their group, to laugh at their jokes, share their stories and offer her own. Now all she could do was remain on the outside looking in.

Darting out from behind the tree, she quickly nipped across the road, making sure she didn't tread on any cracks in the paving stones as she went. Eric Potter was cycling furiously on his return journey back to the post office to replenish his sack. He paid no heed to Phyllis, much the same as he had ignored Clarissa not ten minutes previously, only this time he had met his match. Phyllis quickly sidestepped his approach and discreetly poked the umbrella she was jauntily wielding between the spokes of his front wheel. Poor Eric's eyes bulged in wonderment as his cycle came to an abrupt and jarring halt in the middle of Winterbottom High Street, hurtling him over the handlebars as the rear end of his trusty steed followed him. By the time he had hit the tarmac, Phyllis was already making progress on the pavement towards The Twisted Currant Café, umbrella slightly tarnished but with no one any the wiser as to her part in his downfall. A silent laugh caught in her throat as she pushed open the dark blue door, her eagerness to enter the premises causing the gingham curtain to flutter in the draught she brought in with her. She stood; head held high waiting to see if there would be any acknowledgement of her presence from the little group seated between the potted plant and the coat stand.

As expected, there was none.

'Morning, Gladys. Cup of tea, dear?' Florrie fussed around her, attempting to usher her to the tables that contained Clarissa and her entourage.

'It's Phyllis,' she grunted whilst taking in the lack of response from the ladies. And I'll sit here, if it's all the same to you.' She dragged the wooden chair out from under the adjacent table.

A flustered Florrie hastily made her way back behind her counter, uneasy with her new customer's attitude, but choosing to acquiesce for a peaceful existence. 'Right-oh, dear, any cake with your tea?'

Phyllis stood momentarily watching Clarissa, Ethel, Millie and the gang, deep in conversation, clattering cups and saucers as their aged mouths chomped on a selection of cakes, toast and buns. She shuddered as Millie shovelled another forkful of Black Forest gateau between her lips, decorating her upper lip hair with a smattering of cream. Taking her seat, she made herself comfortable and waited.

Clarissa was the first to proffer something of interest as she tried to lighten the mood.

'Well, ladies, moving on to something a little more uplifting or should I say gossipy, have you heard the latest on Felicity Broadbent?' She gently placed her cup onto the saucer with an air of smugness, confident that they actually hadn't heard the latest and that she would be the one to break it to them.

Millie giggled, pushing her shoulders up to her ears, her lips puckering into a mouse-like pout, the remnants of cream weighing down several whiskers. 'Oooh, is it something juicy?' she squeaked.

Clarissa nodded. 'Escorts!'

A collective clacking of dentures and more 'oohs' and 'ahs' from the ladies filled the room, followed by an eerie silence as they looked at each other for a better understanding of Clarissa's revelation.

'I don't rate them myself; I much prefer the Fiesta. It's more compact. You can still get lots into the boot and you can park it anywhere,' Ethel offered.

Clarissa burst out laughing. Slapping the table with her hand, she sent the little vase toppling over as the crockery rattled like background music to accompany her raucous giggling.

'Nooo, escorts as in high-class ladies of service for gentlemanly needs,' she said as she wiped her chin with a serviette. 'Bella Simmonds from Little Erotica Lingerie told me. Apparently Fliss buys all her underwear from there, sexy bodysuits, thongs, and in particular stuff that has large size quick release flaps for easy access.' She tapped her nose, gave a knowing look, and snorted again, which required another wipe with the serviette.

'Ah, I see. Well you do know you can have an operation for that, don't you?' Brenda took a large bite of her scone and chewed thoughtfully before continuing. 'It's called a labiaplasty. I read about it in a magazine in Doc Brennan's waiting room only last month. I imagine there's nothing more disconcerting than one's flaps dropping down to vigorously slap your inner thigh when you get undressed for a bit of how's yer father.' She smirked.

As the ladies of Winterbottom Tea, Toast & Jam group bellylaughed to their hearts' content, Phyllis sat stoic in her chair, her hand holding the delicate china teacup poised to her mouth, an image of her little 'Minutes to a Murder' notebook forming in her mind's eye.

Wonderful, informative and so very, very fortuitous!

THE INNOCENT

'Okay, okay, Binksy… my, you are impatient tonight!' Pru rummaged around in the kitchen drawer, looking for the fork that was reserved purely for the serving of kitty gunk, direct from tin to bowl. Mr Binks, in eager anticipation wound himself several times around her legs, weaving in and out, almost tripping her up as she reached for a piece of kitchen roll to mop up a small dollop that had missed its target.

'Bloody hell, when was the last time you fed him? He's starving.' Bree knocked back the dregs of her Merlot before offering her glass for a refill.

'Lunchtime. He's just greedy; no wonder he's got a wobbly belly that drags along the floor.' Pru mashed up the chicken-and-liver-in-jelly, scraping the fork on the edge of the bowl while checking out her own midriff. 'Actually, come to think of it, I've just described myself.' She groaned.

Tired of waiting, Bree poured herself another glass and bounced back down onto the sofa. 'Tell me about it. If I carry on like this, I'll be an obese diabetic by the time I'm ready to pop my clogs at the grand old age of ninety.'

'Oooh nooo; all old, shrivelled up and dried up. Who on earth would want to live to be ninety?'

'Er... let me think. Someone who's eighty-nine?'

Laughing, Pru bent down and pushed the bowl in front of the impatient Binks, stroking him gently between the ears. Bree wasn't far wrong. She didn't relish getting old, but she supposed that when the time came it would be natural to grab every ensuing day, week, month or year if they were on offer. As much as she didn't want to be creaking around in a bath chair with a hearing trumpet shoved in her left ear shouting *What's that, Sonny?* while keeping her dentures in place, dying young with firm thighs, bouncy pert boobs and her own teeth didn't fill her with great joy either.

'What was that saying? "Be grateful for old age as it's a privilege denied to many." Maybe we should just be grateful we've not appeared in the sights of our resident "Ladykiller", hey?'

'You're not wrong there, matey. I've been looking at the ages of them all, I think we're safe; we're far too young.' Bree clinked her glass against Pru's. 'I just wish I could figure out what the motive is. It can't be random, so there's got to be something we're missing.' She doodled a flower complete with stem and two leaves on the notepad. 'Means, opportunity, motive. That's what they say on the telly, don't they?'

Pru nodded. 'Mmm... Yep, but all the means have been different. The opportunity has been in varying locations and we don't know what the hell the motive is, so that's us and the police stumped.'

A pleasant silence followed where the two friends, feet curled up under them on the sofa, stared at the torn-out pages from the notebook that were scattered on the coffee table.

'I forgot to tell you; we've been refused access to the parish records. I've tried, even begged, but it's a no go.'

Pru was crestfallen. 'Really? That's ridiculous! I thought

parish records were open to everyone. Maybe we can look online; that's how people do their genealogy, isn't it?'

'It's just one person being awkward, I think I could push it with the church diocese, if that's the right department to speak to, but it could take more time than we've got, and time is something that seems to be in short supply if the rate these murders are taking place is anything to go by.' Bree sighed and shifted her position, placing her wine glass on the table. 'Online will only give the basics. I was hoping for something to do with the school and pupils, something more personal. You won't get that online.'

Slopping more wine into Bree's glass and topping up her own, Pru became pensive. 'Tell you what; you, me and Lucy tomorrow night; 9pm at the library. We'll make a start there; you'd be amazed at what a village library holds. I spotted some old Winterbottom reference books when I was cataloguing last week. No harm done by having a gander through those, is there?'

'Fab idea, you're on. I'll message her now.'

As Bree's fingers deftly tapped out a text message to Lucy, Pru settled herself back on the squishy cushion and closed her eyes, her thoughts quickly diverted from gruesome murders and mottled corpses to the gorgeously toned, very tanned and very much alive body of Detective Sergeant Andy Barnes.

Pru sat in complete silence, reams of notes, books and old papers scattered around her. The dull light from the overhead reading lamp illuminated an expanse that was just enough for her to see what was in front of her. She checked her watch: 8.59pm. The blinds had been pulled down at the windows to the Winterbottom library, but she had left the smaller blind on the window of the door slightly up so she could see out on to the high street.

She checked her watch again. Still 8.59pm. She bit down on

her bottom lip, willing the seconds to pass more quickly whilst she distracted herself by scanning over her notes.

- *Sirdar Wool Shade no. 099 called Maisie*
  - *Small black plimsolls marked with two words, first word beginning with 'MA'*
  - *Handwritten note signed M.M with distinctive crossbar on the Ts*
  - *An Oxford University prospectus brochure*
  - *A retired teacher, nurse and social worker, two shop owners*

She tapped her fingers on the worn mahogany desk, drumming a beat that encouraged her foot to tap along on the crossbar underneath. She cupped her chin in her hand and waited, watching the wall-mounted clock tick to the nine and twelve positions. As if on cue, an excitable rapping on the glass of the front door announced the arrival of her friends. She found herself relieved to have company; there had been something quite uncomfortable about sitting in the gloom on her own. That thought upset her; just when had she ever felt uncomfortable surrounded by her beloved books? But tonight had felt different, almost eerie. She quickly lifted the snip on the door and stood back as Bree and Lucy tumbled inside, their feet shuffling on the worn floorboards.

'Right, whose bright idea was this then?' Bree chucked her multi-coloured wrap, which looked more like a Bedouin birthing blanket complete with stray camel hairs, on to the back of the nearest chair. 'I could be curled up on the sofa with a great big fat G&T in my hand watching *Love Island*. Instead, I'm traipsing the streets of Winterbottom looking for clues to the identity of the "Ladykiller".'

Lucy shook her head in exasperation. 'Why on earth do

people insist on giving offenders a name? All it does is glamorise their crimes and makes them feel important.'

Bree shrugged. 'I don't know; they just do. Maybe it makes people feel less scared if something or someone has a name. It gives them an identity, so it's not like an unknown bogeyman.' She settled herself down at the desk, casting her eyes over Pru's paperwork. 'Anyway, there was that film with Alec Guinness and Peter Sellers in it called *The Ladykillers,* and it was funny. Perhaps that's why, to lighten it all.'

'Jeez, how the hell can anyone "lighten" five murders, Bree? And when did you become an aficionado of *Love Island*? Please tell me you're joking?' Pru rolled her eyes and smirked. 'Tea, coffee – or this?' She wafted a large bottle of uncorked Merlot. 'Wine glasses are over there behind my desk.' She tutted and laughed. '*Love Island*, really? I clearly don't know you as well as I thought!'

Ten minutes later, chatter, gossip, hilarity and innuendo completed, the three of them sat huddled together over the main desk. Pru had brought another reading lamp from the reference section to alleviate their eye strain and Bree had topped up their glasses.

Pru pulled her notepad towards her. 'Right, I've gone over the so-called clues left at each scene.'

'Er... can I just interrupt for a minute? You've both got to promise on your lives that you'll never let anyone, and I mean *anyone*, know that I've given you this information–' Lucy gave a knowing look. '–not even during pillow talk, Pru. I could get hung, drawn and quartered.' She took a gulp of her wine, cricked her neck and popped her eyes, holding an imaginary noose at the side of her head.

Bree cringed. 'Hardly the best demonstration, considering what happened to poor old Avery McIntosh. Anyway, let's get down to business. I think we're all agreed that whoever our suspect is, they're happily leaving us clues, and because all the victims have been Winterbottom residents and WI members to boot, it's safe to say there could be some sort of historical link. It's just up to us to put them all together.'

'Yep, so we've got a strand of wool, a pair of gym pumps, a letter signed M.M and a brochure for Oxford University. Mmm… and we're hardly Miss Marple, Nancy Drew or Vera, are we?' Pru looked crestfallen as she pushed pieces of paper around the desk. 'It's not like Winterbottom has ever been the hotbed of violent crime with a need for female detectives, is it?'

Bree almost choked on the slug of wine she had started to quaff whilst listening to Pru. Crimson splatters dotted the front of her cream blouse, and she tried to stop herself from coughing. 'Oh my God, look at this!' She pushed the scrap of paper that listed the university brochure towards Lucy. '…and we have!'

'We have what?' Lucy stiffened visibly in her chair.

'Winterbottom has been the scene of a most gruesome crime before, years and years ago, and the name on that brochure has just reminded me of it.' Bree jumped up, scattering several sheets of paper to the floor. 'Pru, where are the archived editions of the *Winterbottom News*. Do they go back as far as the 1960s to 1970s?'

'Yes, they're over here.' Pru swiftly nipped between the random formation of several reading tables, eager to show Bree the collection. 'There you go; they date back to the newspaper's first edition in 1819.'

The three of them stood staring at the tall bank of shelving, the ambient lighting in the library casting shadows in the corners as Pru pulled the elephant ladder along to the exact spot she needed to reach the marked decades. 'Here we go. Which one?'

'Try the 1970s, and look for something near to December 1979, I remember my mum telling me I was born during the biggest scandal that Winterbottom had ever seen.' Bree waited eagerly for Pru to pass the large hardback book down from the third to top shelf. Holding it to her chest, she carefully placed it on the desk and opened it at the meticulously catalogued index prefacing the near perfect editions of the *Winterbottom News*. They were clipped carefully into place, each one separated by a clear plastic sheet. A musty, slightly damp, smell filled the air as she traced her finger down the page of the 1979 Christmas issue. 'Here.' She stabbed at the stark headline. 'This'll be it.'

A Tragedy Strikes at the Heart of Winterbottom
On the morning of Tuesday 19 December, the local constabulary were called to the scene of a most terrible tragedy...

As Bree read the newspaper clipping out loud, Lucy and Pru found themselves mouthing the words along with her, in silent reverence to the victim of a most terrible tragedy and an innocent who had been the cause.

FELICITY

$\mathcal{F}$elicity Broadbent stretched out the fingers on her left hand and blew gently on her freshly painted and carefully manicured nails. The topcoat of her Opi The Thrill of Brazil nail varnish, a name which coincidentally matched the style of her recently waxed lady garden, had given a rather rich lustre to the desired finish. She silently lamented the fact that she'd actually plumped for a Bermuda Triangle at Hair Today, Gone Tomorrow, but the girl had been new and a slip of the waxing paper had given her a lot more than she'd bargained for, resulting in the uneven landing strip she was currently sporting. She was just grateful she hadn't ended up with a full hit Hollywood; the regrowth from that would have been like Velcro gripping an old moquette cushion.

She stretched out one stocking-clad leg and alluringly dangled the red patent leather stiletto shoe from her toes, while keeping watch on her bedroom guest in the triple reflection of the dressing table mirrors. Her client, the rather portly Desmond DuPonte, which she knew with absolute certainty wasn't his real name, was spread out on the expensive silk sheets of her oyster-pink clamshell bed. The discreet lighting in the canopy only served to highlight the worst of his features, the sheen of sweat oozing from the pores of his face, the putty-coloured skin of his body, and the dreadful leer on his lips.

Four hundred and fifty quid an hour, Fliss, just keep thinking... four hundred and fifty quid an hour...

She regularly recited this inspirational mantra to herself on the days she had to work. It was rare that Felicity ever had a client that was a pleasure; they were always the type of men that made you close your eyes and think of England, exotic shores – or even the damp, grey sands of Bognor; anything other than the task at hand. Why couldn't a Daniel Craig lookalike book her for an afternoon of delight? Hell, she'd even waiver her fee for something as delicious as that. Come to think of it, she'd happily pay him!

She glanced at her nails again. Jeez, The Thrill of Brazil. How ironic was that when such a thrill was at least a million miles away from reality. Wishing his reflection were more a mirage than fact, she decided South American climes for her mental fantasy would do; it would be where her thoughts would travel whilst her body serviced the Disgusting Desmond DuPonte.

Grabbing the bright yellow pair of Marigold gloves and the expensive Redecker Ostrich feather duster from her dressing table, she sighed to herself as she straightened the white lace apron of her French maid's outfit. Last night her beloved Women's Institute and a tapestry demonstration, and today her role as Miss Trixie LaBelle.

Could my life really get any more bizarre?

Knowing there would be no answer, Felicity straddled the flaccid, corpulent form in front of her, ready to meet his demands.

She fixed a seductive pout. 'Brace yourself, Desmond...' she commanded as she snapped the rubber latex loudly against her wrist, '...this could get messy!'

AS THE WIND BLOWS

*T*he sun shone in elongated shafts through the high windows of the parish hall, picking up dust motes that were quickly scattered through the air by the robust flopping down of several yoga mats at the fair, but not very gentle, hands of Brenda Mortinsen. The slapping noise as they hit the wooden floor echoed from the rafters.

'Make sure they're a decent distance apart, Brenda. We don't want Mrs Ball smacking Mrs Elliot in the face with a rogue leg now, do we?' Avaline Prendergast, the yoga instructor for the Winterbottom Health & Fitness Club, floated between the regimented lines of blue rectangles, her colourful kaftan billowing behind her as she oversaw the setting up of her regular Thursday morning class.

Brenda sighed and rolled her eyes. She'd been doing the mat distancing thing for more years than she cared to remember, and she'd never once overlapped or misaligned one yet, neither had there been an accidental meeting of smelly feet with a wrinkled gob, either. She watched Avaline fussing with the incense wands that she insisted on burning throughout the class. Brenda involuntarily coughed as the plumes of smoke from all six points

185

began to mix in the air, forming a haze akin to Ethel Tythering-ton's forty-a-day Benson & Hedges cigarette habit. She sniffed and coughed again. It was usually a heady aroma of frankincense that filled the hall, a woody, earthy smell that was supposed to promote relaxation and peace, though it never made Brenda feel very peaceful as it was her job to clear the ruddy ash up from the oak flooring afterwards. She turned on her heel, leaving Avaline to set fire to her precious sticks whilst she sorted out the jugs of water and glasses before the arrival of the ladies.

Clarissa, Kitty and Elly Shacklady were the first through the double doors, followed closely by Chelsea Blandish and Cassidy Parks. Next up were Pru and Bree, with Ethel in tow.

'Blimey, look what Chels is wearing!' Bree plonked her gym bag down on one of the chairs lining the panelled walls. Both Pru and Ethel discreetly took in the exceptionally low-cut leopard print leotard that clung to every curve that Chelsea possessed. 'Good God, Chels, you'll never keep them harnessed on the Downward Dog; they'll splat the mat with some considerable force and burst as soon as you bend over!'

Chelsea laughed as she yanked the neckline up, stretching the Lycra material as far as it would go over her surgically enhanced mammary glands. As soon as she released the material it pinged back to its starting position, settling just below her ample cleavage. She held her hands up and shrugged. 'Well, we're all girls together; no doubt you've seen them before.'

'Not 'arf,' Pru whispered, remembering the one and only time that Chelsea had graced the library to borrow a book. She had almost given poor Albert Tytherington a heart attack when she'd leant over a battered edition of *Lady Chatterley's Lover*, bequeathing him an eyeful of something he probably hadn't seen since his wedding night with Ethel.

'Right, quickly ladies, into position. Pick your mats and let's start with a gentle warm up.' Avaline whipped off her kaftan to reveal a turquoise all-in-one body suit. She pulled at the topknot in her hair, tightening the scrunched ponytail that held her blonde curls in check. *'Namaste.'*

The class had begun, and Brenda stood watch from the sidelines as she did each week. There was absolutely no way her arthritic joints could twist into some of the ridiculous shapes that Avaline threw around her mat. In fact, the only joint that Brenda had ever twisted in her life was the one she'd hand-rolled and smoked during a hot and balmy August in 1973 at the Reading rock festival, when she had fallen in love with Rod Stewart. That memory made her smile.

'Bloody hell. Ethel, have you guffed?' Clarissa made an over-exaggerated show of fanning the air between hers and Ethel's mat.

'No, of course not!' Ethel indignantly snapped.

'You did, I heard you. You swung your legs up and you guffed – loudly!' Clarissa took great delight in ensuring that the rest of the class were privy to their exchange.

'Okay, ladies, that's enough, we'll start bringing it down a little, shall we? Let's slowly move into the Garland Pose, slowly, slowly – yes that's perfect, Cassidy.' Avaline threw a look of warning at Clarissa, which only served to make her more mischievous.

'The Burning Thighs of Hell more like.' Clarissa grimaced as she squatted as far as her arthritic knees and muscles would allow whilst watching Ethel mirror her movements.

Paaaaaarrrrrp.

'There you go, you've done it again, Ethel! Come on, all of you must've heard that one!' Clarissa looked around for evidence of support from her fellow yoga enthusiasts.

Bree sniggered loudly as Chelsea produced a hand-held Whoopie bag, giving it another blast with much gusto, making the whole class descend into chaos. Unable to control the ladies or the laughter, Avaline threw her hands up. 'Okay, okay, very funny, Chelsea. You know, just for one minute there, I could almost imagine we were back in infant school. Right, let's break to replenish our bodies with essential fluids.' She checked her watch, grabbed her towel, and wiped the damp ringlets around her forehead.

'Take ten and then we'll regroup for savasana meditation.'

~

Bree flopped out onto her mat, turning her head to face Pru who was similarly positioned looking at the shaped beams that held up the vast hall roof. 'So, where do we go from here, hey?'

'I don't know; it all seems such a jumble of information at the moment. Luce is looking into what we found out from the newspaper archives last night. She wouldn't say much. Well, I suppose she can't really, but she looked so excited as though she was on to something.' Pru sat herself up and took a sip of cool water.

'Yep, I got that impression too. I did try to pump her a bit, but she just kept saying she needed to check a few things out first.' Bree held out a small pack of tropical mix to her friend, encouraging her to take a handful. 'But it's definitely got something to do with the Winterbottom tragedy stuff that got her so excited.'

Pru crammed a handful of nuts, raisins, mango and coconut into her mouth and nodded. 'Mfffhph.' She wiped her mouth with the back of her hand and finished chewing. 'Maga... Magdl... oh blimey what was it called again, the place where it happened?'

Bree thought for a moment. 'Magdalen House. I remember it's called that because I immediately think of those little cakes that have the same name.'

'You mean Magdalenas!' Ethel Tytherington shuffled around on her mat to face them. 'They're little sponge muffins, rather tasty if they're moist.'

Pru cringed. 'Aggghhh that word! Can we just say succulent or juicy, purleeese?'

'What's wrong with "moist"? Moist is such a superb adjective, moist… m-o-i-s-t… moist!' Bree's finger punctuated the air with each letter, fully aware of Pru's aversion to the word.

'It's just gross, Bree! It brings back so many horrible memories of Madison's unwashed hairy armpits and Tom's Betty Swollocks caressing my best Egyptian cotton bedsheets.' They both grimaced in unison at the thought.

Ethel remained unperturbed at Pru's discomfort and reasoning, preferring to stay with the original topic of conversation. She pursed her lips together in thought. 'Aye, Magdalen House, such a terrible tragedy that was; it was an awful place, too. Once the husband upped and left it became a mausoleum to the wife and their young child, until Mrs Magdalen fell down the cellar steps with a kitchen knife in her back. The daughter was taken into care and after that, who knows?'

Pru was excited. 'Ethel, you seem to know quite a lot about the place. What more can you tell us? What was his name, you know, the father? Did they have any staff or maybe a nanny for the little girl?'

Ethel looked pensive. 'Oooh, that's a lot of questions, and you didn't even draw breath! I'm sorry, I don't know much more than that, really.' She tapped her forehead. 'Old age has its snags, I'm afraid. I don't remember as well as I used to. But if you're interested in the history of Winterbottom and who used to live here and in which houses, why don't you have a browse of the parish records? All the births, marriages and deaths are down there. There's probably copies of censuses going back decades.'

She shot out her index finger and animatedly pointed to the floorboards. 'The cellar of this place holds a whole plethora of information for those that have the means to access it.'

THE ELEGANT ESCORT

*F*elicity let the hot needles of water hit her skin and wash over her body. The steam from the shower rising towards the recessed lamp gave a rainforest cloud effect as the threads of light swirled in the mist. This was her cleansing ritual: *cleanse the body, cleanse the soul.* Only she couldn't, could she? No matter how much she scrubbed, no matter how sore her skin would become, her soul would always be tarnished.

It was one of the pitfalls of the job.

The Disgusting Desmond DuPonte had received his money's worth and had quickly left her luxury apartment in town. She had watched him through the window as he hurried down the marble steps, heaving his bulk through the ornate wrought iron gate before disappearing into the back of his chauffeur-driven Mercedes Benz C-Class that had been patiently waiting outside.

She didn't actually hate her choice of career; after all, it paid for her cosy cottage in Winterbottom, her exotic holidays, expensive clothes, first-class restaurants and, with a little bit of help from a legacy or two from satisfied clients, her penthouse apartment, but it did leave her feeling less than worthy measured against other women. From an early age she had been startlingly aware that her combined dark Italian looks and voluptuous figure ensured men's heads would turn and her quick wit and good conversation made her a much sought-after companion by those in need. What had started out as her being a straightforward, no sex involved, professional escort for those gentlemen who required a well-turned-out intelligent woman on their arm had somehow become what she was now. A professional escort with copious amounts of steamy sex involved. She did entertain the odd handful of clients who wanted nothing more of her than conversation, but they were few and far between.

Her shrewd ability for finance and business had ensured her services were upper class and well rewarded. At forty-three years of age, she was self-sufficient with a very healthy bank balance.

Wrapping a white fluffy robe around her, she padded softly into the bedroom of her cottage. Once home and away from her other life, she felt almost normal. She would do normal things like eat pizza, drink hot chocolate and watch *Endeavour* on her wall-mounted television. The simple things that most people took for granted.

She dropped the damp towels into her wash hamper, nudged her feet into her slippers and gently pulled the curtains at the window to one side so she could look down and admire the vibrant flowers in her garden and the small vegetable plot beyond. Engrossed, she didn't hear the door behind her as it creaked slowly open to reveal a small gap.

'Oh, I'm so sorry, Miss Broadbent, please forgive me. I thought you were still in the bathroom, I've just come to empty the wash basket.' The woman stood hunched, almost servile in front of her.

'That's all right, Willis–' Felicity gave what she hoped was a warm smile to her new cleaning lady. '–I've just put the towels in, so that would be wonderful if you could take them now.'

Willis smiled back. 'Certainly, Miss Broadbent.' She waited until her employer had turned back to the window before carefully adjusting the bobbed brunette wig that had slipped slightly when she had shown her subservience. Closing the bedroom door behind her, she shifted the pile of washing in her arms.

'And it's Phyllis!'

AN ENLIGHTENMENT!

The amber light from the street lamp cast an eerie glow over the cobbled entry to the side of the parish hall and Wrinkle in Time. A light shower earlier had invoked the smell of damp earth, leaf-mould and a hint of scent from the honeysuckle that was wildly clambering over the old sandstone wall of Winterbottom St. Michael's churchyard. Pru shivered as she glanced over the top of the wall, taking in the tilted head-stones of Winterbottom's dear departed. The moon intermittently broke through the clouds, becoming a spotlight on the white marbles and grey granites of the grave markers. She held her breath and waited, listening for any out of place sounds, anything that would have her running back to the warmth of her bed.

'How the bloody hell did I get myself talked into this?' she muttered to herself.

Bree had been so insistent on them both searching the parish records, with or without permission; and since that permission had been denied for a second time, she had apparently made her own arrangements. Pru craned her neck around the cornerstone of the parish hall. Taking in the deserted main street she checked her watch, wriggling her wrist to catch the streetlight.

2am.

Pulling her mobile phone out of her jacket pocket, she checked that too. She turned to look along the length of the entry, the cobbles glistening in the half-light, giving it an almost ethereal effect, as though she could follow it to somewhere magical. She was so engrossed in her dream-world she was oblivious to the figure, a mere shadow, slowly drifting behind her until it was no more than inches away from her.

The dark arm reached out, its fingers dancing towards her shoulder until the air between them had all but disappeared.

'Jesus Christ... Bree!' Pru suddenly knew where the expression 'jumped out of your skin' came from; she half expected to find hers in a crumpled heap on the cobbles like a deflated, wrinkled wetsuit.

Bree pulled at the wool beanie hat on her head so that it covered her ears. 'Look, if we're going to do this right, you need to be more on the ball – and what the bloody hell are you wearing? Is that a balaclava?'

Pru immediately fell on the defensive. 'It's so I don't get seen, all black is the best colour to wear at night, I read it in a book.'

'What book? *The Pink Panther*? You look like bloody Cato Fong. Who the hell are you expecting to jump out on?'

'It was a film franchise.'

'What was?'

'*Pink Panther*, it was never a book, only a film.'

'Okay, smart arse. Come on, let's get this show on the road.' Bree pulled at Pru's jacket sleeve, taking her further down the entry. The very same entry she had only moments before viewed as a stairway to heaven but now it had taken on an ominous darkness that chilled her to the bone.

'Look, do you still think this is a good idea? I mean what happens if we get caught? Can you imagine how embarrassing that will be? And what about Lucy? She could end up arresting us for breaking and entering.'

Pru's rushed and almost hysterical plea seemed to amuse Bree. She laughed. 'Oh come on, live a little.' She pointed her finger and gently poked Pru in the stomach. 'Feel the excitement – right – there!'

'Excitement! If my stomach flips and barrel-rolls one more time, I'll put my name down as a gymnast for the next Olympics.'

'We're not breaking and entering. We *are* entering, but with the help of this!' She held out a large, old-fashioned key. The dull metal, barely picking up the street light, sat flat in her hand, the ornate swirls of the handle added to its feel of antiquity. 'There's a door down there.' She pointed to a flight of steps topped by wrought iron railings. A track had worn its way down the middle of each fashioned stone. 'It's rarely used these days; it used to be the escape route between the church and the hall.'

'Escape from what? Religious persecution?' Pru was wary but fascinated. She loved a bit of history.

'Nope. Story has it the vicar was in the habit of playing footsie with Clara, the church cleaner. Their secret meeting place was in the bowels of the parish hall amongst the spare prayer books and kneeling pads. If anyone came in, she'd carry on sweeping her feather duster around the crypt and he'd scarper sharpish out of this door and back to the vicarage unseen.'

'Crypt!'

'Sort of. They used to keep the bodies laid out down there, waiting their burial next door.' She caught the worried expression on Pru's face, side-lit by a brief appearance of the moon. 'Hey, don't worry though, there's not been a stiff down there since the early 1800s – apart from the Irreverent Rev's rigid splendour during his last meeting with Clara in 1947!'

It took a lot of jiggling and twisting with the key; it would catch and turn slightly a rusty squeal showing its lack of use over more years than Pru could care to count, then it would pop back again to its starting point. Bree indicated for her to have a go, as though Pru's touch would succeed where hers had failed.

Pru removed the key from the keyhole and inserted it again, listening for a sign of give as she turned it, first one way and then the other. It caught on the second attempt and the barrel dropped with a dull *thunk*. She stepped back and released a lungful of air; only then was she aware that she had been holding her breath the whole time. She took in the huge, weathered oak door and the rusted black iron strap hinges, her heart thumping against her chest. 'Are you sure we're not going to go tripping over dead bodies in there?' She gave her friend a look of expectant terror, her eyes darting from side to side.

Bree bit the inside of her lip and shook her head. 'Honestly, if you want me to take you seriously, you've got to get rid of that bloody balaclava; it's very disconcerting just seeing the whites of your eyes. Keep it for the bedroom; you never know, the Delectable Detective might appreciate it!'

'Mmm... maybe, but only if my eyes are actually open and I'm not drooling into my pillow.' Noting Bree's look of puzzlement, she quickly added, 'It's a long story. I'll tell you about it over a whole bottle of gin one day.' She tentatively pushed the door with one hand, it barely moved a centimetre. Her left hand joined her right, side by side, her fingertips touching the rough wood. She put the weight of her body behind her and slowly the gap between the door and the frame widened, releasing a rush of stale air.

'We're in!'

Before she could stop her, Bree squeezed past and slipped quietly into the inky blackness. Pru followed, the beam of her torch cutting through the darkness as she swept it from side to side. It picked out a higgledy-piggledy array of chairs stacked one on top of each other and piles of small leather-bound books teetering on a huge bookcase against the far wall. Everywhere she pointed, her torch lit up treasures and junk from previous decades. The musty dust-ridden air was cloying.

'Here, over here!'

Bree's excited voice echoed from underneath the mottled stone archway. Pru quickly sidestepped a pile of prayer pads that were scattered in the middle of the room and vaulted over two trestle tables that were folded and laid edge up. When she reached Bree she saw that she was already poring over an immense thick wooden bench that almost filled the apse they were standing in. Spread out in front of her was an array of boxes, scrolls and files that had clearly been stored and forgotten. Relief washed over her; they had found exactly what they had come for, which meant they wouldn't have to stay long. She was desperate to put this risky escapade behind her and be back home tucked up in her cosy bed.

Pru tugged the balaclava over her head and stuffed it into the pocket of her jacket, her hair settling into a warm sweaty mess around her shoulders. The two of them began to scan every label and handwritten entry that adorned the books and boxes. The years were carefully recorded but appeared to be randomly filed.

Picking up two boxes, one from 1889 and the other from 1930, Bree wailed in despair. 'Oh gawd, this isn't going to be as easy as I thought; we could be here for hours; they're all over the place!'

Pru shook her head and grunted her displeasure. As far as she was concerned, that wasn't going to be an option; she wanted out of this creepy place as quickly as possible. Using her skills at cataloguing to work out the filing sequence that had been used, she began to deftly and with purpose pull out boxes in an ordered fashion. Bree watched her, fascinated.

'Bingo!' Pru reverently held a leather-bound file out in front of her. The meticulous handwriting declared:

Parish Records
January 1960 to December 1969

'This is it; this is the one.' Pru held it aloft. 'If we've got the dates right, then this should cover the daughter; that's if she was born here. Have a look and see if there's anything marked "Deaths" between, say, 1975 and 1985.'

'These are just the births and marriages this side; the deaths must be somewhere else.' Bree began searching in the next apse along. This one harboured wall-to-wall carved cabinets with grille fronts filled again with ledgers and boxes. 'They're locked.' She rattled the door. Looking around the small area, she began to hunt for a key, her fingers picking over the layers of dust and cobwebs that years of neglect had allowed to flourish.

Distracted by their mission, neither Pru nor Bree heard the soft footsteps of a third person who was embracing the corners and dark shadows of the basement. Neither did they see the hand that wielded the heavy wooden candlestick as it hovered over poor Pru's head as she finger-scanned the pages of her leather-bound treasure by torchlight.

'It's got to be here somewhere, I'm sure–'

Thwuuuump–

Pru didn't get the chance to finish her sentence. A searing pain tore through the side of her head, flashes of white tumbled before her eyes as she stumbled forward, frantically grabbing hold of the bench before slipping to the floor as darkness descended and took hold of her.

MAISIE, MAISIE

'Oh God, it's all my fault!' Bree wailed as she watched Pru being trundled into the back of an ambulance still unconscious, a large white gauze pad covering one side of her head. The flashing blue lights that came from the emergency vehicles randomly parked in the narrow street bounced from the glass panes of the parish hall, Winterbottom St. Michael's and Wrinkle in Time. Even the window of The Twisted Currant Café opposite managed to absorb some of the impromptu light show.

'What on earth possessed the pair of you?' Andy unclipped the Klickfast Stud blue light from the roof of his unmarked Ford Fiesta, threw it in the footwell, and slammed the door. 'She could have been killed. In fact, both of you could. I can't believe you'd do something so stupid.'

'I... er... we...' Bree sighed and shook her head. There was nothing she could say to defend herself, or Pru for that matter. What had seemed like a good idea and a bit of a laugh had suddenly, in a split second, become terrifying. She could see how controlled and professional Andy was trying to be, but she could also sense not just his annoyance with them for their idiocy, but something much more. It wasn't only a police officer/victim concern he was showing for Pru, she was sure of it.

'Don't go anywhere. I'll need to speak to you before I follow up at the hospital.' He indicated to Bree to jump in the rear of his car before making his way over to the main doors of the parish hall.

Bree slipped herself onto the back seat, leaving the car door open. She needed some air. The basement had been stuffy and dusty but she had tolerated it because her mind had been focused on their task, but once the chaos had kicked in, the panic that ensued had left her short of breath. She wanted to cry, but held back, choking down a huge lump in her throat. In the seconds that had followed Pru's yelp and the subsequent clatter of books, ledgers and boxes falling to the floor, her heart had almost stopped. Swinging her own torch to sweep the depths of the basement, she had picked out a shadowy figure moving furtively on the far side. The moon had broken through the slightly open door they had sneaked through, forcing a shaft of light to fall on to the stone tiles. Before she could react, the figure momentarily cast its own elongated shadow before slipping through the gap and disappearing into the night.

Her torch had taken that exact same moment to flicker and die. Frantic, she had begun to shout for Pru as she stumbled around in the darkness, trying to get her bearings. Her eyes had picked up a faded arc of light that was fanned out across the floor. Picking up Pru's torch she scanned the apse and that was when she had found Pru, slumped and unmoving, on the cold tiles, a pool of dark liquid spreading outwards around her head like a macabre halo.

Just remembering that terrifying split second of terror when she thought that her friend was actually dead, opened up the floodgates.

Bree dropped her head into her hands and soundlessly wept.

~

Phyllis slammed the door behind her. Stumbling into the kitchen, she turned on the tap and thrust her hands under the running water, relishing the coolness on her skin. She watched mesmerised as the blood mixed and then separated before flowing into the drain.

Her breath was still coming in short gasps as she blew out slowly, trying to control the pace of her heart.

'Well, Captain, that wasn't my finest moment if I'm honest.' She vigorously dried her hands on the olive-green towel. Captain sat in complete disinterest on his perch as she rambled on. 'If there's one thing I hate, it's not having the time to plan appropriately.' Her proverbial hand had been forced, and the result had been sloppy. Still, she'd got what she had set her sights on. 'It was rather fortuitous for me that I heard Ms Bryony Richards making her arrangements for tonight, wasn't it?' Grabbing a glass from the cupboard and a bottle of gin from the sideboard, she poured herself a good measure. She checked. Two fingers.

'Ah, I think I deserve three fingers tonight, don't you agree, Captain?' She sloshed an extra measure into the glass and followed up with a splash of tonic before settling herself down at the table. 'I almost made it another one for the tally tonight.' She poked at the cuttlefish that was hanging between the bars of Captain's cage. He cocked his head to one side, fixing her with his beady black eyes. 'I didn't hit her too hard, after all she's never done me any harm, but admittedly it was a little harder than I expected.' She chuckled to herself. The candlestick had been the first thing to hand; it hadn't felt that heavy until she'd swung it in an upwards arc, which meant that at the last minute she'd been forced to pull the power from her strike. 'I bet it still stung, though.' Her chuckle gave way to a cackle and the cackle to a full-on belly laugh. She took a large gulp of her gin and tonic, which made her choke noisily. She grabbed a tissue and wiped her mouth. 'The other one will be counting her lucky stars right about now, but it simply wasn't her time.' She checked her list, her 'Minutes to a Murder' and marked a cross against the name of Bryony Richards. That done, she turned her attention to the treasure she had snatched from the limp arms of Prunella Pearce.

'They almost had me, Captain, almost but not quite. I'll have to keep a very close eye on the librarian; she thinks she's too clever by half.' Phyllis took another swig of her gin and cursed the warmth; a few cubes of ice wouldn't have gone amiss. 'My work is not yet finished; there's still more to be done so that I may rattle the Winterbottom WI bell with vigour once I'm president.' Tracing her fingers across the embossed pattern on the leather-bound ledger, she paused to admire the workmanship as her hand hovered over the label. 'All in good time, Captain, all in good time.'

Parish Records
January 1960 to December 1969

Opening the aged pages, she slowly flicked through until she reached the second to last page. Scanning the neat handwriting, the ink having matured from black to a sepia brown, she traced along the line with her finger until she found what she was looking for.

Seeing the child's name, so beautifully scripted, brought an unnatural tear to her eye as a deep sadness crushed at her heart. A child hidden. A child forgotten. A child that was sentenced not to exist.

A silent child.

But she had existed, the ledger gave proof to that.

Maisie Martha Magdalen.

Maisie.

Or sometimes just simply: M.M.

Maisie, Maisie pretty as a daisy...

She closed her eyes and remembered. The silence pulsing in her ears, her breath sharp and painful.

And then 'The Rage' began again.

HOOKED

Opening her eyes, Pru took in the subdued lighting in the cubicle she was occupying; the pale green curtains billowed as someone walked briskly past. The gentle hum of voices, electronic beeping and telephones ringing added to the backdrop of what she at first assumed was a dream, until sharp spikes of pain flashed inside her head before giving way to a throbbing sensation of mammoth proportions. Her fingers slowly reached up to touch her matted hair.

'Oh gawd, a hangover that's not a hangover. What the hell happened?'

The chair that Bree was sitting on scraped noisily on the floor tiles as she leant forward to hold Pru's free hand, the hand that wasn't currently picking at bits of lint, cobwebs and dried blood. 'We were attacked... Well, you were... I wasn't, I... I... I'm so sorry, it's all my fault; you could have died.' Hot tears welled up and spilled onto her cheeks for the umpteenth time in the last two hours.

'Hey, hey don't do that; it's not your fault at all. I'm a big girl, I chose to come. You didn't make me. Well, not once you'd released my arm from your grip of imminent death!' Pru gave a wan, comforting smile to her best friend. 'Who was it?'

Bree shook her head. 'We don't know; it all happened so fast. My torch went out and I panicked.' She looked down at her hands and bit her bottom lip. 'I did see someone, though, but it was only a shadow as they ran through the door.'

Pru grimaced as she tried to sit up. Adjusting the pillow behind her, she thought for a moment. 'We're getting close, aren't we? Why else would someone be there the same time as us? Were they searching too? Or maybe they were worried we'd find something.' No sooner had those words left her lips and before she had given Bree the chance to reply, she remembered. 'Oh my God, the book. Quick, have you got the book?'

Puzzled, Bree shook her head. 'What book?'

'The records book I found, I held it up to show you, then you went to look for the death records. It was just before my lights went out.'

'There was nothing, just you lying on the floor. At least I don't think there was. I'll go back and check.'

'No you won't, young lady; you'll leave the investigating to me!'

Andy stood where the curtains had failed to meet. His face was a mixture of relief that Pru was awake and talking, concern for the funny, sassy woman who had only just entered his life but in doing so had made quite an impact, and annoyance that the two women had decided to play amateur sleuth.

Pru and Bree at least had the decency to look slightly embarrassed and suitably chastised. Bree kept her focus on the bed blanket, whilst Pru looked pleadingly into his eyes. 'We didn't mean any harm, Andy; we just wanted to help. We thought that if we could find something down there that would give you and Lucy a lead–'

Andy quickly interrupted her. 'Ah, so you've become some sort of Agatha Christie in your spare time, then? Pru, it's dangerous. Extremely dangerous. Whoever this is, they'll stop at nothing. Five murders so far. Do you really want to become number six?'

Pru pinched her lips together and shook her head. 'No, of course not, but I don't think I would. You know yourself these are not random; they're planned, they're linked, and I don't have any history or past with Winterbottom. I seriously don't think I'm in their sights.'

Bree shifted her elbow to rest on the bed, nestling her chin in her upturned hand, preferring to let Pru do the explaining – which made her feel even more guilty as it had all been her idea in the first place.

Andy sighed and kissed Pru on the tip of her nose, the only part of her that wasn't too bloodied. 'That's all well and good, but we don't tempt fate, do we? Please, Pru, leave it to the experts, that's what we get paid to do.' She nodded meekly as he touched her chin and tipped her face to look at him. 'I'll see you later. As soon as they say you can come home, I think you should stay at mine for at least a day or two.'

Her reply was barely a whisper. 'Okay.' She watched him walk away from her with Bree following reluctantly in his wake.

She allowed her very sore head to gently mould back into the pillow whilst she wrestled with the realisation that she just might be falling hook, line and sinker for the very Delectable Detective.

THE CURTAIN CALL

*I*t was at times like this that Felicity actually wished that the client, who was currently thrusting away like a Boeing 747 on top of her, was the corpulent Desmond DuPonte rather than the clinically obese Sir Carmichael Shytes-Smith. She was almost fully enveloped by his wobbling flesh, pushing her down into the memory foam mattress of her luxury bed. He was a marshmallow of a man, who left a lot to be desired in the underarm sweat department too. She turned her head to one side to avoid his festering left armpit, feeling his breath on her ear and neck as he grunted with exertion. Holding her breath wasn't an option, as what little remained in her lungs was slowly being forced out like a set of Victorian bellows.

Six hundred and fifty quid an hour, Fliss, just keep thinking... six hundred and fifty quid an hour!

The extra two hundred pounds an hour for this client was for her discretion and silence. Sir Carmichael never resorted to an assumed name; his arrogance made him untouchable. He was head of one of the biggest international banks, which had been the result of a conglomeration of two families with historical financial expertise: the Brownes and the Shytes. His wealth, initially inherited, but latterly boosted by ambitious business projects, ensured that he would continue to enjoy the privileged lifestyle to which he had become accustomed, whilst pandering to his strange pastimes and deviancies.

Felicity couldn't help but be amused to think that she was currently servicing a man who had the misfortune to be associated with a financial institution called The Browne-Shytes Banking Foundation. If she hadn't been so devoid of oxygen, she might have laughed. As Sir Carmichael pounded away, her mind wandered to sunny climes: Fort James in Antigua, Matira Beach in Bora Bora, Seven Mile in Jamaica; the turquoise-blue seas, white sands and tropical cocktail–

Her dreamy thoughts were suddenly obliterated by Sir Carmichael's final snort of gratification, which was akin to a hog discovering a rare truffle in dense woodland. As disgusting as it was, it was also welcomed by her as it signalled proof of his satisfaction and the end to her near-death suffocation. He flopped back onto the pillows beside her.

'One should try to be a bit more enthusiastic, my dear. After all, I am paying you for the privilege.' He didn't even try to make eye contact with her, remaining supine, staring at the folds of fabric in the clamshell canopy.

Fearing her six-hundred-and-fifty-quid-an-hour client could slip through her fingers, Felicity turned to him, running her index finger along his chest, the long red talon puckering his skin as she took on the role of mistress. 'Oh, Carmichael darling, there is so much more I can do for you once you have rested.' She traced her finger along the bloated mahogany-tanned skin of his belly until she was less than an inch from his credentials. 'We can't always have everything at once now, can we?' Sliding out from her side of the bed, the silk sheet slowly settled in a pile of soft folds as she made her way to the drinks cabinet. Pouring from the large, chilled bottle, she watched the bubbles pop and float to the surface before holding out a glass to him.

'Champagne?'

As their glasses chinked together, not so much in celebration but to seal the deal of further sexual favours, Felicity and Sir Carmichael remained blissfully unaware of the silent intruder who was acting as voyeur through a chink in the curtains that draped the immense bay window.

Phyllis held her breath and grimaced. The gentle tingle of pins and needles in her right foot had spread at an alarming rate up the sciatic nerve, sending a spasm to the back of her thigh muscle. She curled her toes, stretched, and wriggled them in the vain hope of alleviating the discomfort. She hadn't quite counted on Felicity being so bloody thorough when it came to her services.

Whatever happened to the good old days of the wham, bam thank you ma'am type of sex which was over and done with before you'd even realised it had started?

She rolled her eyes and concentrated on the deft weave in the fabric of the curtains, tracing the stitches and patterns whilst simultaneously pondering her current predicament. She had used the spare key to Felicity's plush apartment in Chelsea, but had then found she had less time to find a hiding place than she had originally planned. After the stress of furtively gaining entry to the building and then utilising the private elevator key code she'd discovered in Fliss's desk diary at the cottage, the lift doors had opened out onto a plush carpeted hallway that serviced a lounge, bathroom, kitchen and, of course, Felicity's boudoir, better known as her Chamber of Delights. Entranced by how the other half live, Phyllis had still been floating around the rooms, touching and caressing exotic materials, ornaments, soft furnishings, and laughing at Felicity's fancy underwear, when she'd heard the mechanical clang of the elevator mechanism starting up from the hallway. The soft whirring as it made its way up to the penthouse filled her with horror. Gripping the small bunch of keys she had found during her in-depth search of Felicity's cottage, whilst supposedly wielding her feather duster and mop, she had quickly hidden herself in the bedroom as her target exited the lift. The walk-in closet had initially presented itself as the perfect location, but she couldn't be sure that Felicity wouldn't be using it for her costume changes, so the bay window had become her hideout.

Phyllis had remained rooted to the spot, hidden by the heavy brocade drapes enduring the grunts and groans of Felicity's bedroom gymnastics and the clinking of champagne glasses, whilst mentally berating herself for once again being sloppy in the execution of her plan. Her poor timing would now mean the demise of two people rather than just one.

Unfortunate? Yes.

Avoidable at this stage? No.

Cosseting the ring-grip handle of the World War II Fairbairn-Sykes commando knife that had once belonged to her grandfather, she closed her eyes and measured her breath, her fingers clasping the neatly stitched edging of the curtain. Waiting … for just the right moment.

She grinned as she watched the couple enjoying their final moments of lust, grateful that Carmichael's back presented such a large and unmissable target. If her calculations were anything to go by, this would be perfection. Two birds with one proverbial stone.

'Lights, camera, action…' she breathlessly murmured to herself.

It was time for curtain up and the performance of her life.

VIVA VOCE

'Death is a delightful hiding place for weary men.' – *Herodotus*

*B*ut for the fact that poor Felicity was orally engaged at the point of impact, she would have screamed.

Sir Carmichael, kneeling before her in all his obese glory whilst she performed her speciality, had suddenly stiffened, but not in the sense that Fliss had come to expect in her line of work. This was different. His whole body jerked violently before becoming rigid, his eyes bulged, a loud grunt filling the air as the knife was buried to the hilt between his shoulder blades. His startled expression was the last thing that she saw before he fell heavily forward, pinning her underneath his 152 kilograms of flesh that had taken him over sixty-five years to nurture and expand.

Feeling her whole body crunch into the mattress, the sheer weight of Carmichael slowly crushing her, she gagged uncontrollably, desperately trying to turn her head away from him to no avail. She wanted to shout, she wanted to scream, but those simple acts were beyond her. She curled the hand of her one free arm into a fist and pummelled his back, all the time knowing in her heart that her efforts were futile. A warm scarlet stickiness clung to her palm, forcing her hand to slip with each frenzied blow.

Carmichael released one long chilling exhalation, and then there was nothing. Just the sound of her heart throbbing a slow, desperate beat that pounded in her ears.

Her frightened eyes picked out a shadowy figure as it stood menacingly at the side of the bed watching her last moments, the sing-song lilt emanating from her voyeur acting as a haunting backdrop to her own gurgling melody.

I do not know, says the great bell of Bow...

Her face familiar, her stance familiar, her voice familiar.

Willis!

As Felicity's final breath was squeezed from her limp, broken body, a ridiculous thought crossed her mind. She had always believed that when her time to die arrived, she would dramatically declaim a final, passionate speech, or at least hold a decent memory to project as a lasting impression of her life on this planet. Sadly, she was not being gifted with anything so special or profound, her mind had all but returned to the mundane memories of her childhood.

No last words, no earth-shattering memory or poignant message – only the sad confirmation that her mum had been right all along.

It's terribly rude to talk with your mouth full, dear!

SWEET DELIGHTS

'It's not okay, Pru, no matter how many times you say it, it doesn't make it okay!' Andy gently tucked a strand of hair that had curled and dropped down over her face behind her ear. 'Promise me you won't do anything as stupid as that again?' He inspected the blush of red and purple smudged across her cheek. 'You've got quite a bruise there, you know.'

Pru sat perched like a garden gnome on Andy's sofa, clad in his huge cotton pyjamas that hung from her arms, her hands barely peeping out from the cuffs. She tucked her feet up underneath her and hugged the fluffy cushion that little bit tighter. 'We thought we were helping, and I know we're on to something. Lucy knows too. She's looking into that Winterbottom murder in the 1970s. That could give us a lead.' She paused to draw breath, her stomach churning again, half with the excitement of solving the murders, half with the knowledge at how close she had come to being a fatality herself. Undeterred, she rambled on. 'It was in that book; that's the key; you've got to find the book. I didn't get chance to read inside, but whoever hit me took it, so it means something!' Her fingers subconsciously felt for the tender spot on her scalp that had been subjected to a deftly applied blob of NHS glue.

'Listen to yourself! You just can't let it drop, can you.' Andy rubbed his temple in exasperation. 'I get paid to investigate. I've told you this before; it's my job. Please, Pru, just let me do my job without having to worry about you!'

Pru pouted, unsure if this was going to be their first row as a couple. 'It's personal. I can feel it here.' She patted her chest, just above her heart. 'This is revenge; there's a psychological background to this. I've read enough crime books in my time.'

Andy plonked himself down beside her, handing her a glass of red wine. 'Ah, I see. So now we're an expert on the criminal mind and the human psyche?' He grinned. 'I'm not worthy to be in your presence.'

Indignant at his dismissal of her literary credentials, she gave him a playful punch on the arm. His glass wobbled, dripping small spots of wine on to his shirt. 'Kiss me, Delectable Detective, kiss me now.' She coyly giggled, pulling him towards her.

As they met, she bit down tenderly on his bottom lip, savouring not just the moment, but him. It really couldn't get any more perfect than–

'Damn.' Andy flinched as his works pager burst into life, the high-pitched, pulsating note making them both jump. He quickly broke away from her as his mobile phone began to ring, drowning out the pager alert. He checked the display screen. 'I've got to get this.'

She nodded, understanding of his role.

'DS Barnes.' His opening was blunt. 'Yep, have you informed the DI?'

She watched him become someone very different from the man she had just kissed and desired. His stance changed, his jaw set firm, and a grey wash painted his skin.

'I'm leaving now.'

~

Frustrated for the second time in as many hours, Andy threw the CID pool car keys onto his desk. They hit the battered grey stapler that carried his force identity number daubed in Tippex and came to rest just shy of his tattered blotter. Holmes, who actually looked worse than he did, hair springing in several directions and a tie that hadn't quite made the grade in a Windsor knot, was nursing a large mug of black coffee as he examined the crime scene photographs. A gentle hum of activity ran around the incident room.

'Okay, everyone, settle down.' Holmes stood up and addressed his team. 'This–' He pointed to the photograph of a very elegant Fliss that was pinned to the murder wall. '–is Felicity Jayne Broadbent, forty-three years. She's a born and bred Winterbottomer and has lived here all her life. She has a property called Lilac Cottage on School Lane, and also owns a penthouse apartment in Chelsea which is used for her, er... business dealings, shall we say.'

A murmur of recognition from some of the team brought Holmes to a halt. He looked again at the file in front of him. 'Ms Broadbent was a high-class escort, a solo operator with extremely prestigious clients.' He turned to the next sheet. 'It will be no surprise to you all to know that she was also a member of Winterbottom Women's Institute, one of our common denominators in all of the murders.'

Andy scribbled notes as he listened to Holmes, glancing briefly at his own copies of the scene photographs. He couldn't help but feel for Felicity Broadbent. Not just because she had lost her life at such a young age, but because of the circumstances. She had obviously been an elegant, well-educated woman who had chosen a career that most would curl their lip at, so to have her last moments lit by flash, gawped at by investigators and documented for eternity, was one of the more brutal aspects of the job. He shuffled through until he reached a close up of the body of Sir Carmichael Shytes-Smith. Strangely enough, he couldn't feel any sympathy or empathy for him at all. He did for his long-suffering wife and children; their loss would be heightened by the utter humiliation of his indiscretions once it hit the headlines.

He was aware of Holmes still droning on about an extra two detectives being sent from the Met to assist. They'd been more than happy to work hand in hand once the suspected links had been confirmed and had helpfully seconded two of their own finest investigators to join Andy's team. He wondered if that would work well with the others, or go down like a lead balloon. He knew some of his team could be quite precious about their own methods.

'I'm still waiting for the final reports from Melvyn, but he's sent over the photographs from the scene.' Holmes ran his fingers over the keyboard, the images scrolling across the screen on the far wall. 'So far there has been nothing that has glaringly jumped out. Two champagne glasses from scene; DNA confirms the donors on both are our victims, no trace fibres as yet, and as beautifully maintained as the apartment was, there were several semen donations recovered, which – putting it mildly – was to be expected.' He clicked the slide along.

'And then we have this…'

A vibrant yellow confectionary pouch with two comical characters on the front filled the screen. Nestled in the thick cream tufts of the bedroom carpet, it sat stark and out of place. Felicity's blood-covered hand could be seen dangling over the edge of the bed in the background.

'An empty packet of M&M chocolate-covered peanuts!' The tone of Holmes' voice accentuated the last word. 'Now unless this is a new one on me, and somehow I don't think Mrs H would be particularly enamoured if I brought a packet of these home for our bedroom romps as she's always on a bloody diet, this needs focusing on. There was no trace of either victim touching or consuming them.'

An uncomfortable snigger ran around the room, partly influenced by their respect for the victims, but mainly at the image now etched on their brains of their detective inspector indulging in a bit of firkling with Mrs Holmes whilst playing oral catch-it with a quid's worth of confectionary from Morrisons.

MINUTES TO A MURDER

Phyllis smugly sat in her first-class carriage on the Kings Cross to Winterbottom train. The upgrade had been a treat to herself for a job well done. She stirred her cup of tea with the silver spoon she always carried with her, watching the amber liquid spin. She carefully polished her treasure and returned it to her bag. It was one of the few things that remained with her from her childhood, the spoon and her Holly Hobbie rag doll with the golden plaits and patchwork frock.

They hadn't allowed her to take anything else.

The jerk of the train as it set in motion rattled her cup against the saucer before the carriage quickly settled to an even tempo on the rails. She watched the station platform and buildings pass by her window before it played host to the glass-fronted office blocks and metal gantries above. Soon there would be fields and trees, which were so much better for her soul. She delved deep into her tapestry bag that housed a dog-eared copy of Agatha Christie's *The Sittaford Mystery*, her 'Minutes to a Murder' diary, a pair of reading glasses, a banana, and a handful of chocolate-covered peanuts that were rolling around loose at the bottom. She picked one out and popped it into her mouth, savouring not only the crunch as she bit down but the sheer brilliance of the clues that she left behind and the confidence that even if they did solve her conundrums, they would never link the solutions to her.

This was such a fabulous game. It mirrored her childhood; she didn't have any playmates who would join in the jollity back then either, but in all honesty, friends were terribly overrated. She'd managed long enough without any, so why change the habit of a lifetime?

Opening her 'Minutes to a Murder', she placed a careful tick against Felicity's name.

Six WI ladies down and only one to go.

Phyllis smiled, *Imperfect but perfect for purpose* had been her childhood mantra, and now she knew exactly what that purpose was.

She was perfect for murder.

She checked her watch. Satisfied that she would arrive in plenty of time for the Winterbottom ladies send off for Betty, she reclined her head back against the seat and closed her eyes.

DYING TO BE POPULAR

*C*larissa huffed in annoyance. 'She was a social piranha; everyone knew what she was. I mean to say, would you relish chomping your dentures into one of her spotted dicks at the WI bake sale? You'd have no idea of where it had been, would you?'

'Blimey, 'Rissa, say it as it is, why don't you!' Millie Thomas adjusted herself on the hard wooden pew, trying and failing to find a more comfortable position. 'And it's "pariah", a social pariah, she wasn't a bloody flesh-eating fish; she was a flesh-fondling floozy.' Millie shifted again, nudging Clarissa further down the pew. 'Heavens to Betsy, I think my bum's gone to sleep!'

'And don't I know it,' snapped Clarissa. 'I've heard it snore twice already!'

'It's not my fault, I get a little windy when I'm upset.'

'A little! Millie, dear, that was a howling gale! Look at Kitty's hair.'

Overhearing the conversation, and in an effort to suppress an inappropriate snicker, Pru snorted loudly, making several heads from the row in front spin like a scene from *The Exorcist*. 'Sorry,

220

sorry…' she reverently whispered, as Bree gave her a sharp dig in the ribs.

'Here she comes. Oh my God, look at the heels she's wearing!'

They both turned to see Chelsea and Cassidy tottering down the flagged aisle of Winterbottom St. Michael's Church towards the front, arms linked in an effort to stop one or the other from falling over. Chelsea was sporting a nifty feather fascinator perched on top of her head, matched to a black high-cut jacket and a pair of leopard-print leggings that petered down to a tight cuff around her ankles, and finished off with a pair of Max 150 Jimmy Choos with six-inch stiletto heels gracing her feet. Cassidy was in similar garb, but in a shade of powder blue.

'Didn't anyone tell them it's a funeral not a ruddy wedding?' Kitty Hardcastle hissed to no one in particular.

Before Pru could reply, Chels and Cassidy came to an abrupt halt two rows from the front. As if in slow motion, Cassidy squealed and Chelsea, arms thrown out in front of her, momentarily floated in limbo before dropping to the floor as if she'd been taken out by a sniper.

'Now you see her, now you don't!' Pru giggled in awe at the acrobatic way Chelsea had disappeared from view. The third, fourth and fifth rows of the congregation craned their necks to see what all the commotion was about.

'Would you bloody credit it, me fecking heel's stuck in the grid!' Chelsea screeched loudly from the depths of the sacred aisle, much to the disdain of Reverend Horace Baggott who, having quickly moved forward to assist, changed his mind and beat a hasty retreat to the altar steps upon hearing such blasphemy. 'Cassidy, get your arse here and give me a hand!' Chelsea begged.

No sooner had those dulcet words left her lips than Ethel Tytherington set to on the church organ with a rip-roaring rendition of 'I Do Like to be Beside the Seaside' at the behest of the undertaker, who had signalled Betty Prince's arrival with six pall-bearers and a fine oak casket. As Ethel pumped her feet and pulled at the array of knobs forcing the tuneful air through the huge pipes, the irony of the song, completely lost on Ethel herself but not the congregation, poured out and filled the church.

Scenes of chaos ensued, with Kitty attempting to stop Ethel's unfortunate performance of what should have been 'Abide with Me' by bouncing along the pews in an effort to reach Ethel before Betty did, whilst the pall-bearers played hopscotch over the entangled bodies of Chelsea and Cassidy as Chelsea frantically tried to extricate her Jimmy Choo heel from the ornate metal floor vent.

'Don't snap it; these bastard shoes cost me six hundred and fifty quid!' Chels howled over the second verse.

Watching the casket slip and slide on the bearer's shoulders from one side to the other as they passed Betty over the squealing mass of dubious elegance and class that was Chels and Cassidy, Reverend Baggott stayed Ethel's organ recital with the wave of one hand, leaving Kitty mid step-up to the chancel.

He waited until Betty was respectfully laid at the front, the bearers had returned to the front pew, and his congregation was attentive before he began his opening.

'May the memories of your loved one begin to bring comfort rather than pain. May the words touch and presence of others bring solace, and may you be blessed in your coming in and going out–'

Pru grinned and whispered from the corner of her mouth. 'Somehow I don't think Chels feels blessed with her "coming in", do you?' She jiggled the first and second fingers on both hands to emphasise air quotes whilst jerking her head towards the still prostrate lump of leopard print splayed out on the uneven flagstones.

Bree knew that if she tried to reply, she'd produce an even bigger snort of laughter than the one Pru had generated earlier. She'd been kicked out of some places in her lifetime for bad behaviour, but tempting fire and brimstone by getting ejected from a church at her age seriously wasn't on the agenda. She bit down on her bottom lip and squeezed her eyes tightly shut, which duly prompted Millie to pat her on the back and offer her a tissue for her perceived grief.

Reverend Baggott continued.

'–and grateful for a life lived and a legacy left behind.'

Unseen by her fellow WI friends, Phyllis sat quietly at the back of the church watching events unfold. Her fingers curled so tightly her nails dug painfully into the palms of her hands as she held back a sudden avalanche of sorrow. She hadn't cried once since that fateful day, the day she had keened and wept with such anguish and fear, her small hands covering her face, painted with her mother's blood.

She closed her eyes, desperate to shut out the memory. Her grief today was not for Betty or for her other victims. It was for herself.

The legacy that she had been left was nothing to be grateful for, and in time the ladies of Winterbottom Women's Institute would know why.

Pru gratefully sat down in their usual window seat in the Dog & Gun, slipped her feet out of her court shoes, and wriggled her toes. 'Mine might be flatties, but they still pinch.' She sighed, giving one foot a rub whilst taking a large gulp from the gin balloon that Bree had given her. 'I can't believe Chelsea spent the whole service sitting on the floor in the middle of the aisle; she wouldn't be parted for love nor money from her Jimmy Choos, would she?'

Bree was going to reply but hadn't quite finished chewing the sausage roll she'd stuffed in her mouth. Waving her hand as a sign for more time, she gave an exaggerated swallow and attempted her first unsuccessful word, which resulted in Pru being showered with a smattering of puff pastry crumbs. 'Ooops! Apologies, Pru...'

'Less of the P's whilst your still getting rid of it.' Pru laughed, brushing the flakes from her blouse.

'It was still stuck in the grating when they carried Betty out; they had to step over her. I bet they're not even real Jimmy Choos, although the price she said she'd paid is about right, so they're either genuine and her dramatic angst was warranted, or someone saw her coming!' Bree sniffed whilst examining the paper plate in front of her. She peeled back the top layer of the wholemeal triangle. 'Egg and cress! Why do they always have egg and cress at funerals?'

Pru shook her head. 'Cheap, probably, and less likely to give anyone food poisoning I would imagine. Talking of poisoning, how about after here we nip into town to the main library and have a look at their national newspaper archives for anything on Magdalen House? I'm off for the rest of the day if you've got nothing else planned.'

'Mmm... good idea, but won't Andy read you the riot act again if he finds out? He's told you to keep out of the investigation, hasn't he?' Another sausage roll went the same way as the first.

'Well, yes I suppose so, but what harm can this do? The worst that could happen would be a paper cut from a 1979 edition of *The Guardian!*' Pru drained her glass and hesitated, wondering if she should have another one. Bree made the decision for her by beckoning Juicy Jason over.

'Nice shirt, Jase,' she teased. 'Would you be in a position to assist two middle-aged ladies who haven't got the energy or,' she pointed under the table, 'the shoes to make it to the bar for two more G&T's?'

'Middle-aged!!' Pru spluttered. 'I'll have you know I'm still very much in my thirties.'

Bree pulled a face. 'Only by the skin of your teeth, girlfriend!'

'At least they're my own. You've got more porcelain in your top set than Ethel Tytherington's got in her china cabinet!'

'Touché!' Bree hugged her friend and playfully punched her on the arm. 'Drink up we've got some investigating to do!'

AN APPLE A DAY...

*E*thel Tytherington sat rigidly on one of the bright orange plastic bucket chairs in the doctor's surgery. She glanced at her husband of over fifty years, Albert Barnard Tytherington, shook her head and sighed at the copious amounts of hair and crusted wax he'd been cultivating in his left ear since last Christmas.

'There'll be no stopping you once you get those ears syringed, Albie. Next door but one will be over the moon at not having to hear *Coronation Street* through three walls and a fence–'

'Eh?'

'*I said there'll be no sto–* oh forget it!' Ethel grumbled loudly before settling back into her chair again. She rummaged around in her handbag and pulled out a crumpled paper bag containing a few solitary mint imperials that had become wedged in the corner. Ethel's heart suddenly felt very heavy.

'Aw, Albie, look, mint imperials.'

Albert's hand quickly dipped into the paper bag; his fingers plucking at the round white ball. Holding it aloft, he admired it for all of two seconds before promptly popping it into his mouth.

'Bloody heard that, though, didn't you?' Ethel snapped. 'Sometimes I think there's nothing wrong with your hearing; you just pretend so you can ignore me!'

'Eh?' Albert cupped his hand to his ear and winked at her. He gave a grin that any naughty schoolboy would have been proud of as he sucked furiously on the mint.

'I was thinking of Betty; the mints reminded me of Betty. We always got a bag each from Martha's sweetie shop for trips and days out. Oh I do miss her terribly, Albie.' She shook out the delicately embroidered handkerchief from the side pocket of her bag and dabbed at her eyes. 'I just hope she's with Jack and Hugo now, together again at last.'

Not for the first time Albert was at a loss for words. He loved Ethel dearly, but the passing years had somewhat dulled the first flushes of exuberance and riveting conversation they had once shared. Those facets of their relationship had now been comfortably numbed down to short sentences peppered with grunts of acknowledgement, empathy, understanding and pleasure. He could feel a sympathetic grunt constricting his vocal cords at that very moment, but was also cautiously aware that if he released it, the next thing to restrict his throat would be Ethel's bony fingers.

'I know, dear, so very sad indeed. Are they no closer to catching who did it?' He relaxed back in his chair, content that he had made the correct type of conversation and had shown just the right amount of empathy for his wife.

Ethel shook her head and looked wistfully out of the window next to her. She watched the white clouds scoot across the blueness of the sky and then turned her attention to an empty crisp packet as it was lifted by the breeze, swirling and tumbling down the path until it was suddenly stamped on by a very feminine two-tone Oxford brogue. She watched the figure bend down and pick it up, the fingers holding the corner of the bag as though it were a prize. Raising her head so the angle to the brim of her cloche hat became thinner and her face more evident, the wear-er's eyes bore into Ethel, making her shift uncomfortably in her chair.

Phyllis Watson!

A shiver ran down Ethel's spine. She didn't know why her presence made her blood run cold and, what was more, she couldn't tear her eyes away. She watched as Phyllis slowly and deliberately crushed the bag in her hand, all the while not breaking her gaze. Alarmed, Ethel grabbed Albert's arm.

'Clarence Clutterbuck to consulting room four, Clarence Clutterbuck to consulting room four.'

The tinny voiceover blared out from the speakers and filled the waiting room, causing a hum of activity as doors creaked and people exchanged seats in anticipation of being next.

'Albie, Albie, look. It's Phyllis. What's wrong with her?' Ethel frantically jostled Albert's shoulder trying to gain his attention, but he was too deeply engrossed in a dog-eared copy of the *Heritage Railway* magazine.

'Eh?'

'Phyllis! Look at her, she looks – oh dear– she looks crazy!'

Before Albert could reply or even think of another way to comfort his wife that didn't involve the laying on of hands, a commotion broke out at the reception desk.

'I'm so sorry, Mrs Alcock, but I don't think we'll be able to give this back to you after it's been sent away for testing.' The receptionist held a plastic container aloft.

Mrs Alcock tutted in disbelief. 'You said to tinkle into a container and bring it in, so I did.' She jabbed her lumpy arthritic finger in the air in a schoolmarm manner. '*This* is a container, but it's my container and I want it back when you've finished with it.'

'But it's a… er…' The receptionist pulled her glasses up from the string around her neck and perched them on the end of her nose. 'A Tupperware box!'

Mrs Alcock rolled her eyes and sighed loudly. 'I'm well aware that it's a Tupperware box. I'm not a silly woman, you know. It's my best one, and Mr Alcock won't have any other box for his sandwiches.' She sniffed indignantly, ensuring her pique was not wasted on the receptionist. 'When Percival goes fishing that's the only one he'll use so I need it back!'

Albert puckered his lips and side-eyed Ethel as Mrs Alcock continued to argue her dilemma over her prized plastic tub and urine sample, whilst the receptionist, trying to maintain calm, began to turn several shades of green at the thought of poor Mr Alcock and what his future butties would be encased in.

Albert leant in close and produced an alarmingly loud stage whisper. 'Well, all I can say, my dear, is that really is taking the pi–'

'Albie!' Ethel slapped him hard on the back of the hand. 'Don't be so disgusting.'

Albert rubbed the injured area and grinned. 'I was just about to say, until you committed spousal battery on me, that that really is taking the piscatory out of Percy, isn't it?' He laughed long and hearty at his own joke. 'Now what were you saying?'

'It's too late, she's gone.' As Ethel scanned the path and street outside looking for Phyllis, she could only afford him a slight smile for his comedic efforts as her mind was now on other things.

WHAT'S IN A NAME?

interbridge library sat behind a regimented ridge of elm trees, their dense and heavy branches giving shade to the windows that faced south, absorbing the late afternoon sun. The red brick façade of the eighteenth-century building offered an imposing frontispiece to the backdrop of the original town graveyard. Aged and weather-worn headstones peppered the grass, standing like drunken soldiers lining the paths that wound their way towards the sandstone chapel in the centre. No one had been buried there in the last twenty years, but it was still maintained, not so much by the Winterbridge council but by local volunteers keen to uphold tradition and history.

Pru and Bree stood at the threshold to the large carved oak doors, a feeling of excitement, curiosity mixed with trepidation, and the general wooziness of a gin and tonic too many before they'd left the Dog & Gun.

'Now I know why Miss Marple only ever drank tea.' Pru hiccupped loudly and then followed up with a burp that a docker would have been proud of.

'Blimey, after you with the trough!' Bree sniffed, holding her finger under her nose. 'You've only got to produce one more bodily function to have the complete set.'

Pru pushed open one side of the doors, a large brass sign that heralded the entrance to Winterbridge library caught the sun as it dappled through the trees. A rush of air hit them as the rubber draught seals parted, the smell of woodblock flooring, polish and musty books eliciting memories of her old school hall. 'I'll have you know I'm a lady and a lady never passes forces unknown – well not loudly, anyway!' she cheerily retorted.

'Talking of forces unknown, how's the Delectable Detective?' Bree delved into her Sloppy Joe bag and retrieved a lip balm, smoothing her finger across the wax she liberally applied it to her lips.

'Mmm... still incredibly delectable, but decidedly missing in action at the moment; he's on nights all this week.' This was something Pru had yet to get used to: Andy's erratic working hours and a frequently empty bed. She pointed to the bifurcated staircase that was lit by a prism of colours shining from the stained-glass windows overlooking the first landing. 'Here we go, archives this way.' She ushered Bree up the stairs towards the mahogany sign that bore a gold-coloured hand with a pointy finger that seemed to be eagerly showing them their rightful path. 'Doors at three o'clock.'

Again, another hiss of air greeted them as the doors opened to Bree's less than gentle touch. 'This ain't going to be easy, my dearest Pru.' She looked around the expanse of filing cabinets and floor-to-ceiling bookshelves that stretched ahead of them, their imposing presence broken by grand marble pillars that held the vast ceiling in place above highly polished wood tables that hosted green glass reading lamps. 'Where the hell are we supposed to start?'

Never one for immediate defeat, Pru marched up to the main reference desk and quickly plastered on her best professional *I'm in the same game* smile for the stern-faced librarian. She was convinced the woman was fully aware of their presence but had chosen instead to continue the deft flicking of her fingers over the filing cards whilst making satisfactory clucking sounds in her throat.

Pru cleared her own throat. 'Excuse me, would you be able to point me in the right direction for the National Newspaper Archives for 1979 to 1983, please?'

Cecily Tucker, her name badge proudly displayed on the polyester print blouse she was wearing, dropped her glasses to the tip of her nose and studied Pru intently. 'Aisle 13b, search online for the year and that will give you the reel or plate code and storage location. Readers are over there.' She pointed a finger that sported a joint misshapen through arthritis at the furthest part of the room.

Ten minutes later Pru was set up in front of the reader and was scrolling slowly through her findings, the pages slipping from right to left, the print and photographs appearing in screen view for a second before disappearing and being replaced by another. She quickened her pace, watching the months of 1979 flicker and shift like a scene from an old black-and-white movie reel. December 1979 whizzed across the screen, forcing her to stop and backtrack.

'This is it.' She held her breath as she focused on the date displayed by the faded edition of *The Telegraph*: 19 December 1979. '**Winterbottom Tragedy unfolds...**'

Bree leant in close as the pair silently mouthed the words to the article, a feeling of despair hitting them both simultaneously.

'It's not telling us anything different from the *Winterbottom News*. It's just basically a rehash from their report.' Bree was bitterly disappointed.

'Mmm... I know, and if you search forward there's nothing. It's like there's been a news blackout on it. Apart from the daughter being taken away by the authorities, there are only details of the victim and a brief statement from the DCI who led the investigation, saying it had all been a "terrible tragedy", and that they weren't looking for anyone else in connection with the death of Dorothy Anne Magdalen. That bears out what Ethel vaguely remembered; that it was matricide.' Pru puffed out her cheeks and scrolled back to the original newspaper report. 'Hold on a minute, there's some photographs.'

They sat quietly, Pru zooming in on each photograph, trying to find detail where there was none. Magdalen House sat bleakly against the snow; slush and tyre marks from the gathered police vehicles had left a criss-cross pattern on the vast driveway. 'Not much, is there?' She flicked between photographs. 'I think we've been on a wild goose chase; we've made something out of nothing, haven't we?'

Bree put her arm around her friend's shoulder and gave her a hug. 'Well, we did say we're not exactly like Miss Marple, didn't we?' She pinched her lips together in thought. 'Then again, the clues that Lucy told us about, the ones that had been left at the scene, they did sort of point towards the Magdalen Murder, didn't they?'

'Suppose... or maybe we're just– aww, will you look at that?' Pru pointed to the expanded newspaper photograph. 'She looks so sweet, so innocent. Hard to believe she would have it in her to commit such an awful crime.'

The grainy black-and-white photograph sat centre screen, the pixels becoming more prominent as Pru zoomed in. The scene was Magdalen House again, the police cars still in their same positions. A large forensic unit had joined them, but the photographer had focused on the main doors to the house. Standing on the steps, flanked by a uniformed WPC and two ladies dressed in dogtooth check coats and boots with Russian style hats to ward off the still falling snow, was the smallest figure Pru had ever seen, dressed in what looked like a thin nightgown peeping out from the opening of the overlarge jacket that was around her shoulders. Her feet in wellington boots stood stark against the snow.

The little girl looked lost, swamped by those around her; the image of her face as she clutched an old-fashioned Holly Hobbie doll in her small hands tore at Pru's heart. The caption underneath was simple.

The child, still holding her treasured doll, is believed to be the daughter of the victim. She is shown here being escorted from the property by representatives of social services and the police.

Pru touched the screen with her finger, tracing the outline of the little girl. The girl was identified in the next paragraph as Miss Maisie Martha Magdalen aged nine years.

'I can't imagine what must have happened to make an innocent child turn into a killer, can you?' Pru scribbled the two names that appeared in the article on the notepad next to her. 'I wonder where she is now, hey? D'you think she could be free and roaming Winterbottom?' That thought terrified her, a rampant killer on the loose playing a macabre game of Cluedo.

Bree tutted and sighed. 'Who knows, but who in their right mind would leave clues pointing to themselves as a murderer? They'd have to be barking mad to do that!'

Clicking the reader off, the low light returned to their corner of the library as the two women sat in quiet contemplation.

'Is that the Magdalen case you're looking at?' Cecily Tucker, three large tomes tucked under arm, paused in her penguin-like progression towards the reference section.

Startled from their train of thought by her unexpected interruption, Pru was the first to respond. 'Yes, we're just doing some research for er... checking up on er...'

Bree quickly interrupted. 'For our local historical buildings and antiques society, *The Wrinkled P-ruins*. Nothing gives us more pleasure than nosing around old mansions, digging into the past, finding out about previous owners, that sort of thing.' She tilted her head, more to dare Cecily to challenge her.

Cecily pointed her slightly bent and lumpy index finger at Pru's notepad. 'I remember it well, a terrible business, quite a scandal, actually. So sad, too, that poor child.' She became pensive. 'She was sent away, you know. America, I think. The house remained part of the Magdalen estate but was leased out as a boarding school. It became vacant again about twelve months ago, and now it's up for auction as far as I'm aware.'

'Do you know where she is now?' Pru expectantly held her pen in readiness. 'The little girl, Maisie?'

'Dead, I believe. That's why the house and grounds are up for sale; there are no living relatives; end of the line. It'll probably be snapped up by a developer. Anyway, must get on, things to do.'

They both watched Cecily waddle away with determined purpose.

'Well that's scuppered that idea then, hasn't it? If she's dead and there's nobody else in the family left, we haven't got any suspects from the Magdalen murder linked to our murders!' Pru slumped down in her chair, defeated. 'Terribly young to die, too. Even if it was recent, she could only have been in her late forties.'

Silence reigned once more.

'We're pretty shit at this detective malarkey, aren't we?' Bree doodled a dagger with droplets of blood falling from the lines of her notepad.

Pru's heart felt heavy with disappointment; she had been so sure they were on to something with the Magdalen clues. Ripping her notes from the pad, she shoved them into her bag. 'Only one thing for it.'

'What's that?'

'The Dog & Gun, a lot more gin and then let Lucy know what we've found out!'

Bree shook her head. 'No, don't tell her yet. I'm enjoying all this cloak and dagger stuff! We need to be absolutely sure that every single link to Magdalen House and what happened there is definitely ruled out of the investigation. How do we know that the little girl is dead? We've only got old sour-faced Cecily's word for it. I vote we do a bit more digging before we tell anyone – and *that* includes the Delectable Detective!' She shot her hand in the air to register her choice.

'All right, Mrs Richards, motion carried. We'll wait.'

A BOOKISH CONFESSION...

'*L*adies, ladies, please settle down.' Kitty Hardcastle tinkled her brass hand bell several times, but the good ladies of Winterbottom WI were seemingly oblivious to her presence or her need for order. She pressed her knuckles into the embroidered tablecloth and leant forward, drawing in a deep breath in the hope that a good intake of air would allow her voice to resonate to the rafters of Winterbottom Parish Hall and beyond.

'*Ladies!*'

A sudden silence fell over the gathered group. Some looked suitably chastised; some pulled faces and rolled their eyes; some laughed; and some quickly sat down in their carefully selected seats. Apart from one.

Phyllis.

Phyllis stood at the serving hatch to the kitchen, one arm resting on the work surface and a hand firmly planted on her hip. The cups and saucers were already neatly laid out and Brenda's cakes and scones stacked in Tupperware boxes sat ready to be devoured during the tea break. Her eyes hooded and narrowed as she watched Bree Richards throw back her head in laughter, probably at something funny that had slipped from the lips of Pru Pearce. It was such a shame that Pru would be losing her good friend very soon. She slicked her finger along the middle of the Victoria sponge. Curling up the butter-cream on the tip, she examined it and quickly popped it into her mouth. She still hadn't devised a deed most foul to despatch Bree as yet, but she was sure she'd think of something devilish and delightful to rid herself of her final bit of competition.

'All in good time, Phyllis my dear, all in good time,' she muttered to herself.

'Right, ladies.' Kitty's voice had returned to a more acceptable volume. 'We have a short amount of WI business to attend to and then we have our guest speaker for the evening, Jill Doyle from Jill's Book Café.' She paused, waiting for her ladies to make themselves comfortable and for the hum of anticipation to cease.

Pru and Bree had grabbed themselves a seat near the front, Pru being the more eager of the two to listen to their guest, her love of books and, of course, her librarian background driving her excitement. Chelsea Blandish followed them, edging her way along the row, dragging a rather reluctant Cassidy Parks with her, pausing only to extricate the leopard print chiffon scarf that had snagged on Clarissa's wicker shopping basket.

'Bleedin' hell, almost carrotted meself then!' she squealed as the fabric tightened around her neck, yanking her backwards.

Pru chuckled loudly. 'Garrotted; I think you meant garrotted, Chels.'

'I knows what I meant. Anyways, what's this woman talking about? What's so interesting about a café? That's what I want to know.' Chelsea plonked herself down on the chair next to Pru and pouted momentarily before plucking at a long blonde hair that was adhered to her skin-tight hot pink leggings.

'It's the name of her book blog.' Bree rolled her eyes and gave

Pru a dig in the ribs as a way of highlighting Chelsea's stupidity. 'She reads books, lots of them, then reviews and blogs about them online.' She could almost hear the cogs whirring in Chelsea's brain as she tried to digest that snippet of information. Feeling the need to help her out further, Bree bit down on her lip in thought. 'Okay, look, it's not like *Take a Break* or *Jackie* magazine, Chels; it's books, proper reading books, you know, stories.' Bree used both index fingers to draw the outline of a book in the air.

'Oh aye, yeah.' Chelsea, jaw dropped and mouth open, quietly contemplated her knowledge of books. 'I did have a book once, yer know, when I was a kid it was–'

Before Chelsea could finish her sentence, which if past conversations were anything to go by could take between two minutes and a full half hour depending on how many bottles of Lambrini she had consumed, Kitty stood up to halt the chatter.

'Right, ladies, may I introduce you to Jill? Jill is originally from Hull, and after many years as a chartered librarian and a reference specialist, her love of books brought her to the realms of book blogging and reviewing. She has an excellent online blog called Jill's Book Café, which I avidly follow, and I think she's as excited to tell us about her journey as we are to hear it.'

A polite ripple of applause filled the hall as a cheerful-looking petite woman with elfin hair took to the podium. She adjusted the microphone to suit her height and took a sip of the water that Kitty had thoughtfully placed on the table next to her before clearing her throat.

'Good evening, ladies, my name is Jill and I have a problem.'

A shocked hush blanketed the hall, a sea of bemused faces taking in their guest speaker and her awkward revelation.

'Oh blimey,' Clarissa gasped as she clutched her wicker shopper in shock. 'I think she's come to the wrong place; can someone tell her this is not an AA meeting.' She almost fell off her chair trying to attract Kitty's attention to the evolving situation.

Jill playfully stayed a hand towards her audience, and in particular to Clarissa. 'Yes, ladies, my problem is that when reading books I get easily distracted... by other books!' She gave a warm, knowing smile to the ladies of Winterbottom WI who reciprocated with a ripple of laughter. 'I have a desire to share what I read and, as Bertrand Russell once said: *There are two motives for reading a book: one, that you enjoy it; the other, that you can boast about it*, although in this sense it is more a case of me sharing that enjoyment rather than bragging of my ability to pick up a book and turn its pages...'

'Wow, can you imagine meeting all those famous authors? That was a fantastic talk, Jill.' Pru took a bite of the Victoria sponge, thankfully unaware that an index finger belonging to Phyllis had already been swept along and poked into the butter-cream. 'Lee Child, Harlan Coben, Linwood Barclay and Ann Cleeves, that's amazing. Do you get the books you've bought at the festivals signed by them?' She felt like a star-struck-by-proxy teenager.

Jill Doyle nodded. 'Yes, if possible. There's nothing I love more than having an author-signed copy; it makes it that little bit special. My go-to books are crime; you can't beat a good murder.' She graciously waved away the offering of a slice of lemon drizzle cake proffered by Brenda Mortinsen.

Bree was just about to shove the remainder of a scone in her mouth but hesitated instead. 'Mmm... Well you can say that again.' She conspiratorially tipped her head towards Pru. 'We've had our fair share here over the last few months, haven't we? Six to be exact, or seven if you count the "gentleman friend" that Fliss was with at the time!' She gave a saucy smirk as she emphasised his questionable relationship to Fliss.

Jill looked aghast. 'Nooo! You're winding me up! *Seven* murders? Not real ones, surely?'

Pru and Bree nodded in unison.

'Yes, real ones. We thought we were on to something, but it didn't pan out. It's all been a bit Agatha Christie and *Midsomer Murders* around here lately.' Pru was really enjoying the company of a fellow librarian, someone who loved books and mystery as much as she did. 'Talking of which, I'd love to stay at the Old Swan Hotel for the Theakston Crime Festival. You made it sound really interesting and fun.'

Bree wiped the crumbs from her chin with the back of her hand. 'What's so special about that?'

Pru jiggled on the spot with excitement, slopping tea down the front of her blouse. 'Agatha Christie, that's what. It's where she stayed when she went missing in the 1920s.'

'Now *there's* an idea for one of our trips. Hands up, ladies, who would be interested?' Kitty quite rudely interrupted. It was evident that when the spotlight had been taken from her, she felt the need to claw back the attention and decision-making by jostling in on their conversation.

Jill popped her eyes at Pru and grinned. 'Well, it's only a few months away. I would imagine the tickets for the main panels will have already sold out, but there's nothing to stop anyone from going and just enjoying the atmosphere.'

'I think there will be quite a few of us up for that, I'll get the dates and speak to Frank straight away, see if the coach is available. A little jaunt will do us all good. More tea, Jill?' Kitty held her pinkie finger out as she proffered the cup and saucer to Jill.

'I'd much prefer a bucket of Harvey's Bristol Cream, to be honest. I don't suppose there's a decent pub around here, is there?'

Lost for words, the cup teetering on the edge of the saucer, Kitty's lips pursed into what Pru thought resembled Mr Bink's arse end disappearing through his cat-flap into the garden. 'Well, there's the Dog & Gun, but I really don't think it's a suitable place for a lady on her own,' Kitty spluttered.

Pru quickly linked her arm through Jill's arm and grinned. 'She won't be on her own, Kitty.'

'And I ain't no lady!' laughed Jill.

AGATHA

*M*aisie lay in bed, pulling the sheets up to her chin. She wondered if she pulled them over her head whether she would just disappear momentarily, or, if she wished long and hard enough, could she disappear forever?

Forever is such a long time for a child.

Forever is an eternity.

It's a 'no going back' sort of word.

She really wished her forever could be a nice one, one that would make her feel happy and hopeful, not just as a means to escape.

Her curtain billowed slightly in the breeze that had found its way through the crack in the corner glass of her window. Although she did not feel particularly cold; her thin sheet and blanket having warded off some of the chill, she still involuntarily shivered. She could hear Mother moving around outside her bedroom door. The third and fifth floorboard creaking as her weight pressed heavily down on the aged oak before her feet shuffled on to the threadbare runner. And then a silence followed.

Maisie hated that moment of silence.

She watched the handle to her door, waiting for the latch to click and for the polished knob to turn.

She held her breath.

Nothing.

No sound. No movement. No click.

The third and fifth floorboard creaked again, the silence, the shuffling feet on the threadbare runner.

'Maisie Martha Magdalen...' *the voice howled, loud and chilling.*

Maisie leapt from her bed, pushing the small blanket chest away from the corner she dropped herself behind it and curled into the smallest ball she could make from her slight frame. She wanted to be smaller than the smallest bird, tinier than the tiniest mouse as the incessant pounding on the panelled door forced her to press her hands against her ears to shut out the terror.

'...You've been such a wicked, wicked girl!'

Phyllis woke with a start.

The persistent pounding from downstairs almost matched the pounding of her own heart. A slight sheen of perspiration coated her neck and chest, her breathing ragged, almost panic-struck.

Nightmares.

The pounding began again in earnest. She checked the bedside alarm clock and grabbed her dressing gown; still half asleep, she threaded her arms through the sleeves and tightly tied the belt around her waist before pushing her feet into her slippers.

'Okay, okay, I'm coming...'

Her feet hitting each stair independently stirred Captain from his slumber in his covered cage. No decipherable words, just a loud, high-pitched squawking that set her early morning nerves on edge. She reached her front door just as the letterbox rattled. Yanking the front door open in annoyance, she squinted as the sunlight pierced her eyes.

'Break my door down, why don't you?' she testily snapped at

Eric Potter who, surprised at her uncharacteristic outburst, took a step back away from her.

'Morning, Phyllis, I couldn't fit this one through the letterbox without crushing it.' He offered the A4 sized envelope to her.

She took it from him and tried to provide a smile of apology. 'Sorry, Eric, it's not like me to oversleep, I've had a busy few days. And by the way it's Dil... oh forget it, it doesn't matter.'

Eric nodded, choosing to take her advice and indeed 'forget it'. He had plenty more deliveries to make before he could put his feet up and enjoy a nice cup of tea, so wasting time talking to a woman that had given him the heebie-jeebies from the first day he'd met her had not been an option he'd entertained. He tipped his cap at a jaunty angle and set off along the path, whistling a pretty fair rendition of 'Jolene'.

Phyllis shut the door behind her and made her way into the morning room to unveil Captain and give him his breakfast. The envelope was carefully placed on the table, ready to read once she had brewed her morning cup of Yorkshire tea.

'I'm not fit to be company until I've had my cuppa, am I, Captain?' She rattled the lid of the kettle into place and put it to boil. Two pieces of wholemeal bread were inserted into the toaster before she laid a side plate and knife on the worktop. 'I see you are your usual chatty self!' She chuckled, watching her stupid bird bounce up and down the perch several times before half drowning himself in his pot of drinking water. 'Right, let's see what we've got here.'

Phyllis knew only too well what had arrived in the post. The franking stamp had given the game away as soon as she'd taken it from Eric. She carefully picked open the seal and slid out her treasure. 'Perfect, absolutely perfect.' She sighed, a slight smile gracing her usually pinched thin lips.

She held it up so that the sunlight shining through the bull's eye glass in the morning room window scattered a rainbow of colours across the paper. Ever since Kitty had announced that the trip to the Theakston Old Peculier Crime Festival had been a non-starter, on account of every available hotel, B&B and guest house being fully booked that week, and had duly offered an alternative, Phyllis had been busy making plans.

'This couldn't get any better, old boy,' she crowed, forcing a twinkle to her eyes. 'This is going to be such a spectacular and totally unforgettable finale.'

Kitty had suggested a midweek break prior to the hustle and bustle of Crimefest. There had been some good offers available, and several of the ladies had jumped at the chance of a few days in a nice hotel and a bit of sightseeing. Frank, after a little persuasion from Kitty, was providing the transport.

'Hmm... It doesn't take much to wonder what she's offered Frank, does it, Captain? I bet he'll be happily partaking of horizontal refreshments once the sun goes down.' Phyllis laughed as she carefully slipped the cellophane from the box of chocolates in front of her.

She hadn't taken Kitty up on her offer of a place on the coach and a room. No, she had politely declined due to 'other commitments', not that anyone would be bothered by her absence or even think to miss her. She dropped the booking confirmation which solemnly confirmed a single room at The Old Swan Hotel in Harrogate in the name of Ms M. M. Magdalen onto the table.

The idea of despatching her last remaining WI candidate, the rather lovely but still on the list Bryony Richards, at the same place Agatha Christie had chosen to disappear in 1926 under an alias, was her *pièce de résistance* and quite simply delicious...

...and as an added bonus it would be by someone who had for all intents and purposes been dead for some considerable time.

CARRY ON CARRYING ON...

'Bloody hell, Pru, what have you got in this?' Bree dragged the unicorn-coloured hard-shell suitcase across the pavement towards the side of the coach, making a meal out of the strength she needed to move it. Frank stood expectantly with the up-and-over door, revealing a cavernous depth to the luggage storage compartment.

'Oh you know, just a few clothes to see me through whatever the weather, and you can never have too many pairs of clean knick–' Pru's explanation was cut short as Frank grabbed the offending suitcase from Bree and heaved it with much gusto onto the ribbed flooring of the coach. The clink of bottles being inadvertently knocked together sounded from inside the pink and lilac valise, causing Bree to double up with a fit of the giggles.

'Mmm… you don't say! Would that be your collection of Droopy Drawers Dubonnet and Camiknickers Claret by any chance?' She draped her arm over Pru's shoulder. 'I'm almost sure they'll have a minibar in our room. After all, The Old Swan catered for Agatha Christie herself, and I'm sure she must have enjoyed a tipple or two!'

'Actually, she didn't drink or smoke!' Pru jumped the first two steps onto the coach, with Ethel following close behind her.

'Dearie me, I bet she was a bundle of laughs at cocktail parties.' Ethel hastily pushed between Pru and the first row of seats, eagerly making her way to sit next to Clarissa.

Kitty Hardcastle stood at the front counting heads, taking charge as she always did. Satisfied everyone was accounted for, she gave Frank a coquettish nod. 'Right, are we ready, ladies?' She paused to take in the show of hands from her motley group. It had only been the ones that were likely to cause her a headache over the next three days and two nights that had excitedly put their names forward when she had compiled her booking list for their little jaunt to Harrogate. Some had been disappointed to miss the book festival but were still eager to revel in a little literary history and, of course, visit the delightful local tea rooms.

'Come on, Kitty, get a move on; or I'll be sober before we even set off.' Chelsea hiccupped loudly from the back seat, her pre-journey visit to the Dog & Gun with Cassidy very much in evidence. 'At this rate, by the time we get there you'll be retired and Bree will be the new president!'

Kitty looked as though she had sucked on a lemon. Her lips pursed and her eyes narrowed as she held her hands firmly on her hips. 'And what makes you think Mrs Bryony Richards is going to be the next president?' Slightly flustered, she nodded to Bree. 'No offence of course, Bree, but we do have a voting system to follow.'

Bree shrugged her shoulders and held her hands up to show that she was not in the least perturbed. 'None taken, Kitty.'

A sudden, high-pitched squeal heralded a eureka moment from Cassidy Parks as she waved a half-eaten packet of cheese and onion crisps accusingly at Bree. 'Oh my God! Has nobody noticed? She's the only one left.' She jumped up, excitedly show-ering what remained of her crisps over poor Ethel, who was sitting directly in front of her. 'They're all dead, every single one of them, all of 'em... 'cept her!'

Pru heaved her suitcase onto the bed, unzipped it and delved deep between her favourite angora jumper and her pyjamas to retrieve the bottle of Merlot that had been wrapped in a pair of bed socks. 'Well, that was an uncomfortable few hours, wasn't it?' The two bottles of Shiraz that had given the game away earlier by clanking together loudly, followed.

'You can say that again. The way everyone looked at me, you'd have thought I was the murderer, doing away with the nominees just so I could jingle the bell, sniff the flowers and be the first to pick sultanas out of my teeth on cake night!' Bree flopped backwards onto the double bed. 'I thought Kitty had booked single rooms for us.'

'She did, but there were not enough available, and rather than allocate this room to Ethel and Clarissa because Ethel apparently snores like a trooper, she asked if we'd take it.' Pru produced two disposable cups and began to pour a good measure of the rich red into each one. 'You don't mind bunking up, do you? I don't talk in my sleep.'

'Do you nocturnal fart though?'

'Very funny. I've told you before, I'm a lady!' Pru tipped the plastic cup at Bree and took a sip. 'Cheers! Amazing feeling wasn't it, when we swivelled through those revolving doors at the entrance? We've actually just walked in the footsteps of Agatha Christie!'

'Suppose so. I know books and writers are your thing and I'd never knock it, but it just doesn't do it for me.' Bree took a gulp of wine, relishing the warm burn as it slid down her throat. 'Now, if you had asked me about the guy that was checking in at the same time as us... that's a different matter. He was rather lush.'

Pru smirked and shook her head. As much as she loved her friend and her company, if she were honest, she would much rather be sharing the mahogany bed with the Delectable Detective and his manly muscles and hairy chest than with Bree's noticeably furry legs.

'Come on, drink up. We've got some exploring to do before dinner.'

Bree inspected her cup. 'Mmm... do you really think the others are going to sit next to me happily at the dinner table now they think I'm a mass murderer?' she snapped. 'They'll probably choke on their crème brûlée!'

'It *is* a bit odd, though, isn't it? And having Cassidy holler it in her classy tones makes it all the more comical, really. It sounded like a scene from a *Carry On* film.' Pru sat thoughtfully for a few minutes before she spoke again.

'Murders aside, we're here to have a nice break, so our investigating can wait until we get back to Winterbottom.'

Pru had a few ideas up her sleeve, and one of them was to find what had happened to the sad little girl from Magdalen House and more about her untimely death. She still couldn't shake off the feeling they were missing something. No matter how many times they had tried to dismiss the notion there was a link, or accept they had finally hit a dead end, she was loath to give up. She watched Bree as she gazed out of the window, the late evening sun casting an orange glow around her. That was another worry now. As much as they had laughed at Cassidy's 'two plus two makes five' moment on the coach, the more the idea bounced around her brain, the more she was actually coming up with a big fat number four herself. Maybe Cassidy's presidential eureka moment hadn't been quite as absurd as they had first thought.

EVER DECREASING CIRCLES

*T*he train journey had been quite a pleasant one, giving Phyllis plenty of time to work through her plans as countryside, towns and industrial estates rushed by her carriage window. So far, she had thought of at least two different modes of despatch for Bryony Richards, one of which was safely ensconced in her tapestry bag. She gave it an affectionate pat. They were both quite imaginative and fun methods of murder, even if she did say so herself. All that was left to do was to confirm that they were possible, given the surroundings and the layout of The Old Swan. Kitty and her crew would have already enjoyed their first night at the hotel, but by choosing to remain behind and arrive a day later she hoped to avoid recognition. She was also pretty confident that not one of them would have missed the old WI stalwart Phyllis Watson.

As always, overlooked, forgotten, ignored – and most definitely underestimated!

The taxi she had commandeered at Harrogate train station wasn't the most comfortable; the well-worn leather seat in the rear was particularly lumpy in parts, and she was quite convinced the windows hadn't seen even the lightest of feather touches from a cleaning cloth in a decade. There were also the mixed aromas of man sweat and a faint whiff of cigar smoke from her driver. Still, it was a short journey to the hotel, and she had suffered for her art on many occasions, so this would be no different.

The tyres hit a large pothole, making her leave the seat by several inches; she narrowly avoided hitting her head on the padded roof. Phyllis grabbed at the peacock-blue tapestry bag that had teetered on the edge, almost spilling its contents into the footwell. 'Good grief, my dear man, can you not be a little more considerate?' she barked. As discreetly as she could, she wriggled the index finger of her right hand under the fibrous band of her copper-coloured wig, just behind her ear. The firm pressure of her nail hit the spot as she gave her scalp a vigorous scratch. She was rather pleased with her appearance. Gone was the drab, predictable, old-before-her-time Phyllis, and in her place was the rather glamorous and totally wicked woman she had always longed to be.

She caught sight of the driver, his eyes watching her from his rear-view mirror. She rather liked the feeling of being noticed. Fluttering her lashes, heavily laden with mascara, she secretly hoped the Revlon gold eyeshadow would, at the very least, catch the weak sun to glitter and sparkle. Rummaging around in her bag, she pulled out the mother-of-pearl embossed compact and flipped open the lid, taking the time to admire what she had become before applying a liberal slick of Passionate Plum matte lipstick, paying particular attention to her cupid's bow.

'Here you are, Miss, The Old Swan Hotel.' The driver leant forward to check the digital meter on the dashboard. 'That'll be £3.50.'

Phyllis tilted her head to get her first look at the imposing façade of the Grade II listed building that hosted a multitude of white framed windows against the gritstone rubble bricks. She clicked the metal clasp on her purple silk money bag and counted out three one-pound coins. Hooking her forefinger into the corner of the lining she teased out a solitary fifty pence piece.

She was far too enamoured with the building to notice the expression of disgust on her driver's face as he glared at the exact amount of money she had placed in the palm of his hand. It wouldn't take a genius to work out that Phyllis would now be lugging her own suitcase from the boot to the doors of the hotel.

As the wheels of the taxi found purchase on the tarmac, sending small stones bouncing across the car park, Phyllis stood in sombre reverence, totally oblivious to the middle finger farewell the driver gave her through his open window as he sped off. Shivering with pent up excitement, she watched the entrance portico as fellow guests came and went, pausing only to navigate the three steps into the foyer.

'My oh my, how absolutely delicious...' she murmured to herself.

Her heart beat just that little bit faster as her hand pressed against the polished wood of the stunning revolving doors, the gleaming brass plates on the lower sections projecting a welcoming warmth, a feel and sense of bygone days. She stepped back, her fingers gripping the edge of one section of the wood. She pushed hard, allowing the door to revolve, the slight swish of rubber draught trim catching, the woosh of air expelling as the sun hit the brass providing a kaleidoscope effect.

'This is just perfect!'

In that instant, Phyllis knew the final curtain to her tableau of revenge would take place in this exact spot. It would be so very fitting, so very satisfying, and so very Isadora Duncan – but without the fancy open-top car, of course.

LOST PROPERTY

The commotion that filled the first-floor corridor of the Old Swan heralded the arrival of an extremely irate and flustered Ethel, closely followed by a very exasperated Clarissa. The leaves on the large aspidistra plant fluttered as she swept past, her pink candlewick dressing gown producing a draught of epic proportions.

'I left them in the gla*sh* on the bed*sh*ide cabinet!' Ethel wailed whilst giving a show of jazz hands.

Clarissa desperately tried to console her friend whilst proffering apologetic nods to the guests who had ventured from their rooms to see what the fuss was about so early in the morning. 'Ethel, for goodness' sake calm down; they can't have gone far. Maybe someone from housekeeping has taken them. Have you checked your room properly?' She placed a comforting arm around Ethel.

'Of cour*sh* I have, they're not there! I'm telling you they were in the gla*sh* and now they're not.' Ethel's pink, shiny gums crashed together. 'I can't go down to breakfa*sh*t without them, I'll be redu*sh*ed to *ssch*lurping the *sh*crambled egg and *sh*ucking the *sh*au*sh*ages!'

Clarissa wanted to laugh at her choice of words to describe her angst, but she didn't dare for fear she would elicit a further gnashing of gums and loud wailing. 'Dearie me, that will never do, will it, sucking on a sausage at your age!' Eyes twinkling and a knowing grin she looked just like an impish child. 'We'll find them, don't you worry. You pop back to your room; just leave it to me, I'll sort it.' Ushering Ethel back down the corridor towards Room 10, Clarissa felt a little peeved that her quip had been wasted on her friend's current lack of humour.

Happy that Ethel was contained and unable to cause further disruption, Clarissa almost leapt the stairs down to reception. She had a feeling Ethel's false gnashers were probably still marinating in water next to the industrial dishwasher in the kitchens; at least she hoped they were. She dreaded the prospect of them not being found. Without them, Ethel's emotional fall out and her mithering would ruin the rest of their stay.

Twenty minutes later, Clarissa and the efficient and cheery young girl on reception were still trying to source Ethel's errant dentures. The only ivory the kitchen had yielded was a set of 1920s fish knives. They were now reduced to delving the depths of the hotel's lost property box which, surprisingly enough, held several sets of unclaimed dentures. Clarissa could only wonder as to what type of guest would arrive with teeth but happily depart without them. Almost to the point of being beyond caring anymore, she animatedly pointed to a set that looked the part.

'There, that's them!' She gave the receptionist a look of gratitude.

'These? Are you sure?'

'Yes, yes definitely. They'll do!'

Clarissa had high hopes for the set she had chosen, they looked fairly straight and, if memory served her right, not dissimilar to the ones that Ethel normally sported. Wrapping them in a serviette, she popped them into her handbag.

'She doesn't smile much anyway...'

~

'How do I look?' Bree gave Pru a twirl, the curls of her vibrant red hair bounced over her shoulders with the momentum.

'Beautiful! I can't believe you've gone to so much trouble just to have dinner with me and the ladies!' Pru's tongue-in-cheek retort elicited just the right response.

'Well, you never know who you might bump in to, do you?' Bree double-checked her lipstick in the mirror and swept her finger under her eye to even out the teal eyeliner.

Pru clicked the clasp on her bracelet. 'Now that wouldn't be Mr Alex Delaney in Room 108, would it by any chance?' She had cleverly managed to find that much about him during a brief conversation with a fellow book aficionado on their afternoon stroll in the grounds. He was apparently part of a crime guild group who each year undertook a pilgrimage to places that had a specific author connection. This year it was Agatha Christie, and the delicious Mr Delaney was part of that group.

Bree stood open mouthed. 'Oh, wow, how did you find that out?'

Pru laughed. 'I have my ways.' She checked her watch and held the door open. 'Come on, we're running late. The last thing we need is to end up sitting next to Chelsea and Cassidy for a three courser!'

As Bree danced along the corridor, a cream and gold chiffon ribbon scarf floated behind her, the delicate fabric gaily wrapped around her neck and thrown over her shoulder.

Pru caught up with her. 'This is absolutely gorgeous.' She reverently caressed the material between her fingers. 'Where did you get it from?'

Bree stopped in her tracks, a frown gracing her forehead. 'Mmm… now you mention it, I can't remember. In fact, I don't even recall packing it, but it was draped on the coat hanger with this top, so it must be one of mine.'

Linking her arm through that of her friend, Pru smirked. 'It comes to something when your wardrobe is that extensive you can't remember what you've got. Jeez, I'm wearing a pair of shoes I bought almost twenty years ago!'

Bree looked down to check out the offending footwear. 'Christ, Pru, did you inherit them from your nan?' she quipped before skimming each carpeted stair with her own fake Manolo Blahniks.

Giggling in unison, both were oblivious to the woman with the copper-coloured hair and glittery gold eyeshadow clutching an empty but fancy Morgan Clare Accessories bag, who watched their every move, hidden from sight by the same aspidistra that Ethel had exuberantly fanned that very morning.

THE BUTTERFLY

The ladies of Winterbottom WI sat together on one long table for their much anticipated last night dinner in the magnificent Wedgwood Restaurant at The Old Swan. The stunning glass ceiling and elegant Victorian proportions were a sight to behold. Behind them, the ornately carved half-panelled oak walls gave an impression of richness, alongside the brilliant white columns topped with light fixtures that Pru thought resembled gold crowns.

Much to their relief, Chelsea and Cassidy had been budged along to the far end of the table, and Clarissa and Ethel had become their immediate table partners. Pru had a soft spot for both ladies, for completely different reasons. Clarissa was a feisty woman with a very dry sense of humour, some would say bordering on sarcastic wit. She had eagerly taken Ethel under her wing since Betty's sudden and shocking demise. Although Ethel could lead poor Albert a merry dance as his wife, when it came to friendships, she actually needed someone to temper her moods and tame her incessant gossiping, and that was where Clarissa came into her own. Ethel was, well – she was just Ethel. Comical without knowing it, sharp of tongue, her cupid bow lips pursed together as her beaming cheeks preceded an outburst. There had been many times she had brought a WI meeting to a standstill with her flair for a hilarious riposte, or a juicy bit of gossip, much to Kitty's disdain.

Ethel, aware that Pru was looking at her, paused mid-slurp, the spoon containing the pea soup starter hovering by her chin. She grinned, showing a huge set of ill-fitting, yellowed dentures that a village vicar would have been proud to possess.

Pru almost choked on the chunk of pâté and melba toast she had just shovelled into her mouth. She gave Bree a dig in the ribs.

'It'*sh pheeeeep* really ni*sh*e *sh*oup i*sh*n't it?' Ethel gurned, spraying dots of the pale green liquid across the white tablecloth.

Unable to contain herself, Bree squealed. 'Bloody hell, Ethel, where on earth did you get those gnashers from? A joke shop?'

Pru caught Clarissa waving frantically behind Ethel's head, her eyes popped and her mouth silently mouthing 'Nooo'.

'Mmm… now I come to think of *pheeep* it, they do feel a little *sh*trange *pheeep*–' Ethel wedged her thumb under the top set and pulled. '–it'*sh* like they're *sh*omeone el*sh*es.'

Bree used her serviette to wipe the front of her blouse where Ethel had pebble-dashed the delicate cream material when she had uttered the word 'someone'. 'Er… no shit, Sherlock, you can say that again!'

Ethel opened her mouth to repeat as requested, much to Bree's horror.

'Actually, no… on second thoughts, don't.'

Ms M. Magdalen dined alone. Her table for two, that had been transformed into a table for one, sat tucked away behind one of the ornate pillars, a sheer white drape that cascaded from it, affording her further cover between herself and the Winter-bottom Women's Institute table.

She had almost laughed out loud at the fiasco with Ethel Tytherington and her teeth, but had quickly reined herself in lest she reveal her true self to the gathered ladies. She loved that she could be so close and yet remain unrecognised. Not ignored or overlooked this time, just simply unrecognised. She admired her carefully manicured nails painted in a vibrant shade of red as her fingers clutched the crystal wine goblet, the crisp white Pinot Grigio radiating a pleasant chill to the glass.

It was like watching a slow, silent movie of yesteryear, the gentle hum of conversation, the clattering of cutlery on white china plates all muted as she delved into herself.

The real Maisie Martha Magdalen.

Not the child.

But the woman.

She had been hidden for so long she was unsure if she could actually be anything other than dismal, drab Dilys Watson, or Phyllis to her so-called friends.

Just when the caterpillar thought the world was over, it became a butterfly.

Was that what she was becoming, a butterfly?

She spread a little more butter on her Melba toast, her head cocked to one side as she daintily chewed.

Maybe it was something less elegant, like a moth, transfixed and drawn to the light. Attracted to the contrasts in her life. The darkness that became so overwhelming it forced her up towards the light.

A knowing.

An awakening.

And suddenly she knew.

This wasn't about loneliness or jealousy. It wasn't about a presidency that in truth now cared extraordinarily little about. Her victims had all been collateral damage. Wrong place, wrong time. An excuse.

This was all about her.

She had not been born evil.

She had been nurtured evil.

THE BUCKET LIST

*T*he hum of idle chatter, mixed in with the tapping of fingers across keyboards, filled the incident room. Two telephones rang simultaneously from opposite ends of the office and were quickly answered.

'Hello DS Barnes.' Andy held the earpiece close to him, listening intently. Lucy sitting opposite him looked up and waited to see if there was any reaction from him that would be worth taking an interest in. 'Yep.' His face gave nothing away. 'Nope, same as before, nothing further… and no you can't quote me on that. Just put "Detectives are continuing to appeal for any information".' He puffed out his cheeks and blew upwards, his normally perfectly gelled fringe succumbed and flopped to one side. 'Peter, just do as I ask and keep it simple, if we get any breakthroughs, you'll be the first to know, okay?'

Lucy could tell he was starting to lose his patience with Peter Bryant from the local rag. Peter was handy to have on your side, but frequently needed to be reined in if he started getting ahead of himself, particularly if he thought he was on to a good story. What he didn't know or what wasn't offered to him by their office, he would just invent himself to grab a headline.

Andy dropped the phone back into the slot. 'Bloody press.' He took a slurp of his coffee and grimaced. 'It's cold; you couldn't get us another brew, could you, Tim?' He proffered the chipped mug to Tim Forshaw.

Lucy flipped her file closed, the most recent update to the 'Ladykiller' case had yielded nothing more than a Crimestoppers call that offered assistance from a psychic medium called Valentia Valentine. Ms Valentine had apparently been contacted from the other side by the first victim, Mabel Allinson. Even though she knew it was a wasted line of enquiry, she had still followed it up, just in case. It had been an eye-opener, to say the least, watching Ms Valentine commune with the dead, especially when a random great aunt Sybil had come through to provide the winning lottery numbers for the following week. Lucy had found herself furtively scribbling them down in her book under the guise of taking notes, just on the off-chance an afterlife really did exist. When Valentia couldn't offer the smallest shred of information that even remotely matched the first murder, Lucy knew she had to draw a line somewhere. She had returned to Winterbottom nick minus two hours of her life that she would never get back and a hastily purchased lottery ticket from the corner shop.

'How well do you know Pru, Luce?' Andy's blue eyes twinkled when he mentioned Pru's name.

'A bit, I'm more Bree's friend originally, but I've got to know Pru quite well over the last few months. We've shared a few bottles of gin and had some good girly nights out. Why?'

'I've got some leave coming up and thought it might be nice to take her away. I'm thinking a quaint hotel, you know, four-poster bed, nice romantic walks. That type of thing. What d'you think?' Andy looked at her eagerly.

Lucy thought he reminded her of a puppy, all pleading eyes and keen expectations. 'You're missing her, aren't you?' She grinned.

'Is it that obvious?'

She was certain there was a flush of embarrassment touching his cheeks, which actually made him appear quite cute, for a colleague. Heaven forbid she would ever get involved with anyone from work, though. 'Definitely! I think it would be a lovely idea. Maybe you could pick up a few staycation brochures from Hay's Travel in town. Then you could look through them together, choose a nice hotel.'

Tim angled himself between Andy and the stacked storage files to place a steaming hot cup of coffee on the UK Cop Humour coaster that took pride of place next to the new black stapler which bore Andy's collar number of 8462. 'Oooh holidays! My favourite time of the year. Me and Emily love looking at holidays on the internet. We've actually made a bucket list of all the places we want to go to before we die.'

Andy looked at the child-like features of Tim and wished he had as much time left as his young protégé did. 'Bloody hell, matey, you haven't even nurtured a bit of stubble yet; you've got years left!' He blew on the coffee, trying to cool it.

Lucy looked on amused as she watched Tim vigorously rub his chin in the vain hope the friction would elicit a few sprigs of bristle. Trying to pass over Andy's sarky comment, she gently smiled at him. 'So what's on your bucket list, Tim?'

Tim brought himself up to full height, a look of sheer pleasure on his face. 'Ah the Maldives is top of our list; you know those bungalows they have in the sea? Then Florida. Emily is really big into anything Disney, and definitely Canada to see, er...' he paused, deep in thought, 'er... the water place, what's it called? Oh yep, Viagra Falls.'

Andy spluttered loudly, spraying spots of coffee over his paperwork. 'It's Niagara Falls, son, unless you really do want to be up all night!' He guffawed.

'Sarge!' Lucy tried her best to look mortified, but she didn't have to worry; it had gone right over Tim's head. She watched him happily amble back to his own desk. 'You are totally and completely incorrigible, Andy!'

'Mmm... that's easy for you to say.' He laughed. 'Right, back to work, I've got a possible lead here, fancy coming with me?'

She nodded. Grabbing her briefcase she stuffed her notepad and a pack of spearmint chewing gum inside. 'Sarge, if I had a sort of an idea that might be worth following up, would you go for it, even if it was a bit pie in the sky at the moment?' Now it was time for her own cheeks to flush. She'd been trying to find the appropriate moment to mention the possible Magdalen link without looking stupid. It was early days in this team, and in her potential future career as a detective was gut instinct worth bringing to the table? She couldn't be sure.

THE MERRY-GO-ROUND

'*I*t was a fruit cobbledegook and it was deeeeelicious!' Bree hiccuped, rather the worse for wear after several wines, the dregs of Ethel's glass, and a nightcap of two gin and tonics.

Pru held her friend up in a desperate attempt to stop her from falling into a nearby flower bed. Her idea of taking Bree for a little stroll in the fresh air to vaporise some of the alcohol hadn't been her best plan to date. 'Upsy-daisy!' She steered her clear of one of the edging posts but failed to see the link chain between it and the next post along. Before she could react, Bree's legs swung skywards as she toppled over backwards, landing with a loud thump on the grass.

'Marks out of ten, judges?' Bree squealed with laughter, throwing her arms in the air in triumph. 'I think that dive was well worth a nine at least!'

Pru bent down to help her up, laughing just as much and to the point of not being able to breathe. 'Oh for feck's sake, what am I going to do with you, you bloody dork! Come on, give me your hand.' She tried to pull, but without assistance from Bree herself she was on a hiding to nothing. She flopped down next to her and lay back to admire the moon that was just starting to shine more brightly as dusk descended.

'Excuse me, can I help?'

Bree looked up into the eyes of the Delicious Mr Delaney, who was now showing an amused concern for her and Pru. Embarrassed, she brushed away the lock of flame-red hair that had fallen across her face. Tucking it behind her ear, she stretched out her hand to him.

Alex Delaney didn't know if he should grab it and haul her up or kiss it. 'Had an enjoyable evening, have we, ladies?' He smiled.

'Er... just a bit.' Pru scrambled to her feet and stood back, allowing him to 'rescue' Bree, who for once was actually stuck for words. 'We're just going back to our room now, thank you.' Desperate to give Bree time to compose herself, she grabbed her arm and pulled her towards the entrance of The Old Swan.

Bree hiccupped again and added an unfortunately loud burp to the mix. 'Ooops.' She quickly covered her mouth with her fingers. 'I might see you at breakfast, Mr Delicious, if you're free.' She tottered ahead, gaily, spinning around, her chiffon scarf floating in the breeze as she passed Ethel and Clarissa who were deep in animated conversation.

'You lied to me, Clari*sh*a; you told me the*esh* were my teef and they're not!' Ethel's peeved voice went up a notch.

'I was just trying my best for you; how would you have felt without teeth for three days? At least you could eat, and you wouldn't have noticed if *she* hadn't said anything!' Clarissa flung an accusing finger towards Bree, who, totally oblivious, was still skipping ahead towards the hotel entrance. 'Anyway, they think they've found yours now, so you can give them that set back.'

'That'*sh* not the point. I've had *sh*omeone el*she*s bodily part in me mouth. I can't tell you how di*sh*gusting that i*sh*!' Ethel spat.

'Oh come on, it's not the first time you've had something in your mouth that didn't belong to you, Ethel. You've had more than your fair share of–'

'Ladies, *please!*' Kitty appeared from nowhere to admonish her charges.

Looking on, Pru let out a deep sigh, their chatter fading as they too made their way back to the hotel. She turned to Alex. 'I'm so sorry and thank you again. We've all had a trying couple of months in our ladies group; these last few days have allowed us to relax and have a bit of fun – as you can see!'

Alex smiled and tipped his head. 'Absolutely nothing to apologise for; it's rather nice to see people enjoying themselves. I hope to catch you both in the morning.'

'I'm sure my friend would like that,' Pru offered. 'I must dash; I don't think she'll make the staircase without me!'

Phyllis sat in the hotel's lobby, happily ensconced in a rather fancy and extremely comfortable high-backed wing chair, watching the revolving doors. With each grand sweep they turned, only to pause momentarily as they spat out a guest or visitor. The rich wood reception desk was directly opposite her and was fortunately vacant. The young girl, ever so smart in her two-piece suit, had only moments ago gathered up her paperwork, sidestepped out from behind the desk, and bustled along the corridor that was cornered by the ticking grandfather clock.

A quietness had fallen over the hotel; Phyllis was alone. She checked her watch and quickly made her way outside, secreting herself to the left of the doors just inside the foyer. She hoped the cover of the large planters and hanging baskets would be enough, and as everyone pushed to the right of the revolving doors, the odds of them looking left and spotting her would be minimal.

Her heart beat that little bit faster as Bree appeared on the steps.

Alone.

The little gift that she had left for her was still draped around her neck, just as she had planned. She waited.

Bree staggered slightly as she approached the doors, her hand pressing on the edge of the wood. Pushing hard she entered the chamber; the swish gave a brief hiatus as she drunkenly kicked the bottom plate and giggled.

This was the chance that Phyllis needed.

Quick as a flash she grabbed at the floating end of the scarf and pulled it tight as she slipped herself into the next chamber behind Bree, whilst at the same time pushing on the panel ahead of her. She saw Bree's head jerk backwards as her scarf caught between the door frame and the revolving capsule. She kept pushing until Bree's chamber had bypassed the reception hall and had come to a stop on the next quarter turn, her scarf still firmly caught. Through the separate squares of glass, Phyllis could see Bree's terror and panic as she gripped her neck, desperately trying to claw the scarf away.

Phyllis wrapped the delicate material around her hand keeping it taut, her foot wedged against the back plate to stop the doors from moving. She checked behind her in the reception hall; she was still alone, there would be no witnesses. It would be the perfect murder, *'Just an unfortunate accident,'* they would say. *'How terribly sad.'* She smiled as she pulled tighter. Once the deed was done, she was in a prime position to just quietly slip away up the staircase ahead of her, unnoticed.

Just a little bit longer, my dear, and it will all be over, she thought to herself as she started to sing.

Here comes a candle to light you to bed,
And here comes a chopper to chop off your head!

THE FINAL PIECE

*T*iny lights sparked and danced before Bree's eyes as she desperately tried to hook her fingers between the scarf and the skin on her neck. Using her left hand in a fist, she pounded the side of her hand against the wood of the revolving door, more involuntary than by design. She felt her tongue swelling in her mouth, her chest contracting savagely, almost exploding.

She waited for her life to flash before her. She waited for the release that would be death itself. She wanted to cry for her son, Nathan, her mum, for her friend Pru. There was so much more left to do, so much left unsaid...

'Oh for goodness' sake, Ethel, it's a set of bloody dentures, not the Crown Jewels. We can get them in the morning.' Clarissa waddled after Ethel who was on a mission, a set of yellowing teeth fixed on a pink palate in one hand and her handbag in the other.

Ethel pushed forcefully on the revolving door. It stuck fast.

'Even the bloody doors are against me!' Ethel barked. 'Oh look, there's Bree on the other side. Dearie me she *is* the worse for wear, isn't she? She's on a starboard tilt!' She laughed and waved to Bree before shoving her full weight behind the wood frame. It gave slightly, which only served to infuriate her more. She heaved her ample bosom in front of her and gave a shoulder barge that a SWAT team member on a drugs bust would have been proud of.

The door popped, hissed, and Ethel went flying forward. Simultaneously, Bree was thrown out onto the front steps on the next revolution, with Phyllis, copper wig awry, following her a split second later, the force spilling her out from her section of the door too.

And then all hell broke loose.

Bree's lifeless body lay slumped on the steps, her scarf still taut against her neck, draped out beside her. A scream filled the night air as Phyllis staggered down the steps and disappeared into the gardens.

'Somebody please help, oh my God–' Clarissa bent down to touch Bree's face. She was quickly joined by Pru and Alex.

'It's the scarf.' Pru began to loosen the fabric around Bree's neck, her fingers trembling, a sick feeling pushing up and making her heart beat faster. 'She's not breathing!' She could feel Alex right beside her, his fingers testing for a pulse on Bree's wrist. She was aware that someone was calling for an ambulance as hot tears stung her cheeks. 'Come on, Bree, please, please–'

And then she heard the sweetest sound ever. A low gurgle escaped from Bree's lips. There was a brief pause before her chest rose, taking in huge gulps of air that forced her to cough and retch simultaneously. A blanket brought out by someone, Pru didn't know who, was draped over her friend as she held her head gently in her lap. Blue lights lit up the canopies of the trees and bounced from the white pillars of the portico entrance announcing their much needed assistance.

'It's okay, I'm here, you're going to be okay...' she recited over and over like a mantra, one that if she believed in, it would be so.

SUSPICIOUS ACTIVITY

*P*ru lay in Andy's arms, staring at the ceiling of her bedroom, her eyes tracing the shadows cast by the dimmed glow of the bedside lamp. His body heat was comforting, as was the rhythmic rise and fall of his chest. She eventually broke the silence.

'It wasn't an accident.'

He propped himself up on his elbow, the knuckles of his fist pressed into his cheek. 'Pru, we've been through this a dozen times since you got back. There is nothing to suggest otherwise at this stage.' He traced a finger across her shoulder. 'Bree's scarf got caught in the revolving doors; she'd been drinking and panicked, and that exacerbated the situation. The more she struggled, the tighter it got.'

'What about the mystery woman then?'

'What mystery woman?'

'The one I saw running off when Bree was lying on the steps, that one.'

Andy sighed. 'Just another guest using the revolving doors who wasn't aware of what was happening, no more than Ethel did. Blimey, Ethel even waved to poor Bree. Thank goodness the old bat put some welly into that shoulder barge, or it could have been a different story. Bree's got Ethel to thank for saving her life.'

She knew he was talking sense, but something wasn't right. She had only caught a fleeting glimpse of the woman with the coppery hair and vibrant choice of dress, but there had been something vaguely familiar about her. 'Don't you think it's more than a coincidence that on the way to Harrogate Cassidy points out the link between the ladies who have been murdered and the WI presidency candidates, and then jokes that Bree is the last man standing – and then *this* happens?'

Andy had to admit it had set his spider senses tingling a bit, but his colleagues in North Yorkshire had assured him that so far their investigation and the ensuing Health and Safety input hadn't flagged anything more unusual than an unavoidable accident.

'It should really be the last *woman* standing, but I do think you're reading more into this than there really is on this occasion, although we are already looking at the WI link.' Andy brushed her hair away from her face and kissed her gently on the cheek. 'Are you seeing Bree tomorrow?'

Pru nodded. 'Yes, I've got some flowers from the WI members to take to her and some cake. They're doing a "bake sale" this week to raise funds for the local animal rescue, so Brenda has thrown a scone or two in before she starts touting them around the village in the evenings, trying to catch people in.'

Andy made a mental note not to open his front door after 6pm. He'd seen Brenda Mortinsen in full flow after the murder of Mabel Allinson. Unnecessary gossip over a dollop of spotted dick didn't fill him with glee.

Pru continued chattering away. 'Oh, and then I've got to pop to see... er... you know, the one that normally opens up the hall, Glynis... Willis... or is it Phyllis...? Watson. Kitty's asked me to deliver the new itinerary to her; some of the days out have been changed. I think everyone has lost the zest for hopping on one of Frank's buses for a jaunt.'

She dropped back into silence again, contemplating how close she had come to losing one of the most important people in her life: her best friend.

DREAMS

*M*aisie, Maisie, pretty as a daisy...
            She danced and skipped in the ray of sunlight that
shone through the mosaic glass of the library window, marvelling at the
dust motes as they drifted up and joined her. Holding tight to the hem of
her opal fruit dress, she paused to curtsey at the large sepia-toned
photograph that hung over the fireplace.

Daddy!

She stood and gazed into his eyes; her heart filled with sadness. It
was a real ache that hurt lots, a bit like when you stubbed your toe on
the end of the bed. She missed him so much, no cuddles on his knee, no
stories at bedtime, no laughter.

There hadn't been any laughter at Magdalen House for such a long
time. Mummy didn't believe in having fun.

'It's a wasted energy, my girl, you'll soon learn!' she had screamed in
Maisie's face, when she had caught her having an imaginary tea party
with Holly Hobbie. The smile on Maisie's face was quickly washed away
by the angry spittle that flecked her cheeks as her mother continued to
rage at her.

'Why did you leave me, Daddy?'

She waited, eagerly watching his portrait, hoping that by some touch of magic he would reply. Her sense of abandonment was still raw. She couldn't understand why he would go without even saying goodbye. She could understand him not wanting to be with Mummy anymore, but not without her, his pretty daisy.

How Mummy had laughed the day he left. She had danced from room to room, spinning in circles with her head thrown back as she cackled and hollered loudly, the garden spade she was using as a dancing partner showering the gold and red brocade of the sofa with lumps of soil. It had frightened Maisie; she had clung to the spindles on the staircase watching her, her little fingers turning white at the knuckles the harder she squeezed.

Round and round she goes,
When will she stop?
Nobody knows.

～

Phyllis woke with a start. Her foot jerked out involuntarily and kicked the fireside companion that sat in the hearth next to her armchair. Before she could rescue it, the brush, shovel and poker parted company with the stand and fell with a resounding clatter.

'Bugger me!' Captain squawked loudly as a swirl of white feathers drifted up and then lazily swung to the bottom of his cage.

Phyllis looked at him in amazement, totally lost for words herself. Twenty years she'd had that bird, and never once had it uttered one bloody word.

'Well hark at you; you wait all this time and suddenly you're swearing like a navvy!' Phyllis laughed as she pushed a peanut through the bars. 'I wonder who you picked that cuss up from, that's what I'd like to know!'

She checked her watch. 'Time for Mummy to have a nice cup of tea and then I've got a little bit of writing to do.' She laid out her 'Minutes to a Murder' book on the table and straightened the pen next to it. 'A murderer's work is never done, is it, Captain?'

She had never expected a reply from the bird, but it didn't stop her from sharing all her woes, adventures and ideas with him. In some ways she was glad of that; at least he couldn't contradict her or tell her what to do.

She was definitely her own mistress.

Leaving Captain to enjoy his peanuts, she nipped into the kitchen to pop the kettle on. Rubbing at the corners of her eyes, she yawned. She hadn't slept well at all since her failed attempt on Bree at The Old Swan. She couldn't believe how it had gone so terribly wrong. She shuddered, remembering the panic when one of the police officers had knocked on the door of her hotel room wanting to interview her. The vibrant wig and clothes had been a huge mistake. Far too easily remembered. The train journey home had been spent planning another attempt, and this time she wouldn't fail.

The cup and saucer rattled on the tray as she ambled back into the morning room. 'Right, where were we?' She took a bite from a digestive biscuit. 'Ah yes, the last moments of Bryony Richards and my escape pla–'

Phyllis's one-sided conversation with Captain was interrupted by the sound of the long harsh ring of her doorbell.

'Oooh! Mummy has a visitor.' She snatched her little book from the table and quickly pushed it into the pocket of her pinny. 'Back in a minute.'

BLACKTHORN COTTAGE

*P*ru stood on the doorstep of Phyllis Watson's neat Victorian cottage, Kitty's new itinerary carefully secured in a plastic ziplock file under her arm. She admired the balance of the architecture on the building. Door in the middle and four windows; two at the top, two at the bottom, a grey slate roof and a chimney at each end gable. She liked balance, which was why her shelves at the library were so neat and ordered.

It was funny how she knew of Phyllis but didn't really know her. She was a bit of an enigma, really. Everyone at the WI could relate a Phyllis story, mundane though they were, but could not offer anything about her private life, her home or her family. She thought that quite sad: to be so invisible that nobody cared. Then again, maybe that was what Phyllis wanted. Pru was still uneasy in her company; she always had the feeling that she wasn't actually a very nice person, and her reaction when Rita had her near miss with the Portaloo still didn't sit right with her.

Pru's finger hovered over the original Foley bell press on the wood frame. She wondered if she could do an adult version of knock and run. Ring the doorbell and just shove the file through the letterbox before legging it down the path and out onto the high street, but a sudden image of Kitty berating her in a high-pitched voice made her shudder.

Mmm... maybe not...

She pressed and waited.

It took Phyllis a matter of seconds before she opened the door to greet her.

'Prunella! What can I do for you?' Phyllis simpered.

Pru, wide-eyed, fought to find her voice. It eventually squeaked out, making her sound like she'd been rabidly inhaling helium. 'Oh, er... Kitty asked me to drop this off for you.' She meant to offer the file to Phyllis politely but found herself shoving it at her as though it were a hot potato she had to pass quickly.

Phyllis ignored Pru's agitation, holding the front door open a little wider. 'I was just having a cup of tea. Please join me; it would be nice to have some company and you can tell me all about your trip to Harrogate.' She smiled. 'I was so disappointed to miss it, other commitments and all that.'

This was the last thing Pru wanted to do, but she knew it would be rude to refuse and besides, her brain just wasn't working quickly enough to think of an excuse. Any lie that left her lips now would sound very obvious. 'Oh thank you, that's very kind. Maybe just a quick one. I've got to er... call in at the library soon, er... ah yes, there are a few limited-edition hard-backs being delivered today.' She gave a hopeful smile, one that said, *You do believe me, don't you?*

Phyllis reciprocated with a wry smile of her own. She stepped back to allow Pru into the hallway. 'Down there, just to the right.' She didn't trust this woman in the slightest; there was a little imaginary bell that jangled every time she saw her, and she had a feeling that Pru felt exactly the same about her.

That was what made her ever so dangerous to Phyllis's ultimate plan.

Pru made her way to the morning room. Phyllis followed,

indicating for her to take a seat. She chose the armchair that didn't have an indent in the cushion, preferring to leave the well-used one for Phyllis. As Phyllis rattled cups and saucers in the adjoining kitchen, she took the chance to look around the cosy room. Nothing out of the ordinary, a small bookshelf with some of the classics: *Oliver Twist*, *Great Expectations*, *Hard Times*, *To Kill a Mockingbird*, *Tom Sawyer*, to name a few. She was surprised to see Phyllis was a connoisseur of Dickens. A few old-fashioned ornaments adorned the sideboard and next to that was a fancy bird cage. The occupant, a large white parrot, eyed her suspiciously. Next to the cage was a small mahogany chair with a cane webbing back. Perched on a small cushion, slightly tilted to one side, was a doll.

A Holly Hobbie doll...

Pru's heart dipped slightly in her chest, which in turn made her stomach flip. What were the chances of seeing a Holly Hobbie doll twice in a matter of weeks? She scanned the room again, looking for anything that was out of place, anything that would either fuel the tinge of suspicion she was feeling or, better still, quell it.

'Here we go.' Phyllis placed the cup and saucer down on the small side table next to her. 'Would you like a piece of cake?'

Regardless of how deliciously moist the cake looked, Pru had a feeling that it would without doubt choke her at this very minute. Her mouth was so dry her tongue was sticking to its roof as her throat constricted. She was frozen to the spot and so was Phyllis.

Mid-bend with a floral plate topped with a slab of chocolate sponge in her hand, Phyllis cocked her head to one side and studied Pru. She followed Pru's gaze to the chair that held her beloved doll. 'Oh dear,' she whispered in a sympathetic tone. 'You've discovered my secret.'

Pru felt sick. Was that a confession? A threat? She mumbled as she tried to push the words she needed from her lips. 'Gosh, yes, she's beautiful. I think my aunt had one of those when she was younger, they were so popular.' She coughed, giving herself time to think. 'Just about everyone had one; there must be loads knocking about in charity shops these days. How long have you been collecting dolls, Phyllis?'

Phyllis paused, taking her time to work out just how much Prunella Pearce knew or at the very least suspected. 'Oh for quite some years, my dear.'

At that exact moment, Pru sensed she would need more than just a Holly Hobbie doll to throw at Andy to prove her suspicions, but as their eyes met, she knew.

'Oh my goodness, is that the time?' Pru made a huge show of looking at her wrist. Her heart sank as she realised she had left her watch on her bedside cabinet at home. She quickly scanned the oak beam of the inglenook fireplace. She was in luck, there was a clock.

'I'm so sorry, Phyllis, I'm going to have to run, I'm late already.'

Before she could object, Pru was up and halfway down the path doing a good impression of a grandma-gallop; a half-run, half-walk that would take her as far away from Blackthorn Cottage as quickly as possible without arousing suspicion.

Phyllis slammed the door shut behind her. Her breath coming in short, sharp rasps, she bit down hard on her lip as her fingernails dug into the palms of her hands, allowing her to savour the pain.

'That bloody woman will be the death of me!'

Her plans of a grand finale and a great escape could so easily slip through her fingers if she didn't act quickly.

DOROTHY

DECEMBER 1976

'Mothers are all slightly insane.'
— *The Catcher in the Rye*, J. D Salinger

*S*tanding in front of the wood-worn butcher's block in the
kitchen, Dorothy Magdalen tipped her head to one side and
listened intently. The squeals of laughter drifted along the corridor,
curled around the door frame and, like notes of an opus, bounced and
peaked across the vast kitchen until they reached her. She visibly winced
as the sound bore deep into her heart. She gripped the handle of the
knife until her knuckles turned stark white against the raw red skin of
her wet hand.

'Daddy, Daddy, play it again, please; please play it again!'

Small footsteps pattered and tapped over the black-and-white
chequered tiles, followed by the simpering tones of her husband as he
overindulged the brat, the vile cuckoo in the nest who had kicked her out
and stolen his affections. Her grip loosened and the knife rattled onto
the table, falling short of the doughy mass that spread across the scat-

tered flour. Her jealous and unnatural rage would be channelled and pummelled into her teatime creation, her outlet.

'I gave her life and this is how she repays me!' Dorothy slammed her fists into the warm sticky mixture and then rammed her fingers down, squeezing it tightly, just as she would choke the life from the brat given half the chance.

One last family meal, a civilised meal, a farewell meal; he was leaving her and taking the wretch with him. He had pleaded with her, begged for her to release him from their promise. She had thrown her head back in laughter and mocked him relentlessly, his eyes haunted and afraid. The power of his reaction overwhelmed her, made her stronger and suddenly she knew what she had to do. She had composed herself, curtly nodding in false agreement before calmly making her way to the kitchens to prepare.

'Ernest, Ernest... you silly, foolish, weak man,' she growled to herself as she reached for the shiny, sharp meat cleaver hanging from the mantle hook. Caressing it gently, her fingers stroking the cool steel, she marvelled at how it would complement the garden spade that was leaning in readiness against the back door. 'I do so hate long and overly emotional goodbyes,' she hissed.

And there it was.

The madness.

It had festered and grown and for poor Maisie Martha Magdalen, life would never be the same again.

THE SET UP

*P*ru slumped down on her sofa, a large mug of hot chocolate between her fingers. She checked her mobile phone for the umpteenth time, Andy still hadn't responded to any of her texts. She had tried calling him, but his phone had gone straight to voicemail. She had left one breathless message saying she needed to speak to him as soon as possible, but until she had further evidence, she wasn't going to go all out and accuse Phyllis of being the 'Ladykiller'. She'd be so embarrassed if he laughed at her or, worse still, told her off like he did the last time she got involved at the parish hall.

She kicked off her shoes and wriggled her toes before tucking them underneath her. Did Phyllis really fit the profile of a serial killer? She thought for a moment, two or three gulps of the hot chocolate helping the process. In all honesty, what did a serial killer look like? Her idea of Phyllis being somehow linked to Magdalen House and a child murderer made her shiver. She took another sip, her tongue savouring the sweetness. But why would she want to bump off just WI members? That simply didn't make sense. What could it be that made them targets? Too many questions were starting to give her a headache. She rubbed her forehead and checked her phone again. He was probably tied up with a job; she just hoped he wouldn't panic when he saw all her missed calls and texts. That made her feel all warm and fuzzy; it was so lovely to be part of a couple again, to have someone care about her. She couldn't wait to tell him about her little visit to Phyllis's. She'd make sure she missed out the flutter of histrionics she'd had and just stick to the facts. She really wished she had something more than a doll to present to him.

Mr Binks, who had been curled up fast asleep next to her, startled suddenly, his ears upright on alert, his tail swishing angrily. She smoothed the top of his head. 'It's okay, Binksy, it's just the letterbox.'

She got up and padded down the hallway to the front door. A Manilla envelope lay on the rug, her name flowed across the front in black pen.

'Oooh, what have we here?' She slipped her finger under the flap and pulled out a small note.

Hi Pru,

Can you meet me at Magdalen House tonight, 7pm?
I've got the keys.
Lucy

'Yessss!' Pru excitedly punched the air. 'Magdalen House, Binks, where it all began!' She eagerly clicked Bree's number to let her know. Bree still wasn't well enough for adventures, but the very least she could do would be to let her know and share some of the fun. Her call went straight to voicemail. 'Blimey, is it something I've said, Binksy? It would seem nobody wants to talk to me today!'

She listened to Bree's recorded voice telling her not to be a dipstick by hanging up but to leave a message and she would get back to her as soon as possible. She laughed to herself; she really did miss the daft bat.

'Lucy has got the keys to Magdalen House; I'm meeting her there at seven. We'll have a good mooch round and I'll let you know if we find anything significant. Bye!' She went to end the call when she remembered. 'Oh, hope you're feeling a bit better; I'll see you tomorrow.'

She quickly left another message for Andy, letting him know she would be late as she was meeting Lucy for a drink at the Dog & Gun. She definitely didn't want him getting cross with her for interfering again. Throwing a sachet of Felix into the bowl for Mr Binks, she checked the time. Changing into her trainers, she grabbed a warm jacket and a torch, patted her pocket to ensure her house and car keys were there, turned on the porch light for later, and quietly closed the front door.

As she made her way to her car, it never once crossed her mind that protocol would never have allowed Lucy to include her on an investigation. Nor would Lucy take such a risk with her own career by obtaining the keys to a property under the guise of police business whilst taking a civilian not involved in the case along with her on an evening jaunt.

'*M*aisie Martha Magdalen.' Lucy breathlessly flopped herself down on the chair next to Andy.

'And that should mean something, because?' He gave her a wry smile and went back to threading the green tag through the punch holes of his court file for the CPS.

'The clues, all the clues point to a murder that took place in 1979. Here look–' She unceremoniously dumped her own file on his desk. '–murder scene of Mabel Allinson, a thread of wool identified as Sirdar DK Shade 099 in… *Maisie!*'

Andy stopped what he was doing and gave her his undivided attention. 'Go on…'

Lucy was on a roll; she'd spent half the night wide awake putting everything into a semblance of order. 'Okay, murder scene of Avery McIntosh; a child's pair of plimsolls with a faded name inside. All we had were the initials of two words beginning with "M" and "M". From that, forensics could only make out two letters of what we assumed was the beginning of a first name… "*Ma*".'

'Er… I'm not sure where you're going with this.'

'Humour me. Let's say it's the name "Maisie" and the second

M stands for "Magdalen". Then we've got the murder scenes of Rita Charlesworth and Felicity Broadbent.' Lucy grabbed a sheet of paper from her file and pushed it towards him.

'You've missed out Phillipa Jackson and Betty Prince.'

'No, no I haven't, I'll come to them in a minute. Right, Rita Charlesworth, the note that was left by her body was signed *M.M* – that could just as easily be Maisie Magdalen again, couldn't it?'

'If you say so.' Andy was more than a little intrigued; he was actually feeling quite hopeful.

'And then we've got this.' She dangled the crime scene photograph from Felicity's demise. 'A discarded but carefully placed packet of M&M peanuts – again M.M for Maisie Magdalen.'

Andy grabbed the photograph from her outstretched fingers.

'And next, but definitely not last, Phillipa Jackson and the brochure.' She punched the air in anticipated triumph.

'Now you have lost me on that one, a brochure for, er... what was it you said, "Maudlin" College in Oxford? I'd say there's not much of a link there and nothing came back from forensics for it either; it was clean.' Andy rummaged through his stack of files for the 'Ladykiller' case, trying to find the forensic photograph that had been taken of the brochure.

'That's it; that's my point. It's pronounced *Maudlin*, but it's actually spelt *Magdalen*! Whoever's committing these murders is telling us that it has something to do with Maisie Magdalen, who just happens to have been a Winterbottom-born child and committer of matricide in the late 1970s.' Lucy sat back in her chair, her arms up above her head in a victory V shape, totally exhausted but elated.

She could see the excitement building through Andy's body language as he flicked between each piece of paperwork that she had presented him. Where his shoulders had been slumped when she had first entered the room, his back was now straight and tense with anticipation.

'This is brilliant, it's the first concrete thread we've had so far;

it can't be a coincidence.' He ran through the names and the links from the list. 'We're forgetting one victim, though, Betty Prince. There's nothing here for her. If we're going down that road they've all got to link to the same thing.'

Lucy smiled. 'I pre-empted that.' She delved into her file again and pushed the personal property list from Betty's scene towards him. 'It didn't mean anything at the time, why would it? An older lady with a screwed-up packet of mint imperials on her lap when she died. They were ruled out as a cause of death from choking or poisoning, so they were just designated to her property, along with her handbag and contents.'

'I don't get it, what's the link?'

'They're from a small independent sweet-maker called Martha's Marvellous Confections. I went down to the property and had a look. Once the bag was flattened out, the logo was as plain as day!' She felt like doing a lap of honour around his desk but decided it might come across as incredibly childish. Still, it would have been fun. 'I got Melv to photograph it and it's been bagged up for a forensics run; you just never know.'

Andy jiggled a mug at her. 'Coffee? I think you deserve it.' He laughed. 'We'll work this out into a semblance of order, research the 1970s murder, and drop it on Holmes. It might bring a smile to his face.'

Lucy gave a slightly smug grin as she placed another file on his desk. 'It's already done; newspaper articles, the original crime report and investigation notes, although sadly some bits are missing, probably during the station move in the late 1980s, and the scene photographs are in the wallet at the back.'

'Well, well, Detective Constable Lucy Harris. I'd love to call you a smart arse, but at the moment I could actually hug you!'

Lucy grinned. 'Oh, and to add to the mix, I spoke with the team at North Yorkshire. The woman in the revolving doors at The Old Swan that they spoke to with the funny colour hair – she gave her name as Alice Jones.' She savoured this one; it was

289

her finale. 'Well they've checked against the register at reception.' She waved a sheet of A4 at him and waited.

Andy picked up his mobile and switched it on. A stream of alerts rattled through, one after the other. 'Go on, hit me with it.'

'She was actually booked in under the name of Maisie Martha Magdalen!'

THE AWAKENING

*P*hyllis stood outside the imposing Victorian manor, her fingers tracing the weather-worn lettering on the nameplate.

Magdalen House.

The amber sandstone entrance had faithfully shielded the double oak doors from some of the inclement weather over the years, but they had seen better days and were as unwelcoming as ever. She stepped back to take in the bricks and mortar that were once the foundations of her home. The tall chimneys stood menacingly against the rapidly darkening sky, the rustle and swish of the trees in the gathering breeze offered some comfort. They had been her sentries in her childhood, their whispering the only voices to soothe her at night.

The windows reflected the already waxing moon. She shivered.

They were still watching her, still judging her.

She pushed the key into the ornate escutcheon lock on the front door and turned the ringed handle. A flurry of leaves whipped themselves into a mini maelstrom, pushing past her to enter first as they scattered across the black-and-white chequered tiles. The huge centre staircase that hosted the galleried landings to the east and west sat dormant, the curved side banisters like open arms, gathering her back into the family.

She pushed back her shoulders and held her head high. She was returning in strength as a woman, not as the beaten child.

Magdalen House had awakened.

~

Pru's trainers crunched on the gravel driveway as she swept her torch from side to side. She could make out the silhouette of Magdalen House just ahead of her, the vast trees providing an eerie backdrop. It was more of a mansion than a house. She wondered if an hour or two with Lucy would be long enough to explore the building and to find what they wanted.

'Mmm... I think a few weeks with a team would be more like it!' she murmured to herself. She switched her mobile phone to silent. The last thing she wanted was for it to start ringing and give the game away. She wasn't sure how 'secret' this jaunt with Lucy was supposed to be.

She had parked her own car in the lane leading to the gates for Magdalen House, and had half expected Lucy's car to be either in the same place or actually outside the property, but it was nowhere to be seen. Her torch picked out the main entrance doors; they were slightly ajar, a warm light radiating from inside.

'Luce, it's me, Pru.' Her voice sounded a little wobbly, which annoyed her. It made her sound scared. She pushed the door open and involuntarily released an appreciative gasp. It was beautiful, ancient smelling but beautiful. She stepped inside, turning circles as she took in the stunning architecture, the oak panels, carvings and ornate ceilings around her lit by the dim overhead globed glass drop lights.

'Oh my, how the other half live!' Her voice no longer weak,

she touched the smooth surface of the immense stair newel, her fingers curving around the swirls.

Footsteps behind alerted her, she turned and froze to the spot, her heart missing a beat.

'Or sometimes it is how the other half die!' a familiar voice rasped.

Pru had only a fleeting second to see Phyllis Watson, her arm raised above her head, bearing down on her. She flinched and tried to turn away, her heart hammering in her chest as her feet slipped from underneath her.

I can't, no purchase, tiles, leaves...

A searing pain split through her skull and for the second time in a few short weeks, blackness overtook her.

THE LEGACY

ranges and lemons said the bells of St. Clement's...
Phyllis's sing-song voice filled the entrance hall of Magdalen House, accompanied by the swoosh of Pru's body as she dragged it across the huge expanse of floor. She couldn't pull holding both of Pru's ankles, so Phyllis had utilised just the one, allowing the other leg to remain on the ground bent at an angle. Pru's trainer gave off a staccato squeak as it trailed across the tiles, her limp hand hit the deep skirting board as Phyllis continued on her mission towards the cellar door.

You owe me five farthings say the bells...
She stopped suddenly and tilted her head, listening. Her eyes glazing over, she dropped Pru's leg and slid down beside her, leaning against the very door that had caged her as a child. She closed her eyes, a single tear silently slipped down her cheek, a small whisper escaped from her lips in a voice that wasn't hers.

'*Stop snivelling and eat it up, my girl, or it's the Dark Place for you...*'
How could she ever forget?

'You're nothing like him, it's me you've got running right through you, like a stick of Blackpool rock.' Dorothy Magdalen wiped her wet hands on her apron. 'Mark my words, it'll show itself in you in the end, it always does. There's no goodness in the Birch family, just pure wickedness, touched by insanity.'

Maisie cowered in her chair; the bowl of chicken broth left untouched in front of her. 'But, Mummy, I'm good, I say my prayers every night like a good girl. My daddy says I'm a good girl—' She noticed the change in her mother's face and suddenly wished those words had not left her lips. She balled her fist tightly and tried to push it into her mouth to stop any further words from escaping. She watched Dorothy become rigid, her breath coming in short, sharp rasps, her lips thin as her black eyes pierced her tiny soul. She flinched, knowing what to expect.

Dorothy exploded.

She grabbed Maisie by one pigtail and dragged her from the chair. 'My daddy this, my daddy that! You don't have a daddy anymore. Why would a brat like you need a daddy? Your daddy is dead – I got rid of him myself!' Dorothy cackled loudly as she yanked and pulled Maisie from the kitchen, oblivious to her little hands grasping at anything she could hold on to to stop from being dragged to the Dark Place. Her fingers touched something cold, something metal. She took it. Her other hand gripped the door frame, but Dorothy was too strong for her. Maisie resisted momentarily but then let go, her nails scraping the paintwork.

Her tiny feet stumbled over each other as she desperately tried to keep her balance as Dorothy hauled her along the corridor. The door to the Dark Place opened and a rush of damp air hit her nostrils.

'Please, Mummy, please don't, I'll be good I promise—' Tears streamed down her cheeks, but her cries were in vain. Dorothy, cold of heart, pushed her child into the black depths. Maisie's feet scrabbled to find a stair, something solid to stand on. She grabbed for the stair rail but missed it, her fingers skimming the worn wood. In a frantic last ditch attempt she managed to clutch on to her mother's apron.

Dorothy, taken by surprise, slipped on the top step as Maisie pulled her mother towards her. She fell on top of Maisie, the two of them entangled on the wooden risers. Maisie's heart beating so fast she thought it would burst through the front of her pretty opal fruit dress. She pushed her away and brought her fists down on Dorothy again and again, hard and deliberate, she needed her to pay for what she had done.

Maisie didn't stop until the energy had exploded, bursting before her eyes like fireworks. And then it was gone, like a switch being turned off.

She sat with her head in her hands, her mother heavy and motionless by her side, no breath, no heartbeat, no words. The dim light from the grated coal drop caught Dorothy's glassy dead eyes...

...and glinted from the handle of the kitchen knife that was buried deep to the hilt in her back.

'Oranges and Lemons say the bells of St. Clement's...' sang Maisie as she fingered the patterned fruit on her frock whilst rocking her dead mother in her arms.

'You owe me for my father,
Said the bells of Maisie Martha.'

The childish laughter echoed up the cellar steps, along the corridor, across the vast black-and-white chequered entrance hall and out through the open door of Magdalen House.

The madness had finally arrived for her like an unwelcome guest.

THE SECRETS WE KEEP

𝒜ndy positioned the 'Ladykiller' file neatly in front of
him, then rearranged his pens, pencils and finally his
treasured stapler. 'She's not picking up!'

Lucy coughed loudly, the harsh salt and vinegar flavouring
catching in her throat. She hastily wiped crisp crumbs from the
front of her blouse. 'What did she say in her texts?'

'Just that she needed to speak to me. She didn't say anything
about going out unless she's gone to visit Bree. She did say she
was going to pop round.' He pinched a crisp from Lucy's packet.

'Hey, that's my tea! If you're making me hang around for the
boss, I need something to stop my guts from grumbling!' She
laughed, grabbing the packet from him. 'What did her voicemail
say?'

Andy looked puzzled. 'What voicemail?'

'The one you mentioned she'd left before. You said she'd left
you zillions of text messages and a voicemail.'

'Ah, yep, I did, didn't I? I forgot about that.' He pressed 121
and listened. It didn't take long for Pru's voice to fill the room.

*'Hi, Andy, only me again. I can't get hold of you. I sent you a text or
two, or three or four...'* She laughed. *'I've left a lasagne out for you. I'm*

going to be a bit late getting back as I'm meeting Lucy for a drink in the Dog & Gun. Middle shelf in the oven, 180 for forty minutes, and no matter how much Binks does his eyes, he can't have any! Moocho kisses.'

The door to the incident room swung open, heralding the arrival of Murdoch Holmes. For once he almost had a smile on his face. If it weren't for the fact that Andy's brain was now working overtime, fuelled by the look on Lucy's face, he would have made some smart-arse comment.

'Sorry, boss, just a minute. Lucy, you didn't tell me you'd arranged to meet Pru; we're on a late shift with no time off. What's that all about?' His gut instinct was telling him that something was very wrong.

'I didn't say because I haven't.' Lucy looked just as puzzled as he did. 'She knows I'm on duty until ten tonight.'

Andy quickly dialled Bree. She answered on the third ring.

'Bree, sorry, quick call, just trying to find out where Pru is. Is she with you?'

The knot in his stomach grew bigger the longer it took for Bree to reply. The silence between them was a giveaway. Eventually she spoke.

'No, she popped in this morning, but she's not here now–'

Andy interrupted. 'Bree, this is important, I won't be annoyed, but with everything else that is going on, I need to know where she is.'

Another silence.

'Bree?'

'Bloody hell, talk about rat out a mate! Look, just don't get cross with her again will you, she's only trying to help, especially after what happened to me. I mean I'd have gone with them if I'd been up to it–'

'Gone where and with who? Where is she, Bree?'

'She's gone to mooch around Magdalen House with Lucy. Luce left her a note earlier on; she's apparently got hold of the keys, probably from the estate agent and told Pru to meet her there. She's convinced it's got something to do with the murders. We'd found links that could help you solve the case, but we needed more evidence. She wanted to find it before she told you.' Bree fell silent again.

A chill wormed its way along his spine as his eyes met Lucy's. She held her hands up and shook her head. 'I haven't left any note, Andy, but someone obviously has!'

Without finishing his conversation he cut Bree off and turned to his team, acknowledging Holmes with a wave of his hand.

'Magdalen House, now! Get back up!' he barked at Lucy.

The busy incident room suddenly became the Marie Celeste in less than thirty seconds as everyone took up the call for assistance. Only a sheet of A4 paper blown from a desk, drifting from side to side before coming to rest on the floor, was evidence of a previously occupied room.

THE SEVENTH

She could hear a voice singing a nursery rhyme, one with which she was familiar. It was distant, as though she were under water. Fading in and out, loud one minute, an almost silent whisper the next. She tried to move but a burning pain coursed through her shoulders. It took her breath away.

Why can't I feel my fingers? Why does my head hurt? Where am I?

Pru blinked several times, her eyes becoming accustomed to the dim, orange lighting. Her mouth was dry, a metallic tang on her tongue. She knew what it was. Blood.

If I can taste it and I'm aware of it, then I'm still alive.

Nausea washed over her, making her gag as she struggled against an invisible force. She paused and took stock. She was on a chair, her arms looped around the wooden spindles, hands tied together behind her back, her feet bound at the ankles. She could smell damp mixed with fresh earth. Her eyes darted left to right, up and down, trying to make sense of where she was.

A room. A dark room, basement, cellar... a shed?

The last thing she remembered was being inside Magdalen House and seeing Lucy. That was who she expected to see, but had it been Lucy? The image was there on the periphery of her consciousness. A face looming over her.

The Old Swan... Bree... a scarf... the woman with the red hair... the rag doll... inside Magdalen House... think, you idiot, think!

'Oh my God... Phyllis Watson!' Pru grunted. She had remembered.

A shuffling sound gave away the position of someone or something in the far corner, the arc of light not quite reaching the blackness. Pru silently hoped it wasn't rats.

'You called, my dear?' The dark silhouette emerged from the shadows and like a panther it slowly slinked around its prey.

A deep stab of fear forced its way up from Pru's stomach into her throat as she saw who was standing before her. 'Phyllis! Oh my God, I knew there was something not quite right about you. Why?' she croaked.

'Mmm... and why not?' Phyllis laughed. 'You tell me why not. Make it a good reason and I might let you live.' She caressed the kitchen knife she held in her hand and placed the tip onto her own palm, marvelling at the puckering of her skin as she gently pushed. The sharp stab of pain was a pleasure. She knew she should really allow Pru to live; after all she wasn't on the list, but this was so much fun. She was a cat toying with a mouse on home ground. She was in control.

Mmm... this was going to be ever so delicious...

'What have I ever done to you, Phyllis? What has anyone ever done? The others, they didn't deserve what you did to them, they did nothing.' Pru choked back a sob. She knew she was babbling, but fear was keeping her talking.

'That's just it, they did nothing... *absolutely* nothing. No recognition, no acknowledgements; overlooked, ignored, invisible.' Phyllis raged. 'Why them? I asked that myself, I had just as much right to the presidency as they did, but no, good old Phyllis didn't count, good old Phyllis didn't matter!'

'Please, we can talk about this, can't we?' Pru tried again.

'Talk? I don't think so. I had years of talking about it in the institution, and then one day they just spat me out with a battered suitcase and a new identity to be forgotten all over again.'

Pru watched her pace up and down the small, dank room, spittle flying from her lips as she mumbled under her breath.

'This is my home!' Phyllis slumped down on the stairs, her head low, the kitchen knife limp in her hand. 'I came back, I wanted to try again, but it was just the same as it was before. No one looked out for me when I was a child and desperate for help.' She pointed the blade of the knife in Pru's direction. 'Nobody asked why I wasn't at school or why I was so thin, why I wore long sleeves in the summer, why I cried all the time. They didn't look for my father, they listened to *her* and not me. They didn't care, just as they don't now. You *all* abandoned me.'

Pru's eyes widened as the pieces fell into place. 'You're Maisie Magdalen! But we... we thought you were dead!'

Phyllis threw back her head, a hoarse, thick laugh bursting from her throat. 'Just as I wanted, I'm very adept at disappearing and when I've completed the seventh, one murder for every year I had a father, I'll disappear again.' She got to her feet, the sadness gone, the desolation brushed aside to be replaced by a malevolence. 'The game has changed; you are going to be the seventh, Prunella. You really should have kept your interfering nose out.'

A ripple of sweat ran along Pru's spine. Her brain was being overrun by escape ideas that fell over themselves in a jumbled mess and were just as quickly dismissed. She decided her only option was to beg for her life and point out some harsh realities.

'Phyllis, you'll never get away with it. My friend is a police detective–' The thought of Lucy being in danger too brought a huge lump to her throat. She coughed to clear it. 'She knows I'm here. You won't have time to get away and... and... how can you look me in the eyes and use that knife on me? Even you can't be that devoid of feeling.' She wanted to appeal to whatever sliver of decency Phyllis still had.

'Ah that's where you're so very wrong!' Phyllis sneered. '*Can you meet me at Magdalen House tonight, 7pm. I've got the keys,*' she mimicked in a sing-song voice. 'That was so, so easy, my girl, and you really fell for it. Your friend has no idea where you are!' Smirking, she glanced at Pru's feet.

Pru's heart missed a beat as she leant as far forward as her tied hands would allow. An electric cable snaked out from the darkness, across the earthen floor, ending by her legs, the wires exposed and taped to her ankles.

Phyllis revelled in the horrified look on Pru's face. She checked her watch. 'A ten-minute head start should be all I need and then... zap!' She keyed in a number and sat the timer on the floor in front of Pru. 'Don't you just love technology?'

Pru started to sob. 'Please, Phyllis, don't do this, I'm begging you–'

Phyllis had already started to climb the stairs. She paused and looked down at Pru. Her seventh.

'It's Dilys... *D-i-l-y-s,*' she spat, as she slammed the door behind her.

This one is for you, Daddy...

THE VANISHING

The weak light from the lamp on Brenda Mortinsen's sit-up-and-beg bicycle that had once belonged to her grandmother picked out the main gates to Magdalen House. She gripped the brakes and dropped a foot down onto the gravel, holding the bike upright to protect her precious cargo in the wicker basket on the front. Henry, her miniature Yorkshire terrier poked his nose out from underneath the grey blanket that sported a pattern of little black paw prints.

She had cycled this route so many times over the years, but this was the first time she had seen the windows of Magdalen House illuminated. She checked the 'Sold by Auction' sign attached to the sandstone gateposts.

'Looks like Creepy Manor has new owners, Henry.' She checked her watch. 'Maybe they'd like some delicious cake to go with their cocoa. It's not too late to call, what do you think?'

She pushed off, wobbling along the driveway, small stones scattering in her wake and Henry's ears fluttering in the wind.

~

Brrrrrrrrrriiiiiiiiiing. Brrrrrrrrriiiiiiiiiing.

Phyllis stopped in her tracks as the piercing ring from the old doorbell to Magdalen House echoed out, filling the entrance hall, before bouncing from the walls of the corridor and finally coming to rest in the kitchen. She looked up at the old butler's bell plate and watched the curved metal arm vibrate. It was a sound she had not heard since her childhood. She slipped the kitchen knife into her tapestry bag and held her breath, leaning heavily on the butcher's block.

They'll go away, just wait.

She checked her watch.

Seven minutes remaining.

Brrrrrrriiiiiiiiiing. Brrrrrriiiiiiiiiing.

She waited.

Six minutes.

Silence.

Tap, tap, tap, tap...

Her heart sank as she turned and looked toward the large sash window, bare and devoid of any soft furnishings.

'Cooeee, anyone home?'

The rotund little face of Brenda Mortinsen peered back at her as she shrieked to be heard through the glass whilst frantically waving at her, a 1940s-style floral knotted head band comically flopping with each wobble of her head.

Five minutes.

Panic took hold of Phyllis. She turned the rusted key in the stable door, only opening the top half as an unwelcoming barrier between them.

'Oh my goodness, Glynis, what are you doing here? I came round the side as I didn't think the bell was working.' Brenda gasped. 'You haven't bought the place, have you?'

'What do you want, Brenda?'

Quite put out by Phyllis's abruptness, Brenda harrumphed loudly, which in turn caused Henry to bare his teeth and growl.

'Lemon drizzle cake, it's to die for; would you like some? It's all for charity, you know.'

'No, Brenda, I wouldn't. Now I'm busy, I need to get on.' Phyllis went to shut the door, but Brenda was having none of it. She held her hand against the peeling wood.

'You're not working here, are you? Are you the new cleaner?' The excitement of anticipated gossip was just too much for her.

Four minutes.

'Just piss off, Brenda, and take your bloody cake with you! Is that clear enough?' Phyllis spat.

Brenda's lips pursed together. 'Well, I never–'

In the distance, sirens sounded and blue lights bounced from the heavy boughs of the trees lighting up the grounds and beyond. Voices shouting in varying pitches echoed along the corridor from the entrance hall as doors banged and static from police radios began to fill Magdalen House.

'Bugger!' Phyllis yelped. Grabbing her bag, she yanked open the half barn door and ran, leaving poor Brenda on the stoop holding a slice of her finest lemon drizzle cake, an apoplectic yappy dog, and a puzzled expression.

COUNTDOWN TO MURDER

Two minutes...

Pru watched the red digital countdown, feeling utterly helpless and lost. She tried again, pulling her hands apart until she couldn't bear the pain any longer as whatever bound them cut into her wrists. It was the same with her legs.

One minute thirty seconds.

She slumped forward, her chin resting on her chest. Defeated, the tears flowed freely. She didn't wail or howl, she had not an ounce of fight left in her. She knew in her heart it was too late.

One minute.

'Pru, if you can hear me shout so I can find you!'

Oh my God, Andy! Am I dreaming? Is this just wishful thinking or hysteria?

Her head jerked up, alert.

'Pru, answer me!'

His voice was loud and urgent.

'Andy, Andy–' she screamed, her throat painfully hoarse. *'I'm down here. I'm in the cellar.'*

The red numbers changed again.

Twenty-two seconds.

She could hear footsteps above her, a sudden strip of light appeared at the top of the stairs, muffled voices becoming louder and Andy barking out orders.

Fifteen seconds.

'It's too late, Andy, it's too late,' she sobbed as the counter clicked steadily down.

Seven, six, five...

And then he was there, fear etched on his face as he took in the electric cable secured to Pru, his eyes tracing its destination as it disappeared into the dark recess. Her terrified eyes lit by the dim light met his as he raced down the steps.

...four, three, two, one...

She closed her eyes and prayed it would be quick. She didn't want to die painfully or without dignity.

Four red flashing noughts dropped into place.

A finality.

Andy's arms reached out to her. 'No, no, no!'

A loud click filled the small dank space, followed by a flash of light that temporarily blinded him. A tinny crackling sound echoed in his ears as he desperately tried to adjust his eyes and focus. It bounced from the stone walls, reminiscent of an old 1920s movie track, as the strains of a jaunty melody cut through the air. The tuneful whistling from the song 'Always Look on the Bright Side of Life' drifted out from the darkness making Andy stop dead in his tracks. If it had been any other time than this precise and rather urgent moment, he would have joined in with the chorus whilst cheerily adding a couple of *dedoo beedoo bedoo's* for good measure.

The ridiculous and totally out of place strains of the comical Monty Python song continued, permeating a moment that had only seconds before been filled with absolute terror.

Pru opened one eye and squinted, waiting for the nothingness that didn't come. The light from Andy's torch stabbed the dark corner and illuminated an old red and cream Decca portable record player. The black vinyl record spun, the stylus crackling as it picked up the song.

'What the actual fu–' Andy caught himself before he let a rather rude expletive pass his lips. He quickly ripped the tape from her ankles and kicked the cable to one side, clearly not taking any chances, a sense of relief washing over him.

Pru threw her head back and let out a very inelegant snort followed by uncontrollable, hysterical laughter as her beautiful chestnut hair, slicked with sweat, fell behind her. 'Yeeeow, you bloody idiot! You've just stripped what few hairs I had left on my legs – and I think the word you're looking for is *fu–*'

Suddenly the cellar door slammed open, cutting her short as the cheery, high-pitched voice of Brenda Mortinsen hollered out from the darkness, her plump cartoon-like silhouette framed at the top of the stairs by the light behind her.

'Lemon drizzle, anyone? It really is to die for!'

A SIMPLE MADNESS

*M*urdoch Holmes poked the slab of cake with his pen. 'So, we now know who the "Ladykiller" is.' He grabbed a knife that was poised on his plate and inspected the crumbs on the blade. 'We've got the motive – she's bloody barking mad. We've got the confession to a witness–' He poked another hole in Brenda's creation, but this time with the knife. '– but we've got no ruddy prisoner! What the bloody hell were you lot playing at?'

The atmosphere could have been cut with the knife that Holmes was now exuberantly waving in the air. Lucy quickly dodged a lump of butter-cream that came flying towards her. It breezed past her ear and landed with a splat on Tim's cheek. If it hadn't been for the fact they were all getting a good rollocking, there would have been at least one of the team that would have shouted 'goal' and executed a lap of honour around the photocopier.

Murdoch took in the sombre faces of his murder team, letting the ensuing silence speak for him. He was furious, his one chance to shine and maybe make DCI had been flummoxed by a forty-nine-year-old on-the-run psychopath with a warped sense of humour and a mute parrot. He could feel the tension radiating into his jaw. 'Well?'

Andy was the first to speak. 'Sir, we've created a police national computer wanted/missing marker. Special branch, the NCA and all ports have been given a notification in her birth name and what aliases we know she's been using.' He paused to check the file in front of him. 'She does hold a passport in her assumed name from the new identity she was given by the authorities: Dilys Margaret Watson.'

Lucy looked puzzled. 'I thought her name was Phyllis. They always called her Phyllis at the WI meetings.'

'Mmm... that seems to have been one of the triggers to her recent spree; everyone's inability to either notice her, appreciate her, or get her name right.' Andy slammed his desk drawer shut.

'Aww bless her, my sympathy knows no bounds for some old trout who has murdered six innocent women as well as one man, in addition to torturing a seventh woman with a repeat rendition of Monty Python on a 45-rpm single.' Holmes took a bite of the lemon drizzle cake and savoured the moment before using the rest of the slice as a pointing stick. 'My arse is on a plate with this one, so get *your* arses out there and bring her in!' Another blob of butter-cream took to the air.

'Sir.' Andy nodded an acknowledgement and indicated to the team to vacate the incident room as quickly as possible lest they should feel a second wave of what was jokingly called the 'Wrath of Holmes'. 'Lucy, you're with me, there's some CCTV footage to view from The Old Swan that's just been booked in, and I've just received confirmation details for the original hotel reservation.' He shook his head in disbelief. 'Bloody hell, look at this, she even had the audacity to have it posted to her own home address in Winterbottom.'

Holmes sat down at his desk, elbows cocked and his head in his hands. 'Seven murders, Andy, plus one abduction, and I've just had confirmation that an eighth body has been found by the search teams in the grounds of Magdalen House. What the hell is going on around here? It's supposed to be a leafy, tranquil village for God's sake!'

'Mr Ernest Edgar Magdalen I take it?' Andy puffed out his cheeks.

'Yep, not a tremendous amount left of him after forty years of festering under a bushy *Viburnum Opulus* and a ton of soil, but dental records will confirm if it is.' He sneaked another bite of the cake as he sifted through the paperwork from the original Magdalen file. 'Daughter always maintained that mum murdered the father, ill-treated her and kept her prisoner until she snapped and buried the nine-inch blade of an antique Sabatier kitchen knife in her back during a tussle in the cellar. They did a search of the grounds at the time and newspaper appeals asking Ernest to come forward if he had, as Dorothy Magdalen had claimed, abandoned them for his mistress, but it was all in vain; he was never seen or heard of again.'

Looking at the photograph of Maisie on the steps of Magdalen House clutching a doll, Andy found it hard to believe a child could be capable of such a brutal act. The thought of the cellar and Pru forced a shudder to jar his spine. 'It's actually a sad story but for recent events. The problem we've got now is not knowing what name she is using, or if she even looks the same, taking into account some of the disguises we know she has already used.'

Lucy nodded in agreement. 'And she's got plenty of money with which to change her appearance and do a vanishing act. We're still trying to track the funds that came from the sale of Magdalen House, but she's had such a good head start on us. It's not hard to filter money and make it disappear if you know what you're doing.'

Holmes ran his hand through his hair, which seemed to have got greyer than it was at the start of the shift. 'How's Pru?' he asked with genuine concern.

Andy offered a wan smile in return. 'She's good, she's quite a tough cookie to be honest, but it has left its mark.'

'Aye, being held at knifepoint and then that bizarre cellar scenario; it's enough to stop anyone from sleeping for a few weeks.'

'I think it's more the earworm of *Always Look on the Bright Side of Life* that's keeping her awake, boss!' Andy laughed. 'Come on, Luce, we can't stand here talking all day; there's things to be done!'

Lucy grabbed her jacket from the back of her chair and shrugged one arm into the sleeve. Tilting her head to one side, the wisps of a memory niggled her. 'Sarge, the parrot!'

'What about it?'

'It wasn't there when we searched the cottage. Pru saw it just before she went missing; she's confirmed it was there when she called round, but it wasn't there when the teams went in.'

'What are you saying, Luce?'

'Wherever she's gone, whatever arrangements she's made, she's definitely not coming back. We need to find out who has the parrot; they might know something!'

TO THE STARS AND BACK

'What do you mean you've got the parrot in protective custody?' Pru looked incredulously at Andy who was playing a pretty fair game of 'po-face'. She prodded him in the ribs, trying to elicit some response from him. 'The parrot, Andy! What about the parrot?'

'It's deceased; it has ceased to be; it's bereft of life–' He pulled the duvet up under his chin and pinned his elbows to his side, a makeshift barrier between his remaining unpoked ribs and Pru's finger. '–and now it's evidence.'

Pru's face fell. 'Oh no, how did that happen? It looked so fit and healthy when I saw it.' She actually felt a small stab of sadness. First the bird had lost its mistress of many years, then it had been farmed out to Avaline Prendergast and her yoga studio under the pretence of Phyllis having a week's holiday in Bognor Regis, where it had then endured regular infusions of aromatherapy odours, incessant chanting, tinkling of triangles and a deluge of chia seeds, and now it was dead.

Andy remained deadpan staring at the bedroom ceiling. 'It was a right little snitch too. Its last words were '*The old trout did it.*' He attempted a look of remorse. 'It then let out a loud squawk and fell off its perch, stone dead and bereft of life.'

'Oh my goodness, how awful, the poor thing.' A reverential silence enveloped the room as Pru digested the sad news.

He watched her beautiful face in profile, her hair tumbling across the pillow, falling softly over his own shoulder. She turned and smiled at him, the soft light from the candles reflected in her eyes, which made his heart beat just that little bit faster. The fear he had felt in Magdalen House had been something quite alien to him, he had never before cared enough about another person to elicit such a response. He turned and kissed her gently on the lips, tenderly stroking her forehead whilst being careful to avoid the vivid bruising and painful stitches, a gut-wrenching reminder of how easily he could have lost her. He still couldn't understand why Phyllis had ended her reign of terror by being lenient with Pru. He would be eternally grateful for that one act, but he would never rest until she was caught and convicted.

She entwined her fingers in his; the electricity of her touch took his breath away. He had never loved anyone more.

'Pru?'

She nestled her head onto his shoulder, nuzzling his neck. 'Yes, my Delectable Detective.'

'About the parrot... er... you've never been a Monty Python fan, have you?'

It took a few moments for her brain to assemble the link between parrots and Monty Python. 'You absolute twa–' she grabbed one of the bolster cushions and smacked him on the head with each word she uttered.

'Whoa, librarians shouldn't know words like that!' He laughed, holding his hands out to stay the onslaught.

'Librarians know lots of words; they are very familiar with bloody dictionaries!' She lost her grip on the cushion as Andy gently grabbed her wrists.

'Police! Drop your weapon, put the cushion down!' He quickly turned her so that she was underneath him. He pressed himself against her, holding her, protecting her. 'I love you to the moon and back and all the stars, Prunella Pearce, my Loony Librarian.'

'And I love you too, my Delectable Defective,' she whispered and sighed.

Silence.

'Andy…'

'What?'

'Is the parrot *really* dead?'

THE WOMEN'S CLUB

'All for one and one for all!' Pru held the slim champagne flute out in front of her, eagerly waiting for Bree and Lucy's glasses to join hers. The swelling to her left eye was now minimal and the florid purple bruising had tempered down to a gentle mustard yellow and puke green flush. She had done her best to cover it with a slightly thicker foundation, adding a slick of lipstick to make herself feel better.

Bree laughed. 'Er... I think you were on your own for that one. I still can't understand why you went to Magdalen House by yourself, particularly with our suspicions and after what happened to you before in the dungeon.'

'Oh don't be so dramatic, it wasn't a dungeon, it was the parish hall cellar,' Pru popped open a bag of crisps and swung her leg over the arm of the sofa, 'and I thought I was meeting Lucy, who happens to be a police officer. Nothing scary about that.' She grinned. The wrinkling of her eyes crinkled the stitches on her forehead and made her wince.

'Thanks for that; it's nice to know I don't hold a presence that could make a criminal shake in his boots!' Lucy topped up her own glass from the bottle of Prosecco she had brought to Pru's house as a celebratory offering. They had all agreed the Dog & Gun wasn't the best place to meet up as it was still awash with gossip and incredulity that a member of their own little village had been responsible for the recent macabre events, and understandably Pru had been very reluctant to show off her war wounds. 'What are we celebrating, anyway, the fact you're not dead?'

'Yep, I'll drink to that!' Bree held her own glass up for a refill. She glanced at Pru who was sitting opposite her, seemingly mesmerised by the dancing flames from the log fire and without warning, a surge of emotion caused her throat to tighten. 'We came so close to dying didn't we?' She touched her neck, the marks from her own brush with death still visible above the curve of her sweatshirt collar.

Pru didn't break her gaze from the fireplace. She nodded. 'We did, so very, very close.' She took a sip from her glass. 'But bloody hell, it was exciting wasn't it? I don't think I've ever felt so... so... so alive!'

Lucy and Bree side-eyed each other in surprise.

'Exciting? Jeez, Pru, it wasn't a bloody Enid Blyton adventure, it was real life. You both could have been murdered. It was only sheer dumb luck that you weren't!' Lucy snapped. 'Six women are dead, and wherever she is, Phyllis is still on the loose.'

Pru felt a little bit guilty, but it was quickly replaced with the exuberance she was feeling for an idea she had been nurturing. 'I know, but c'mon, Luce, you must feel the same doing your job. The excitement amidst tragedy you still feel for the victims, but there's a flutter of trepidation mixed with an eagerness to dive headfirst into the investigation. Surely that's why you do the job?'

Lucy had to admit she was right. Nothing beat that feeling of pitting your wits against an offender, trying to get one step ahead rather than trail one step behind. The thrill when clues and intelligence begin to fit together revealing the right path to take was exhilarating; there was no denying it. She sighed and nudged her glass towards Bree who was now holding the bottle and examining its contents. 'Yes but, and it is a big but... I'm trained and get paid to put myself at risk; that's my role, that's my job. You can't play at these things, Pru.'

Bree hiccuped loudly as she peered down the neck of the bottle. 'Well, ladies, I'm investigating the case of the disappearing alcofrol – alcopoop – alcohool!' She waved the bottle at Lucy.

Pru jumped to her feet, her arms windmilling in excitement as she slopped Prosecco over the rug. 'That's just it! That's what I've been trying to say to you.' The fire behind her gave a warm, silhouetted glow. 'Can you just imagine the three of us investigating things together? The fun we would have, not to mention plenty of buttock-clenching moments?' She tipped back what was left in her glass, her tongue darting out to savour the remnants on her lips. 'And by that I don't mean an unfortunate bout of Montezuma's revenge!' She puckered her lips into a wry smile.

'I'll drink to that!' Bree screeched whilst rummaging in the fridge for another bottle.

'You'll bloody drink to anything!' Pru retorted as Lucy, shoulders slumped, rolled her eyes and grinned.

Three women.

A librarian, a film researcher and a detective.

And a deliciously exciting idea that had suddenly popped into Pru's head.

The Curious Curator & Co Detective Agency...

Now that was something to consider.

LET THEM EAT CAKE

Two months later

'And the successful candidate for the next president of Winterbottom Women's Institute is…' Kitty paused, almost in expectation of a drum roll. She took in the eager faces of her ladies, the very fabric of the ethos and values that the Institute promoted and supported. She felt a swell of pride: they were all shining examples of those four important words.

Fellowship, Truth, Justice and…

'Bleedin' hell, Cassidy, watch where yer goin', will yer, yer fat bint – you've just trod on me new Jimmy Choos!' Chelsea's voice screeched out from the second row to such a pitch Kitty could feel her teeth setting fast on the proverbial edge. Chelsea rubbed the toe of her shoe, horrified at the scuff mark Cassidy had left behind. 'You stupid, clumsy trollop,' she snarled.

… and Tolerance, Kitty mentally continued.

If she could have rolled her eyes she would have done so. Unfortunately, the set of Russian lashes that had been glued to her lids to flutter at Frank on their up-and-coming secret weekend away were too thick and too heavy to allow for much movement. 'Ladies, ladies!' She tinkled the WI bell savagely. 'If I may be allowed to continue!' Her glacial stare was sufficient to freeze the testicles off a polar bear and quickly brought her audience to rapt attention once again.

'The successful candidate is...' She fluttered the Russian lashes with such force several sheets of A4 paper wafted off the tablecloth. 'Prunella Pearce.' Kitty tapped her fingers together in a wet squib of a handclap. 'Well done, Pru.'

Although Pru had been expecting it, she still blushed profusely. Bree slipped her hand into hers and gave it an encouraging squeeze. 'Go for it, girl,' she whispered. 'You deserve it.'

Edging between the rows to make her way to the small podium, Pru's mind raced, trying to think of suitable off-the-cuff witty responses to her new position within the WI. She had lain awake until the early hours penning an acceptance speech that would not have been out of place at the Oscars. Bree had not unexpectedly stepped down from her own nomination, and in light of recent events no other candidates had been forthcoming, so Kitty had played on Pru's kind nature. She had begged her to put her name forward as a balanced, courageous and forward-thinking new member, and with the ladies of Winterbottom WI's encouragement, Pru had agreed. She had at last been integrated into the village ways and its social life.

She nervously stood at the front as Kitty, slightly reluctant to give up her cosseted role and her place behind the table, eventually moved an inch or two to allow her to have her moment in the spotlight...

'Ladies, after such a short time with you all, I can't thank you enough for having faith in me to take on this prestigious and coveted role.' Pru looked at the six empty seats on the front row. Each seat bore a single rose of a different colour. Each seat held the name of one of the ladies of The Winterbottom Women's

Institute who had each given so much towards their ethos, and ultimately had so sadly given their lives too.

Mabel Allinson
Avery McIntosh
Pip Jackson
Rita Charlesworth
Betty Prince
Felicity Broadbent

Six chairs, six roses.

She paused, a small lump forming in her throat as she caught sight of Ethel dabbing at the corner of her eye, Clarissa pursing her lips together tightly as her chin wobbled, a shredded tissue wrung tightly in her hands. And she knew. She knew that her speech should not be about herself, but about those who were the very essence of The Winterbottom WI.

She took a deep breath.

From the heart, Pru, say it from the heart...

'Agatha Christie had *The Big Four*, Enid Blyton had her *Famous Five* and we ladies, we have our very own *Stupendous Six*.'

A collective nod of heads and warm smiles radiated back at her. Ethel stopped dabbing her eyes and placed her hand on the back of the chair in front of her, the chair that had once been Betty's. A touching moment that was not missed by many in the Winterbottom parish hall.

Pru continued. 'If anyone would like to say a few words for Mabel, Avery, Pip, Rita, Betty and Felicity, please do. This meeting is for them, I think it would be lovely to share our special memories.'

A chair scraped on the wood floor as Millie Thomas slowly rose to her feet. She held her hand over her heart, head bowed as she collected her thoughts.

Reeeeeeeeerrrrrrk.

Every head turned towards the kitchen door in the corner as it noisily swung open on its aged hinges to reveal Brenda

Mortinsen, tea tray in hand, cups rattling against saucers as she waddled over towards them. Shoving her finger in between the slices of a rather sumptuous looking delicacy, she popped the creamy contents into her mouth and smacked her lips together.

'Do you know, ladies, and for the life of me I don't know why, but lemon drizzle certainly seems to have lost its appeal lately.' Brenda quizzically tipped her head, allowing for a brief comedic pause. 'Strawberry shortcake, anyone?' she gaily trilled.

EPILOGUE

'THE RAGE'

18 DECEMBER 1979

*T*he little girl with the red tartan scarf and ill-fitting wellington boots stood in front of the huge entrance doors to Magdalen House. Her brow furrowed, her eyes full of sadness. The icy damp seeped through her knitted mittens, the snowball clutched in her hand was already beginning to melt and disappear.

Just as she was.

The house looked down upon her, its many eyes holding judgement as she felt herself becoming smaller and smaller.

Just like Alice in Wonderland.

A smile touched her lips as she waited for the last tiny remaining piece of Maisie Martha Magdalen to enter the darkness.

You will be safe here, little girl, promised 'The Rage'.

As the swell of the waves rolled the white horses in a rythmic and mesmerising dance, Miss Meredith Myrtle Sitwell, elegantly draped on a very comfortable steamer lounger, took another sip of her chilled champagne. She watched the solitary strawberry bob amongst the bubbles, admired the deep blue skies and revelled in the rich wood shine of the deck. The gentle heat that radiated warmed her bones and made the years of having lived so frugally float away.

'Would madam care for a refresh?'

Meredith shielded her eyes from the sun with a delicately placed hand, taking in the handsome young steward in front of her. 'Yes, yes I think I will. In fact could you leave the bottle please, Barney?'

Barney nodded respectfully and placed the ice-bucket on the table next to her. 'Is there anything more I can do for you, madam?'

Meredith sighed as she gazed at him through slightly hooded eyes.

Oh, my dear boy, there is quite a bit you could do for me, I'm sure – and it certainly wouldn't involve fetching more peanuts!

'No, I'm quite fine thank you, Barney, I don't wish to be disturbed for the rest of the afternoon,' and with a wave of her hand she dismissed him. She stretched out her gaily painted toes, wriggled them in pleasure, and then kicked her leg up high in wild abandon. This was most definitely the life.

A round-the-world cruise.

A luxury round-the-world cruise, to be exact.

And in a suite with its own private deck and balcony.

Well, she could afford it now. In fact she could afford anything she wanted, including this new life she had meticulously chosen for herself. She took another sip of champagne and toasted the real Meredith Myrtle Sitwell.

'Saluti, my dear girl, saluti.' She raised her glass as a mark of respect. 'And farewell, Phyllis, Dilys, Willis and Phallus!' That made her laugh again. It sounded like a line-up from an episode of *Trumpton*.

Meredith Myrtle Sitwell had been born on the 14 December 1969 and had passed away on the 16 December 1969. Her tiny untended and neglected grave in Winterbottom St. Michael's cemetery bore a simple epitaph, *Treasured memories of a little life*, and the dates that Phyllis had so desperately needed to progress her plans and forge a new identity. She had felt a small stab of guilt, but only because the child had been so innocent... then again, hadn't she been an innocent once upon a time?

She replenished her glass to the brim, popping a few select peanuts into her mouth before she tipped her head back to allow the sun to touch her face. The slight smile gave way to a grin and the grin to a full-on belly laugh as she pictured Prunella's face. What a jolly jape that had been. She had intended to do away with the interfering bint, but just at the last minute she had changed her mind.

Why?

Time and time again since she had fled across the grounds of Magdalen House that fateful night, she had asked herself the same question, and in all honesty she still couldn't answer it. Maybe 'The Rage' had abated and allowed the gentle and kind little Maisie to pop her head out briefly, or maybe it simply didn't matter anymore. Suddenly remembering the rather delicious detective almost breaking his neck on the old threadbare runner in the corridor, trying to figure out where the shouting was coming from, made her giggle. He'd fair skated along the length of the floor before his progress was halted by the heavy hallstand making contact with his head, giving Phyllis the opportunity to grab the only thing that mattered to her before almost knocking stupid Brenda, the bloody cakes and her yappy rat to the ground in her haste to leave Magdalen House behind her.

The cables strapped to Pru had actually led to nowhere but the darkness and the timer had been set to the record player. The song? Well, that had been their favourite and it had tickled her pink when the strains had once again drifted through the hallways, corridors and rooms of Magdalen House. She smiled at the memory.

'Daddy, Daddy, play it again, please, please play it again...'

And he had. Over and over, whenever she asked for it, and they would dance along the corridor, through the entrance hall, skipping the black-and-white tiles before jumping the central staircase. Her father would always dance to the left of the galleried landing and Maisie would dance to the right. They would finish sitting together on the top step laughing fit to burst.

And then the darkness would descend in the form of a furious Dorothy Magdalen standing at the bottom of the stairs. Her paisley pinafore smudged with blood, a knife held in front of her and a limp, glassy-eyed rabbit dangling from the tense fingers of her other hand.

Phyllis shuddered. That was not the kind of memory she wanted. She wanted happy thoughts; all she had ever wanted was a happy life and to do just as the song had begged her; to look on the bright side of life, but in her heart she knew that her past would forever haunt her.

Just how long would she have to wait for 'The Rage' to gnaw at the pit of her stomach once again before sparking into life? Would it always be there, just biding its time like an unwelcome guest? How many more would meet the same end as Mabel, Avery, Pip, Rita, Betty and Fliss... and that disgusting perverted bloater Sir Carmichael Shits something-or-other, when she could no longer control it?

Well, she had warned them never to piss off a full blown, professionally certified, time-served psychopath, hadn't she?

'I'll drink to that!' She chuckled in amusement and took another gulp of champagne. Viewing the ocean through the half empty glass she looked to the horizon that held her dreams. She pulled her faithful tapestry bag onto her knees; it had been the only thing she had allowed herself to bring with her to her new life. She knew she could never part with it. She delved her hand inside, her fingers touching the contents, not wishing to reveal to the world the small treasures it held. A pair of earrings that had belonged to her grandmother, her father's amber stud cufflinks, the silver spoon, her Holly Hobbie doll, her special little note-book and...

'Oh my goodness, what have we here?' Her fingers touched a small box. 'Mmm... now they'll go wonderfully with my cham-pagne!' The bright emerald green foil of the chocolate mint cremes glittered in the bright sunlight as she carefully unwrapped and popped one into her mouth. She retrieved her beloved Holly Hobbie and sat it on her knee.

'Well, how much better can life get, Holly? Champagne *and* chocolates!' She unwrapped another and pretended to give the doll a taste before impishly eating it herself.

'Right, story time. This one is called "Minutes to a Murder" and trust me, it will have you on the edge of your seat, Holly, and when we get to the bit where the police haven't got a clue and are still chasing their tails trying to find me, that's as sweet as a nut with perfect planning, wouldn't you say?'

And so it was that Phyllis, soon to be better known as Meredith Myrtle, settled herself down to read a tale of resent-ment, horror and revenge to Holly Hobbie as *The Regent Seven Seas Splendor* sailed the warm Caribbean waters, ploughing through the waves to her new life.

'...And this one was quite delicious in the planning, Holly, but I changed my mind at the very last minute and went for a more dramatic but failed strangulation by scarf rather than my intended modus operandi of a box of poisoned *Whitaker's Mint Cre-*'

Phyllis's eyes bulged as her hand involuntarily gripped the wooden arm of her sunlounger, scattering several shiny green wrappers in the process. They fluttered slowly to the deck, a further convulsion shaking her body as the sudden realisation of where those delightful little mints had originated from tore into her brain.

'The chocolates– I... I... oh how ridiculously silly of me!'

How could she have forgotten? A whole box, carefully prepared and laced with strychnine by her own fair hands as a means to despatch Bryony Richards at the Old Swan in Harrogate, but due to her odd fascination with a revolving door and a bloody expensive chiffon scarf; had remained unused and completely and utterly overlooked at the bottom of her threadbare tapestry bag.

Until now.

'Bugger–' she groaned before her jaw clamped shut from another convulsion and the glass slipped from her hand hitting the deck, the champagne frothing and spreading across the mahogany planks. Her eyes focused on the deep red of her toenails as her feet involuntarily spasmed and kicked down on the sunlounger, a low strangled grunt forcing its way out from her curled lips as it set into a rictus grin.

'Buuuugaaaaah...'

An eerie silence then overcame Phyllis, leaving her with one last thought, just as she had predicted as a child all those years ago.

Mouths were trouble. A mouth could be opened.

And this time hers had.

It had willingly opened to fatefully accept the method of her own demise.

The tip of her finger gently stroked her treasured doll. 'Oh how terribly ironic, Holly,' she mumbled. Her breath weakened and laboured. 'Farewell my faithful fr–'

Phyllis's chest rose and fell for one last time before she slumped to one side, her chin resting on her shoulder, lips stilled, as death finally claimed her.

As the sun began its evening descent, the gentle breeze brushed through Phyllis's hair, skipped over her skin and fluttered the pages of her unintentional confession where it lay open on the deck beside her, her limp fingers barely touching the lined paper. A beautiful half-glow of radiant light rippled a path across the waves and kissed the water's horizon...

...A horizon that the sightless eyes of Maisie Martha Magdalen would never see, one that Phyllis Watson would never enjoy and one that Meredith Myrtle Sitwell would never reach.

THE END

'How we live our lives from the beginning to the end is what we leave as a legacy.
That is the measure of our existence...'
— Gina Kirkham

ACKNOWLEDGEMENTS

I never quite know where to start with acknowledgements.

As those close to me will tell you, I am always so very grateful for the smallest of things as much as the biggest of things in my life. I could probably write something akin to War and Peace trying to thank everyone from our postman (thanks Phil) to an old trout called Phyllis who once trod on my toe in Sainsbury's and whilst exchanging apologies, gave me the idea for a character in this book.

In 2015 I began to scribble words on a sheet of A4 paper, never dreaming that seven years later I would be the published author of four books with a fifth in progress. That success has only been possible because of you. It's all the more special and fun when you can share that happiness with the people that mean something to you, so I am grateful to be able to have the chance to say 'thank you' and to count my blessings.

Firstly, to the wonderful ladies of The Women's Institute. Without you there would be no *Murders at The Winterbottom WI*, no Kitty, Ethel or Clarissa and no tale to tell. Your kindness, generosity and fabulous sense of humour became the inspiration for my characters and the story, although I'm sure I didn't chance to meet an actual, real-life Phyllis – or did I?

Joking aside, thank you for inviting me to speak at your meetings and thank you for all you selflessly do for others.

To Fred and Betsy at Bloodhound Books. I know you were forewarned about my quirky humour and personality, and even though there have been no humongous thongs to use as a PR stunt this time, you have without fear, warmly embraced me and my ways. I couldn't ask for a more inclusive, fun and professional team to look after me, my words and my characters. Thank you for giving *Murders at The Winterbottom WI* a home and for loving Pru and Phyllis as much as I do.

A big thank you to Loulou Brown and Abbie Rutherford. It was an absolute pleasure to work with you to get *Murders* into shape, you made the whole process so simple, straightforward and stress free and best of all, you 'got' me and my style of writing. Thank you too to Hannah Deuce for rushing a few things through for me to meet deadlines, I really appreciate all you do for me.

This is a special thank you to Tara Lyons. Now this is the strangest thing, we have never met, but I feel as though I have known Tara all my life. Our only connection has been through the numerous emails we ping each other, mainly for work but we do also enjoy chats about our respective families and life in general. Tara, you have been an absolute dream to work with, you keep me level when my head is so full of ideas and floaty bits of nonsense – and when that floaty nonsense has tied itself in knots making me reach for a bottle of gin, you gently steer me in the right direction, giving me great suggestions to work on. Not only did I gain a fabulous Editorial & Production Manager when I signed with Bloodhound, I also gained a beautiful friend. We will meet for that drink one day!

To Sally Ann Fidler and Christine Iddon Parry for keeping me updated with the nuances of policing since my retirement, thank you, your help was invaluable, without it I would have been swinging the lamp on how it used to be. To my cousin, Dr Robyn Powell, Consultant in Emergency Medicine, for your valued expertise on medical procedures and how to kill someone efficiently and properly. To say I'm a bit proud and in awe of you and your achievements is an understatement, Robyn.

To Nia Ireland for her proofreading skills and support before submission, I still howl with laughter at the comma omission that almost got poor Rita arrested!

I very quickly discovered how amazing readers and book bloggers are. There are too many to mention individually, and I would hate to miss someone out, so this is a collective thank you. A bit like a group hug. As writers, where would we be without them? Our words wouldn't be heard, our stories wouldn't be told. They would lie dormant on paper or screen, meaningless. They only come to life because people read them, enjoy them and spread their love of our books.

Once again (I have to mention him as I truly am the doting elder sister), to my very handsome, debonair brother, Andy Dawson – for no other reason than him being handsome, debonair and of course, my brother. Love you, Bro.

To my sister Claire, so far away but you will always be in my heart.

To my beautiful daughter, Emma and my gorgeous grandchildren, Olivia, Annie and Arthur. You are my sunshine, you make me smile every day, I'm so very blessed to have you in my life.

And last but definitely not least, to my handsome and very funny hubby, John. The love of my life, my bodyguard, chauffeur and human Satnav. The man who makes me laugh every single day (and frequently think of murder too). He has endured hours of torment as my muse and 'go to' for ideas for this book. Trying to find out how long it would take to suffocate face first in a lemon drizzle cake from Aldi or if his 6'2" tall, 18 stone bulk would snap the coat peg in the under-stairs cupboard if he was hanging from it, have been just a few. He rolls his eyes and groans but still continues to reluctantly participate in the most bizarre acts all in the name of research – well, at least that's what I tell him it's for!

Without his love and support there would be no stories to tell – and I'd still be driving around various parts of the UK, panic struck and lost.

I hope I haven't missed anyone out, but knowing me and my scatter-brained head-thoughts, I probably have. My track record is to write names down as I go along and then promptly lose the piece of paper. This time I excelled myself and recorded it all on my laptop, which two weeks ago curled up its keyboard and died a death, taking with it lots of stuff that wasn't saved to cloud which included – yep, you've guessed it – my list! I'm so sorry if you haven't appeared here, but please know there's a humongous thank you in my heart for you. You will always be very much appreciated.

Gina x

A NOTE FROM THE PUBLISHER

Thank you for reading this book. If you enjoyed it please do consider leaving a review on Amazon to help others find it too.

We hate typos. All of our books have been rigorously edited and proofread, but sometimes mistakes do slip through. If you have spotted a typo, please do let us know and we can get it amended within hours.

info@bloodhoundbooks.com